CW00523893

FORCED TO FORGET

Melissa Morgan

Please be aware that this book discusses themes including domestic violence, self harm and homophobia. There are also scenes of a sexual nature.

Forced to Forget

Copyright © 2020 Melissa Morgan

All rights reserved.

This is a work of fiction. Names, characters, places and incidents are either the product of the author's imagination or are used fictitiously, and any resemblance to actual persons, living or dead, business establishments, events or locales is entirely coincidental.

ISBN: 9798556353619

For Grandma.
Thanks for always believing in me and giving me a hug when I needed it.
You will never know how much it meant to me that you cut out little
writing competitions from the newspaper for me.

TRIGGER WARNINGS

Please be aware this book contains storylines about domestic abuse, self-harm and homophobia. If this may trigger you, please read with caution or hand the book to a friend.

PROLOGUE

Bex was nervous.

Her hands were fidgeting, she kept tripping over her words and she knew the eyeliner on her right eye was somewhat crooked. Her jeans felt too tight and her jumper too big, her scarf was too itchy and, now she thought about it, her coat clashed with her entire outfit.

What the hell was wrong with her?

Bex Wright did not do nervous. She did not do scared. She did not do uncomfortable.

Her eyes flicked to her right.

Him.

That was what was wrong with her.

The tall, handsome, ever so slightly intimidating gentleman next to her, who currently had his left hand in her right, was the first - and only - man who made her feel nervous. Nervous, but in a good way. Nervous, excited, full of butterflies, and yet deep down, calmly content all at the same time.

And that was why she was so scared.

"Why do you keep looking at me all funny?" he said, without even looking at her.

"I'm not."

His smile grew. "Yes, you are. I can feel your laser gaze across a room, let alone up close."

"Laser gaze? My God Daniel, you do know how to make a girl feel attractive."

He laughed, finally looking at her. "Come on, spill. What's

wrong?"

"Nothing is wrong."

"You keep staring at me and you've been practically silent since we met."

"You're always silent after work."

"Yes, but *you're* never silent."

"I'll have you know I'm a demure, classy, elegant woman who is very capable of being quiet." Her eyes snapped to him as his lips twitched. "Don't laugh!"

"Bex, I love you, but I don't think you have a single atom in your body that is silent."

Daniel Williams was thirty-seven-years-old. Six foot one, dark brown hair that he always managed to keep tidy, and cheekbones that could cut glass. He was the epitome of a gentleman and, in all honesty, the complete opposite from Bex's usual type.

And yet, nearly three years after they'd had extremely hot but unplanned sex in his parents' study, here they were.

His eyes were grey but in the mornings Bex had realised they were more a light blue, reminding her of calm and cosy winter days where she'd want to spend the day tucked into his side under a duvet. He had a small line between his eyebrows which sometimes appeared when he wasn't even frowning, and he had at least ten different types of smile that only a few ever got to see.

As Bex stared at him, not caring that he was still frowning at her in amused curiosity, the realisation that she could read Daniel better than anyone sank deeper into her chest. Her mind flicked to the letter in her pocket and she felt a sense of calm settle over her emotions.

Precisely two years and seventy-three days ago, Daniel Williams had told her that he was in love with her.

Bex had never said it back.

When he had said it they'd been in bed. He'd held his breath. She had smiled, kissed him on the lips and had proceeded to try and thank him for his kind words in kisses and touches. But she had seen the frown between his eyes, and still remembered the feeling that had punched through her as his cheeks had flushed with embarrassment. Despite her attempts, they hadn't slept together that night. When he had fallen asleep, she'd listened to his breathing, feeling it tickle her shoulder and an acidic taste had risen in her mouth where the words she had wanted to say should have been.

But she hadn't said them.

She *still* hadn't said them.

And kind, patient Daniel hadn't pushed her. He hadn't said those words again until at least three months later when they had been at the beach. Bex had been playing with Amy – his daughter from his previous marriage – in the sea, and they'd formed a team to drench him with as much water as possible. Finally, when they had let him come up for air, he'd just smiled and said it so easily it was as if the awkward first time had never happened. And from then on, he hadn't stopped.

And still she had never said it back.

Bex had learnt a long time ago that trusting someone with that kind of information made you vulnerable. She wasn't prepared to be vulnerable with anyone until she was one hundred per cent certain that they wouldn't hurt her. That they wouldn't use it against her.

And that was why the letter she had in her back pocket felt like it was pressing against her hip, burning a hole through the material and scorching her skin. Instead of voicing it, she had written her love down on paper. Every emotion she felt for him was scrawled in black biro on a page ripped from an old notebook so that when it came to telling him, hopefully, she wouldn't chicken out. She had decided she was going to read it to Daniel on his birthday - seven days away.

But now that she had officially signed the letter, now that her feelings were open and exposed on a piece of paper, she kept feeling an overwhelming need to tell him.

"Bex, honestly, what's wrong?"

She realised he was still watching her. "I'm just being quiet."

"I know, which is why it's scaring me." He squeezed her hand. "Was it a hard day-? Amy, shoelaces!" Amy Williams was a couple of metres ahead of them, jumping between pavement slabs and trying her hardest to get her shoes as wet as she possibly could as she splashed in nearly every puddle. Amy had curly red hair, long freckled limbs and dark brown eyes.

"Daaaaaaad!" Amy groaned, throwing them a look over her shoulder. She bent down, did a very good job of pretending to tie her shoelaces when in fact she just shoved the ends back under the lip of her trainers, before jumping up and running away again. Daniel shook his head and Bex leaned into him.

"At least we have a doctor nearby if she falls over and cracks her skull open." She patted him on the arm.

"Oh, thank God for that," Daniel replied sarcastically. "I'm off shift. She falls, we're calling an ambulance. Talking of which, she's told me you've been teaching her how to walk in heels."

"She asked! I did tell her to ask you first in case you got jealous. I know how good you are in heels."

His lips twitched and she saw how hard he was trying to hold back a smile. Affection filled his eyes despite the dry look he was giving her.

She grinned. "Besides, the girl has got to learn otherwise she'll end up like Lizzie."

Daniel laughed. "She's eight."

"My little brother was wearing them from when he was four."

Their eyes met for a second and she saw the affection in Daniel's expression grow.

"I'm really looking forward to meeting him. And Jason and Marco."

She smiled, faking confidence. "Good, so you should."

Another thing she had decided recently was to introduce Daniel to her family. The weekend after next he was going to meet them all - Kyle, Jason and Marco. She'd never let any 'adult' boyfriend officially meet her family. Meeting the family made things serious and highlighted that she cared. But Daniel had chipped away at those fears. Over the next month not only was he going to have a great thirty-eighth birthday party - she'd arranged it so of course he would - but she was going to tell him she loved him, accept his invitation of moving in with him, agree that they needed to tell their friends they were dating and introduce him to her family.

Bex Wright, she thought to herself with an inward smile, *you're growing up.*

He squeezed her hand. "Is that why've you've been quiet? Are you worrying about me meeting them?"

She had a sneaky suspicion Daniel found her quite easy to read too.

"Nervous excited. It means a lot to me."

"I know." He smiled at her. "I really do." He let out a long breath. "And if it's really worrying you, we can delay it."

She grinned. "Is me being quiet really that much of a red flag?"

"You have no idea."

She shouldered him playfully. "I can't quite figure out if that's a good thing."

"Even in your sleep you talk."

"Do I?" Bex said, her eyes rounding in surprise as a giggle left her lips. "Why have you *never* told me that?"

He shrugged. "It saves me putting the radio on in the background when I'm getting ready for work. Great for my energy bills."

"You dick!"

The smile on his face grew and his grey eyes danced with amusement.

"What do I say?"

"All sorts of random nonsense."

"Can you record it next time?"

"Why?"

"I want to know what I say!"

He shook his head at her. "Fine, but only if—" His head snapped away from her, his eyes wide and alert.

The air stilled.

Bex felt it too.

Her stomach clenched involuntarily and the fine hairs on the back of her neck stood up. It felt as if the earth had just taken a breath, like the stars had vanished for a second and the ground had shifted beneath her feet. Daniel's hand tore away from hers, a shout in his throat as he began to run. Cold, white, painful fear flooded into Bex's system and made her head spin as she tried to understand why she was suddenly so afraid. Her head spun to look in the direction Daniel had run and she saw Amy trying to push herself up from the middle of the road. Her hands slipped against the ground and she fell forward onto her front. She was just out of reach of the nearest streetlight, her red hair only standing out because Bex knew her, knew to look for it, knew to spot it in a crowd. The car metres away from her however, did not.

Bex was running too, her feet pounding against the pavement as the headlights pierced the darkness. Daniel was metres ahead.

Amy looked up. Her body stiffened as she saw the car. Instead of running, her body locked, still on her hands and knees.

The sound of brakes ripped through the air.

"AMY!" she screamed before relief slammed into her.

Daniel was there.

Daniel had her.

He grabbed her under the arms, yanking her up off the ground and throwing her forwards.

But the relief dissolved into horror.

She was screaming, her feet still pounding against the pavement.

She could get there.

She would-

Daniel's eyes met hers for less than a fraction of a second before the car hit him instead.

PART ONE

CHAPTER ONE

Now

"Matt, give me back the phone!" Bex snapped, squeezing Neil's ear painfully one last time as he clawed at her arm. She stretched her other arm as far as she could, gesturing at Matt wildly with it.

He gave her a wary look, pressing the phone in question slightly more firmly to his ear. "Lizzie, I'm going to have to go before Bex does that ear twisty thing that she just did to Neil to me."

Wise move, Bex mouthed before he passed the phone to her. She let go of Neil's ear, ignored his swearing, and walked over to the corner of the living room.

"Violence is not the answer, Rebecca," her best friend laughed down the phone.

"It is when it comes to Neil Grayson," Bex snarled, but at the sound of Lizzie's laughter her anger wavered. It felt like an age since she had heard happiness in Lizzie's voice.

Over the last two weeks, Bex had not left Lizzie's side. She had discovered, literally with a slam to the head as she had hit her mat in the Crossfit box, that thirteen years ago Lizzie had made a wish on top of Primrose Hill and reversed their lives by thirteen years. Everyone else had forgotten their past lives except for Lizzie – and later, they realised, Lottie Williams – and she had changed her life. At nineteen, she had left Charles instead of marrying him, she hadn't told him she had fallen pregnant, she hadn't told him when Leo had been born sleeping, and she had started living her life again but without her previous husband by her side.

Last time Bex had met Lizzie, a buzzing, young office receptionist sat at the squeaky-clean front desk of Lightswitch Productions, when she was twenty-one and Bex was twenty-two. She had seen the wedding ring and thought *that'll never last*. That had been until she had met Charles roughly six months later. A tall, lean, scruffy English teacher with a child-like smile and bright blue eyes.

Then she had witnessed the two of them together and they simply *worked*. Silently communicating with one another, knowing the other's thoughts before they even had a time to think them, and she had caught the both of them, on more than one occasion, stealing glances at the other and looking as if they couldn't quite believe their luck.

But when Lizzie had reversed time she had split up with Charles before they had even married, knowing that in the future her inability to have children would put a strain on their relationship. She wanted Charles to be free to have a family of his own.

But Lizzie and Charles were back together now. And that's all that mattered. This life had finally caught up with the last, and they were all the same age as they had been. None of them knew what was coming anymore.

There were a few small differences between this life and the last. Charles was now a celebrity, Maria Williams hadn't died from cervical cancer, Lottie Williams hadn't been part of her family for the past decade and Bex was single.

Not that anyone picked up on *that* last small difference because as far as they all knew she had been single the last time as well.

All of their lives had been affected in one way or another.

Grey eyes, brown -

Inwardly she shook her head, dismissing the thought.

After they had all remembered, Charles hadn't seemed to forgive Lizzie for what she had done. That was why Bex had been playing babysitter slash best friend slash parent for the last two weeks. Lizzie and Bex didn't know that Charles was dealing with his own feelings of guilt, blaming himself for what had happened and he'd forgiven Lizzie almost straight away.

Two days ago, Matt had rung her and confided Charles's plan to win Lizzie back. And now, after a painful twenty-four hours in Matt and Neil's company, they had discovered the plan had worked. Charles had won her back.

Hearing Lizzie laugh made it worth it. She was happy. And Lizzie deserved to be happy. She deserved it more than anyone Bex knew.

"Anyway, I'm done with you. Can you put Charles on the phone?"

Lizzie's laugh once again travelled down the phone before she heard a slight rustle and then a chin hit the receiver.

"Hi Bex."

"Right, the move in Lizzie's flat, where you didn't tell her instantly that she was an idiot to think you wouldn't want to be with her if she couldn't have children, dickhead move. Don't be that guy. I want to like you again but right now, you're on rocky ground, even with the grand romantic gesture. You understand? You've got a lot of grovelling to do."

His laughter echoed down the phone. It was familiar but foreign. Before Lizzie had reversed time, Bex had been extremely close to Charles. He was older than her, but she had always felt protective over him, like he was a little brother.

"Do you understand?" she repeated.

"Yep. Ya-uh."

She heard him mutter something to Lizzie and her answering giggle made Bex roll her eyes.

"Charles, are you even listening to me? Stop flirting. Charles? Hello!"

"Bex, I'm not going to hurt her. I promise," Charles replied and Bex smiled triumphantly as she had finally got his full attention.

"Good. Because she literally gave up her life to make you happy."

The beat of silence down the phone was so strong she felt it lodge in her throat. There was a rustling as she heard him shift in his spot.

Nevertheless, she continued, "Never forget what she went through, just so you could be an actor and potentially go off and have a family with someone else."

"Yes," he said quietly, "yes, I know." Bex felt the smallest flicker of guilt in her stomach. She pushed it away. Charles needed this wake-up call. He needed to understand that Lizzie was far more fragile than she let on.

"So you realise how much that girl loves you, yes?"

"Yes." His voice sounded gravelly.

"And you're not going to pull whatever the shit that was in the flat when you didn't put her feelings first, yes? Because that was not acceptable."

"Yes. I agree. It was bad of me." He sighed. "I'll make it up to her. I promise."

Bex turned to face the rest of the living room and glanced at Matt. He was sitting on the sofa watching her, wearing grey jogging bottoms and a black t-shirt. His hair was a dishevelled mess and the slightest hint of stubble showed across his jawline. Catching her eye, he shook his head and her shoulders slumped ever so slightly.

Okay, maybe she was being a bit harsh but no matter how much she liked Charles, Lizzie was her priority.

"Okay then," she said simply.

"Is that the end of my bollocking?" He attempted to laugh but she heard the way it got stuck in his throat.

"Not by a long shot but it'll do for now. Oh, and tell her that Neil has installed an app on her phone so she can't silence his calls. That's why his came through and mine didn't."

Neil pulled a face and mouthed, *tell-tale*.

Charles laughed and the warmth of it made her realise how much she had missed him.

"You better tell her!"

"Yes, I'll tell her."

"Right then, well, we will leave you two to it. Sorry to have interrupted your aloooooonnnnneeeee time-"

Matt groaned and Bex raised her eyebrows at him. "Grow up."

"My little sister," he said, pointing at himself.

She jabbed a finger at the phone. "With your best friend who you plotted with to make this happen." She turned her attention back to Charles. "Have fun!"

Matt groaned even louder this time.

"That was mean," Neil said, shrugging his coat on over his shoulders with a smirk. For once, Neil approving of her actions didn't instantly dampen her mood.

"Oh, before you go, quick thing," Charles said as Bex was about to hang up.

"Yeah?" Bex replied.

"Call him."

The words hit like a sucker punch to the chest.

Matt was no longer looking at her but she saw curiosity spark in Neil's eyes. She turned away from them both, staring at Matt's living room wall as Charles's words curled around her throat.

"I don't know what you're talking about," she muttered, trying to sound casual.

Charles laughed. "You know who I mean, call him."

How did Charles know? Had he told him? Had Lizzie figured it out?

No.

If Lizzie had figured it out she would have already confronted her. She would be the one on the phone.

"Why is it my responsibility? He could call me, you know?" she snapped, wincing as she felt Matt and Neil's curiosity pierce into her back.

"Yes, I know," he sighed. "But you know what he's like."

"That's not a good enough excuse."

"Just do it, Bex. He won't think there's a chance in hell you're still interested."

Anger flared in her chest.

"Then he's a fucking idiot!" Bex snapped.

For a second her anger was hot enough to distract her from the growing intensity of Matt and Neil's gazes.

"I agree."

"Charles-"

"Please call him. I'll see you soon, okay?"

"No, just a second-"

And then Charles had the audacity to hang up on her. She swallowed, letting her rage drum through her body for a couple of seconds before she peeled the phone away from her ear to stare at it.

How had he found out?

How had he known?

Grey eyes, brown hair, chis-

The face of the man Charles had been referring to flashed before her eyes in high definition.

Idiot. Complete and utter idiot.

"Soooo, what was that about?"

Bex turned and saw both Matt and Neil were watching her. One looked confused while the other looked delighted.

Neil's grin widened as their eyes met and he repeated his question, enunciating every word. "So, what was that about?"

"Why are you still here?"

He dipped his hands into his pockets. "This is Matt's flat not yours."

"You alright?" Matt was watching her carefully.

"I'm fine." She walked over to Neil and handed him his phone. "Thanks for your help."

Neil smiled at her, his keen eyes flicking across her face. "What were you talking to Charles about?"

"Matt, can you ask him to leave?"

Matt laughed. "No, Bex."

Neil smirked as irritation swelled in Bex's gut. She took a step forward and Neil lifted his hands in surrender, a cocky grin still across his face. "Fine, fine, I'm gone! Thanks for having us, Matt."

Matt gave him a nod and a smile, which made Bex's eyes narrow even further.

"Anytime."

"Your scheme seems to have done the trick. Little Miss Whiskers is happy again."

"Let's hope so." Matt raised a fist up and Neil paused for a second before bumping his own against it, looking extremely out of place as he did so.

When the front door finally shut behind him, Bex turned on Matt. "Why did you take his side?"

"I didn't take anyone's side." Matt stretched his hands above his head, clicking his head to the right. "The guy's alright."

Bex huffed in response which made Matt's smile grow. "Come on, Bex. He cares about Lizzie. He helped us."

"He did nothing except make sure she got on the bloody train to Tring."

"Why do you hate him so much?"

"He represents every single thing I hate about the male species."

Matt laughed again, shaking his head at her before yawning ever so slightly. "Breakfast?" he asked, standing up and pulling at the bottom of his t-shirt so it lay flat against his stomach.

"Yeah, alright."

Matt's flat was nearly the exact copy of Lizzie's just above him with a few minor adjustments. For example, he had knocked down a wall – the advantage of owning the flat instead of renting it – and combined his kitchen and living room area, making the space look a lot bigger than it actually was.

Bex had a feeling it was because Matt considered the flat his home, whereas Lizzie had subconsciously been holding off on thinking anything was a home until Charles walked back into the picture.

Bex moved to sit at the thin, long island Matt had in the middle of his kitchen and watched her friend as he moved around the room. Matt was a good cook, he enjoyed creating dishes and he had a knack for throwing things together.

He was also ridiculously good looking.

Tanned skin, a scruffy mess of almost black hair, and muscles that were built from spending more hours in the gym than even she did - and that was saying something. He was also a nice guy. Beneath all the commitment-phobic, male bravado she knew him to be a loving brother and a great friend.

It was kind of frustrating that Bex wasn't attracted to him.

It would make so much more sense if she was; he went to her gym, he was cheeky, he didn't take himself too seriously, he was just her type. He was even an inch shorter than her, and all her boyfriends had been shorter than her. He fitted the mould.

But she and Matt were just friends and always would be. They'd kissed once at a Halloween party. The moment their mouths had pressed together they'd simultaneously burst out laughing.

It had been revolting.

No - instead, ever since the past had squarely punched her in the head, her mind had been filled with one man only.

Grey eyes, brown hair, chiselled jaw.

She felt Matt's eyes on her slightly too late and looked up guiltily, smiling at him as he raised an eyebrow at her.

"So, what were you and Charles talking about? Who do you need to call?"

Bex pretended to check her nails. "We going to the gym after this?"

"Bex."

"Matt."

He shook his head, a smile across his lips. "Haven't we learned anything over the past two weeks? Keeping secrets leads us to some shitty situations."

"I have no idea what you're talking about."

"Ya-huh." He turned back to continue making omelettes, tilting the frying pan this way and that. "I was planning on going to the gym

14

but didn't know if you might want to go home and sleep first. We had a late one."

They'd been up all night, Bex pacing up and down the room whilst neither Lizzie nor Charles rang them to tell them what was going on. Neil, annoyingly, had predicted what had happened.

"They'll have reunited and probably be screwing. Why are we waiting for an update on that?" he had groaned, having just been elbowed off the sofa.

"Mate, that's my sister."

"Yeah, and you're the weirdo who took time off work to make sure your best friend could definitely have sex with your sister."

Matt had thrown Neil an irritated look at that point and Bex had simply elbowed him again.

Now, she smiled. "Whatever you can do, I can do. I'm up for the gym if you're going."

Matt laughed. "Thought you'd say something like that."

"You're not tired at all then?" she asked, getting up and moving towards the coffee machine. She could feel tiredness beginning to creep into her body now that the adrenaline rush from hearing Lizzie and Charles happily together had faded. But if Matt was going to the gym, she would go too. Her competitive side wouldn't let her refuse.

"Not really." He began plating up their food. "It'll probably hit me later but I said I'd see Zoey after she's finished work so no napping for me."

"Ooooo," Bex said, nudging him in the side with a small smile. "Still going well then?"

His lips thinned and he avoided her gaze.

"Oh, God. I know that look."

"She wants me to meet her parents." He sighed, running a hand over his jaw. "Think I'm going to have to end it."

Bex opened her mouth to respond but then thought better of it. Telling Matt off never worked. Trying to analyse him *never* worked. He was so set in his ways he would need to be hit by something bigger than just a cross word from her to derail him.

Bex began making them both coffees. Matt had a fancy coffee machine with even fancier coffee, one of the only items of luxury he had in his entire flat. Luckily, Bex had worked as a barista for most of her teenage years so she was one of the only people besides Matt who could use it easily.

"She's not *the one* then?" she said simply.

"The one to what?"

"The one to change your mind." Their eyes met and something dark moved behind Matt's expression.

"I'm not going to change my mind, Bex," he said quietly. He turned away from the counter, the two plates of food in his hand.

She grabbed the cutlery and their coffees before sitting down, smiling her thanks as she looked down at the omelette in front of her.

Matt was a health freak. He never seemed to have a day off from exercising and barely ever strayed from his healthy diet plan. It was protein, complex carbohydrates, good fats or nothing. He'd drink occasionally. Once in a blue moon he would join them for a takeaway. She watched him as he picked up a fork and noticed the small line between his eyebrows.

"I thought," she said carefully, "that because of Charles and Lizzie and us all remembering everything...well, that it might have made you think twice about the whole, love-doesn't-exist thing."

"I had the exact same opinion last time."

"Yes, but now, it's different."

"How?"

"Because it's almost like it was fate that they got back together. Soulmates. That sort of thing."

He smiled. "Soulmates? Really Bex?"

"You don't think so?"

"I don't believe in that kind of thing."

"But Lizzie-"

"Lizzie and Charles are just an exception to the rule."

She let a small smile cross her lips. "What about me?"

His eyes flicked up, the hard look behind his eyes softening ever so slightly. "You'll be an exception too. Don't worry." He kicked her leg affectionately under the island. "You've got to find dream guy after all."

Bex's back stiffened but she threw Matt a convincing smile; all white teeth but nothing behind it.

Dream guy. The man who she had been dreaming about for the past year. So much so that she had finally broken up with Ryan. Not because of the cheating, or the stealing, or the photos, but because she was convinced she was having a mental affair and she couldn't cope with the guilt of it.

Every night her mind had been filled with dreams - some sweet, some frustrating, some hot – of being with this mysterious man. They were so real she could have sworn she could really taste the food she was eating as they sat opposite each other on a dinner date, or the salt on the air when they were by the beach, or his lips on hers. Gradually the dreams had got darker. At the end of them, just before she was about to wake up, the world would shift, lights would shine in her eyes and the imaginary man would be hit by a car, crumpling as if he were made of nothing, his head hitting the road hard.

Blood would fill her vision.

Her heart would break as she would scream, knowing before she even reached him that he wasn't going to make it.

And then she would wake up with puffy eyes and a sore throat. Sometimes she even woke with the smell of blood still thick in the air.

Two weeks ago, when she had fallen from the ropes at her Crossfit box, the thirteen years that had been deleted from her memory poured back into her head within a couple of seconds. It hadn't been painful but it had felt weird, suffocating and comforting all at the same time, and she had finally realised none of her dreams had been imaginary.

None of it had been fictional.

Dream guy was real.

Very, very real.

And on the night everyone believed Lizzie's wish had turned back time, nobody knew she had made one too.

Nobody knew that she had held Daniel William's lifeless body in her arms. They didn't know she hadn't just wished he would open his eyes, she'd screamed it with everything she had.

And then everything had changed.

CHAPTER TWO

"Dad!" Amy squealed as she was swept up into Daniel's arms. He squeezed her to his chest, kissing the top of her head before letting her drop back onto the kitchen floor.

He caught his sister's affectionate smile over his daughter's head and gave her a grin. "I could try and pick you up too if you wanted."

Lottie laughed, throwing her head back and cackling in the witchy way she always had.

"No, I'm fine, thank you. Don't want to break you." She gestured at a mug on the table. "I made you a hot chocolate."

"Thanks." He picked it up and turned to look at his daughter. She was still in her school uniform, her mass of red, curly hair scraped back behind her ears and there was definitely a chocolate smudge running just along the bottom of her mouth. She sat down again at the kitchen table, homework spread out in front of her and Lottie to her left, a smile across her face as she watched his daughter.

She was responsible for the chocolate.

Lottie had this weird ability to always have sweets or chocolate on her - like she was her own permanent candy store. And he knew whenever she babysat his daughter it meant Amy would officially be so high on sugar that she'd practically be shaking by the time he got back from work. It had been exactly the same last time. "How was school?"

Amy pulled a face. "Okay. I got into trouble though."

Daniel's eyebrows rose. Amy enjoyed learning. When she wanted to she worked hard and excelled in anything she put her mind to. But that was only *when she wanted to*. He sat down next to her.

"Oh?"

She turned to look at him, her eyes rounding innocently. "I was so tired this morning I forgot about my shoes and I went to school in my slippers."

Shit.

That was his fault. He'd been in a rush that morning, Fi from work had texted him saying he needed to get in early as Colin had been sent home sick. He had practically bundled Amy and her school things into the car and hadn't thought to check if she had been wearing real shoes.

"Sorry, Amy, I'll ring the school and explain. That's my fault."

"I have to do lines as extra homework."

"What?" He ran a hand around the back of his neck, guilt flickering in his gut. "Which teacher was it? I'll ring the school, I'll explain-"

"Amy." Lottie's voice was stern.

His eyes flicked across the table. There was a wry smile on Lottie's face and she had folded her arms across her chest. Her dark brown eyes glinted with amusement.

"What?" Amy asked, innocently.

"Miss Tonstone had a different story as to why you got told off."

Cottoning on, Daniel turned to look at his daughter. She shot him a sheepish grin.

"Okay, so I might have actually been given lines because I was showing off that I had managed to come to school in my slippers."

Lottie caught Daniel's eye. "Miss Tonstone was prepared to let it slide until Amy told her friends how she had purposely hidden her feet from you."

Daniel could feel a smile growing on his lips at his daughter's cheeky expression but he tried his hardest to supress it.

"May I ask why you wanted to try and go to school in slippers?"

"Because they're comfy. Lottie always says that being comfortable is the most important thing about clothes."

"Don't drag me into this!" Lottie said, choking back laughter and leaning forward to ruffle Amy's hair.

"You know she wasn't talking about school uniform," Daniel said, trying to keep his tone serious.

Amy heaved a dramatic sigh. "I know. Sorry, Dad."

Their eyes met for a solid five seconds, Amy's mouth slowly becoming a pout whilst Daniel had to press his lips together even harder so he wouldn't laugh.

"It's fine, I should have noticed. But don't try and pull that kind of trick again."

Her eyes widened. "Moi?" She pressed a hand to her chest. "How could you think such a thing?"

Daniel's eyes flicked towards Lottie, who was trying her hardest not to spit out her own hot chocolate. Her shoulders were shaking hard and her eyes had turned glassy.

"It's been two weeks. Two weeks and she's acting just like you."

Lottie laughed then, the cackle breaking across the room as she held up a hand for Amy to high-five.

"Dad, it's not been two weeks for me," Amy said happily after high-fiving her aunt. "I remembered way before you adults did."

"That's because adults are stupid," Lottie said, catching her breath. "Especially male ones."

"Okay, thank you, enough of that!" He pointed accusatively at his little sister, who was laughing again. "Go and get changed for bed, Amy. Have you had dinner?"

"Lottie made us salad."

Daniel felt the corner of his mouth lift. "Well, that sounds like utter rubbish."

"Amy," Lottie groaned, shoving her playfully as the young girl stood up. "You were meant to say something *convincing*."

"We had...peas?"

Daniel stood up and walked over to the bin, flipping it open. "You had McDonalds."

"We saved you some," Lottie replied, holding her hands up.

"Well, at least that's something." He winked at her.

Amy pushed back her chair and walked towards the door. She stopped just before she left the room and looked hesitantly over her shoulder. Daniel leant back against the worktop and folded his arms across his chest.

"Yes?"

"You're not really angry at Lottie are you?"

Lottie laughed. "No, kid, don't worry about your dad. He loves McDonalds."

Amy's eyes flicked towards Daniel and he saw the whisper of

worry threaded behind them. His heart soared for his sister. It had been two weeks since Lottie had come back into their lives, two weeks since they had all remembered their life from another era and had realised that Lottie Williams had been telling the truth all along when she'd declared they were living in some weird, continuous Groundhog Day. Amy had grown attached to her aunt so quickly it was as if Lottie had never been away.

Since Helen had died, Amy had very few older female influences.

Her grandmother, Maria, adored her but lived in Tring and still worked hard as a midwife at the hospital meaning that their visits were often interrupted by her running out in a hurry - something he understood all too well - and were often dominated by his father, Kenneth, instead. Patricia, his eldest sister, had children of her own but didn't actually *like* children. She made sure her own two boys were enrolled in every activity under the sun so that by the time they got home they were too exhausted to disturb her. And Daniel hadn't ever brought any woman back to meet Amy. He had been on three dates since Helen had died and each had been a disaster. Two had immediately enquired about his younger brother, Charles, and he had realised the point of the date was so that they could get closer to a famous actor, and one hadn't realised he had a daughter and had immediately made her excuses when he had started talking about her.

After a while it had become easy. He didn't feel the need to date or to be with anyone as he became comfortable in his singleness. His job kept him busy enough and Amy filled up the rest of his time.

And there had always been the echoes.

Helen's words going around in his head, the slight sting on his back, the shadow of betrayal reminding him that, even if he dated anyone, there wouldn't be much point.

"You're just so bloody boring! Since Amy arrived I feel your personality has got up and walked out of the building."

And this time around he hadn't had a certain blonde makeup artist in his life trying to help push those memories away.

Snapping out of that train of thought as quickly as he could he saw the worry had intensified in Amy's eyes at his silence.

"I was only joking, Amy," he said calmly, holding her gaze. "I'm not mad at Lottie."

She smiled slowly, the dimple on her cheek appearing before she quickly ran out of the room.

Daniel watched her, seeing her little legs dash up the stairs as quickly as they could and felt something pull in his chest.

"She adores you," he said, ever so quietly.

Lottie laughed. "And I adore her. Now come sit back down before your drink gets cold. How was work?"

Daniel walked over to the table, sitting down and taking a long sip of the hot chocolate she had made him only to cough sharply as the taste of liquor ran across his tongue.

"I made you a grown up one," Lottie said with a grin. "Thought you might need it after," she glanced at the clock on the wall, "a sixteen-hour shift."

"We had a stab victim come in when I was about to sign off." He rolled his shoulders, feeling the effects of the day more than he usually did. "Thanks so much for staying. I didn't derail your plans, did I?"

"I never make plans when I'm looking after Amy. I know what your job is like."

He gave her a grateful smile. "Thanks. And thank you for this." He raised his mug towards her and she leant across the table to clink her own against it.

He hadn't asked Lottie to look after Amy, she had simply volunteered, insisting she needed to see more of her niece. Part of him suspected she was also looking after him.

Really, he should be the one looking after her.

In their last life, their arguments over her then boyfriend had meant their relationship had crumbled.

In this life, he had dismissed her just like everyone else had.

He'd been the one to suggest to his parents that they needed to get her professional help when she had refused to stop saying that they'd lived their lives before. He'd even called her 'crazy' on one or two shameful occasions. And then she had run away.

Guilt pinched in his gut.

He had missed her terribly. She always had this energy about her that lit up the room, and a way of talking that made whoever she was talking to feel like they were the only person in the world. With a mane of curly blonde hair, deep brown eyes and a dress sense that made no sense, she was one of the kindest people he'd ever met.

"I think Miss Tonstone likes you," Lottie said.

"Yeah, right," he scoffed, coming out of his thoughts. Who was

Miss Tonstone again?

"She *so* does. When I picked Amy up, she came to talk to me about just how hard it must be on you being a single dad. Her eyes went all gooey and her cheeks were a nice shade of pink. Last week, she was glaring at me. Literally *glaring*. I think she thought you adding a 'Lottie Williams' to the approved list of people able to pick Amy up was because I was your wife, not your sister. Obviously someone told her otherwise."

"Shut up," Daniel said, shaking his head.

"She totally does, Daniel." Lottie grinned as he shifted again in his seat, taking another long sip of the boozy hot chocolate.

He was pretty sure that he'd met Miss Tonstone at the last parent's evening. He racked his brains to try and put a face to the name but he couldn't. It all seemed a blur.

That had happened a lot since they'd all remembered the life Lizzie Cartwright had wiped from their minds. He didn't feel any older but his brain felt fuller, as if it was crammed with too many memories.

It was hard to distinguish one life from the other when it came to less important things.

It also meant some things stood out much more clearly.

He cleared his throat. "So, what are your plans for the weekend?"

Lottie eyed him, her lips turned into a sweet smile but there was a mischievous twinkle behind her eyes.

"Would your disinterest in the pretty teacher have something to do with a certain blonde?"

He stared at her.

She couldn't know.

They hadn't told anyone last time.

"Blonde?" he asked cautiously.

"Have you rung Bex yet?"

Shit.

He spluttered, almost spilling his drink down his chin as he turned away and got up to find a dish cloth.

"I...why would I ring Bex?" He grabbed the pink one off the side that Amy had insisted he buy last year and wiped down his face quickly.

Lottie's cackle bounced around the room.

"Real smooth, Daniel. That was perfect. You didn't look bothered in the slightest."

"I just swallowed it the wrong way."

"Ya-huh. So, back to the question. Have you rung Bex?"

He took a deep breath and turned to look at her. "And I said, why would I ring Bex?"

"Because on the night that I finally rang you to apologise, Bex was the one who picked up the phone. Sobbing hysterically. I was too emotional at the time to really think about it but over the past few years I have always wondered why Bex was with you... that night."

The night he'd died.

"She was my friend."

"It was late, Daniel. Really late."

"Amy was with us."

She smirked. "Is that meant to convince me you were just friends? That is just another huge indicator that says something was going on between you two." Lottie raised her eyebrows. "Am I right? Or am I right? I'm right, aren't I?"

He sighed, chucking the dish cloth on the side and assessing his sister coolly.

"Yes, okay, we were in a relationship."

Her eyebrows raised in surprise. "In a relationship? In a bloody relationship and you didn't tell us!" Lottie exclaimed, putting her hot chocolate down with one hand and jabbing a finger towards him with the other. "Why the hell didn't you tell us?"

"Why are you now acting shocked? That is what you just implied."

"I thought you might be fooling around or seeing each other. Not in an actual relationship. How did you keep it secret? Why did you keep it a secret?"

He sighed. "Mainly for Lizzie. She was going through a lot and Bex didn't want to upset her or stress her out. We both kind of thought it wouldn't go anywhere at first. We were such a bizarre combination so we decided we should just keep it to ourselves for a while."

"But you told Amy?"

"That's when things got more serious. Amy's a good secret keeper." He glanced towards the stairs. His daughter was also very good at appearing at precisely the wrong time.

"She talked about her today."

Daniel's jaw tightened and he pushed himself off the side.

"What?"

"Amy asked when Bex was going to come around. Which simply confirmed my suspicions. Amy likes her. A lot."

He winced. "I didn't think...I didn't think she would remember."

The memories hadn't slammed into Amy the same way they had into the adults closest to Lizzie and Charles. His daughter had started behaving oddly since Charles had signed up for the film *Censorship* and thus set everything in motion. She had talked to him about things she couldn't have known, and remembered things Daniel could not. She had started talking about Lottie, and Charles's wife, and how happy she was that Maria was alive this time.

It had caused him to worry and he'd believed she was starting down the same path as Lottie.

She had started to have night terrors, screaming for him as she had dreamt of him dying. He'd been about to take her to be checked out when the same nightmares had plagued him too.

When they had all remembered, she'd already regained most of her own memory. She'd kept saying her imaginary friend had explained it to her, which he put down to her younger brain's way of dealing with such absurdity. The human body was a clever thing, and a child's brain could adapt more easily to the impossible than an adult's.

"You don't think she would remember the woman who was with her when you died?"

He ran his hand along the back of his neck. "Okay, when you put it like that, I sound stupid."

"Have you called her?"

He shifted on the spot. "No."

"Then yes, you are stupid."

"Lottie," he said firmly, taking the chair opposite her once again and leaning across the table. "Bex will have moved on, please be realistic."

"What?"

"Up until two weeks ago, she didn't remember who I was. We had never met in this lifetime. She'll be in a relationship. She'll be fine. It would be embarrassing to call her."

"But you don't know that! She might be single."

He smiled ever so slightly and a cold laugh left his lips. "Sure."

Lottie's gaze hardened. "Daniel, she was single once otherwise you two wouldn't have got into a relationship."

"I was lucky, once."

She pushed her chair back, anger flaring behind her eyes and she stood up, placing her hands on her hips. "Are you being serious right now?"

"Lottie." He gestured for her to sit down but she didn't move, instead her eyebrows furrowed even further. Despite her angry expression it was hard to be intimidated by someone wearing bright pink dungarees.

"Lottie, sit down. It's fine. Please relax."

"It's not fine, you're being pessimistic."

"No, I'm being realistic. Not all of us have to be optimistic all the time." He smiled at her.

"I wasn't optimistic when you guys all wanted to send me to hospital." The air in the kitchen stilled. Daniel felt his stomach clench sharply and pain rippled across his chest. "I wasn't optimistic when one minute I was on the phone to Bex, hearing that you had died, and the next I was waking up as a sixteen-year-old. I wasn't optimistic when I was begging Mum to get a smear test because I knew she had died last time because she hadn't got one in time. I wasn't optimistic when I found the e-mails between Patricia and the private hospital offering me a space. I wasn't optimistic when I turned to you, telling you what I had found out, only for you to admit it was you who had suggested the idea."

His breath caught at her last few words and he felt more pain settle between his shoulders.

"Lottie," he whispered, his voice slightly strangled.

She blinked back angry tears. "I'm not some optimistic fairy who skips around only believing in happy endings anymore. Trust me, Daniel, I've grown up quite a bit since last time."

He'd never wanted her to. Lottie's constant need to believe in the good of people, her want for everyone around her to be happy, her love of the simplest things made her *Lottie*.

"I'm sorry," he said, meeting her eyes. "Lottie, please know I am so sorry."

Lottie's angry expression broke apart like a page being torn in two. He saw the instant flash of guilt across her eyes and she blinked, as if she was gaining consciousness. "Sorry, sorry, that was a low blow from me. Sorry. I said it was forgotten. You've already apologised enough. I didn't mean to bring it up again."

"It wasn't a low blow. You're right."

She walked around the table and wrapped her arms around him from behind, leaning over the chair and burying her face into his shoulder.

"It was. You weren't to know. I get it." She squeezed him tightly. "It's all forgiven. I told you that."

"That's because you're too good."

"I wasn't that good last time."

He knew what she was referring to. It had been in their last timeline and it was one of the memories that stood out to him. The night they had stopped talking. He had confronted her, telling her he knew that her injuries were due to abuse and not her clumsiness like she claimed. He'd been able to read it easily, not just from his professional experience but for reasons Lottie herself didn't even know. The argument that had followed had torn them apart. He had tried his hardest to get back into contact with her, scared for her own safety, but she had picked her boyfriend over him. On the night she'd finally accepted that what Felix was doing *was* abuse and had rung Daniel for help, he had been hit by a car.

"That wasn't your fault. Felix was manipulating you-"

"Daniel, stop." She pulled away from him and placed a hand on his shoulder, hovering just above the table as if she were about to sit on it. "Look, once again, my stupid mouth ended up hurting you. Please, can we forget what I just said? I didn't mean it."

He raised an eyebrow at her.

"Daniel, please."

"Just know I'm always sorry for what I did. For trying to send you away. I'll never forgive myself for that."

Her guilty smile turned playful. "You know how you can make it up to me? You can ring Bex."

He laughed, the tension in his body easing. "No."

"Daniel! Please? Why not? What if she isn't in a relationship? What if she is waiting for your call?"

"She won't be," he said as gently as he could. "She'll be dating someone else."

"Bex is dating someone else?"

Daniel looked around and saw his daughter standing in the doorway. Her face was pale and there was a shimmer to her eyes.

Shit.

"Amy," he said, his tone hardening. "How many times do I have to tell you it's rude to eavesdrop?"

"Is Bex not coming back to live with us?"

"She lived with you!" Lottie said, the hand on his shoulder briefly moving away and returning with a punch.

"Ow!" He threw her a look and stood up quickly. "No, no she didn't." He was trying his hardest to keep his voice calm. "Amy, she never lived with us."

"She was here allllll theeeeeeee time."

He winced, a new kind of pain settling in his stomach.

Yes.

Yes, she had been here all the time.

And for a short while he'd been the luckiest bastard in the world.

"She was here a lot." He ignored the look Lottie was throwing him and walked over towards his daughter. He smiled affectionately down at her but she was staring at him warily, her shoulders up by her ears and her hands curled around the book she'd brought down like she was about to use it as a weapon. "Amy, things have changed, sweetheart. Technically, Bex and I have never even met."

"But you have."

He knelt down in front of her. Due to his height he still was taller than her even on the floor. He'd hoped his action was reassuring but he saw Amy's lip quiver gently.

"But we haven't. Not in this lifetime. And I'm afraid that might mean she doesn't want to...hang out with us as much." He reached across and brushed a strand of hair away from Amy's face before letting his palm rest on her shoulder. "She might be with someone else."

"But you don't know that." Amy's eyes flicked to Lottie and then back again. "That's what Lottie said."

He raised his eyebrows. "How long were you eavesdropping for, exactly?"

She looked away, scuffing her slippers against the floor. "It doesn't take long to get into pyjamas, Dad."

"So, Amy agrees with me then. You should ring her," Lottie said cheerily from behind him.

He didn't have time to throw her an irritated look before Amy's face broke out into a grin and she nodded quickly. "Yes."

"Things have changed."

"You're starting to sound really boring, Dad." She put a hand on her hip and rolled her eyes dramatically.

He had to resist the urge not to laugh.

"I completely agree with you!" Lottie said, happily.

"Can you two stop ganging up on me please?" he said, looking between them.

"If you ring her, we'll stop," Amy replied, crossing her arms across her chest and widening her stance.

Power pose, huh?

She was eight, for God's sake. Where had she learnt that?

"Say you'll ring her, or I'll tell Lottie *the* secret."

Daniel narrowed his eyes. "What secret?"

"The one you told me that I couldn't tell anyone."

He frowned, racking his brains as he heard Lottie's laugh fill the kitchen. He turned to glare at her. "This is all you. She never used to have this kind of attitude."

"Really?" Lottie's smile widened. "I was just thinking how much she reminded me of Bex."

His stomach dropped and he felt pain and warmth fuse in his chest at the same time. Pain for the woman he missed and warmth at the memory of how much she had meant to the both of them.

"I'll tell!" Amy sang.

"I thought you were the best secret keeper there is?"

"I am but this is important."

He straightened up. "Well, I can't remember any secret of mine you're keeping. Especially one you can't tell Lottie so I'm going to say no. Now," he glanced at the clock, "it's Friday, do you want to stay up and watch something with me?" He glanced at Lottie. "If you don't have anywhere to go you're welcome to join?"

His little sister ignored him and turned her gaze to Amy instead. "Well, looks like your dad's made his decision. What was this big secret you needed to tell me?"

"It was from last time, Dad said no one could know." She clicked her heels together. "I wasn't meant to hear."

"Oh, you were eavesdropping again were you? What a surprise!" he said dryly. He shook his head, wondering what on earth she could be talking about, before reaching for his drink on the table and stepping away from them.

"It was in the summer. I remember I was too hot so I came downstairs to ask if Dad could plug the fan in."

Something uneasy stirred at the back of Daniel's mind but he still had no idea what she was talking about. His hand curled around his mug of cold hot chocolate and he walked over to the microwave, opening the door and pushing it inside.

"And Dad and Bex were at the bottom of the stairs."

Shit.

That memory he did know.

Fuck.

"Amy-" he said, quickly, spilling the hot chocolate across his hand as he quickly straightened up.

"And he told her-"

"Amy-"

"He told her that he'd never loved anyone in the world as much as he loved her." Her grin grew. "Although he did tell me later he loved me more just in a different way. That he was *in* love with Bex, which made it different, but-"

"Amy, stop talking!"

Electric silence crackled around the room, sparking before it landed heavily all around them. He was staring at his daughter, his jaw locked. She smiled gleefully, her eyes flicking back and forth between Lottie and him as her cheeks flushed delightedly.

There was a beat of silence.

"Well," Daniel said, clearing his throat and rubbing his right hand down his left sleeve. "Anyway-"

"HE SAID WHAT?!"

CHAPTER THREE

Bex stared at herself in her mirror. She had got home from work about three hours ago, done a quick workout using the sofa and the kitchen table for equipment and had just about managed to get herself ready. Unfortunately, the endorphins that had been soaring through her body and making her feel on top of the world whilst she sang Lizzo very, very loudly had started to fade away. Instead, worry was now niggling at the back of her mind again.

And she hated herself for it.

She didn't get worried. She didn't get nervous.

And it was *his* fault.

Her reflection stared back at her, looking slightly deflated. Her shoulders were rounded, her hands crossed over her body and her eyes clouded by the thoughts rushing through her head.

"None of that," she whispered fiercely to herself.

Straightening her posture, she narrowed her gaze and placed a hand on her hip.

Power pose.

Better.

She was wearing a scarlet dress. It fell to just above her knee with a slit up the side which made her body look even taller. Talia, her old roommate, had called it her revenge dress. She smiled at the memory and felt her confidence edge up a few more points. Next to the mirror were her nude heels which brought her up to six foot one.

Was it slightly too obvious she was trying to make a point?

No.

It could never be *too obvious* when it came to men.

Her phone buzzed on the bed and she picked it up.

Matt.

"I'm about five minutes away," he said, without preamble.

"Cool, I'll be outside."

"Fab, see you soon."

Matt had rented a car and was picking her up. They had both had to work on New Year's Eve so it had made sense for them to drive up to Tring together. It would be weird being back inside the Williams' house. She felt like it had been decades, but at the same time, she could see the front door as clearly as if she had been there last week. She knew the smell of the living room and had seen the state of the garden last time, but now the house would be different. She had a feeling that now Maria Williams was alive and well, it would feel more like a home. Bex wondered what she would be like. Everyone had always spoken highly of her but still, Bex felt wary. Mums of men she had dated before hadn't been the friendliest.

Not that she was dating Daniel anymore.

Her phone buzzed again.

Can't wait to see you tonight x

Lizzie.

She smiled and returned the feeling.

She had seen Lizzie twice since she had reunited with Charles and the difference in her was obvious. There was a lightness to her step and a smile constantly on her face. She seemed more relaxed, more comfortable in herself and there was a spark behind her eyes that Bex hadn't realised had been missing. She hadn't seen Charles yet. *Censorship* had finished early for Christmas and he hadn't been back to the studios since.

Bex quickly slipped her phone into her small black clutch before grabbing her overnight bag off the bed. She could already hear cheering from outside and smiled to herself as she shut the window. The night sky was purple with clouds of firework smoke already dotted throughout it.

Bex rented a small flat in Ealing, west London. Originally, her flat was the attic in a large country home: the house had been converted into four flats roughly twenty years previously. Bex loved it because it meant her windows were all skylights, and being able to look up into the mass of blue, white or purple gave her a sense of freedom.

Her bedroom was simple. There was one double bed pushed up against the wall, a couple of motivational posters on the wall and a yoga matt curled up to the side. She knew it looked like the bedroom of a twenty-year-old - her whole flat did - but then again, that was living in London in the current climate. She had risen up high enough in her job as a makeup artist at Lightswitch Productions that she could afford somewhere more roomy, but she'd always preferred to spend her money on experiences, holidays, nights out and makeup – which was technically a business expense - rather than spend it on a bigger flat. Especially when she didn't need more space.

Her phone buzzed again.

"Hello?"

"Hey, Bex." It was Matt. He sounded ever so slightly like he was annoyed with her.

"Hi? What's up?"

"What did I just say?"

"Oh, shit," she said, quickly sliding into the kitchen to shut the window. "You're here."

"Yes, I'm here!" he said, his voice breaking into a laugh. "Your bloody Pitbull of a traffic warden is down the next road, can you hurry up please?"

"It's New Year's Eve! Why is he working?"

"Funnily enough I'm not going to go and ask him. Come on!"

"Sorry!"

She quickly hung up, grabbed her stuff again and hurried to the front door. She had to take the stairs slowly in her heels. They were particularly deadly and she'd fallen down them many a time.

As had Lizzie.

As had Matt.

They were lethal.

The night air bit at her arms as she hurried to shut and lock her front door. It sucked any bit of warmth from her skin, especially as her coat was slung over her arm rather than on her shoulders, and she felt the tip of her nose sting painfully. Her mind briefly flicked to the scarf she knew she had left on the kitchen table but she dismissed it. She'd be in Matt's car before long. Turning, she glanced up to see if she could spot him and her step faltered.

If Matt rented a car usually it would be a small little thing. Tonight, however, the car stopped on the road just outside of her place was huge. It was a black Jaguar, its sides gleaming in the lamplight and its body purring happily. Two men were resting against it, watching her.

"Charles!" she shouted loudly, practically sprinting the rest of the way so she could throw her arms around him.

He grunted as she slammed into his chest but it quickly turned into laughter as he returned the hug, his arms closing around her as he brought his head down to kiss the top of hers. "Hello, you."

"It's been forever."

"But weirdly no time at all at the same time."

Bex pulled away, placing her hands on his chest and smiling at him. Even in her heels he was just a tad taller than her. All smiles, startling blue eyes and dark, blonde hair, which was a lot thicker on the top than it had been whenever she had caught him in the corridors at Lightswitch Productions. Her chest filled with warmth at seeing her old friend, he even smelled the same, and the spark behind his eyes matched the one she had seen in Lizzie's for the past few weeks.

She patted his chest before lowering her hands. "You've gained some muscle there."

His cheeks pinkened. "I don't think I have."

"Hey, I'm not saying you're a new born gym addict but your personal trainer has got you into the best shape you've ever been in."

"I don't know if that's an insult or not," Charles said, glancing at Matt.

"Take it as a compliment, that's what I do whenever I'm not sure what Bex really means." Matt turned his green gaze on her. "On that note, hello, nice to see you too. Thanks for the lift, *Matt*. So generous of you, *Matt*. Thanks for waiting for me, *Matt*."

Bex fanned herself dramatically. "Sorry, *Matt*, I just got distracted by the fact that Charles Williams is on my doorstep."

"Oh, shut up!" Charles said, straightening up and shaking his head at her, his blush turning to red.

Matt sighed dramatically before leaning over to grab Bex's overnight bag from her. "Get in the car before anyone drives up behind us or that traffic warden shows up."

Charles squeezed Bex's arm and walked back around the front to passenger side whilst Bex went to jump in the back.

"You look great, Bex."

She stopped, catching Matt's eye as he put her bag in the boot. He smiled at her.

"Thanks!" She grinned. "You look very handsome yourself!"

"Why, thanks very much."

As she said it, she realised just how true it was. Matt was always handsome but tonight he'd made an effort. His hair was styled and he was wearing a smart navy shirt that was tucked into black trousers. It showed off his frame, hugging his strong arms and emphasising his broad shoulders. Even the coat he was wearing could be considered stylish and Matt didn't do fancy clothes.

"What?" he asked, closing the boot and moving around past her. She frowned.

"Nothing." Bex said, inwardly shaking away her curiosity. Matt was allowed to dress nicely for a New Year's Eve party without it being suspicious. Just because she had an ulterior motive didn't mean he had to have one too. Hopping into the back seat of the car the smell of leather hit her with force and she smiled at the luxury of it all. "How come we've got such a fancy car?"

"It's mine," Charles said quickly, turning to check she wasn't sat behind him before pushing back his chair and stretching out his legs.

"And you're trusting Matt to drive?"

"Hey! No car, no opinion!" Matt said, checking behind him quickly before shifting the gear stick and the car began to move. It was a nice change not to feel every bump, nook and cranny in her road whilst they drove down it.

"He wanted to drive."

"Haven't driven a Jag in years," Matt said.

Bex rolled her eyes. "You can be such a kid sometimes."

"Kids don't drive."

"No but they get excited about big cars," she teased.

"Shall we leave her at the next petrol station?" Charles asked.

"Think that sounds great, get it up on your maps, yeah?"

Bex laughed and the anxiety and tension that had been threaded through her mind took a back seat as Matt manoeuvred them through the small streets of London. This felt so easy. She was back with her boys, chatting away, laughing at one another's jokes and occasionally singing along when a good song came on the radio. As they left the busier streets of London, the twenty-mile an hour zone royally pissing Matt off, Bex took a moment simply to watch them. Their easy banter back and forth, the way Charles got exactly what Matt was referring to even if he wasn't making much sense, the natural quality to their friendship, in its own way, was beautiful. She was sad they'd missed so many years together but, they were back now. Stronger than ever. And Charles had only a slight adjustment to his jaw line as a reminder that Matt had once hated him.

Charles had been in London for a last-minute radio interview. He'd felt like he owed his agent after having made her life hell by cancelling the last two weeks of filming for *Censorship*, so had agreed to do the radio interview when she had asked him to. He explained it'd been a rather difficult one as it was the first he had done since his relationship with Jennifer publicly came to an end – only a few people knew it had never been real to start with.

"Petrol," Matt announced, pulling over into a small station on the A41.

"How much?" Bex said, reaching down for her small clutch.

Charles waved his hand. "Don't worry about it." He handed Matt his card, reeling off his PIN.

"In any other circumstance I would insist but seeing as you're now a rich celebrity…" Bex teased.

Charles groaned. "Please don't call me that."

"I'd argue too but I can't be bothered. Thanks, mate." Matt took the card and jumped out of the car. Even the prospect of filling the car up looked like it excited him.

The moment the door closed behind him, Charles turned in his seat to look at her. There was a childish glint to his eyes and a smile across his mouth.

"Have you rung him?"

Her stomach lurched at the question. She looked out of the window, her eyes focusing on a couple in the car opposite. It looked like they were trying to decide what sweets to open first.

"Bex?"

"We haven't spoken."

"Why? Why wouldn't you just ring him?" Charles groaned.

"I did try, actually," she snapped. The couple had selected the packet of Skittles but were now laughing as the man struggled to open them. Something stirred in Bex's chest. Normally, she wouldn't have cared. She would glance at couples and look away without interest. But now…a sense of missing out slid between her ribs.

She looked away.

"Really? You tried to call him?"

"It was a moment of weakness."

It had been three days ago. She had woken up, another nightmare having played through her brain, and before she was fully conscious, her phone had been pinned to her ear. She had rung him, desperate to hear his voice again, desperate to confirm he was still alive and instead she had got his voicemail. As his recorded audio message had begun to play in her ear, embarrassment had run down her spine. At the same time her chest had lifted just at the sound of his voice. She had hung up, humiliation winning the war of emotions inside of her and she had deleted his number. The number that had magically appeared in her phone when they had all remembered.

Bex crossed her arms across her chest. "He probably told you."

Charles shifted in his seat. "I haven't told him I know actually."

She frowned. "Why?"

"Never found quite the right moment."

Silence filled the car. It was itchy and uncomfortable. Bex pretended to need to find something in her clutch bag just for something to do instead of feeling Charles's questions pressing down on her. He turned away from her and looked out of the front window. The loss of his intense gaze made her muscles relax somewhat.

"Why did you two keep it a secret?"

She sighed dramatically as if he had asked the most irritating question in the world. "Because we didn't want to jinx it! We wanted to keep things quiet in case they didn't work. And you and Lizzie had so much going on already, I didn't want to add to that."

She saw a frown cross his brow. "It would have hardly stressed us out."

"I know but...it was nice being just our thing, you know? He's so different from my type and I'm not smart like Helen was. I guess I didn't want people getting their noses in and telling us we were making a mistake before we had a chance to even figure out what we were."

"Firstly, you're intelligent, just in a different way. Secondly, I didn't like Helen. And thirdly, I wouldn't have thought you were making a mistake."

Bex laughed, shaking her head at him fondly. "That's because you're a romantic, Charles."

A small smile crossed his face. "Well then, as designated romantic, I think you should talk to him."

"I tried to!"

"Once."

"Once is enough!"

"Sometimes it isn't, Bex."

"I'm not talking to a guy who refused to call me. A guy who didn't even have the decency to call me back. We were dating for two and half years-"

"Two and a half years!" Charles turned around in his seat to stare at her.

"Yes." Bex jutted out her chin defiantly.

"Two and a half years and you didn't tell us?"

She swallowed. "Yes."

"Two and a half years and you were still trying to figure out *what you were?*"

"I get it! It's a long time! So, when we all remembered he should have had the decency to call me."

"I can't believe you didn't tell us!"

"He was part of the relationship too!"

"Oh, I'll have words with him too, but you were dating for two and a half years and didn't even tell Lizzie!" He narrowed his gaze. "And the Bex I know would have no qualms in calling him if he had ignored one phone call."

This was different. Daniel was different. Her whole relationship with him was different. The other men she had dated she didn't mind chasing because she didn't really care what they thought of her. Rejection would have felt like a mere brush of disappointment.

Daniel...well, with Daniel she did care. Ringing him again would have made her even more vulnerable than the first phone call had.

He made her vulnerable.

Charles shook his head. "You're so stubborn."

"It's a quality your girlfriend and I share."

He snorted. "Don't I know it."

Matt opened the door. "What are you two talking about?" he asked, slipping into his seat and looking between the two of them.

Charles sighed. "The fact Bex and Daniel dated for two and half years and none of us knew about it."

"CHARLES!" Bex shouted, glaring at the back of his head.

"What the fuck!?" Matt said, turning his own seat to stare at her. His eyes widened in delight. "Oh my God, does this mean-?"

"Don't you dare-"

"Is Daniel the dream guy?"

Bex groaned, throwing her hands up in the air. She would have run them through her hair if not for the fact she had spent so long perfecting it.

Why did Matt have to say *anything?*

"Dream what?" Charles asked.

"Nothing!" Bex quickly snapped, giving Matt a look.

Matt simply grinned in response and turned back to the front, facing Charles. "Dream guy is the man Bex has been dreaming about for the past year."

"Matt!" She kicked his chair. "I'm not liking the fact I've clearly been downgraded in your friendship list. Your loyalty should still be to me, remember?"

Matt continued to ignore her. "She dreamed about him every night for the past year. She actually broke up with her boyfriend because of it."

Charles threw her a look. "And you still refuse to call him?"

"I did call him! I called him once and he never called me back!" She kicked the back of Matt's chair again. "I'm going to kill you, Matthew Cartwright."

"Not from back there you're not. I knew something was up the moment we picked you up."

She huffed in annoyance. "What do you mean?"

"Bex, the dress code was New Year's Eve glamour, but you look insane."

"Good insane or bad insane?"

Matt laughed, starting up the car. "Stop fishing for compliments, you know I mean good."

"I'm just making an effort."

"A special effort because Daniel's going to be there." Matt shook his head. "You and Daniel, I'd never have guessed."

"Why?"

The two men exchanged looks.

"What?" she asked leaning forward.

Silence followed her question and the two continued to look at each other. One of their silent conversations playing out between them. Ever so slightly Charles shook his head, his eyes locked onto Matt's. In response, Matt shrugged.

"Bex...you're kind of terrifying."

"I am not! I'm not terrifying!" She looked at Charles who was deliberately looking out of his window. "Charles, am I terrifying?"

She saw his reflection in the glass wince ever so slightly. "Well…" He let out a sigh. "Yes."

Matt flicked on his indicator and smoothly left the petrol station, laughing as Bex made an irritated noise in her throat.

"I hate you-!"

A flash of white exploded within the car. It was so blinding that Bex screamed and Matt slammed on the brakes causing a car behind them to honk loudly.

The sound of the brakes echoed in Bex's mind, crawling up her spine and she felt as if someone had just stamped hard onto her chest.

Breathe Bex.

Screech.

Brakes.

Amy.

She could hear voices.

Her heart thumped painfully in her chest and her temples hummed.

"Bex!"

"What?" she said, sounding out of breath. She looked up to see Matt watching her from the driver's mirror and Charles was turned towards her, one of his hands on her forearm.

"I said, are you okay?" Matt asked.

She swallowed, "Yeah, course. Sorry."

"You sure?" Charles asked gently.

"Yeah, yeah, I'm fine." She forced a smile across her face and leant back in her chair, trying to stop the slight tremble dancing across the back of her calves. "What the hell was that?"

Another flash of white went off and Bex flinched.

"Someone's got a camera," Charles muttered darkly, looking around. They were just outside of the petrol station, in the small slip of road before they pulled back onto the A41. "Drive Matt, quickly."

Matt didn't need to be told twice. As the car was once again filled with white light, they smoothly rushed forward. Even through the thick glass, Bex heard someone screaming Charles's name and he visibly shrank in his seat, placing his hand over the side of his face nearest the window.

"We are at a bloody petrol station!" Matt snapped, speeding up to pull out onto the dual carriageway. "How did they find you?"

Charles glanced behind him. "Might have been coincidence. They might have been waiting for someone else."

"They were taking tons of photos when I picked you up too," Matt said gruffly, glancing in the mirrors of the Jaguar as he increased their speed.

Charles sat up straight, lowering his hand and turning to look out of the window. "They're on my case at the moment. They keep trying to speculate why I took two weeks off work, why *Censorship* had to wrap up filming early, and who I'm dating." He rubbed his hands along his thighs.

"Is Patricia going to tell them?" Bex asked softly.

Patricia was not only Charles's oldest sibling, she was also head of his PR. As intimidating as she was, she was also very, very good at her job.

Charles shook his head. "I'm not ready to put Lizzie through that yet. I almost lost her, I don't want-" He stopped himself, and Bex watched as his shoulders rose and fell heavily. "I can't - I don't want her to regret..." He turned his head and looked out the window, his lip caught between his teeth.

"Mate." Matt reached over and patted him on the shoulder. "My little sister is the most loved-up, starry eyed sucker in the entire world. She's been in love with you since she was, like, ten? You've nothing to worry about."

Some of the tension in Charles's body eased but he still looked like he was holding something in. Bex undid her seatbelt and leant forward, wrapping her arms around Charles's shoulders as best she could.

"Bex! Seatbelt!" Matt barked but she ignored him.

"Lizzie only did what she did because she loved you so much. Now she's got you back, trust me, she's never going to be able to give you up again." She kissed the side of his cheek and felt the muscles in his shoulders relax.

"Thanks, Bex," Charles said softly. "I just can't risk it yet, you know?"

"I know. But I am her best friend, she tells me *everything*. So, I can say, categorically, I know how much she loves you and *exactly* how much she has loved being back with you these last couple of weeks."

"Thanks," he said but his tone sounded heavy.

"The paparazzi being dickheads won't scare her off. I've never seen her happier than in these last few weeks." She lowered her tone to make it deliberately suggestive. "And like I said, she's told me everything. I don't think she could give up being back in your bed every night either."

Charles spluttered in shock and she practically felt the blush radiating off his cheeks.

"Bex!" Matt groaned. "Older brother still in the car!"

Bex let Charles go, sitting back down properly. "Don't be jealous, Matt. I'm sure your conveyer belt of women show off about your bedroom skills too. Charles just clearly didn't need the practice."

Matt shook his head in mock anger. "You bitch."

Charles had started to choke on his own laughter.

"Charles is just a born natural."

Matt rolled his eyes. "Bex, shut up!"

Charles leant his head back against the headrest and laughed loudly, closing his eyes as his body shook with it and Bex smiled triumphantly. She caught Matt's eye in the driver's mirror and despite his words he winked at her, silently thanking her for lifting Charles's mood before shoving an elbow into Charles's side.

"Seriously, you're a celebrity now, has no one tried to train you to laugh normally?"

CHAPTER FOUR

Every room in the Williams house was blazing with yellow light. It shone out and lit up the driveway, making everything look alive and warm even in the crisp, cold air. The car bounced slightly as they pulled up onto the drive and the stone crunched beneath their wheels. A huge Christmas tree sat just beside the porch, lights wrapped around it over and over, while hundreds of baubles hung haphazardly along its branches. Bex smiled as the car stopped and a sense of homesickness flipped in her stomach.

She had so many happy memories of the Williams home.

So many that, until a few weeks ago, she'd completely forgotten about.

The front of the house combined modern architecture with the old Tudor style. The top floors had white exterior walls with long, brown, wooden beams every few feet, whilst the bottom floor's exterior was brick. Grand steps led up to the porch, where a huge black door stood looking slightly at odds with the bright lights and warmth that seemed to seep from every other corner of the house.

"Leave your stuff in the car," Matt said as they all jumped out. "We can just grab it later." He walked around to the back and grabbed a crate of beer and two bottles of champagne.

"Want a hand?" Charles asked.

"No." He waved one of the bottles at Charles. "I went to great lengths to get your dad's favourite. Want him to know it was from me."

"How do you know it's his favourite?"

"He told me, last week." Matt shrugged.

Charles paused. "You spoke to my dad last week?"

Matt clicked a button on the keys and the boot smoothly shut. "Yeah."

"Why?"

Matt shrugged, now not looking at either of them but instead at the bottle in his hand. "To apologise."

Charles's gaze softened. "Matt, I've told you, you don't need to do that."

"Yeah well," Matt smiled and even to Bex it looked a little sad. "Tell your broken jaw that."

"You didn't break Kenneth's jaw," Bex pointed out.

"I know, but I still punched his son and humiliated him in his hometown. Needed to apologise. I'm a big boy." He flashed them a smile. "I can admit when I'm in the wrong. Don't want him thinking I'm some kind of thug."

"No one thinks that, Matt," Bex said, shaking her head at him. "You don't have any menacing face tattoos for a start."

He smiled at her teasing.

Charles walked over to put his arm around Matt's shoulders. "Well, that's it now, yes? No more apologies. If I thought you'd got my sister pregnant and run, I'd have done the same thing. No one thinks you're a thug."

Matt didn't say anything but he nodded. "Come on, let's not get soppy, let's get inside. It's freezing out here.'

Bex turned to walk back up the drive, the stones beneath her heels only bothering her slightly, when she caught sight of Daniel's car. The dark blue Volvo had scuff marks around the wheels and a bunch of stickers on the back window that Amy had put there sporadically. She swallowed.

He was definitely here then.

She forced her feet to move and caught up with the two men as Charles slipped his key into the door.

Light spilled out onto the steps, as did the distant sound of Christmas songs and the smell of pizza, roast dinner and pancakes. Lizzie's round green eyes were the first thing she saw. She was stood on the bottom step of the stairs, wearing a black dress that showed off her curves and her brown hair fell in waves down by her shoulders.

"Hi guys!" she said, delightedly. "That was good timing." She opened her mouth to say something else but was stopped as Charles swooped in to kiss her, crushing his mouth against hers and curling an arm around her waist to pull her into him.

Bex laughed, glancing at Matt.

Matt wasn't looking at them, instead he was staring fixated down the hall. The earlier look of weariness that had been on this face when they'd been discussing Kenneth had faded, the smile was back behind his eyes. "We have a deal. He's allowed ten seconds and then he gets off her."

Bex used the distraction to quickly ask him, "Are you okay?"

He frowned. "Yeah, why?"

"With the whole 'feeling the need to apologise' thing?"

"I'm fine, Bex. I'm always fine." He threw her a smile before raising his voice. "And that's ten seconds!"

Charles pulled back but not before he whispered something in Lizzie's ear that made her cheeks redden and Charles's smile grow. Even though she was a step up she was still a good few inches shorter than him.

"Hello gorgeous!" Bex said. "You look incredible!"

"Stop it!" Lizzie flushed even redder, batting away the compliment but then her eyes dropped on Bex. "Especially stop it, look at you!" She left the stairs and the two hugged each other hard. "Seriously, you look incredible. Where did you get that dress? And don't those shoes hurt?"

"Oh I have had plenty of practice in these kinds of shoes, you know that." Bex stepped away and winked at her.

"Is this what it's going to be like now? I get greeted last by everyone," Matt said dryly.

"Sorry," Lizzie winced, turning to her brother and giving him a hug as best as she could around what he was carrying.

"Who else is here?" Charles asked, glancing down the hall as the sound of laughter travelled up it.

"Everyone."

"Shit." Charles brushed a hand through his hair. "I'll go get changed and meet you back downstairs."

"What's wrong with what you're wearing?"

"I've been wearing this all day." He waved a finger in Bex and Matt's direction. "And if everyone is dressed like you three, I'm severely underdressed."

"This is just a black dress, Charles. You're in a suit!"

Charles met her gaze and raised an eyebrow. "Trust me, Cartwright, that's not *just* a black dress." He pulled her into his side and kissed her on the head. "Right, I'm going upstairs. See you guys in a little bit." He turned and quickly paced it upwards.

"Were you two always this sickly?" Matt said, scrunching his nose up.

"They weren't," Bex confirmed. "But I guess that's because they'd been married for ages. Now it's all fresh and new."

"I'm still here!" Lizzie said, folding her arms across her chest and trying her hardest to look cross. Her blush and the spark behind her eyes gave her away though. "And why are you guys dressed so nicely?"

"Excuse me?" Bex said, placing her hands on her hips. "I'm always dressed nicely."

"True, but Bex, you look like a supermodel."

She grinned at the compliment.

Lizzie turned her gaze onto her brother. "And Matt, you look like you actually washed."

"You're so funny."

"I'm being serious! You've combed your hair!"

"Leave it, Lizzie." He shook his head.

"And he's wearing cologne." Bex wiggled her eyebrows. "We all know Matt's trying hard if he wears cologne."

"Are you going to show us towards the booze or not? Don't know if you've noticed but I'm carrying quite a lot here?" Matt said, ignoring the pair of them. As if to emphasise his point he raised the crate of beer.

Lizzie rolled her eyes - Bex noticed they were neatly lined with eyeliner and she smiled, feeling proud. It had only taken eleven years of knowing each other for Lizzie to finally get the hang of it. "Come on then."

As Lizzie led them down the hallway, sounds of voices and laughter grew louder and louder. She opened the door at the end into the living room and vibrant colours, bodies and music greeted them. Instead of turning on the lights, Kenneth and Maria Williams had lit the room with reel after reel of fairy lights. They were hanging from the walls, along the back of the sofas, and lining the mantelpiece above the roaring fire. There were plates of food on every surface and the glass doors through to the conservatory had been thrown open to create extra space.

The moment she entered the room she felt a shiver up her spine.

Despite the heat radiating from the fireplace and from the groups of people stood around, she felt her skin goosebump and awareness danced across the back of her neck. She followed Lizzie, smiling occasionally at people she didn't recognise as they caught her eye.

"Ta-dah!" Lizzie said, throwing her hands up towards a table that had been laden with alcohol.

Matt placed the crate of beer down upon its surface but hid the two bottles of champagne under the table and out of the way.

"What can I get you?" Lizzie asked. "We literally have everything."

"Would kill for a gin and tonic."

"Coming up!" Lizzie began to make her a drink as Matt asked his little sister how her day had been.

As they spoke, Bex took a deep breath and looked over her shoulder, her blonde hair tickling her bare skin as her eyes searched for the person she was pretty sure she had felt was watching her from the moment she had stepped into the room.

As if pulled by a magnet, all too quickly, her gaze slammed into him.

Damn.

The moment their eyes met, she felt the air around her still, as if the world was pausing to let her have this second in time.

He was near the fireplace, leaning against one of the bookshelves, dressed in a white shirt, black waistcoat and black trousers. His dark brown hair was smooth and mess free.

He looked perfect.

Sharp cheekbones that belonged to vampires in teen dramas, grey-blue eyes that always looked brooding and mysterious, and a manner about him which made people feel safe.

Daniel straightened up, his mouth parting ever so slightly as his eyes pinned her to the spot.

All six foot one, handsome, well dressed *him.*

She swallowed, her pulse in her throat banging away as if it were having a party of its own and she felt her palms turn sweaty. He swallowed too, she saw the dip in his throat and it made her blood thunder louder around her body.

Prick.

A month and he hadn't called her.

Royal prick.

She let her eyes narrow, her anger burning out of them and she saw the shock register on his face, his eyebrows raising as he stepped forward, much to the confusion of whoever he was meant to be talking to. She turned, dramatically flipping her hair back over her shoulder and stepping closer to Matt and Lizzie.

The back of her head burned and a shiver chased its away across her shoulders. Emotion after emotion bubbled up inside of her and she tried her hardest to control them, to slam them down and forget them.

But she had never been good at that.

Swallowing, she leaned over and took the drink Lizzie was still pouring for her.

"You okay?" Lizzie asked, her eyebrows raising instantly as she tried to pull the glass back.

"Absolutely perfect." Bex successfully took the glass from her and shot it in one.

Matt's gaze skated past her, finding the person she'd just been staring at. "I need to go see someone," he said, his tone light.

Bex handed Lizzie her glass back, throwing Matt a warning look. "No, you *don't.*"

He winked at her. "Relax, Bex, it's not who you're thinking of. See you later, Lizzie."

Matt slipped past her.

"Bex." Lizzie's eyes narrowed. "What was that about? What was *this* about?" She shook the glass she was now filling with tonic again. "You're all tense."

"I'm not." Bex shook herself out, letting her shoulders fall away from her ears and trying her hardest to relax her forehead. Her eyes, however, still followed Matt as he crossed the room. He still looked like he was definitely heading in Daniel's direction.

Don't you dare.

Don't you dare.

At the last second he turned to his right and squeezed between two couples, moving away from Daniel. Bex felt her body slump, as if she had been holding her breath.

Lizzie reached over and placed a hand on her arm, pulling her attention back to where she was. "You looked after me so much for the last few months and I love you for it, but now it's my turn. If something's going on, I want to know."

Bex looked at her best friend, staring down into her startling green eyes and she found the words got stuck on her tongue. She had meant to tell Lizzie. Of course she had. The first time around she had kept finding herself wanting to confess, wanting to tell her how hard she had fallen. But, simultaneously, she had enjoyed the secrecy around seeing Daniel, she'd enjoyed the rush of excitement that zipped up her spine when he'd brush his hand across hers when they were in public and no one but them knew just how important they were to each other.

If she was really honest with herself she'd enjoyed the drama.

And at the same time, she'd been terrified. Terrified it was going to end and if everyone knew about it then the break-up would make an unrepairable dent in their friendship group.

And now, she couldn't bring herself to tell Lizzie. Not when Lizzie already felt so guilty about every little thing in life, let alone reversing time and changing their lives. If she knew Bex had been in a relationship at the time and by reversing everything she had guaranteed they had never met...well, she just couldn't do that to her best friend.

One day she'd tell her.

But not right now. Right now, she was still too vulnerable.

Right now, she deserved to be happy.

"I'm fine, Lizzie. Just a bit tired from work. It was a long day."

Lizzie winced, handing Bex the fresh gin and tonic. "How early did you start?"

"I was in the studio at 5 a.m."

Lizzie shrugged. "That's virtually a lie in for you."

"Not on New Year's Eve it isn't. Especially when I had no friends around to distract me."

Lizzie laughed. "None of the usuals were in?"

"No one was in. I would have even welcomed Neil's company..." She considered what she had just said. "Actually, no, I would have hated him being there."

Lizzie laughed but it didn't quite meet her eyes. "And that's all it is?"

The question hung between them. "Of course it is." Bex forced her smile up higher. "Now, let's go have fun and forget about boring work. Who the hell are all these people? I thought you and Charles were keeping things on the down low!"

"We are." A smile crossed Lizzie's face. "But these are all Kenneth and Maria's friends and they aren't going to say anything. They don't watch many of the things Charles is in. Unless he's doing Shakespeare. Then they all go. I've heard from fifteen people today how they wished he would do *Much Ado About Nothing* again. Then there's you, Matt, Lottie and her boyfriend-"

"Oooo new boyfriend?"

"Yeah, he seems nice. His name's Bry. He's American with short brown hair, quite muscular. He's really into fitness too so you two might get along."

"Might?"

Lizzie hesitated. "Well, like I said he's nice..."

"But?"

"It's nothing." Lizzie shook her head. "I'm probably just being overprotective because of what we found out about Felix. I think I'm just going to always be suspicious that she's picked another idiot."

"Surely a good guy wouldn't make you worry?"

"That's what Charles said. I don't think Bry's her *one*. But he might be *the one* for right now. He might just be nervous...but there's just...forget it. Just something I can't shake. Then there's Patricia, Simon and their two kids. Daniel, of course, and Amy."

Bex hummed in agreement.

"Have you seen him yet? You two used to get on so well." Lizzie turned her head to look for him and Bex felt her stomach drop.

"Lizzie, it's fine. I want to spend the evening with you!"

"Amy was asking about you earlier. Think she wanted to see you too." She went to turn around and Bex used her free arm to grab her shoulder. She realised she had been slightly too forceful as Lizzie winced.

"Sorry, I just - stop being *the* amazing host. It's not even your house. You don't need to make me socialise. You know I'm hardly the shy type."

"I just thought you'd want to see them! Remember that time Daniel and you got stuck on the rollercoaster at Thorpe Park? That was hilarious."

"That was one of the most horrifying moments of my life."

Bex and Lizzie stuck together for most of the night, weaving in and out of the different groups of people and occasionally being introduced to someone neither of them had met. Bex was impressed by Lizzie's easiness. Usually she was the confident one but tonight, Lizzie was the perfect host, smiling, relaxed and completely calm. She hadn't even checked her work phone. Not even once. Although Bex could see the outline of it tucked into the armpit of her dress.

Bex glanced across the room to see Charles talking to his parents, the smile across his face wide and his hands animated as he spoke. When he finished talking she saw him glance up to check on Lizzie, his eyes warming at the sight of her.

"You two are a bit sickly."

"What?" Lizzie said, turning her head ever so slightly away from Mrs Peanook who was telling a circle of people about the time she had fallen into a hole her husband had been digging to make a pond.

"You and Charles."

Lizzie looked over Bex's shoulder, her eyes seeking her boyfriend. "No, we're not."

"You are. It's cute. When's the wedding?"

Lizzie's eyebrows shot up, her face reddening in alarm. "We've been back together a month."

"Yeah, but you've been married before."

"Bex," Lizzie hissed.

"That's my name." She smiled. "Come on, Lizzie. You two are basically already married. If it hadn't been for your little time travelling trick-"

"You always rant about people jumping into marriage too quickly."

"Yeah." Bex shrugged. "But they aren't you and Charles. Like I said, you're basically already married."

"I've not even moved in." Lizzie turned properly to face her, stepping away from Mrs Peanook and her friends.

"What are you waiting for?"

"I-I-" Her eyes skated over the top of Bex's head again, looking for Charles. Bex saw the indecision floating behind her green eyes, sparking back and forth.

"What is it?"

Lizzie sighed, her chin dropping down. "I'm waiting for an

invite."

Bex's eyebrows shot up. "Hold my drink, I'll go get you one-"

"Don't you dare!" Lizzie grabbed her, spilling her drink. "We're not even going out *officially* yet."

"Charles is full on in love with you."

"Then he'd have asked me himself."

"He's probably worried he'll scare you off. Look, I'll go ask him-"

"Don't -"

Lizzie's work phone began ringing.

It had buzzed with texts a few times throughout the evening and Lizzie had ignored it but now, she paused, worry flickering behind her eye as she glanced at where it was hidden.

"You don't need to get that," Bex said firmly. "You owe Tyrone nothing. Especially after this year."

Tyrone was Lizzie's boss and Bex felt, as did many at Lightswitch Productions, that he took advantage of her conscientious nature.

"I...I should though-it's my job."

"Not at 11.30 p.m. on the 31st of December it isn't."

The phone stopped ringing for a couple of seconds before it started again, now attracting the attention of people nearby. Lizzie glanced around nervously.

"I need to take this."

"Fine, you do that and I'll go talk to Charles."

Lizzie's hand slammed down on her arm, her eyes turning pleading. "Please don't. Bex, I'm begging you. I just got him back, I don't want to scare him away."

The similarity of her words compared to what Charles had said in the car crossed over each other in Bex's head. One side of her wanted to ignore Lizzie's wishes and do exactly what she knew needed to be done, but she couldn't resist Lizzie's terrified expression. She didn't want to scare her.

"Fine. But Lizzie, just talk to him."

Lizzie sighed in relief, grabbing her phone from her armpit.

Bex winked at her as she watched her leave.

Idiots.

The pair of them.

Looking around the room, she tried to see if she could spot Matt. Not that she was against joining back in with Mrs Peanook's conversation, she just felt finding her other best friend would be a more fun alternative. Even in her heels she couldn't spot his head of black hair. She was surprised he wasn't near Charles. She turned to try and see if she could spot Lottie's curls instead. Maybe she could introduce herself to this new boyfriend, see if Lizzie's worries were justified.

Someone tugged her hand and with a slight jump, she looked around only to realise the person on her arm was considerably smaller than her.

The smile was instant, breaking across Bex's face gleefully.

"Amy!" she said, happily, ducking slightly so she could get even closer to the girl.

Amy looked adorable. She was wearing a dark blue dress that fanned out at the bottom, her hair fell in reckless abandonment over her shoulders and she had so many bangles on one arm she was reflecting light against the closest window giving the weirdest illusion that snow was falling outside. There was a slight etch of worry behind her eyes and the smallest of lines between her eyebrows that reminded Bex of Daniel but the smile on her face was genuine.

She really was the cutest little girl Bex had ever seen.

"You remember me?" Amy said, the uncertainty fading as she clocked Bex's wide grin.

"Of course I do!" Without even thinking about it, she slipped off her shoes and squatted down at Amy's side, not caring that they were amongst a sea of standing adults. Amy's brown eyes squinted happily at her. "How's my little Amy been?"

My Amy.

It had slipped off her tongue easily and she tried not to let the shock of that register on her face.

Amy wasn't hers. She had no right to call her that.

Especially now.

But she had meant it affectionately, right? That was okay. You could say that kind of thing to kids and it not mean a thing, right? Teachers did all the time…surely.

"I've been okay. School's over. So that's good."

"I thought you liked school."

"I do but it's boring at the moment." Amy sighed heavily, the line back between her eyes and Bex had to conceal a smile. She had missed Amy's flare for drama. The young girl folded her legs under her and sat down, blinking at Bex and tilting her head to the floor as if to say, *you coming down?* Bex obliged, moving the small distance from squatting to sitting. The carpet was warm from the amount of people who had trodden on it that evening but it was also soft against Bex's bare legs.

"Boring?"

"We're doing kiddy stuff." Amy shook her head. "And we aren't learning anything important."

A laugh escaped Bex's mouth but she quickly swallowed it back up at Amy's serious expression. The gin had loosened her mouth but she didn't want Amy to think she was laughing at her. "Surely it can't all be bad?"

"I'm enjoying science." Amy shrugged. "But I want to learn medical stuff and the teachers keep telling me off when I ask. I'd find that way more exciting than if my cress can grow on a window sill."

Bex rested her chin against her knuckles, propping her elbow up on her knee. "You want to do medicine?"

Amy threw her a perplexed look. "Obviously. I want to be able to help next time."

Bex raised her eyebrows. "Next time what?"

Amy looked behind her, her eyes scanning around the room. When she'd done a whole circuit, she turned back to Bex and leant in closer. "I want to make sure when Dad gets hit next time I can fix it."

Bex's stomach dropped, her grip tightening around her empty glass to an almost painful degree and she felt fear clutch her shoulders.

Daniel.

Running.

Car.

Slam.

Glass.

Tears.

Screams.

Daniel.

Daniel.

Daniel.

The snapshots of that night flashed through her mind, more vividly than usual and she had to look away from Amy's earnest and determined expression.

She swallowed, trying to bring some moisture into her mouth and feeling as if her chest was struggling to expand.

That night.

The night everything had changed.

"Bex?"

She quickly righted herself. It had been so long since she had been around Amy, she'd almost forgotten that you couldn't have a quick moment to yourself.

Kids picked up on everything.

"Your dad isn't going to get hit again, sweetie." Bex reached forward and squeezed Amy's hand. "He's far too clever for that."

Amy looked down at her lap, her thumbs fighting against one another. "You never know. What if it has to repeat? What if it *has* to happen?"

"Amy, look at me," Bex said gently. When Amy didn't she tapped her on the chin and finally Amy's brown eyes met hers. There was a shimmer behind them that made Bex feel as if all the noise in the room had quietened. "It was never meant to happen. It's not set in stone. Your dad is going to be with you forever."

Amy held her gaze for a short few moments before nodding, swallowing hard as she clearly pushed the thoughts in her head away. "Okay."

Bex tucked a strand of Amy's curly hair around her ear before squeezing her shoulder. "I promise."

Something snapped open behind Amy's gaze as her eyes flicked to Bex's hand on her shoulder and Bex quickly removed it. Maybe she had become too familiar with Amy too soon. She couldn't just swan into this kid's life like she had never left. What was she thinking?

"Sorry," she said, quickly leaning back.

"You...you and Dad do the same thing."

"What?"

"The hair-tucky-pat thing. You both do it."

Something hard formed in Bex's chest. "Do we?" A faint, high-pitched laugh left her lips. "How strange." She looked away, taking a sip from her drink before remembering it was empty.

Amy's sad expression had been replaced by something sharper, her eyes narrowed and there was a slight tilt to her mouth that chillingly reminded Bex of Neil Grayson.

"Do you have a boyfriend?" she said, out of nowhere.

A bark of laughter left Bex's lips but she quickly stopped it when she saw seriousness flash behind Amy's gaze.

"Why are you asking?"

"Dad says you'll have had lots of boyfriends by now."

Bex's eyebrows shot to the top her head.

"Did he now?"

He, what?

The anger she had felt when she had clapped eyes on him at the start of the night flared back to life in the pit of her stomach with even more petrol added to the mix.

"Yeah, he said you'd be in a relationship by now and have been on tons of dates. He said it was why you weren't going to come around to play."

It took a second for Bex to answer, she felt her jaw tighten and her nails dig into her right thigh.

"Interesting," she said sharply, trying her hardest to keep her anger out of her tone.

How dare he. How fucking dare he.

Even if that had been true, he had no right to assume it.

She let her gaze bounce around the room, pretty sure if she spotted his familiar shape she would do a Patricia Williams and stab him with her shoe.

"So, do you have a boyfriend?"

Bex was about to lie. To tell Amy that yes, she had tons of them, so hopefully she could relay that to her dad and see how he liked it. Before she could open her mouth though, Amy spoke again.

"I wouldn't mind. It's okay. Really."

Bex's eyes flicked down to the little girl in front of her and felt the lie die between her lips. The way Amy was looking at her, all innocent brown eyes and careless red hair, made it impossible.

"No."

Amy's eyes lit up. "Really?"

"Really."

"So, why did Dad say you did?"

"I don't know, sometimes men try and insult women by saying they have lots of... friends. Your dad isn't being very nice."

Amy frowned. "But Dad-"

"Amy, there you are!" A gravelly Irish voice spoke above them and Bex looked up to see Kenneth Williams. He had curly grey hair, a slight beard and red cheeks. Amy jumped up, flinging her arms around her grandad's waist and squealing as he bent and picked her up for a huge hug. "You don't mind if I steal her, do you? Need someone to help me cut the cake at midnight and Amy promised to be my right-hand girl." He smiled at her.

"No, go ahead!" Bex stood up, smiling back at the infectious smile on Kenneth Williams's face. She'd have to text her older brother later. He'd die to know she was at a New Year's Party with Kenneth Williams - Jason was a huge rugby fan, despite having never played the game in his life.

"Bye Bex!" Amy called as Kenneth carried her away. Her bracelets danced in the light.

"Bye!" Bex waved her fingers at her, smiling, but the moment the girl's head was turned the smile dropped off her face.

So.

Daniel thought she was in another relationship.

Or dating "many men".

Bitterness and anger raged within her.

Did that *stupid man* still not realise how much he had meant to her? Did he have no clue?

She had literally held him in her arms as he had died. Even if she was in another relationship, surely he felt that was worthy of a conversation. Surely he still felt it was worth it to check.

Hurt joined the fray of emotions battling it out inside of her.

She briefly shut her eyes, trying to calm her breathing and not caring how stupid she might look if anyone caught sight of her.

To be fair, she probably just looked drunk.

Bex's skin felt sweaty, her dress too tight and the room too small. She looked around at the mass of people and took another sip of her glass to yet again realise it was empty.

She saw a tray of champagne glasses resting on the side and walked towards them, swiping one quickly and putting her own empty glass down.

The clock said it was exactly ten minutes to midnight. Someone had turned on the television where a radio presenter and that year's *X Factor* winner were chatting about the past twelve months. Bex looked around but she couldn't see Lizzie anywhere.

As quickly as she could she headed out of the living room, squeezing between the sofas that had been pushed together and walked into the conservatory. There was a couple deep in conversation in the corner, raising their voices ever so slightly as they attempted to speak in hushed tones. They didn't even look at her as she walked in but Bex caught the gold spark of curls out of the corner of her eye.

Lottie.

She glanced at the man opposite her.

The new boyfriend.

"I just wanted to show your mum that photo of us at Kew Gardens."

"I know," Lottie said softly, "I'm so sorry, Bry, I have no idea what's gotten into him."

"He's got some sort of problem."

"He…he does get angry at times."

"You shouldn't be near that Lotts, it's toxic. Especially given everything you've been through."

Bex turned her head away so as not to eavesdrop. Bry seemed nice. If he was trying to protect Lottie then maybe Lizzie's worries were just down to paranoia after all.

Spotting a key in the French doors leading out onto the patio, she quickly pushed them open and stepped out.

The cold air whipped her face with the force of a slap and she sucked in a sharp breath as she felt it thread itself through to her bones. The wind slammed the door behind her shut and she jumped. The trees around the garden were swaying this way and that, dancing to a song no one else was allowed to be part of, and sounds filtered across the sky from those in the forest behind and the neighbouring gardens. Despite being outside on her own, she didn't feel lonely at all. Crossing her arms over herself she walked to the side of the house, out of view from the conservatory, and leant against the cold brick staring up at the sky.

She needed the cold. She needed the fresh air.

It calmed her blood and made her anger recede slightly.

Why had Daniel said that about her?

Why had he thought that?

She was so angry at him she wanted to grab him by the tie and …

and…

And kiss him.

"Urgh!" she groaned, leaning her head back and closing her eyes.

Sometimes she hated being a woman. Did men get this confused?

They never seemed to. They never seemed to have emotions literally combating one another. Her youngest brother definitely didn't. He said what he wanted or what he was thinking, occasionally how he felt, and that was it. Job done.

Her older brother on the other hand...well, he was a special circumstance.

Without opening her eyes she took a sip of champagne, letting the bubbles fall against her tongue.

A throat cleared itself close by. "It's quite cold out here."

CHAPTER FIVE

Her eyes snapped open and her gaze tore into Daniel. He was at least six metres away but her skin was reacting as if he'd whispered those words into her ear. Annoyingly, he still looked just as good as he did earlier. Hair slightly less perfect because of the wind but everything else neatly intact. The waistcoat emphasised his angular shoulders, his cheekbones cast shadows across his face and those grey-blue eyes seemed to have a light of their own.

Fire burned through her.

"That's what you've got to say, is it? That's what you're going to lead with?" She pushed herself away from the wall. The wind was barely affecting her now. Her body simply felt hot with anger as she stared at the man who had been living rent-free inside her mind for what felt like forever.

"Bex," he said, gently. Concern flashed across his face and he took two careful steps towards her.

She resisted the urge to step away. She wanted him to see what he'd done. She wanted him to see how furious she was with him. He didn't get to act like he bloody well cared.

Not now.

"I'm surprised you remember my name."

He frowned. "What?"

"Couldn't remember it well enough to pick up the phone though, could you? Couldn't quite muster up the energy to ring me?"

"It wasn't like that."

"Was it because of all these men you've been telling your daughter

I'm dating? The string of guys you'd think I'd rather see than talk to you after we all remembered?"

He took another step forward, his frown growing. "I never said that."

"Your daughter said you did."

"Amy over exaggerates."

"Over exaggerating means there was something to exaggerate."

He ran a hand along the back of his neck. The familiarity of the movement hit her square in the chest and she inwardly swore at herself.

He wasn't going to have this kind of effect on her.

His movements meant nothing to her.

She didn't feel as if nostalgia had just curled its fingers over her shoulders, she didn't feel a sudden need to walk up to him and kiss away the familiar worry line between his eyebrows, she didn't feel the need to tell him how much she'd missed him.

God, how she had missed him.

"I did think...I thought you might be with someone."

"So I've heard," she replied, her words clipped.

"Is that so unreasonable?"

"You didn't even bother to call me to find out! Not one phone call. Nothing. And when I gave in, when I was the one who called you, you ignored my call and didn't call me back."

His eyes shifted to the side. "It was a confusing time."

"Confusing?" she snapped and took another step forward. "I don't know how this whole thing worked for you, *Daniel,* but I suddenly had a rush of images, feelings and emotions slammed into my head that I couldn't explain. They might have been from a past life but my God, did they feel real. Every single bit about them. I could feel *every single thing.* Do you have any idea what that's like?"

His mouth thinned. "Of course I do."

The fire in his eyes equalled her own and for a second it made her own anger falter.

What did he have to be angry about?

What the hell had she done that was terrible?

"Then why didn't you come and find me?"

He swallowed, his throat bobbing ever so slightly. She followed it with her gaze before snapping her eyes back up to glare at him. The line between his eyes was still there and she saw something painful shift behind his expression. He still didn't drop his gaze, however. Not even for a second.

"Like I said, I thought it would be too confusing. It's hardly like you were ever short of offers, Bex."

Bitterness sagged through her, joining the array of confused emotions already churning in her stomach. "I expected better from you."

"What the hell does that mean?"

She met his cold gaze with her furious one. "It means, *Daniel,* that I didn't expect you to slut shame me."

She got minimal satisfaction from seeing his glare drop, from seeing his cheeks pale and his eyebrows raise. "That is *not* what I was saying."

"Isn't it?"

"No!"

"Because today I've heard you daughter tell me you believed I was *playing* with lots of men. *And* you just said something equally as insulting! Even if I was in a relationship, why didn't you want to talk to me?"

"It would have been too bloody hard!" Daniel snapped.

Their eyes locked together but neither of them said anything. Silence stretched between them, interrupted by the faint rustling of wind and sounds of people in far off gardens. Other than his chest rising and falling he was still, like a statue that was slowly coming to life. His nostrils were flared and his jaw hard, frustration threaded through every feature.

"It would have been too hard for me to call you if you were in a relationship with someone else. It would have hurt too much." He closed his eyes briefly.

"Why didn't you take the chance?"

He didn't answer the question, instead he opened his eyes and stared at her for a couple of seconds. "Did you ever dream about us?"

She blinked, heat rising to her cheeks but she wasn't one to outwardly blush.

Not normally anyway.

"No." She laughed awkwardly, the reflex to lie coming too easily. "What a ridiculous thing to ask."

His gaze sharpened. "Well, I think that tells me everything I need to know."

"Wait, what?"

"Bex, please let's just be realistic about this!" he snapped. "I always cared about you way more than you cared me about me. I was always the one pining after you, not the other way around. I was always the one more invested in what we were, thinking long term, planning ahead. You weren't so bothered. So, I didn't ring you because I didn't want your pity. I didn't want to put you in the awkward situation where you told me you had moved on. And I didn't want to put myself in it either, talking to the woman who meant so much to me while she just brushed me off! While she told me she was with someone else and I was made to feel like nothing." Something darkened behind his eyes. "Again."

"I'm not Helen!"

"I wasn't talking about Helen."

Pain stabbed through her gut. The only thing stopping her stumbling away from him was her anger. She felt her nails dig into her palms, her wrists aching as her hands formed tight fists.

Something smashed.

"Shit, Bex." Daniel's angry expression slipped from his face as they both looked down and saw the glass Bex had still had in her hand lay in shards at her feet. Cuts painted her palms and she saw red lines gleam in the darkness as champagne flowed between her fingers. "Don't move." He reached for her hand but she moved it away from him.

"Don't touch me!"

"Bex, you're hurt, let me see."

"No!" She stumbled back, hitting the wall.

"Stop being stubborn and let me look!" he said, following her.

She slammed her uninjured hand into his chest, stopping him. She could feel his warmth beneath his shirt and smell the cologne on his skin. More pain shot through her and she winced. His keen eyes caught it.

"You're hurt, Bex, let me see your hand."

"I couldn't give a flying fuck about my hand!"

He flinched, his body tensing under her palm.

"You're a bastard! You're such a bastard, Daniel Williams. How could you say any of that?"

He rubbed a hand across the back of his neck again, his chest heaving as he glanced from her bleeding hand to her face, back to her hand.

"Bex, you never told me you loved me. Not once. We were together for nearly three years."

"But you knew!"

"Did I?" She felt the ice of his words bite into her skin. "Bex, you *never* said it."

"The words aren't important."

"They're important to me!" he shouted, his voice rising before he looked away to compose himself. She saw him take a shaky breath, "Just like physical touch was important to you."

Her back bristled in annoyance. "I don't remember telling you that."

"You didn't have to." He shook his head. "For the past year or so, I've dreamt about you pretty much every night. That is how much you meant to me."

"Daniel, -"

"Bex, it's fine. I wasn't *it* for you."

His sentence hung between them.

For once, Bex was lost for words, her brain struggling to come up with a response with the emotional tornado raging inside her.

She was so angry at him she could have screamed in his face and not felt an ounce of remorse, but simultaneously, guilt was practically rooting her to the spot.

She had never told him how she had felt. Yes, she had planned to but she had never got to do it. Could she blame him for feeling the way he did?

"Now, are you going to let me look at that hand?"

"No," she said, her anger triumphing over every other emotion. It felt like she was drowning in it.

"Come on," he said, turning to look at her properly and she saw him force his mouth into a smile. "Let me see."

She leant closer to him, briefly registering the fact he inhaled sharply and his eyes blinked a hundred times more than they had just done for the past five minutes.

"Everything you just said," she said in the calmest voice she could muster, "was an utter load of bullshit." She injected as much venom as she could into the last few words but only felt a small sense of satisfaction as she saw his eyes widen in surprise.

She stepped around him, smacking her shoulder against his deliberately as she strode back towards the conservatory.

"Bex!" Daniel called.

"Don't!" she yelled, angrily, whirling around to look at him. Her hand was really beginning to throb but it was nothing compared to the box of emotions up-ended inside of her. "I held you dying in my arms, Daniel, and you have the bloody nerve to come out with that bullshit. You have no idea what I went through. You didn't have to sit in the street with the person you cared about most in the world bleeding all over you. You didn't have to hear their daughter screaming from across the road. You didn't have to feel utterly and completely useless. I had to rely on some random teenager who happened to be nearby to help because I stopped functioning! My body shut down like it was breaking! I begged you to open your eyes. I screamed at you!" She took a sharp breath, her tone quietening. "And you have the audacity to tell me that I didn't care about you."

He looked away. "I didn't say you didn't care."

"No, that I just didn't care enough. Right? Not up to your standards."

"That isn't what I meant!"

"You said I made you feel like nothing."

"No, that isn't...I didn't- that came out wrong."

She stared at him. His ice meeting her fire.

"You know what-"

Something loud exploded around her. Bex screamed, her heart thundering up in speed and she jerked away, tears automatically welling in her eyes.

Brakes.

Screech.

Daniel.

Brakes, brakes, brakes.

The way his eyes had locked with hers. The way they'd communicated a hundred different things.

Brakes.

Screech.

"I was going to tell you I loved you," she whispered into his shoulder. *"Please wake up. I need to tell you."*

Brakes.

Screech.

She couldn't breathe.
She could smell blood.
"Bex!" Daniel was in front of her, his hands on her biceps. "Bex!"
Blood everywhere.
It was everywhere.
The taste of it, the smell of it, the —
"Bex!"
She looked up, her eyes focusing on the man in front of her.

"Yes?" she gasped, feeling as if she had just come up for air. She pushed his hands away from her, taking two steps back.

More screeches and the pair of them looked up into the sky. It was lit up with a billion different colours and patterns. Fireworks streaked across the darkness, painting patterns and obscuring the stars. Cheers erupted from inside as people struck their glasses against one another and began singing songs or screaming 'Happy New Year!' at the top of their voices. Bex placed her hand to her chest, feeling her own pulse racing beneath her palm and reminded herself that the accident was in the past.

The accident was in the past and the man she had screamed for was just a metre in front of her.

A wave of loneliness rushed through her, making Bex shiver, her body finally reacting to the winter night air, and she realised her teeth were close to shattering against one another. Their heads dropped at the same time and Daniel's eyes met hers.

They'd never kissed on New Year's Eve.

Not once.

They'd always been surrounded by other people.

A memory flickered through her mind. Their last New Year's Eve together. As everyone had cheered, wrapped their arms around one another, singing loudly into the ceiling, his hand had skated across hers and he'd pressed a soft kiss to her cheek. No one had noticed. That slight affection had made her heart soar and her face blush — outwardly for once. She remembered the way their eyes had met and she'd leant forward, about to kiss him on the lips and be damned to the fact everyone was around them, but she'd stopped herself at the last second.

Now, for the first time they were alone... but it was just too late.

Daniel opened his mouth to say something but Bex turned, reaching for the conservatory door and sighing as the warmth and sound of happy voices greeted her. It was like she was being pulled into a bath that was too hot - painful but worth it.

She didn't wait for him to follow her, instead she pushed her way through to the living room where she promptly bumped into the back of someone also watching the crowd of jumping, happy people.

"Matt!" she exclaimed, relieved it was him

He turned and for a second, her own problems and emotions vanished as she caught the regret, anger and pain behind his eyes. It was so strongly visible she felt a rush of protectiveness for him bulldoze into her.

"Are you okay?"

"Fine," he said quickly, smiling at her. "Always. What happened to your hand?"

She glanced out into the mass of people, trying to spot what he'd been looking at. She couldn't see Charles or Lizzie, but the other Williams siblings were dotted around. Patricia and Simon had linked arms and were spinning around - very unlike Patricia, Bex had a feeling lots of alcohol was involved - Lottie and her boyfriend were lip locked on one of the sofas and Kenneth was trying to get Maria to put down the tray of champagne glasses and dance with him. She was furiously shaking her head at him, a grin on her face and her cheeks red as she tried to slip out of his grasp. Kenneth was laughing. They looked like the poster models for marriage.

"Earth to Bex, what happened to your hand? You've got blood on your dress."

"What?" Bex snapped, looking down and realising he was right. It wasn't too noticeable against the scarlet material but she didn't want it to stain. She was also dripping onto the carpet. "Shit, I need to go upstairs."

"I'll come with you."

She dismissed him. "No, it's fine. Go find Charles or something and have fun."

"Don't know if you've noticed but Charles and Lizzie seem to have disappeared."

For a second Bex forgot about what Daniel had said outside. The pain eased into a simple whisper as she laughed at the pained expression across Matt's face - he looked comically disgusted.

"Oh, they're sweet."

Matt raised an eyebrow which only made her laugh harder.

"They're acting like they're teenagers. He's breaking every single rule of man code."

"I don't think he has ever paid much attention to man code."

Matt rolled his eyes. "Touché."

"They've got a lot of missed time to make up for."

"Can we not?"

"I'm surprised you haven't called him out on it."

"Call it a broken jaw and dislocated knee. I owe him for putting him in hospital. Although he's pushing his luck."

Bex laughed again and then shuddered as she accidentally brushed her hand against her dress. It stung, painfully.

"Right, come on. Upstairs. Let's get that cleaned up."

Bex turned her head to her left, glancing through the conservatory out into the dark inkiness outside. Daniel hadn't come in.

She hoped he wasn't just standing outside in the cold.

Stop it.

She turned her gaze back to Matt. He was watching her with an all too familiar smile. Lazily, he glanced the way she'd been looking. "Or would you rather wait for a dashing doctor to come to the rescue?"

"Don't be ridiculous. I don't need rescuing," she snapped.

He laughed. "Okay then."

She scooped up her hand, holding it to her chest and quickly made her way out of the living room. Matt's chuckles reached her ears even as they stepped out into the hallway and she leant to the side to swipe a glass of champagne off the side.

Her hand throbbed, the pain pulsing inside her fingers like it was playing the drums.

The pain in her chest was worse.

CHAPTER SIX

The screech of brakes sliced through the air, Daniel's body folded over the bonnet of the car before he fell to the side. His head smacked down against the ground with such force that a sickening thud echoed into the night sky. Bex felt the sounds run through her entire body. The screech, the thud and Amy's screams. It was like a blanket was being wrapped around her head and forced down her throat.

The car came to a stop. Two scared looking boys were sat in the front seat, their eyes were wide, music still bounced through their battered blue car and the driver was crying. He couldn't have been older than eighteen. As their eyes met Bex saw his panic.

"Don't!" she yelled but the car was already moving, scraping against a parked van as it left. The back wheel rolled over Daniel's right ankle and he made a choked gargle of pain.

Bex raced forward, dropping down by his side, trying her hardest to keep her head straight, trying her hardest not to cry and not to panic.

She couldn't panic.

"Daniel?" She was shaking, her body trembling so violently she could hear the chatter of her teeth above everything else. It was like it was vibrating through her whole body. "Daniel!" she cried out again, pulling him onto her lap.

He groaned, his face scrunching up in pain.

A hand touched her shoulder. "I've rung an ambulance."

"Thank you." She turned her head to see a young boy beside her. His green eyes were wide with terror and he couldn't stop running one of his hands through his dark blonde hair. He looked about thirteen but there was a steady calmness about him that suggested he was older. His eyes were fixed on Daniel and a small

part of her wanted to tell him to look away, to not have to see the broken man lying on her knees. "I'll get Amy." He swallowed, looking up and quickly crossing the road over to where Amy was lying on the ground between two parked cars.

A whisper of laughter ran past Bex's ear. It sounded broken and out of place.

Amy looked paralysed with fear. Her eyes open in horror and her body shaking too. The small girl's knees were wet with blood from where she had fallen but she hadn't noticed. Instead her eyes were fixed on her dad.

"Daniel," Bex said, trying to brush some of his hair out of his face.

It was messy.

It was never messy.

"Daniel, can you hear me?"

"Yes," his voice was gravelly. "When can I not hear you? You're so loud."

Bex laughed but it sounded distorted in the air.

She tried to pull him further up onto her lap and he yelled out. "Don't do that!"

"Sorry, sorry," her voice shook. "I'm so sorry."

"It's okay." He grimaced but finally opened his eyes, squinting up at her. She felt the brush of his hand in hers and when he squeezed it she let out a sob. She should be comforting him, not the other way around.

"You're such an idiot."

He laughed, wheezing slightly. "Is Amy okay?"

"She's fine. She's fine, Daniel. You saved her. She's okay."

"That's all that matters then."

His grey-blue eyes met hers and he smiled at her softly. Her chest tightened and she felt like she was going to be sick.

"Don't look at me like that."

"Like what?"

"Like you're saying goodbye!" she snapped angrily.

"I-"

"The ambulance is coming. You're going to be fine. You're going to be absolutely fine. A bump and bruise. That's all this is."

More people were beginning to come over. She saw a jogger stop and quickly cross the street towards them, she felt the presence of people behind her, someone asking another to grab a blanket from the car. Daniel was beginning to shiver. His blood seeping out over her legs and it sickened her to feel how warm it was. She curled her hand around his tighter.

"Where's Amy? I don't want her to see me like this."

Bex looked up and saw the young girl was finally standing up, her hand curled into the young boy's.

"See her dad like what? A heroic wannabe idiot."

He laughed again but then winced, pain closing down around his face and for a second, the mask he'd been clearly trying to wear in front of her slipped. He was pale. Very pale. His cheekbones making his face look more gaunt than defined and anguish was in every feature.

"Daniel!" she said desperately. "Daniel!"

"I'm right here, stop shouting! I'm injured, not deaf." He smiled.

"Not the time to be making jokes!"

"Dad?" Amy said, her voice wobbling as she kneeled next to him. He winced. "Amy, I'm fine-"

"I'm so sorry, I'm- so- sorry." She was sobbing curling in on herself as Daniel reached out with his free hand to place it on her shoulder.

"You're okay?"

She nodded and he stroked a stand of hair back from her wet, red face, squeezing her shoulder affectionately.

"Don't cry, sweetheart."

Once again, panic rushed through Bex. It was in the tone of his voice. Sympathetic, gentle, calming, but there was something so final about it. There was a goodbye behind his words that he wasn't voicing. He should be angry. Angry about being hit by a car. Angry about being in pain. Angry that Amy had put herself in danger.

But he was just icily calm.

"Dad, I'm so sorry."

"Shut up," he grumbled and the words were so unlike him that Amy let out a gasp of laughter. Her sobs briefly paused for breath on her lips. "I love you, Amy. You never have to be sorry. I'd jump in front of a million cars for you, okay?"

She nodded, and then folded down, her head resting on his chest as she cried into him. Her body shook as he looped an arm around her back and held her to him.

"Please don't leave me," Amy whispered and Bex had to look away. She felt a tightening in her chest, making it harder and harder to breathe.

"Your dad's going to be fine, darling, I promise." She let go of Daniel's hand to run it over Amy's curls. "He wouldn't dream of disappearing on us."

She felt Daniel's gaze on her and for a few seconds refused to meet it before, finally, she let her eyes move to meet his. "Thank you."

"For what?" she said firmly, jutting out her chin as she used her other hand to stroke his forehead. The usual frown line between his eyebrows was gone.

"Being the one I was waiting for."

Her breath hitched. "Daniel, I swear if you keep talking like that-"

"I'm really tired."

"I don't care."

"No, Bex, I'm really tired."

"No, you're not. You're fine."

His eyes shut.

"Daniel! Daniel, don't do you dare do that to me!"

Amy's head flicked up from her dad's chest and she began to shriek, grabbing hold of his shirt and shaking him. "Dad! Dad!"

"Don't you dare! Open your eyes, right now! Daniel Williams, open your bloody eyes."

"Open your eyes, Dad! Please open your eyes!"

Bex felt as if her chest was collapsing. Sirens were echoing down the street and her whole body was beginning to shake violently.

"Daniel!" she yelled out. She brought her head down to his, bending over his body as Amy's small hands continued to pull at his shirt. "Daniel, you need to open your eyes. I need you to open your eyes."

She'd never got to tell him.

She'd never got to tell him the truth.

"He's not breathing," The young boy next to Amy said.

"Thank you for your fucking input!" she snapped. "Daniel! Wake up!"

"No, I mean, he's not breathing!" The boy pulled Amy off, pulled Daniel from Bex so he was flat against the floor and placed two hands on top of each other onto his chest.

"Come on, mate!" He pushed down with force, his young face contorting with anger. He was mumbling something over and over, under his breath, repeatedly.

Bex knew she should be doing that. She was stronger than a teenager. She knew CPR. But it was like her body was refusing to move. Amy was screaming now, her shouts echoing down the street. People were looking away, hiding their faces, Halloween makeup running down cheeks as silent tears stripped away the colours. Daniel's head rolled to the side.

Bex woke up, her eyes flying open as she gasped for air. It felt like she had been drowning, misery crushing down upon her chest and sorrow filling her lungs. She flung the duvet away from her and sat up, her body trembling violently as she fumbled for the lamp by her bedside. Sweat coursed down her back and everything felt sticky and unpleasant. Her hand smacked against it and she swore in pain as she knocked the lamp onto the floor.

"Bex, what are you doing?" Matt grunted from the mattress across the room.

"Nothing, nothing, just go back to sleep. I'm fine. Still a bit drunk, go back to sleep."

"Go get a drink of water."

"Yeah, yeah, good idea."

Bex tried to calm her breathing. She placed a hand to her chest and took a couple of deep gulps of air as her eyes adjusted to the dark.

Her hand was still throbbing. The combination of her earlier injury and the fight with the lamp causing it to ring with newfound pain. Her lip began to tremble as the nightmare played over in her brain and she squeezed her eyes shut, trying to drown it out. When it continued to run she slowly got up and walked towards the door, trying to leave the room as quietly as she could. The house was in silence apart from someone snoring down the corridor. It was somewhat comforting.

Real sounds.

Real people.

She walked towards the stairs, taking them as quietly as she could and remembering not to lean her whole weight on the bannister when she got to the bottom: it would make an awful creaking sound.

Matt and her had never come back downstairs after going to fix her hand. Despite Bex's insistence, Matt had been fine with cutting the night short. Surprisingly fine with it. He'd bandaged up her hand as well as he could and then they'd taken it in turns to use the bathroom, change, and go to bed.

They were sharing Amy's room. An extra mattress had been pulled into it which Matt had insisted on sleeping on. She hadn't fought him on that point. Amy was in with...with her dad in his old room.

Downstairs was still a mess. Confetti lined the floor and decorations hung from the ceiling, some slightly swaying as they had been pulled down. Bottles lined the tables and she could still smell the shadow of the food that had been constantly plated up again and again by Maria.

Kenneth would no doubt be up at some ungodly hour tidying.

Maybe she'd get started on it. Give him a nice surprise when he woke up.

The cold had started to ebb out of her chest and the sweat on her skin had stopped trying to drown her. She felt tired, a shadow of a headache hummed at the back of her skull and her face felt dry.

She walked into the kitchen, enjoying the feel of the cold tiles against her bare feet and moved over to the sink. Taking a semi-clean glass from the side, she rinsed it under the tap before filling it up with water.

"Hey."

She jumped, spilling the water into the ceramic basin of the sink.

With everything going on, with every single emotion battling it out inside her, his voice was the only one she wanted to hear and yet, at the same time, she didn't want to hear it at all. Her emotions from earlier were still present in her gut. The anger his words had caused was still running through her blood whilst her mind was desperate to see him, to check that he was real, to hug him.

Her body was completely at war with itself.

"Hi," she whispered. It felt wrong to talk normally in the dark.

Daniel walked up beside her. He was no longer wearing a jacket or a waistcoat, but he was still in his shirt and trousers.

She took a long drink of water before putting it down on the side and placing her palms against the wooden worktop, not trusting herself to face him yet. Daniel's side brushed hers.

"What the hell have you done to that hand?"

She laughed and a tear slipped out of her eye as a consequence. She wiped it away quickly, embarrassment warming her neck as she felt him watching her.

"Matt wrapped it up."

She finally turned, holding out her hand towards him.

"Oh, dear," he whispered, his tone slightly playful.

His hands closed gently around her forearm and she managed to resist the urge to flinch at his touch. A jolt passed through her blood stream, however.

"He wrapped it up in a sock?"

"Hey, it was the best we could do."

She inwardly scolded herself as a sob threaded its way through her words.

His eyes flicked up, catching it. They stared at each other for a fraction of a second and for a terrifying moment, Bex thought he could see exactly what she had just witnessed.

"Sit down, let me have a look at it." When she didn't move, he inclined his head closer to hers. "Please?"

Her inner turmoil twisted again but she pushed it aside and despite her earlier prickliness, she nodded. The dream had shattered her and she felt too tired to fight him on the matter. He gently took her by the arm and led her into the living room.

CHAPTER SEVEN

Bex sat down on one of the long living room sofas as Daniel went to get a first aid kit. In the darkness, it felt like the iron clad walls she'd set up for herself had the strength of cloth. She hated the fact she had liked the way he had taken her arm and led her into the living room. She hated the small warmth that had grown in her chest as his caring eyes had scanned over her poorly bandaged hand. She hated how his very presence eased the ache the nightmare had left in her head.

There was a duvet over one of the sofas, the cushions all piled at one end looking spread out and messy. "Were you sleeping in here?"

He glanced at the sofa she was looking as he came in with the first aid kit. It had been pushed back against the wall for the party.

"Yes."

"Why?"

"I'm going to go get a bowl of water, two seconds." His long legs strode past her again and she resisted the urge to watch him leave the room.

Their argument seemed a lifetime ago.

She shivered. As the aftereffects of the dream began to fade, she realised she'd left the dressing gown she had brought with her upstairs. She was wearing a simple two-piece lilac chemise. The shorts were just long enough for her not to feel completely exposed but her arms were bare and a pattern of goosebumps decorated her skin as the late night chill settled over her body.

Daniel's footsteps came back into the room. He paused as his eyes met hers, placing the bowl down on the small coffee table that had been shoved up next to the sofa. He didn't sit down, however. Instead he moved back over to the sofa he'd clearly been sleeping on and picked up the duvet with one hand.

"You're shivering."

"Thank you," she said, gratefully, taking the duvet from him and wrapping it around herself, quickly covering her chest.

Not that he had even noticed the fact the chemise coupled with the cold had left very little to the imagination.

That really shouldn't have irritated her...but it had.

"Now let me see that hand." He sat down and waited for her to offer him her hand before moving closer towards her. His knee brushed hers as he took her wrist and another jolt ran through her.

Stop it!

"Wow, it's worse than I thought." He raised an eyebrow. "A sock with Sellotape wrapped around the end." The corner of his mouth kicked up into a smile.

"It was the best we could come up with!"

"I'm going to have a word with Matt. He's in serious need of some basic first aid skills." His warm eyes caught hers. "As are you. This is appalling."

"Hey! We were a bit tipsy, okay?"

"Poor excuse!" He began to unwrap the Sellotape, which Matt had determinedly wound around her arm, his fingers brushing her skin. "You look as if you're about to go and put on a puppet show."

"Stop it," she laughed.

"Honestly, which character is Matt's sock? Did you at least name him? Or her?"

"Or them!" Bex pointed at him and the easy grin across his mouth made her heart hurt.

"Or them. Quite right."

Dropping his gaze, he leant forward and took the sock off carefully. Bex grimaced and a hiss of air escaped between his teeth as the material snagged against her skin. Daniel's other hand tightened around her wrist in response.

It was worse than she remembered. She really had cut her hand pretty badly and now she was looking at it, the pain was beginning to increase. The sock had soaked up some of the blood but because it was black, she hadn't noticed her hand was still bleeding. Now she could see trails of it fanning down her hands and she winced at the state she'd left it in.

"Right, let's clean this properly, shall we?" He placed her hand gently on the top of his thigh before he began to take things out of the first aid kit. "Mum is messy in every aspect of her life except when it comes to her job and her medical items. Thank God for that." He began to rip small white packets open, taking out wipes. "I'm just going to turn on the light."

"Don't!" she said the word so sharply that he looked up, surprise across his features.

"Why?"

Because you'll see I've been crying.

"I...errr..."

"Bex?"

"I just...it's night time. I've been drinking. No one needs to see this dehydrated nonsense under a spotlight." She made her tone light and breezy and gestured good naturedly at her face.

Daniel opened his mouth, a half smile across his lips as he frowned in amusement. But whatever he was going to say, he quickly stopped himself, returning his gaze back to her hand.

With a flicker of alarm Bex realised she really wanted to know what he'd been about to say. And why it had now caused a red flush to warm his cheeks.

He took her hand gently by the wrist and raised it ever so slightly. Bex pretended the touch of his careful fingers did nothing to her nerves...or her pulse...or her body. He sighed. "I'm sorry, I need the light to work. Unless you want me to do as good of a job as Matt?"

She shifted. "No."

"Okay then...I'll put on the lamp, okay? Less light. Compromise?"

"Okay."

He leant away, reaching for the switch by the side of the sofa and the lamp on the coffee table just behind him flickered on. She looked away quickly, pretending to be focused on the curtains across the other side of the room but she felt his gaze on her face.

"Right then," he said, softly.

Daniel let go of her hand briefly to roll the sleeves of his white shirt up to his elbows. Her eyes followed the movement and she felt a jolt of lust run through her. He was lean but muscular, the bit of skin he'd just exposed was carved and solid, a few prominent veins stood out in the semi-darkness and she felt her mouth dry.

"Are you okay? You look funny."

"Fine!" Bex said, shrilly. Her eyes darted up quickly and a blush brightened her own cheeks as she realised he had caught her staring. "All good."

Shit.

She was blushing. Why was it always around him that her body tried to betray her emotions?

"Are you sure? You're not feeling faint are you? You can lie down?"

Don't flirt. Don't flirt. Don't flirt.

"I'm fine." She forced back an acceptable response.

He placed the back of his hand to her forehead and studied her face. She could see the medical glint behind his eyes but still, her face became more flushed as he leaned towards her. This close she could smell his cologne again.

Was she that needy for someone's individual attention?

Or was it just him?

"I'm fine," she forced herself to say. "Honestly Daniel, I'm not about to faint."

He eyed her, unconvinced, but then dropped his own hand before turning his attention back to hers.

Bex's breathing returned to normal as he began to carefully clean the cuts across her palms. She watched him work, methodically and precisely, his eyes solely trained on what he was doing and she felt herself leaning in to watch him.

She liked to think she was independent, that she was completely fine with being on her own and fiercely happy in her own company.

And she was.

Most of the time.

But there was something undeniably attractive about being cared for, about someone taking the time to really look after her and care for her. She couldn't remember the last time it had happened and it was spreading havoc through her emotions.

"You're not the first person this evening, I've had to patch up," Daniel said, breaking the silence.

"No? Who else was this stupid?"

"Mum's friend, Diana. She decided that this new year was the time to relive her youth and do handstands against the wall."

Bex snorted with laughter as a grin crossed Daniel's face. "I'm guessing that didn't go down too well."

"No, she fell into the bookshelf. It would have fallen on top of her had Dad and Diana's husband not been there to grab it. She had a pretty bruised ankle though."

"Never a dull moment for you, is it?"

"I almost expect it now. Especially at parties. Someone is always going to get injured."

"Do you still enjoy your job?" Daniel flicked his eyes up to meet hers, surprise hiding just behind the grey.

"I do, yeah." He shrugged. "Always wish I could spend more time with Amy but I love my job."

"Do you still want to be part-time?"

"Um, yeah. In an ideal world but alas, can't really afford that. How about you? Still loving your job?"

"Yeah."

"Still working with Jack and Jill?"

Warmth flooded through her.

He remembered.

"Yeah, still stupidly early mornings but it's worth it."

He smiled. "Good. That's really good." He looked down and took out a small box of skin closures from his pocket. "Just in case."

"Have they been on you all night?"

"I'm not that organised."

"I'd disagree."

"They were in the cupboard with the first aid kit."

"Sure."

He laughed again, his shoulders falling from his ears as he sat back to open the packet. He looked relaxed. His hair was slightly scruffy and he'd undone a few buttons at the top of his shirt. Combined with rolled up sleeves, the look reminded Bex of early mornings and nights they'd spent together. She wanted to tell him how good he looked. A part of her itched to compliment him and watch him blush in response. It was like the alcohol and nightmare had loosened her tongue.

She desperately searched for something else to say.

"I never actually met your mum before."

He paused. "To my shame, I'd never actually thought about that." A smile broke out across Bex's face and his eyes turned curious.

"What?"

"You still say stuff like *to my shame*. You've not changed in the slightest."

"I don't know if that's a good or bad thing."

"It's good. Trust me, it's good."

His eyes sharpened causing her skin to bristle with heat. She quickly looked away.

"She's nice."

"Yeah, she's great. Fusses over everyone and everything. I don't think she sat down once this evening. Right, nearly here." He took a bandage from the green kit and began to unwrap it. "This is probably a bit excessive but you use your hands a lot so want to just cover it up as much as I can."

"Makes sense."

He pressed the thicker part of the bandage into her palm before wrapping the ends around her hand in a neat and organised manner. By the time he'd finished, it looked almost elegant, like she was wearing a pale, white sleeveless glove.

"Thanks," she said, trying not to be affected by the fact that he'd moved away once he had finished, quick to place all the items back inside the first aid kit and move the bowl back onto the coffee table. Even his knee had stopped touching hers and she felt the loss of its warmth.

"No need to thank me." He put the first aid kit to the side and cleared his throat. "It was...it was my fault after all."

"You did make me quite mad."

"I gathered that. The broken champagne flute kind of gave it away."

"Not the bloody hand?"

"It was a close second."

They looked each other and both laughed softly. Daniel shook his head, rubbing his hands against his trousers before standing up. "I'd better let you get back to bed."

Something cold settled back into her stomach. Daniel had completely distracted her from the very reason she had come downstairs but now his words acted like a trigger.

She didn't want to go to bed. She didn't want to shut her eyes.

And she also didn't want to lose this moment. He'd been a bastard outside. An absolute git. But in the lamp light, a part of her began to listen properly to what he had said. They were the words of someone who had been hurt too.

"I owe you." She stood up, clutching the duvet to her still.

"You don't," he said softly, dismissing her with a wave of his hand. He reached across towards the lamp and they were once again plunged into darkness. It painted the furniture in a purple, navy light and made Bex feel braver.

"I owe you the truth at least."

He turned his head to look at her. "The truth?"

She took a deep breath. "I lied. Earlier."

He cocked an eyebrow at her, straightening to his full height and turning to face her fully. "Sorry?"

Without her heels on she was reminded of just how much of a difference their few inches in height felt to her. There had been something about Daniel's height that had always made her feel safe. Her eyes flicked up to him now and she swallowed. Hard.

"I dream about you every night." Daniel's body stiffened. "I have had dreams for the past year and a bit. I even broke up with my boyfriend because I felt I was having a mental affair with someone I must somehow know. They were great dreams, amazing dreams." She ran her teeth across her bottom lip. "Now I realise they were memories. Memories of us just hanging out, memories of us getting to know one another, memories of us...just being us." He watched her carefully, the small line between his eyebrows prominent. "But they slowly began to be turn into darker ones. I began to dream of the night you got hit. And since we all remembered, it seems to be the only dream that wishes to be repeated." The memory of it was still so close to the surface. She felt a sharp string of tears threaten to build behind her eyes. "That's why I didn't want you to turn on the light. Another lie. I was scared you'd see I was upset. The reason I was downstairs was because I'd had another nightmare."

He stepped closer to her. "Why didn't you say that?"

"Before? Oh, gosh, must be something to do with the fact I didn't want to be vulnerable in front of someone who had decided I wasn't worthy of a phone call." She intended for her sarcasm to come off light and funny, but it sounded forced and hung in the air awkwardly between them.

"Shit," he whispered, running a hand over the back of his neck. "Bex, I'm so sorry."

"I rang you after one of those nightmares." She swallowed, pushing back the pinch on the brink of her nose. "I needed to hear your voice."

He stepped forward again, reaching out a hand to hold her arm. "I am so sorry."

"I *really* needed to hear your voice." She shook her head, his face partially swimming in front of her as she felt more tears try to crowd her vision. "And you didn't bother to pick up."

"I was a coward."

She looked away, forcing a smile on her lips. "Well, I didn't want to say..."

He laughed. It was short and pained and he squeezed her arm ever so gently.

"I've dreamt about that night too." He nodded towards the sofa just behind her to the right. "It's why I was sleeping down here. I didn't want to disturb Amy or upset her if she woke up to me having a nightmare. Her nightmares, thank God, seem to have ceased."

"She had nightmares too?"

"Yes. And she had more severe reactions to them."

"She didn't want to lose you."

Unable to stop herself, Bex reached forward with her uninjured hand and took his hand in hers, the duvet falling to her feet. For a second, she was scared he was going to pull away. But he didn't. His long fingers curled around hers instead. Bex fought back the urge to sigh with relief. It was the first time she had touched him properly since he'd laid in her lap. His skin was warm and the way she had positioned her hand meant her fingers just traced over his wrist.

She could feel his pulse.

Strong. Solid. Alive.

"Is Amy okay now?"

His eyes crossed over Bex's face. "She's fine."

"Are you okay?"

He squeezed her hand ever so slightly. "Not really. How about you?"

She smiled sadly. "Not really is a good summary."

They stared at each other, their gazes locked together with such force Bex didn't even know if she could blink. Her mouth felt dry and her body was so very aware of him being so close. She could feel the heat of his hand on her arm, just above her elbow, the way his long fingers were tracing the sensitive skin just inside of it whilst the hand in hers felt strong and safe.

But it wasn't enough.

She closed the space between them, noticing the way he sharply inhaled as her chest brushed his own. She didn't feel the slightest touch of cold, around them was something much hotter.

Daniel's nostrils flared as she leaned in closer, his cupid's bow drawing her attention.

"What are you thinking?" he said, hoarsely. He let go of her arm and reached up, tapping her temple ever so gently. "I can see you're thinking about a million different things."

"I'm thinking two things actually." She licked her lips. "Firstly, you were wrong."

"Wrong?"

"Outside, you were wrong."

He swallowed, his breathing become more shallow as she deliberately placed a hand on his stomach and ran it up toward his chest. "Oh yeah?"

"Yes." Her eyes met his firmly. "And you know what the second thing is."

There was a short pulse of silence where she felt Daniel breathe in slowly, the hand she had on his chest moved with it.

"I do?"

"Yes." She slid her hand up to his shoulder, leaning into him.

His eyes scanned her face and he hesitated, she could see the emotions behind his eyes arguing between themselves.

She tilted her head. "I want you to kiss me."

Daniel didn't say anything at first. His eyes were fixed on her mouth and his breathing was shallower and faster.

"Unless you don't want to." She moved to pull away but his grip on her forearm tightened. Before she could blink she was pulled back to his chest, and his mouth slammed down on hers.

Feeling exploded across Bex's lips. It was hot, tantalising and desperate. One of his hands moved to the nape of her neck, his fingers brushing against the sensitive skin and causing more fire to stir in her blood whilst the other looped around her waist, bringing her body in closer to him.

God, she'd kissed many boys in her life. She'd always thought the majority were rather good. Pleasant enough.

They all paled compared to him.

Daniel kissed like *a man*.

The kind of fires he stoked inside made her feel breathless and needy. She could barely concentrate on anything but him. The kiss wasn't just a prelude to something else. The kiss was its own damn show. She threaded her arms around his neck, running her hands through his hair and feeling a rush of desire pool between her legs as she bit down on his lower lip.

"Bex," he hissed against her before coaxing her mouth open and upping the intensity.

Oh, God.

She pressed her body into him harder, trying to ease some of the ache in her core but it did the very opposite. Instead it just stoked the fires as his tongue slid against hers. The hand around her neck tightened.

Daniel. Daniel. Daniel.

Sweet Daniel, calm Daniel, sensible Daniel.

Kissed like a bloody Devil. She'd never known anything like it.

The first time it was such a surprise. It was in this very house, a couple of metres above them, in the study. They'd been arguing, Daniel having found her about to ring her ex in a moment of drunken weakness at Lizzie's thirtieth.

This kiss had the exact same power over her as that one, turning her bones to jelly and unsettling any kind of calm her body had been pretending to possess in Daniel's presence.

Carelessly she gripped onto his hair too tightly.

"Shit." Pain soared down her arm making her flinch. He broke away from her immediately and she felt the loss of his lips more than a kick to the stomach.

"Are you okay?" He was breathing hard, she could feel his shoulders rising and falling underneath her arms and his eyes were practically black. The sight of them did nothing to calm her heart rate so she dropped her eyes to his mouth.

Yep, that wasn't the best idea either.

She bit down on her lip and couldn't hold back the grin slowly growing across her face. A huff of laughter left his lips as a similar smile crossed his own. Their gazes locked again and the way he looked at her made her feel like the most beautiful thing in the world.

He'd always done that. He made her feel better than anything or anyone.

"You okay?" he repeated again, softly. "Your hand?"

"Can't really concentrate on it right now," she said.

Daniel smiled but worry still creased his brow. "You sounded in pain."

"It's nothing." She shook her head, a smile on her lips. "I forgot what a good kisser you were, Dr Williams."

He laughed, his cheeks flooding with colour as he pressed his forehead against hers. "You're being far too generous, as always, Miss Wright."

She tilted her head up and kissed him again, skating her lips across his deliberately slowly and teasingly.

"I'm not."

His cheeks grew redder but as he tried to kiss her back she pulled away, a smile still on her lips.

"If you kiss me again, I will have you here and now, and that's not happening. Not whilst I'm still mad at you."

Daniel blushed so hard he was practically the colour of a stop sign. "That's not...that's not what I was trying-"

"I know," she smiled. "But I've never been able to resist you, have I?"

She watched his reaction to her words. The way he dropped her gaze and shifted his weight ever so slightly whilst his face remained flushed and his cheeks red. Whilst he was distracted, she pressed one of her arms resting on his shoulders gently against his neck. His pulse was still there. Still strong. It was just going at a hundred miles an hour.

"I'm really sorry I didn't call."

"I bet you are, *now*."

He laughed, but when he looked back up she saw a sadness behind his gaze that made her lean in closer to him. "Honestly, Bex. It was cowardly of me. I just...got in my head. I was convinced you...what I said outside. I'm sorry I hurt you, I'm sorry if I got it wrong-"

"No *ifs*. You did get it wrong."

"I'm sorry."

"I'm sorry too." She folded her arms around him, holding onto him tightly and inhaling sharply as she caught the smell of him on his clothes. The slight ghost of his cologne mixed with the smell of books and the laundry detergent he used. He always smelled so good.

She closed her eyes, pressing her face into his shoulder and they stayed locked together, breathing quietly in the darkness.

"Would you come to bed with me?" Daniel asked, his voice very quiet.

"Wow, where did that confidence come from? I said that wasn't going to happen." She pulled away ever so slightly so she could look up at him, a smile across her lips.

His expression, however, was rather more serious. He stroked a hand across her cheek, cupping her jaw in his hand. "Just to sleep. I promise."

She knew why. She could see it in his eyes without him uttering a word. The same nightmare that had been plaguing her had been stuck in his head for just as long. Maybe...maybe if when she woke up and she had Daniel right next to her, his pulse easy and ready for her to find, maybe it wouldn't be so bad. And maybe, if he woke up, scared and afraid, he would realise it was a dream a lot easier if she was tucked into his side.

"Okay." She nodded.

He pulled away from her, reaching for the duvet at their feet whilst his free hand remained in hers. "Sorry, it's just the sofa."

She rolled her eyes. "I've never been picky."

He laughed and he squeezed her uninjured hand.

They both walked over to where he'd been sleeping. It was bigger than the others and there was a bed sheet thrown carelessly over the base cushions.

"After you."

She glanced at him. "You going to bed in your suit?"

"I left my top in Amy's room. Didn't want to wake her."

Their eyes met. She knew the reason why he'd rather have stayed in a shirt and trousers than face Amy finding him in just his boxers in the morning. Or anyone for that matter.

Sympathy and protectiveness for him flared hard in her chest.

The first time she'd seen the scar across his back it had horrified her too.

"You didn't tell anyone this time around either?"

"No...I don't want Amy to find out." He let out a long breath. "If I tell someone, she's bound to overhear them talking about it at some point. She hears everything."

"I get it, I do, but you're going to have to take off your shirt, otherwise you'll melt. Just lie on your back, there is no way in hell you are going to be tossing or turning in your sleep with me next to you. That way, if anyone accidentally comes for a walk in the night, they won't see it. And in the morning, we'll set an alarm on your phone early enough for us to get up and you to change back. Deal?"

He hesitated. "If anyone does go for a walk in the middle of the night, they'll see us."

"So?"

His eyes tracked across her face. "So, they'll think we're together."

"So?"

He blinked a couple of times. "You don't mind?"

She frowned. "I never minded."

He ran a hand across the back of his neck. "You wanted to keep it a secret last time."

She walked up to him and began to undo the buttons on the shirt. His hands landed on her hips and she felt his gaze as she concentrated on getting his shirt off. "Lizzie's happy. Charles and her are great. We don't need to keep it a secret anymore."

"It...it really was just that?"

"It *really* was just that. What else would it have been?" She undid the last button and ran her hands back up his chest, enjoying the way he sucked in his breath at the touch of her skin against his.

"I...er..." Something unreadable passed across his face. "Nothing."

"Daniel?"

"I think I've been a bit too honest today, don't you think? I keep landing myself in trouble."

She pushed his shirt off his shoulders, forcing his hands off her so she could pull it down his arms. "I'll never be cross with you for being honest. I just may correct you when your inner critic tries to make you think a certain way. Turn around."

His eyes tracked back and forth across hers uncertainly before he turned around to let her get the shirt off his forearms. He tensed under her appraisal and she deliberately didn't let her pace stop or falter as she removed it.

The scar didn't look so gnarly in the darkness. It moved from Daniel's right shoulder blade, across his body, down to the lower part of his back. She knew the skin was still red and raised, scabbed over but still vulnerable in a completely different way. She stepped forward and pressed her mouth to the top of it, wrapping her arms around him and feeling his body sigh into her. The sight of it made her angry. Angry that someone could have hurt him like that. She turned him around, smiling up at him and reaching up to flatten his hair. He caught her hand before she dropped it, turning his head to press a kiss against her palm whilst still holding her gaze.

The move was so innocent but it sent a jolt of lust through her.

How long, exactly, are we planning on making him wait before we sleep with him? A small voice in her head asked.

Not now, Bex.

She stepped back. "You can do your trousers yourself, otherwise I will get carried away." She winked at him and he rolled his eyes,

"Yeah, yeah."

"I mean it, I'm going to keep my eyes fixed on the ceiling." She folded her arms and turned her head upwards.

"Stop it!" Daniel chuckled.

He quickly removed his trousers and folded them neatly before placing them to the side. He glanced at Bex, a smile on his mouth. "Thought you weren't watching."

She looked away, a smile playing across her own mouth as she heard him laugh.

He lay down on the sofa, pulling the duvet up towards him and lifting part of it into the air, silently inviting her to join him. She snuggled in next to him, resting her arm firmly across his stomach and resting her head on his chest, ignoring the fact she deliberately placed her ear directly over his heart.

"Ah, damn, I forgot we need to set an alarm."

"No, my normal wake up time is 2.30 a.m., I'll be up earlier than anyone else." She pressed her head more firmly into his chest, enjoying the warmth of him beneath her and feeling his arm around her shoulders.

She knew it should scare her.

And she knew the realisation that she had missed being with him so much would terrify her once she was far enough away from him. But right now, she didn't care. She could push those thoughts to the side.

He was here.

He was safe.

"It's 4 a.m. now? Way past 2.30."

"What I'm saying is, I never sleep in. I'm always up first. It'll be fine, Daniel."

"When we were together you always used to lie in."

"That's because I was with you," she whispered sleepily. She shifted her head upwards and pressed a kiss onto his neck, enjoying the trace of cologne she tasted on his skin.

"I am with you right now," he said, laughter in his voice.

"Yeah but we're on a sofa, not nicely tucked up in your bedroom. It's different. Go to sleep, we'll be fine. I'll wake up in time to give you your shirt."

She felt her body already being pulled into sleep, feeling safe and secure in Daniel's arms and cosily tucked into his side. It had been so long since she had looked forward to sleep. Her eyes were growing heavy and she moved her head again to listen to the steady drum of his heart underneath her ear.

He was alive.

He was here.

He was okay.

She smiled. "We got our New Year's kiss."

She heard his laughter but it sounded like it was coming through fog. "We did."

"Next year let's actually aim for midnight though."

His arm tightened around her. "I'd really like that."

CHAPTER EIGHT

Daniel woke gradually, not in his usual sweaty panic, and not with a jolt. He felt so peaceful he could easily fall back to sleep if he wanted to.

Bex's scent was everywhere.

He could smell her shampoo, her perfume, her body wash and the exfoliator she used. It was a mixture of citrus, orange, lavender and something tropical but it all blended together perfectly because it was *her*. She was still tucked into him, her head firmly on his chest and her arm around his torso protectively. He could feel the slight tickle of her hair against his chin and one of her legs had wound itself around his.

Last night.

He couldn't quite believe what had happened.

He hadn't meant to say everything he had outside and, when he had, he certainly hadn't been expecting her reaction. The sadist in him had believed she would agree with him. And despite being told Bex was single by Lizzie the previous morning - who hadn't cottoned on to why he was asking - he'd still been waiting for her to show up with someone.

But then she'd walked in, all sharp eyes, blonde hair and prickly confidence and the punch he'd felt at the sight of her had nearly winded him. In that moment he'd hated himself for not calling her, for not answering the phone, for not trying. Seeing her had made him realise how much he'd missed her. How much he'd give anything to be the guy who could walk up to her and kiss her on the cheek and offer to get her a drink. But when they had been outside, fear and old wounds had got the better of him. He'd honestly managed to convince himself over the past month that she would be fine without him being part of her life and that he would be stupid to enter into anything with her again.

He hadn't expected her to be upset.

Guilt washed over him and he tightened his grip around her.

Something other than her hair prickled across his face. It was an awareness, like he'd forgotten something.

Slowly, he opened his eyes only for them to widen and slam into the small person stood at the side of the sofa.

"A-Amy!" he stuttered, automatically shifting to sit up but quickly stopping as he dislodged Bex. She grumbled unhappily and pressed her head harder into his chest, her leg curling more determinedly around his own and her ankle jabbing into his calf.

"Hey Dad!"

His daughter's mouth was set in a wide grin and her eyes were practically sparking at him. She was still in her pyjamas, the blue ones Maria had bought her for Christmas, and she had her hands on her hips.

His eyes darted around the room and he saw the doors to the kitchen had been shut. They were wooden doors with small glass panels which meant he could see through them and see Lizzie and Charles just on the other side. They were discussing something animatedly. He watched as Lizzie made to move towards the door and Charles grabbed her around the waist, laughing at whatever she was saying even though there was a thunderous expression across her face.

Shit.

"I brought you tea," Amy said, bringing his gaze back to her.

"W-w-what time is it?"

"Eight."

"Eight!"

He knew he should have set an alarm, but with Bex practically on top of him telling him they didn't need one, he'd selfishly not wanted to move. He pressed his back more firmly into the arm of the sofa. He could hide his scar easily from this angle but he was still very conscious of the fact he was topless in front of his eight-year-old daughter with a woman curled into his side.

"Amy, I-"

"I had to bring you both drinks twice. It got cold the first time. Charles helped me. Then Aunt Lizzie came downstairs and saw you both and they started arguing." Daniel flicked his gaze to the coffee table that Amy had dragged across the room to set beside the sofa. "Charles made Bex's coffee as I don't know how to make that yet."

"Amy, I probably should explain what...what happened."

She raised her eyes comically. "I think it's fairly self-explanatory, Daaaad."

Despite the situation, he laughed.

God, sometimes she sounded far too grown up.

"Where have you got that phrase from?"

"You."

"Be quiet," Bex grumbled into his skin.

Daniel glanced at her and then at Amy, unsure of what to do or say. "Um, Bex. We have company."

"Everyone's still asleep. Stop worrying," she mumbled, her voice partly distorted. She patted him on the stomach.

He laughed, his words getting stuck as he heard Amy giggle. "Think you'll find that isn't quite correct."

"Oh good, you're awake!"

Daniel's head flicked up and he felt Bex flinch against him as Lizzie burst loudly into the room. Charles followed her, grabbing her around the waist again and easily picking her up. He hauled her back against his chest. "Cartwright, come on."

"Stop picking me up!"

"I'll stop when you stop overreacting!"

Bex sat up, her hair sticking out in all different directions. The duvet slipped to her waist and Lizzie flinched before visibly sighing with relief.

"Thank God you're dressed."

"Oi!" Bex snapped, leaning over the edge of the sofa, grabbing one of the spare pillows Maria had left for him and tossing it across the room just as Charles put Lizzie down on the floor. The pillow missed Lizzie and hit Charles squarely in the throat.

"Thanks for that," Charles grunted, coughing slightly as he rubbed his neck.

Lizzie was already striding towards them, "Amy, I really don't think you should be in here. Your uncle shouldn't haven't let you in."

She threw Charles a look over her shoulder.

"Why?" Amy asked, shrugging.

"Because your father and Bex aren't dressed."

"We are dressed!" Bex said, plucking at the strap to her camisole. "Daniel isn't."

"Yes, he is!"

Bex made to lift the duvet off the pair of them but Daniel quickly grabbed it. "As much as I am dressed, I am only in my underwear and maybe let's not demonstrate that."

He didn't need to see Bex's face to know she rolled her eyes and he had to push back the laugh in his throat.

"Fine," she pulled the duvet so she could fold her arms over it comfortably. "But we are dressed! I'm in my pyjamas and Daniel's in his boxers. All very PG."

"Still! Amy's here!"

Bex turned her head to look at Amy. Her blonde hair was partially covering her profile so he couldn't see her expression but suddenly, Amy was grabbed and pulled firmly on top of Bex. A giggle erupted from Amy's mouth as Bex used one arm to trap the young girl to her whilst, with the elegance of a dancer, managed to grab Daniel's abandoned shirt from the ground and pass it back to him without even turning her head or anyone noticing.

The small gesture, the fact she'd only woken up two minutes ago but already knew without looking at him what would be scaring him the most, made his chest lift and guilt flicker in the pit of his stomach.

He'd been a right prick to her last night.

It was little gestures like that that showed she cared.

Just like she had said.

"Amy Williams!" Bex cried dramatically. "Rule number one of childhood, you never see your dad naked."

"I'm not naked!" he said, quickly. He glanced up at Lizzie and Charles. "I'm not."

Amy was laughing, her back to Bex's front and Bex was covering her eyes as the young girl pretended to try and get free of her grip. He could tell she wasn't really trying because if she had been he'd have probably got a few elbows to the face. Even to a young girl, Bex would never lose a wrestling match.

"Well, he isn't now he's wearing a shirt," Bex whispered

theatrically, without even turning to see if he had actually put it on or not.

"I'm not naked!" Daniel said again and Amy burst out laughing, still wiggling in Bex's arms.

"You can't ever see!" Bex said dramatically, still with her hand over Amy's eyes.

"Who's naked?" said a voice from the door.

Daniel turned to see his mum walk in, her short hair sticking up at all angles and her blindingly white dressing gown on – he really had no idea how she seemed to keep it so clean.

"Dad!" Amy cheered.

"I'm not naked!" Daniel insisted again, doing up the last few buttons on his shirt.

Maria's keen eyes flicked between the three of them, a small smile tugging at the corner of her mouth. "It's rude to be naked when you have an audience, Daniel. If Bex has got herself dressed surely you could too. Anyone for tea?"

Bex snorted with laughter as Daniel threw his hands up in the air. "For God's sake!"

"I'll take that as a no."

"Me please, Nanma!"

"Okay, Amy." Maria shuffled past Charles, patting him affectionately on the shoulder as she headed for the kitchen.

"I'm so confused, what's going on?" Lizzie said, looking between them all.

"Keep up, Daniel's dream guy," said a gravelly voice from the other door to the living room.

Dream guy?

Matt walked into the living room, his eyes bleary with sleep whilst he rubbed his head. He smiled at Bex. "Wondered where you'd got to."

"Dream guy! Dream guy!" Lizzie's eyes snapped around to Bex. "What! What?" She then whirled around and pointed at Charles. "Daniel was the guy you were trying to get Bex to ring!"

"You knew?" Daniel said, looking at his brother.

Charles smiled. "I figured it out."

"Dream guy!" Lizzie said, anger in her eyes as she glowered at Bex. "You didn't tell me Daniel was dream guy! Why didn't you tell me?"

"Lizzie, hun, you don't exactly have the best track record for telling me things you should have, do you?" Bex said, finally lowering her hand from Amy's eyes, looping her arms around the young girl and leaning back against the sofa. She glanced at Daniel and smiled coyly.

"Good morning."

"Morning," he replied, still not quite believing that any of this was real.

Matt laughed loudly and Lizzie turned on him. "Not funny!"

He shrugged. "She's got a point."

"It's not the same!"

"Yours was far worse."

"Charles, can you tell Matt to shut up?"

"I could but he won't."

Daniel took advantage of the three of them bickering.

"How are you this morning?" he asked Bex.

"Really good, you?"

He couldn't stop his own smile growing. "Really good, thanks."

"No bad dreams?"

"None," he said gently. He hadn't dreamt about anything. And for once, he felt well rested, despite the fact he hadn't actually got that much sleep.

"Me neither."

"But this is *dream guy*!" Lizzie said, slapping her hands down on the back of the sofa and making them both jump. "We've been talking about him for the past year!"

Bex turned her head back to look at her. "Yeah, well, *dream guy* didn't call me, so I was a bit piss-" her eyes dropped to the back of Amy's head. "I was a bit annoyed about that. Amy, is that coffee for me?"

"Yep!"

"Thanks, doll."

"Dream guy?" Daniel asked.

"Don't get big-headed about it." She elbowed him playfully before reaching up and flattening his hair. "It's like I said last night. I was dreaming about you."

He still couldn't believe she was so calmly sitting with him. Not even sitting, she was leant into his side, the pair of them squeezed onto the sofa, with his daughter in her arms. She hadn't jumped a mile the moment they'd been caught, she hadn't stopped being affectionate with him just because others were in the room and she hadn't denied that they were together. Instead of running away from Amy, who would clearly jump to all kinds of conclusions now she had seen the two of them together, she'd grabbed her and brought her into their huddle.

"I missed our sleepovers," Amy said, nodding back at Bex.

"I missed them too."

Lizzie looked like she was about to explode. She moved her hands as if to tie back her hair only to realise she didn't have a hairband. Bex handed her one off her own wrist.

"Thanks!" she said, still glaring at her but taking the hairband to pull her hair into a sharp ponytail. As soon as her hair was tied she took a deep breath in and slowly, let it out. "Now, would someone please tell me what's going on?"

CHAPTER NINE

The first weeks of January were bleak. The weather got colder, trees were stripped of their fairy lights, decorations were pulled down and moods dropped significantly. People turned their backs on dark nights consisting of hot chocolates, mulled wine and family movies, and replaced them with nights in packed gyms, late hours in the office and pining for summer months. Everywhere one looked there were posters for detox teas and new diets, whilst shiny, white teethed celebrities told anyone who would listen to get their summer body ready.

Bex hated it.

January aged people more than the rest of the year did.

"Stop frowning," Matt said, as he delivered a jab, cross, jab to the pads Bex was holding out in front of her. She dropped them automatically to her waist, pointing them downwards as he swung his knee up hard before slanting her body to the right as he kicked.

"Again, that was weak."

"Fuck off!" he snarled.

But he went through the motions again, striking harder against the pads this time.

"Still couldn't feel it, *mate.*"

"Really, you want to go there?"

He did it again, and this time when he kicked and struck the pads with his right foot, Bex lost her balance. She hissed out in annoyance as a smug grin lit up Matt's face. He wiped his arm across his brow and Bex fixed her stance.

"Spill, what's wrong with you?"

"Nothing. What do you mean?"

"You're more grumpy than usual. I'm used to you being all drill sergeant but you're being moody right now."

"No, I'm not."

He delivered the routine again and this time, Bex fell back when he delivered his knee strike.

"Sloppy, Bex."

"Shut up!"

"Come on, what's bugging you?"

"I'm just a bit nervous, okay?"

"Nervous?" He'd been about to throw his first jab of the routine but he stopped, straightening up and staring at her. "What are you nervous about?"

"Tonight. The premiere." She shrugged her shoulders. "Are you coming?"

A movie Charles had filmed roughly two years ago was about to be released. He'd been doing press back-to-back for the last fortnight whilst also being back on *Censorship*, and the poor man was knackered. She'd seen him that morning and forced him to take a twenty-minute nap whilst she literally sat on the stairs to his trailer, not letting him leave and not letting anyone in.

They had all been invited to the London premiere. Charles would be doing a quick Q+A with the audience and director, before hopping on a plane to New York for the weekend for more press. They'd still be watching the film whilst he was handing over his passport to someone at Heathrow airport.

"Only for the first bit, said I'd give Charles a ride to the airport."

Bex frowned. "I'm pretty sure he's got staff for that."

Matt smiled. "I know, but I volunteered. I know the streets of London, and will actually let the guy get some sleep in the car. You know Charles, he'll be too damn polite and talk to whoever is driving him the whole way there if it's a stranger. The guy needs a bloody break and we are only midway through January."

"Matt," Bex said, studying her friend's face carefully, "you know you don't keep having to *make it up to him*. He wouldn't want that."

Matt shrugged, ducking his head as he readjusted his gloves, pulling the strap tighter around his wrist. "I know. It isn't just that." He met Bex's eyes. "I promise it isn't. Yeah, I feel bad for everything that happened. I feel like a dick but…" he let out a long breath. "I also missed him. Charles is…well, he's like my brother. I'm making up for thirteen years of lost time."

"Even if he's fast asleep in the back of the car?"

"Yeah." Matt smiled.

"And he's completely in love with your little sister?"

"That was never an issue." Matt plucked his sweat ridden top away from his body. "He makes Lizzie happy. As much as it can gross me out at times, I've not seen her like this in such a long time. Not even last time. There's just something…different about them. Makes me feel less guilty."

"What do you have to feel guilty about?"

"I've always felt a bit guilty about the way Dad treated her. He treated me like a bloody God and he ignored her. And as a teenager, I bloody loved it. Loved that my dad showered me with affection. Was completely blinded to the fact he was a prick. Anyway." He cleared his throat. "That's enough touchy feely bullshit for today."

"Matt," Bex groaned. "Don't be that guy- hey!" She blocked him as one of his fists swung up towards her stomach. "You bastard!" He laughed, shifting around to the right and then jabbing straight towards her throat. She blocked him, swiftly bending down and retrieving the second pad she had dropped on the floor. "After this round we are swapping and you best hope-" she blocked his kick and spun to the right, "-that you're on your top form otherwise you're going to that premiere with a black eye for an accessory!"

He laughed, going again for another combination without warning her of it. She dodged and blocked easily, grinning at the challenge and feeling the energy buzz through her body. They continued circling each other, Matt refusing to tell her what he was about to do and Bex laughing as she managed to predict his moves each time. She was enjoying herself, which was why Matt was the one who spotted him, not her. His green eyes sharpened over her shoulder.

"Dickhead at ten o'clock."

Bex stripped off the wrist wrap to her pad, letting it fall to her feet and flexing her hand. "Which one?"

"The worst one."

As she made to pull the other pad off her hand she turned to look him straight in the face.

Her ex-boyfriend, Ryan, was stood over by the weight machines.

He was watching her with disdain, resting against one of the pieces of equipment with such an air of arrogance that she was surprised those around him could continue to workout without choking on it.

Ryan was good looking. She couldn't deny that. He had dark brown hair, a square jaw and muscles carved from hours at the gym. He had a tattoo sleeve down his left arm, the designs deliberately curving around his biceps to over emphasise them, and he wasn't wearing a top so no one could avoid seeing his perfectly muscular stomach. His gaze was one of disgust and dislike. It lingered on her like she was something dirty for him to look at and it made her gut twitch with annoyance.

Suddenly he jerked away from the equipment, anger slamming across his expression as if she had done something to offend him. She looked around in surprise before flicking a glance over her shoulder to see Matt was giving him the middle finger.

"Matt, stop it."

"Couldn't help it. Not sorry." Matt didn't take his eyes off Ryan but he lowered his hand.

Ryan walked over to them slowly, weaving between the people happily going about their workouts and acting as if he had all the time in the world.

She felt Matt's heat at her back. "Can you stop dating people from our gym? Can we make this a no-go zone? It's really bloody irritating."

"Shut up," she snapped over her shoulder, before turning her attention back to Ryan. "Do you mind?" she called as he got closer. "We're trying to work out and your staring act is putting me off."

He smiled, a creepy, sardonic smile which once upon a time she had thought was flirtatious and sexy.

"Didn't know I still had that kind of power over you, babe."

"What do you want, Ryan?"

His eyes flicked between the pair of them. "Still pretending you two aren't shagging then?"

She flinched and felt Matt's anger bristle behind her.

"Say that again, mate?" Matt snapped. Predicting what he was going to do she swung an arm out to block him moving forward. His chest bumped against it.

"You know there's nothing going on between Matt and me, and if there was, it would be none of your business."

"I'm just saying, this is the longest you've gone without calling me, begging for me back. Evidence would suggest you're getting it from elsewhere."

"Don't talk to her like that!"

"I never begged," Bex snapped, ignoring Matt's snarl. She'd had her weak moments, she couldn't deny that, but Bex Wright never begged anyone.

"Potato, potatoes."

A short silence followed his statement before Matt snorted with laughter.

"That's not the phrase, moron." Matt touched Bex's arm briefly, signalling he wasn't about to step around her and punch Ryan in the face. She lowered it to her side.

Ryan shrugged and turned his eyes back to Bex. "You look good, babe."

"Please stop calling me babe."

He grinned, all cocky and arrogant. "You didn't mind it before."

"Yeah, well, I do now." She sighed, placing her hands on her hips and trying to ignore the way his eyes lit up at her action and travelled over her body. "What do you want, Ryan? Or can Matt and I continue our workout in peace?"

"Well, if we're *actually* done, I wanted to know when I can come pick up my stuff?"

"I gave you four dates to come and pick up your stuff and you never showed."

He shrugged. "That was last year. I want it back this year. Unless there's a reason you don't want me to get it back?" He let his eyes trail over her again in what she was guessing was meant to be a flirtatious, sexy way. A long time ago it would have worked. Now, all she could feel on her skin was her sweat beginning to cool.

"What the fuck did you see in this guy?" Matt muttered behind her, quiet enough for only her to hear.

She wasn't sure.

At first he'd been wonderful. He'd been sweet, and his love and passion for fitness had attracted her to him like a moth to a flame.

But over time, that had changed. As he had become more defined, he'd also become arrogant, knowing his figure drew people's gazes, knowing most women would find him attractive. And that's when he had started to let her down.

He'd always known the exact words to pull her back in. He'd known the compliments that would work and the way to persuade her to give him one more chance. He'd realised that beneath her steely exterior there was a romantic side buried under her skin.

"Fine. Come pick up your stuff."

"You *absolutely* sure you want me to-?" His head snapped to Bex's right side. "-Dude, I swear, if you keep laughing at me, I'll deck you."

Matt didn't get agitated this time. Instead she heard him chuckle some more and practically felt him shrug. "You'd have to get past her first."

"Ryan, you have my number. It hasn't changed. Text me when you want your stuff and I'll put it by the door."

"Can't you bring it to me?"

She arched an eyebrow at him. "Excuse me?"

"Just, my new girl don't like me talking to you."

"How does she even know about me? Hang on, why does she think we are talking at all?"

Her eyes scanned some of the curious faces watching them. Did she go to this gym too?

"I told her we'd been talking." Ryan dropped his gaze, shrugging like a prepubescent teenager being told off. "Just to make sure she doesn't get too comfortable, you know?"

"Jesus," Matt said from Bex's right. "You're a total prick, aren't you?"

Ryan's body stiffened with anger and he surged forward toward Matt, cursing at him loudly and drawing everyone's attention. Bex planted a firm hand into his chest and pushed him away.

"Calm down, Ryan."

"He's being a dick!"

"And you're being immature. Stop acting like a child. You're thirty-three, for God's sake. You should know better than to bloody try and wind up your girlfriend by pretending to be pals with your ex." She dropped her hand. "Look, text me when you want your stuff. I'm not coming to yours."

"But if my girlfriend finds out I've come to yours, she'll kill me."

"I'm pretty sure your girlfriend will kill you if she finds out that just now you were insinuating you wanted me to beg for you back." She narrowed her eyes at him and he couldn't hold her gaze. "Send a friend over if you have to Ryan. You've got a month. A month or I'm binning all your stuff."

Bex turned and very nearly bumped into Matt. She pushed him gently back and he followed her lead, still not taking his eyes of Ryan.

"Don't say anything else," she hissed at him but he wasn't listening to her. His eyes were angry. "Matt, please, don't say anything."

"Thank God your new boyfriend is a hundred times better than this dick."

"Matt!"

"New boyfriend?" She heard Ryan snap behind her. The atmosphere around them drew tight immediately and she found herself glaring at her friend.

He caught her gaze and shrugged.

Shrugged.

She wasn't even sure if Daniel was her boyfriend.

Or was that already a given since they'd dated before?

They hadn't exactly discussed it but they were texting every day and he called her at least once a day.

Her mind cast back to that kiss. The way he'd grabbed her. The way he'd kissed her like she was oxygen. Her mouth suddenly felt very dry and she felt her cheeks flush.

"Bex?" Matt said softly.

"Let's just go," she mumbled, grabbing Matt by the t-shirt and forcing him to turn around. "Before you cause a fight."

Daniel adjusted his collar for what felt like the fifteenth time before quickly grabbing the rail above him as the ground jerked forward. He felt nervous, his mouth continually dry and his palms were beginning to sweat. Lottie eyed him knowingly, a smile on her lips. Today, she'd gone for purple lipstick and green eyeshadow but her outfit was tamer than usual. She was wearing jeans and an oversized checked shirt, her fingers were covered in different types of rings and she was wearing a thick blue, chunky necklace around her neck.

It kind of worked.

Daniel had been to many premieres before so he knew by now they weren't formal affairs. The cast and crew dressed nicely so that they looked good in the photos, but as a guest, he simply was expected not to turn up in shorts.

Daniel didn't own shorts.

He also didn't own anything that straddled the line between smart and casual. Consequently, he simply always wore suits. He wasn't nervous about what he was wearing because of the premiere. He was nervous because it was going to be the first time he had seen Bex in thirteen days.

Lottie glanced at him again. He could feel her teasing gaze burning across the side of his face and he turned his head away, preferring to look at the balding man sandwiched next to him rather than his little sister being a pain. Amy was just in front of him. He had one hand on her shoulder because she was trying to read whilst they were on the tube and he was convinced she was going to go flying if the tube driver continued to brake like it was some kind of game.

It was rush hour and, although it was winter, the temperature inside the carriage was that of a tropical island. He could see beads of sweat on nearly everyone's foreheads and their eyes were all dull, irritated or bored. Squished together on the Bakerloo line was clearly the last place they wanted to be but Daniel appreciated the time it gave him to think.

He hadn't been able to see Bex since New Year's Day. He'd been working the later shift which made dates or dinners non-existent and when he'd had a day off, he'd spent it with Amy, not wanting her to feel neglected just because Bex was *potentially* back in their lives. Bex had understood. In fact she'd been fairly easy about it, which in turn had made him relax and simultaneously worry. She'd been so calm on New Year's Day. Lizzie had grabbed Bex for a 'chat' before they'd eaten breakfast and when they had come back the redness in Lizzie's cheeks had turned to a light pink and she hadn't been able to stop smiling at him. He'd pretended to find something in his tea particularly interesting so not to make it obvious he had been waiting for them to return, but then Bex had slid an arm around his shoulders and planted a kiss on his temple. He'd flushed, not used to public displays of affection or sure if Lizzie was going to scream again but she'd simply grinned at them.

He still couldn't believe Bex didn't care.

He winced as he remembered what he'd said to her that evening. It had been a combination of Dutch courage, hurt and fear that had made him say all that he had. Part of him was still wary. Still not sure if they would work in the way he really wanted them to but he couldn't bring himself not to try.

Not after she'd told him that she'd been dreaming about him too.

Not after the feeling he'd gotten in the pit of his stomach as he'd taken care of her.

Not after the way she'd spotted Amy in the morning and pulled her into her chest.

Not after *that kiss*.

He swallowed and pulled at his collar. It really was extremely hot in this carriage.

The three of them got off at Piccadilly Circus, preferring to walk to Leicester Square than have to change onto the cramped volcano that was the Piccadilly line. Amy was still trying to read, tripping up over her-

"You're wearing odd shoes!" Daniel said, staring down at his daughter's feet as he just stopped her from falling over the end of the escalator.

She grinned up at him. "I liked both and couldn't decide. Lottie said I should just wear both."

Daniel gave his sister a look. She simply shrugged. "Life's too short not to wear odd shoes."

When they were finally above ground, they walked towards the hustle and bustle that was Leicester Square. Despite it being January, it was still busy. London always was. Shop windows still blared with colour whilst restaurants hummed with heat and strong smells of good food. 'Sale' signs were every few metres and people left the shops carrying far more than they really could manage. People still queued up restlessly outside of theatres and workers, desperate to get home, were pushing against the crowds with frowns on their faces.

Daniel gripped Amy's hand firmly in his own and they began to walk quickly through the different groups of people.

At first, premieres had scared him. He'd been convinced they would be intimidating and full on. He also hated being anywhere near the centre of attention and Charles usually was just that. He had especially hated it when Patricia had forced him to walk the carpet with his brother - she said that together they generated a lot of attention.

More recently, Jennifer had stepped in and often gone to the premieres with Charles publicly instead. Patricia had insisted on it after the papers had started trying to pick apart their relationship.

He'd been grateful to be demoted and much preferred simply walking in with the public and getting to watch the actual film.

Tonight, Charles was going to walk the carpet alone and meet the rest of them inside.

Daniel, Lottie and Amy lined up in front of the food and drinks stall inside the Odeon. It was a very different atmosphere within the gleaming foyer in comparison to the cramped tube. People were smiling, conversing with one another merrily whilst unwinding their scarves and shrugging out of their coats. There was a smile behind nearly everyone's expression.

He tried not to make it obvious who he was looking for as he glanced around at the different groups but just as he saw Lottie spot what he was doing, he felt a familiar warmth creep up his spine. He turned his head to the right, searching for its source.

Bex was stood by one of the doors into the cinema looking straight at him.

She smiled as their eyes met. It was a slow, delighted smile that made his pulse race.

Her blonde hair was piled into a messy bun, two symmetrical strands of hair falling down either side of her face and she wore black skinny jeans with a slightly oversized navy blue shirt. She looked effortlessly beautiful. He waved and then winced at the awkwardness of it. She merely laughed.

"Go," Lottie said, elbowing him in the back. "I'll get Amy her popcorn."

Daniel glanced at Amy but her head was in her book, her red curls blocking him from seeing her expression.

"Amy, would you mind if I go and say hello to Bex?"

She tilted her head and he saw one eye peering out from beneath her mass of hair. "Can I get chocolate with my popcorn?"

He laughed, reaching forward and roughly patting her on the head whilst he passed Lottie a twenty-pound note. "Fine."

"That was easy." She wrinkled her nose. "Can I get a puppy?"

"No." He winked at her. "Lottie get something too. Will that cover it?" He had no idea how much things cost in fancy cinemas.

"I'm fine," Lottie said brightly.

"Not even your traditional pic-n-mix?"

Lottie laughed. "Good memory but I'm just not feeling it. Now go!" She shooed him away.

Daniel adjusted his collar before he left them and walked over towards Bex. The corner of his mouth kicked upwards as Bex refused to stop watching him, her coal lined eyes making his heartrate triple.

He stepped to the side to avoid two teenagers barrelling through towards the cinema doors and something uneasy stirred in his stomach. It was enough to make him stop for a second, looking around as something cold prickled across his shoulders.

It felt like a warning.

It was the same kind of pull in his gut he'd had moments before Amy had stepped out onto the road the night he'd been killed. The way he'd just known something was about to go wrong. He glanced back at Amy. She was happily gesturing at Lottie about something in her book but the tension in his chest didn't ease. He looked around again, convinced he was missing something but at Bex's confused expression he inwardly shook his head and strode back towards her.

Probably just nerves.

"Hello stranger." She pushed herself off the wall to stand up properly.

"Hello," he smiled, any ill feeling he'd had in his gut disappearing as he took her in. "You look...great."

Bex laughed. "Thanks," she nodded at his suit. "And likewise."

"Hey Daniel!" Lizzie said brightly.

"Hello Lizzie, hello Matt."

Matt nodded at him with a smile before quickly engaging in conversation with Lizzie. Daniel had the feeling he was doing it on purpose and silently thanked him.

He stepped closer to Bex. "How've you been?"

"Okay." Her hands reached out to flatten the lapels of his blazer. "Although I think it would have been better if I'd gotten to see a certain someone. How about you?"

"Feeling very much the same way." They exchanged smiles. "How was work?" he added.

She pulled a face. "Don't mention work." Her gaze flicked to Lizzie. "She didn't get the best news this week."

Concerned, Daniel frowned, asking the question silently only for Bex to roll her eyes and mouth, *Neil.*

"What about him?"

Daniel remembered the blonde haired man who had always been at Lizzie's parties over the years. "He's leaving," Bex said, leaning into him so she could whisper it. "Didn't tell Lizzie until today and he's on his merry way to Australia in two weeks' time for a job. She's a bit upset."

"Wasn't he her best friend?"

Bex eyes flashed. "No, because that would be me."

Daniel laughed. "Okay, male best friend."

"That would be Charles."

"Male best friend who she isn't in love with."

Bex shrugged playfully. "Okay, then yes, that's him. And the git didn't tell her he was leaving. Acted like it was nothing. Acted like he didn't give a shit that they weren't working together anymore."

"Poor Lizzie."

"To put it mildly." She leant even closer to him. "But between you and me, as much as I hate the guy, I feel like there's something else going on."

"Something else like?" he said, trying to concentrate on what she was saying instead of the proximity of her mouth to his.

"I don't know yet."

"Hey!" said Amy's voice beside them, making him jump.

Soon, they were all being hustled into the cinema. Matt disappeared, ready to be Charles's chauffeur the moment he needed him, but the five of them all shuffled in to be seated.

There was a brief Q & A with the cast. Charles wasn't one of the main characters. He was the older brother of the main hero and Daniel was pretty sure Charles had told him his character died at the beginning of the film. It was still weird, sitting in the darkened room and watching his little brother on stage. Especially now he knew that his life could have turned out so differently. Charles had enjoyed being a teacher, but his dream had always been to be an actor. He was brilliant at what he did and he still worked hard at perfecting his craft. Daniel's eyes darted sideways down the row to look at Lizzie. She was smiling widely, sat with Lottie on her right and Bex on her left.

She was the reason Charles was now up there.

She'd sacrificed everything for his little brother and he loved her for it. As he watched her watching Charles, her eyes filled with affection and admiration. He smiled to himself.

Charles had told him at Christmas that he was going to ask Lizzie to marry him again. He still had the ring, and although to the outside world it looked like they'd only been together a month, to anyone who knew them, the truth was a lot more serious. They'd been together their whole lives. However, this time, Charles was determined to propose properly and not on the back of his nineteen-year-old girlfriend telling him that she was pregnant. That probably meant the proposal wouldn't be happening anytime soon. Charles was the biggest romantic Daniel knew and he would want to make it perfect.

An icy prickle ran along the back of his head and he automatically turned in his seat to look behind him. The lights were only partly dimmed as the film hadn't started but he couldn't see anyone obviously watching them. Still, something uneasy stirred in his chest.

"On your left," Bex whispered in his ear. "You've got an admirer."

Daniel looked over Amy's head to where Bex was slyly nodding. A row ahead of them, across the aisle, was an old woman staring directly at them. She had curly grey hair, glasses that were shining in the reflections of the low lights and it looked like she was dressed all in green. He felt something churn in his gut and a frown crossed his forehead.

"Do you know her?" Bex asked softly.

"No," he said, turning his head slightly to talk but not taking his eyes off the woman. Something uneasy was starting to truly stir in the pit of his stomach. It made him want to move. It made him want to leave. His shoulders relaxed ever so slightly as he felt the woman's gaze leave him but then his skin bristled as he saw her eyes land on Amy.

Maybe she was someone from the hospital. A doctor, part of another team? Maybe she was a friend of the family? Maybe she knew Amy from her school? A teacher, perhaps?

None of the thoughts were easing the waves of anxiety in his chest. If anything they were making them pitch higher as there were no obvious answers to his theories.

The lights in the auditorium dimmed and the woman turned in her seat to face the stage just as the curtain was pulled back to reveal the screen behind.

He eyed the back of her head, his heart not quite ready to settle yet.

Why had she been staring?

What had she been looking at?

Bex's arm nudged his right side.

"Relax and watch the film, Daniel."

He nodded, trying to smile but he was still partially distracted.

Why had that woman been staring?

What did she want?

As his breath steadied and he settled further back into his seat Daniel became very aware of something else entirely. A realisation so distracting that he forgot about the old older lady almost immediately.

And that realisation was the woman sitting on his right… and his hands.

He stretched them out in front of him, brushing them down to his knees and feeling a new, unfamiliar tension rise-up around him.

He wished he could have spent some time with Bex in private. They'd been sending texts back and forth and had daily phone calls, but it was nothing like seeing her in person.

Her very presence next to him was causing his pulse to thunder.

Why hadn't he kissed her? Just a quick brief kiss on the cheek when they'd greeted one another.

Instead he'd stood there looking like an idiot. Unable to even call her beautiful and instead had gone for 'great'.

Great?

Really?

Great was how you described food or someone's dog. Not Bex.

His knee knocked against hers and he quickly drew it back, apologising under his breath.

Calm down, you idiot!

And now he wanted to hold her hand, but he couldn't bring himself to do it, just in case she rejected him. So instead his hands jutted out in front of him awkwardly, like they were stuck out on poles, palms pressing into his thighs as the thoughts in his head spoke louder and louder.

Not paying any attention to the film, he watched as Bex very slowly and very deliberately moved her leg to rest against his. Thigh to thigh. And then her hand reached across the arm rest and her fingers linked with his. He risked glancing at her. There was a knowing smile across her lips and he felt his body relax and his mind calm at the playful affection in the sweep of her mouth. Her eyes

flicked to meet his.
    She knew him.
    Thirteen years apart and she still knew him.

CHAPTER TEN

As the lights came up, a chorus of sniffs echoed around the cinema and people began to clap. Daniel joined in, enjoying watching how many people reached for their tissues or tried to discreetly wipe away tears on their sleeves. Charles had undersold his role. His death had been one of the pivotal twists of the film and it had been right at the end. Despite the film's happy ending, Charles's final scene was still having an effect on people. The moment the applause stopped and people began to rise from their seats, Lizzie shoved her hand into her bag and began to search for her phone. Tears were running down her face but her cheeks were flushed with anger.

"That *prick* didn't tell me he was going to die."

"Lizzie, calm down," Bex said laughing.

"No! He insists I don't need to accompany him to the airport, tells me he doesn't want to put me out, makes sure I stay to watch the film, and doesn't even warn me-" her breath caught in her throat as she used her fist to wipe away some of her tears, "that he goes and dies in it."

She slammed the phone to her ear. Daniel caught sight of Lottie just behind her - she was trying her hardest not to laugh.

"Aunty Lizzie," Amy offered, from Daniel's side.

"Yes, Amy?" Lizzie said, holding the phone so tightly he was surprised it hadn't sunk into the side of her face.

"It was just a film."

There was silence between all five of them before Bex and Lottie simultaneously snorted with laughter. Lizzie's eyes flared at Bex and she turned her head to send an evil look in Lottie's direction.

"I know it was just a film, Amy, but I'm still very mad at your uncle."

Amy shrugged and looked up at Daniel. "I tried," she said, so dramatically that a laugh escaped his lips too. He ruffled her hair.

"It was a good point."

"Bloody answer machine," Lizzie snapped, grinding her teeth together. "Okay, hello, yes I'd like to leave a message. Call me the moment you get this. I can't *believe* you would do this to me."

People were beginning to leave the cinema, their backs bowed as they climbed out of their seats, hopping over the few who wanted to stay for the credits. Conversations threaded in and out of passing groups and Daniel was surprised no one had politely coughed at them to move by now.

They were slap bang in the middle of the aisle after all.

"Lizzie," Bex said, her tone stern. She placed her hands on her hips and was shaking her head at the brunette. "Charles is on a plane right now, he'll get that when he lands in a few hours and he'll panic. You'll be in bed, you won't answer your phone and you'll put him in a right state."

Lizzie stared at her, unmoving for a couple of seconds as the two friends seemed to have a whole argument just with their eyes. Lizzie conceded. Her shoulders sagging as she took out her phone again and aggressively punched numbers into the screen before she placed it to her ear.

"It's not urgent. Go to sleep when you get there. We're fine...just please tell me when you're going to die in a film before I have to see it, okay?" She shuffled on the spot and turned her head away from the others. "I love you."

They began to make their way out of their seats, Daniel banging his legs on the seats regularly before merging with the crowd of people. He felt Amy's grip in his hand tighten, her small warm hand curling harder into his whilst at the same time he felt another hand hold his elbow. This hand had the ability to send heat up his arm and caused his shoulders to roll back as he made sure he led the way confidently.

Even her touch made him feel stronger.

He'd forgotten what that was like. As much as the memories had come flooding back into his mind, he'd forgotten the intricacies of how he felt around Bex. The way she made him stand taller, hold himself higher, lift his eyes upwards. She had that effect on a lot of people. It was like she had found the secret to confidence and, consequently, insisted on sharing it, letting it seep out of her in touches, looks and words. He'd seen Lizzie fiddling with her jacket earlier, undoing a few buttons before doing them back up before undoing them again. Bex had only had to touch her arm and whisper something in her ear for Lizzie to relax, for her shoulders to come away from her ears and her cheeks to return to a normal colour.

The whole movie Bex's hand had stayed interlocked with his, their thighs pressed together.

It had filled him with an emotion a lot richer than confidence. It drummed through him and caused him to keep losing focus. It was a feeling he'd missed but would never have been able to describe.

About thirty minutes into the film, he'd finally had the confidence to stroke his thumb affectionately down the side of her hand. He'd seen the answering smile on her face and felt her knee press harder against his own. He noticed the slow way she'd inhaled and thought maybe, just maybe, she had a similar feeling flooding her nerve endings as well.

Outside of the cinema, Lizzie seemed to have calmed down from being a witness to Charles's onscreen death. She was shivering, her arms wrapped around herself and suddenly looked so much younger than she was.

"Lizzie, do you want a coat?" he asked.

She shook her head but he took his off anyway, handing it to her which she took with a guilty smile.

"Sorry. I bought a new one two days ago! I promise!"

He smiled, shaking his head at her fondly.

"Lizzie, you never have a coat," Lottie said, her own big, grey woolly one drowning her frame.

"That's not true!"

The two turned towards each other, bickering in the way good friends could.

"That was nice of you," Bex said, her lips close to his ear as she slid her arm through his.

"I'm glad you think so, it was all for show," he said, the corner of his mouth rising slowly. She laughed.

"Of course."

"I'm actually charging her by the minute."

"She can afford it. I've heard her boyfriend's loaded."

"Oh, he just died, didn't you know?"

"In a tragic ski accident that was actually orchestrated so he could save his brother's life? Someone did just tell me that." She shrugged. "Then again, I might be wrong. I was rather distracted at the time." Her eyes met his.

He swallowed, feeling his mouth turn dry. "Were you?"

"Weren't you?" She was so close to him he could smell peppermint on her breath.

Should he kiss her? Just a quick peck amidst the crowd.

Or was even that too much in front of Amy?

God, he'd completely forgotten how to do this.

Shit, where was Amy? He turned his head away, feeling Bex's huff of laughter against his throat as she theatrically groaned.

Okay.

So that was a yes.

She had wanted to be kissed.

Amy was right next to him. Her head back in her book. She didn't seem to care that they weren't moving or no one was paying her attention. She was simply reading. He squeezed her shoulder affectionately.

"Right, shall we-" Lottie began to say when a shrill, high voice interrupted them.

"I'm so sorry, but are you Daniel Williams?"

Daniel turned to his left to address who had spoken.

His eyebrows shot up and the uneasy feeling threaded through the back of his mind again as his eyes laid upon the old woman who had been watching them earlier. Three friends of hers lingered a few feet behind her, glancing at each other curiously. Her eyes stayed locked onto him.

"Hello, yes." He held out his hand but when her thin fingers closed around his, he felt as if the floor had been shaken beneath him. Something in his gut was telling him this situation was dangerous, his body reacting to the old woman like she was a witch stood with a cauldron asking if she could use him as a sacrifice. He painted on a smile. "I'm so sorry, do I know you?"

"My name is Irene Copperton."

Daniel paused, waiting for her to continue. When she didn't he quickly nodded. "Great, nice to meet you."

"I'm from Tring."

His mind whirled.

Tring, so she was a friend of his parents? Or an old family friend? Had she used to work at the school?

"How lovely! This is Bex, Lizzie, Lottie, and this is my daughter, Amy."

Irene took no notice of the others, even as they were quick to say their hellos but her eyes dropped to Amy.

"Hello, you're a beautiful little girl, aren't you?"

He felt Amy freeze beneath the hand he had on her shoulder and he prayed to God she wasn't giving this old woman a dirty look. Irene was talking to her as if she were three. Her voice had become all musical and high pitched and she had crouched ever so slightly.

"Do you read a lot? That's an awfully good habit of yours."

"Dad reads so I read," she said simply, shrugging.

Bex squeezed his arm ever so gently and he suppressed the smile wanting to break out across his face. Why Amy couldn't say that kind of thing at parent's evening, he didn't know. He cleared his throat. "Well, it was lovely to see you. We best be-"

"Why has she got odd shoes on?"

Daniel blinked. "Sorry?"

"Why is your daughter wearing odd shoes? Why did you let her leave the house like that?"

"I only noticed once we left."

Irene gave a little tut, shaking her head and grasping her hands together. "Careless."

The comment took him so much by surprise that his immediate reaction wasn't anger, but shock. He stared at her. Part of him wanted to laugh. "Excuse me?"

"She's got beautiful eyes."

"Thank you." He glanced sideways at Bex, his brow dipping.

"They're brown," she said, matter-of-factly.

"Yep…" He cleared his throat. "Anyway-"

"I'm right in thinking she is Helen's child then?"

His ex-wife's name was the last one he had expected to hear that evening. He frowned, feeling his hand flex by his side. "Yes. Yes, she is."

Irene took off her glasses, polishing them on her off-white blouse that was just visible underneath her ivory-green knitted cardigan and lime-green winter coat. "Was. Helen's dead."

There was shocked silence. Even in the midst of Leicester Square it felt like everyone stopped just for a moment. The cheer from *The MnM World* dulled, the Mexican music from *Chiquitos* quietened and even those outside of the pub to their left appeared to lower their voices.

"I beg your pardon?" he said, taken aback.

Amy turned towards him, looking up with a small frown over her face. "Dad, I want to go home."

He felt anger spark at his side. "How dare you talk about Helen like that in front of Amy!" Bex snapped.

It looked like she had just beaten Lottie and Lizzie to it. Both women had stepped forward, fire in their gazes.

Bex's eyes flashed dangerously and she pulled her mouth into a sneer, "Have some respect." She walked around to the other side of him so she could place a hand on Daniel's back and her other on Amy's shoulder. "We'll be off now, thank you. We hope you enjoyed the film."

"Is *she* your new wife?" Irene said, the distaste in her tone obvious as she raised her eyes at Bex.

"If she was it would be none of your business," he said, his voice still lacking the venom he felt towards her. He was too shocked to make his anger obvious.

"It will make it far easier."

"What?"

Now Irene wasn't even making any sense.

"I think you need to go home and have a nap," Lottie said, her voice patronisingly calm. "Sleep off whatever *this* is." With the word *this* Lottie drew around the women in mid-air with her palm.

Irene's eyes flicked to her. "Says Mad Goldilocks."

Lottie stiffened, the old nickname making her eyes widen.

"That's enough," Daniel said, his voice gaining strength. He took Amy's hands. "I don't really understand what's going on here but I don't like you insulting my family and hurting my daughter's feelings. Come on everyone. Let's leave Ms Copperton to it."

They walked away together, all exchanging looks as Irene's gaze bored into their backs. Anger and concern drummed through him in equal measures. He squeezed Amy's hand and she squeezed his back, her eyes staring straight ahead and her book forgotten in her free hand.

"Who the hell was that?" Lottie muttered. She glanced over her shoulder, stilled, and then turned to walk backwards in line with them. She held up an arm and began to wave.

"Lottie, what are you doing?" Daniel snapped.

"She's still staring and taking photos by the looks of it so I'm giving her something to look at."

"She looked familiar," Lizzie said, biting down on her lip.

"I thought that too but I have no idea where from," he replied.

"Could she be part of one of Charles's fan groups? One of the obsessive ones?"

Daniel liked that option. He preferred that option to anything else swirling around in his head. But he couldn't shake the image of her eyes landing on Amy. They'd been eager, excited…and proud.

They made their way through the crowds, the six of them huddled together keeping out of the cold January air and fighting against the wave of people desperate to come and party in London even in Baltic temperatures. Inside Piccadilly Circus Station, they began to say their goodbyes. Once they got down to the busy platforms it would be impossible to communicate with one another. Besides, they were all heading in different directions and the station was heaving with people.

While Amy hugged everyone, Daniel stood back, letting the women embrace and smile at one another. Normally, he'd have joined in but now they were underground and far away from Irene Copperton, his mind was once again preoccupied by something else.

How to interact with Bex.

How was he going to say goodbye?

He had no idea.

He had no idea what they were.

They all made to move through the barriers, being pushed along by a sea of people and barely able to keep up as crowds around them cheered and others groaned. Just before they reached the escalator, he heard Bex calling his name. He turned to see she was still on the other side of the barriers, her body pressed up against one of them as she waved her cards at him frantically.

"Lottie, I'll meet you down there. Fourth carriage in. Amy, don't let go of Lottie's hand. Bye Lizzie!" he said it so quickly that he wasn't sure if they had all heard him, before he turned back and moved against the wall of people. Luckily, the man working at the larger turnstile took pity on him and let him back through. It probably had something to do with the helpless expression across Bex's beautiful face as she batted her eyelids at the him.

"What's wrong?" he said quickly. He led her away from the barriers and the main underground chaos, sheltering just behind a sign for tickets for *Dear Evan Hansen* so that they weren't in anyone's way.

"Can't get through the barrier," she said, pulling a face and waving a card at him.

"Bex," he said, taking hold of her hand. "That's a *Boots* card."

"Oh, is it?" She grabbed him by the collar of his shirt and pulled him into a kiss.

For a second he was taken completely off guard, freezing as her lips pressed into his but then, as if his body had been waiting for this the entire night, he gripped her waist, pulling her into him and pressed his mouth back against hers passionately. She tasted like mints. It sent a fire through his body as he slowly moved his arms to wrap around her waist as the kiss heated. Desire bolted through his blood stream as her hips rolled against him.

Public displays of affection were never really something he'd agreed with. He didn't like having to side step around people as they made out on street corners, or having to look sharply away as couples straddled one another on park benches. The worst one was in queues, when the couple ahead would start kissing out of boredom more than anything else and the people around them were just expected to watch the show.

But with Bex it was different. He didn't even think about the people around them. They were just a blur of noise and chaos. He didn't care if anyone was watching. He simply wanted to keep kissing her. Behind the cardboard advert, he felt like they had their own little hideaway anyway. Her hands knotted harder in the collar of his shirt and he deepened their kiss, bringing one hand up to cup her face. Even with the heavy traffic of moving people around them he felt her soft moan vibrate against his mouth and his heart quickened.

She pulled away first, smiling that cheeky smile he found irresistible as her eyes drank him in. He felt a blush rise to his cheeks.

"So, I'm guessing you knew that was your *Boots* card?"

She placed a hand on her chest and batted her eyelids at him dramatically. "Me? Never. Complete blonde moment."

He laughed, knowing full well Bex hated that expression.

"Are you free tomorrow?" he said, out of the blue. The way she was looking at him was making him feel confident. The way she'd kissed him made him feel practically euphoric.

"Tomorrow evening, I can do."

"May I take you out on a date?"

She cupped his cheek and pressed a sweet kiss to his lips. "Sounds perfect."

CHAPTER ELEVEN

"You're a complete softie," Bex said, elbowing him in the side and enjoying the way the corner of Daniel's mouth kicked up into a smile.

"I figured that last time it seemed to go well, so why mess with it?"

Bex laughed, genuinely touched that he had remembered. They stood outside of a small, white restaurant. The name *Alfonso's* was written in large green writing at the top, all swirls and looped letters, with fairy lights hanging in neat semi circles underneath. The restaurant was just three streets away from where Bex lived and it had been where they had gone for their first date last time.

"After you," he said, nodding towards the door and placing a hand on the small of her back.

Bex could feel he had a more confident air about him today. Yesterday he'd been nervous, she had felt his leg jogging up and down the moment they'd sat in their seats and she'd known she was going to be the one taking charge. However, today, he'd picked her up with an easy smile and he hadn't hesitated to give her a kiss when he'd greeted her.

It had been far too short and respectful but she'd work on that.

Tonight, he was wearing a dark grey suit that had the same effect on her as when he had rolled up his sleeves to tend to her hand. She could smell a delicious cologne when she leaned in closer to him and his hair looked freshly washed.

Inside they were greeted by their waiter like they were old friends before being seated. It was mainly couples inside the restaurant and one large birthday party seated alongside the window looking out at the park opposite.

The conversation flowed easily between them, just like it had from the moment he had picked her up. They leaned across the table, chatting about life as if they had never been apart. Daniel asked about her job, about recent looks she'd been working on or if she still enjoyed working solely with Jack and Jill, while she asked questions about Amy, about her school, about how she was getting on now the world around them seemed to have changed so dramatically. The waiter had to come back three times before they actually opened their menus to take a look at what food they wanted.

Bex felt any worries she'd had over the night melt away. Talking to Daniel was easier than talking to any other man, she didn't feel judged in her responses or patronised when he had asked her questions about what she did. Usually men thought her job was frivolous and far too girly to be taken seriously. The nice ones would smile, add the odd question, and move the conversation on, the not so nice ones would openly laugh and usually say something offensive under the disguise of a joke.

Daniel was interested.

He remembered small details from conversations they'd had years ago and sympathised with her unusual work hours.

She snuck a glance at him as he studied the menu. Her eyes were drawn to his jaw and the sweep of his neck. The small line was back between his eyebrows but the rest of his face was relaxed and calm. His eyes flicked up, catching her, and the ghost of a smile tugged at his lips as she quickly looked back down at her own menu.

Their previous first date at *Alfonso's* had been awkward. Daniel hadn't quite realised the restaurant was heavy on the romantic vibe and it had caused him to blush so deeply Bex had been worried for a second he was going to run. For the first five minutes his eyes had been wide and nervous, his words stuttered, and he'd acted like they had never even met before, let alone been friends for years and had sex up against a bookshelf at Lizzie's thirtieth.

She hadn't really minded: the fact it was obviously a restaurant for secure couples and not first dates simply reminded her of the fact none of her exes had ever suggested anywhere remotely like it. They'd never picked a restaurant near her to make it more convenient for her or to make her feel safe, they'd never dressed up nicely to pick her up, and they often hadn't even bothered to apply fresh deodorant.

Daniel had done all of those things, without even thinking it was a big deal.

And that's why, from the start, it had always felt different with him. Like the start of something important.

But, despite the fact she had found his nervousness endearing, she was glad it wasn't quite like that this time.

When they had finally ordered, the waiter shaking his head at them in amusement, they handed over their menus and turned back to each other.

"So, is life drastically different now with Charles being a celebrity?"

Daniel pondered the question. "Well...other than for obvious reasons, no."

"He didn't develop a bad drug habit you had to drag him out of then?"

He laughed. "No, Charles managed to avoid that side of things. I think it was because he wasn't very successful to start."

Bex smiled. "Really?"

"Oh God, yeah. Took him a few years to land anything substantial. He had to really work at it. He was working two jobs for the first three years out of drama school and an extra one every other weekend. I think being with Jenni helped. She's always been into her fitness and I don't think she would have stood for him getting into that world. And there's our parents. Mum would have killed him. And then Dad would have brought him back to life to kill him again."

Bex scrunched up her nose. "I didn't think your parents were that strict."

He raised an eyebrow. "Oh, they can be when they want to be."

"Oh yeah?"

He steepled his fingers, tapping the tips of them on his chin in thought. "Did I ever tell you how Dad caught me with a cigarette at university?"

Bex's mouth dropped open. "You smoked?"

"Socially, and only for a year."

"*You?* Mr Goody-two-shoes who was studying medicine at Cambridge?"

Amusement danced behind his eyes. "Everyone smoked at

Cambridge."

"What did Kenneth do?"

"He was coming down to do a talk on the importance of sport for one of the colleges so he said he would come and take me out for lunch. That evening he was going out for a meal with the man who had set up the talk and caught me outside with a few of my friends smoking. Right there, in front of everyone, he began shouting at me. Full on bellowing at me in the street, and when he shouts his Irish accent gets particularly strong. It's terrifying." His eyes widened as if to emphasise his point and Bex laughed.

"I can't imagine your dad being scary."

"Oh trust me, he can be scary. Mum would tell us off when we were kids but you knew you were in *serious* trouble if Dad raised his voice."

Bex smiled. "That was kind of the same in our house."

"Yeah?" Something passed behind his eyes as he asked the seemingly innocent question but Bex knew what he was thinking. She never discussed her family. Nearly three years into their relationship previously and she still hadn't introduced him properly to her brothers. And as much as she rarely spoke about her brothers, she never spoke about her mum and dad.

"Yeah. Anyway, continue with your story. Kenneth was yelling?"

Smoothly, Daniel continued, "Everyone was staring, Dad's friend looked like he was dying for me, and then Dad plucked the cigarette out of my hand, stamped on it, proceeded to pick it up again and then demanded I ate it."

Bex covered her mouth, her eyes going wide as she began to shake with laughter. "No!"

"Yep."

"You didn't do it?"

Daniel raised an eyebrow. "Have you ever tried to say no to an angry, Irish, ex-rugby star?"

"You ate it!"

"I had no other choice. I was violently sick right there in the street but yeah, I ate it. Never touched the things again in my life."

"That's horrible!" Bex said pulling a face. "Didn't someone say something?"

"What could they say?" Daniel laughed. "He was right though, I shouldn't have touched them. I don't know what I'd do if I found

Amy smoking."

"I've heard making people eat their cigarettes is a good turn off."

Daniel grimaced. "I'd like to think I wouldn't act quite that strongly."

Bex reached across the table and patted the top of Daniel's hand. "I don't think you have to worry about that yet. She is only eight."

"You'd be surprised how grown up she seems to be."

"Yeah?"

Daniel nodded, running a hand through his hair and groaning theatrically. "The other night I was watching *The Echo* on television."

"I tried to watch that. Too gory for me," Bex said, shaking her head and taking a sip of her wine.

"It's not my favourite either, but it's a good distraction after work. But, in between the crazy axe murderer running around that no one's caught, there was a..." He caught his tongue on the top of his teeth and winced, his cheeks reddening ever so slightly.

Bex could predict what he'd been about to say but she didn't come to his rescue. Instead she tilted her head to the left and smiled ever so subtly.

Not subtly enough, however, because without even looking at her, Daniel said, "I know what you're doing."

"I'm not doing anything. Carry on with your story, Daniel." She raised her elbows onto the table, leaning forward and resting her chin in her hands.

"Fine, there was a sex scene - stop it, I know you're doing that on purpose."

"I'm not doing anything."

He raised his eyebrows. "Yes, you are."

Bex held his gaze for two seconds longer before bursting out laughing. He shook his head, a chuckle on his lips as he looked away and Bex dropped her hands, grinning widely as she stopped holding him in her flirtatious gaze. "Sorry," she said, letting her arms rest on the table. Laughter was still on her lips. "I like watching you squirm."

Daniel's eyes slid back to hers, a small wry smile on his own mouth. "Likewise."

Bex's body flushed with heat as his gaze held her still.

How the-?

Where had he-?

Images upon images of nights they had spent together flickered in her mind and she dug her nails sharply into the tablecloth. Daniel didn't drop his gaze but his smirk widened, clearly clocking her reaction to what he had just said.

"Who was having the salmon?" came a voice from above their heads and Bex sat back with a thump as the tension around them broke. She closed her mouth, only now realising she'd been practically gawping at him and humphed loudly as Daniel snorted with laughter.

"Salmon's for me, thanks," she said, glancing at the waiter after she threw a quick glare in Daniel's direction. He was trying his hardest to disguise that he was still laughing.

When the waiter had placed both of their meals in front of them, she pointed her fork over her dish at the smiling idiot opposite her. "That was mean. Where the hell did you learn to flirt like that?"

There was the smallest spike of jealousy in her chest at the idea he had found someone else this time to bring out that side of him. Maybe through Charles's new connections. It made sense, she supposed, and it wasn't like he was in a relationship with anyone now...was it? She hadn't actually asked him if he was seeing anyone else. Her heart faltered ever so slightly at the thought.

His smile softened. "You."

"Ah, so you do remember some things I taught you?"

"Some," he said, winking at her.

She processed that for a second, the worry in her chest easing and when she smiled in response, she liked the way his smile grew too. "So, what happened with the sex scene?"

"Ah, well Amy walked in, I practically had a heart attack trying to turn it off and she gave me this cold look and went *I hope they were wearing protection.*"

Bex slapped a hand to her mouth, snorting with laughter and turning in her seat so as not to spray her wine over her food.

"How the hell does my eight-year-old know *anything* about sex, let alone protection?"

Bex was trying her hardest not to choke. Her sides squeezed with laughter as she buried her head in her hands.

"They do say kids pick up on everything," she managed to wheeze out, grabbing her napkin to dab at her eyes.

"I'm hardly going around talking about sex, am I?"

"No?"

"No, funnily enough it's not a regular subject I choose to talk to myself or anyone else about."

Bex finally managed to sit up straight, turning back to face him properly but the smile on her face was still so wide it was beginning to ache.

"It'll be school. Bound to be."

"I know." Daniel shrugged sadly. "Wish kids would just enjoy being kids. They don't need to know everything straight away, you know?"

She reached across to squeeze his hand. "I get it."

Withdrawing her hand she picked up her knife and fork again, staring down at her food as something stirred in her mind.

"What is it?" Daniel said, laughing slightly. "I can see you're thinking something."

"Oh it's just a question."

"About my poor parenting skills or the fact that I have clearly been walking around the house giving contraceptive talks out loud."

A laugh escaped her lips but she didn't quite meet his eye. It surprised her. It always did. This feeling of hesitancy around him. The scatter of nerves in her chest when it came to voicing things she would normally be fine to ask.

Forcing herself to meet his eye, she asked, "Just whilst we are on the subject of protection, are you seeing anyone else?"

His fork was almost at his mouth, a piece of seabass positioned perfectly. Lowering it slowly, he held her gaze.

"No. I would have told you."

She knew he would have. Deep down she knew that. He would have said before they'd spent a night together on the sofa, before their incident in his parents' guard, before their daily phone calls.

She knew he would have said.

But she had to make sure. She had to tick that box. Just in case.

She couldn't trust him just yet, she reminded herself. No matter how strongly her feelings for him had returned, she couldn't just roll over and let a man walk all over her.

She told herself not to ask anything else. She pressed her lips shut and focused on her meal but the question came stumbling out.

"Have there been many people this time around? Girlfriends?"

Fucking hell, Bex.

Sometimes she did see how Lizzie had once compared her to a

bull in a china shop.

She hadn't agreed with her at the time but the comment had stuck with her.

Daniel looked away hesitantly before looking back. He placed his fork back down on his plate, the slightly chime of it sounding a lot louder in Bex's head than it probably was.

"Truthfully?"

"Obviously."

"No," he said, shaking his head. "My life played out pretty much exactly the same as last time except I didn't meet you and start dating you two and half years ago."

"No one since Helen?"

"No. It's hardly like there's been a queue."

He looked down at his plate, pretending to cut his food, and Bex had an overwhelming urge to hug him. How could a man so beautiful be so unsure of himself? How could he not realise that he could have any woman he wanted? How was he not a prick with that bone structure and those long eyelashes?

She stroked her foot up his inner calf and saw him freeze opposite her.

"Well that's good." She grinned as he looked up at her, deliberately biting her lip the moment his eyes fixed on hers. "Don't have to bitch slap anyone for you then."

He blinked once before snorting with laughter. Bex's chest rose at the sight and she laughed too, joining in as his face flushed red. His knife and fork fell back to the table and he put a hand to his chest as his whole body shook with laughter.

She did *not* notice the way it made his shirt pull against his chest.

She did *not* notice the way the sound sent desire bolting through her.

She did *not* notice how kissable that mouth was when it was happy.

God, she thought, *I'm in so much trouble.*

CHAPTER TWELVE

They left the restaurant roughly two hours later. Without thinking Bex reached for Daniel's hand and he squeezed hers in return. The night was cold and sharp, the air stung at her face and she was grateful for the thick coat wrapped around her. Even still she made sure she stayed close to Daniel's side, pretending to need the warmth of him. She'd opted to wear heels today when Daniel had mentioned they were going somewhere fairly formal, and she liked the fact Daniel didn't care. Being 5ft 11, many previous dates had complained at her wearing heels, saying it *looked weird*. Especially as she had been taller than most of them to begin with.

After informing them that they had no right to comment on her clothing choices, she hadn't been able to stop the insecurities stirring in her gut whenever she had picked future date outfits. She often just stuck to flats as it was easier than having an argument and being labelled as 'difficult' for telling them to stop commenting on her clothing.

Daniel was roughly her height in the heels she had picked for this evening, if anything maybe an inch shorter, but he hadn't batted an eyelid.

He never had.

"Daniel," she said, trying her hardest to think of how to frame this question without it being too much.

He turned his head, waiting for her to finish her sentence.

"What are we?"

She saw the Adam's apple in his throat dip and an anxiousness she hadn't felt in a long time flooded into her. Why had she asked that?

Why had she ruined tonight?

Bull in a china shop.

Bull in a fucking china shop.

"Um, well-"

"I mean obviously you don't have to decide right away," Bex said quickly. She stopped walking and turned to face him. "I mean, obviously, we can't go back to what we were." She swallowed hard. Her heart pulled at her words and her eyes dashed across his face.

The line between his eyebrows was back. "Right," he replied. For the first time all evening he reached up behind his head with his free hand and rubbed the nape of his neck.

Shit.

She had made him nervous.

Stupid Bex. Foolish Bex.

Just because her feelings had returned the moment she'd remembered in November didn't mean his had. Hadn't he made that obvious by effectively dumping her on New Year's Eve? Yes, they'd made up a few hours later but still...God, what had she been thinking?

When she had landed on that mat, her head had just been filled with their memories as if they had never gone away. As if they had never stopped. As if she hadn't had thirteen years away from him. Instead she remembered both timelines so clearly it was as if they had been placed next to one another in her head

What had she been thinking?

She knew what she'd been thinking.

She wanted to go back to being on the verge of moving in with him.

On the verge of telling him that she...

Shit.

Is this how he had felt when he had told her that he'd loved her and she hadn't said it back?

It was mortifying.

Embarrassment crept up her spine and her face burned. Why did he have this effect on her? She was used to just saying what she wanted and not caring about the consequences, but when it came to Daniel and their relationship...things were so much harder to voice.

"We aren't going to jump back into things, of course," she said, hoping that line between his eyebrows would fade with her words.

"What...what I'm saying is I'd really like to start again. To start dating that is."

She couldn't just presume all his feelings had come back too. It was complicated enough as it was, let alone throwing a relationship into the middle of it. She felt like they had been dating the past two and half years but at the same time, the other side of her brain knew that technically they hadn't. Technically, it had been thirteen years but it just didn't feel like that. It was like her emotions were jetlagged and it made the whole thing more confusing.

And yes, Daniel was a sensitive man. He expressed his emotions and feelings, and he wasn't a commitment-phobe but...but, he was still a man.

Men didn't just jump into relationships these days.

Daniel cleared his throat, bringing her attention back to him.

"Bex, stop worrying," he said, gently. "That's fine. If that's what you want, then that's what I want too." Something passed behind his eyes so quickly she missed it. "To start again. Just like last time never happened." He squeezed her hand. "Right?"

"Right," she said, sighing with relief that he hadn't shot her down but also feeling a stab of pain as something inside of her began to scream in indignation at writing off their past.

They walked back to her flat in fairly comfortable silence. She could tell Daniel was deep in thought, the line was still between his eyebrows and his lips were pressed tightly together but she let him be, giving him whatever time he needed. Her fingers itched to be threaded through his again but she couldn't force her hand to even swing close to his direction. Confidence, her fickle old friend, seemed to be momentarily lagging behind and, in its absence, barriers in her torso shot up a few inches. He walked her up to the door and took a step back as she reached for her keys.

Shit.

They'd been having such a nice night, why had she ruined it with something so serious?

Although, thinking about it, 'serious' had never fazed Daniel before.

Maybe that was because *before* she hadn't tried to throw it on him after the first date.

Hoping she could distract him or remind him of how much fun they had been having, she stepped into him, sliding her arms over his shoulders and bringing her mouth close to his.

"Thanks for tonight, I really enjoyed it."

The tension behind his eyes eased slightly. "Me too."

He kissed her, slowly and yet determinedly, one hand coming up to cup her face whilst the other snaked around her waist. It was a chaste kiss, well…more chaste than Bex would have liked, but she felt the care and strength in his touch.

They pulled away and his eyes met hers.

"You can come in if you want?" she said softly, tracing a finger along his jaw.

He closed his eyes and groaned, placing his forehead against hers so she practically felt the sound through her skull. "God, Bex, I want to, I really do, but I've left Amy with Lottie and Bry, and I promised I wouldn't stay out too late."

"Are they going out on a date afterwards?" she asked, enjoying the way he seemed to be leaning into the hand she was stroking along his jaw.

"I didn't promise Lottie. I promised Amy. She doesn't like Bry. If it was just Lottie she would probably have told me to leave for the entire weekend."

Bex laughed gently. "I'd like to have you for a whole weekend, Dr Williams."

"What did we learn earlier about the ridiculous flirting?"

Bex skated her lips against his. "That secretly you like it really."

He groaned and captured her mouth again. Inwardly, Bex smiled victoriously before she was distracted by Daniel's hands on her body and the heat his mouth was generating in her blood. The last kiss was chaste. This was anything but.

It felt like seconds later he pulled away but it couldn't have been because she was now pushed up against the side of the front door and her body was so warm she thought she could have probably stripped naked and still not felt the cold. Her arms were inside the blazer of his suit, wrapped around him. Daniel had one arm pressed against the wall above her head and the other on her neck. His coat had swung forward so she felt as if she were deliciously trapped in their own little bubble. At some point she must have undone the first few buttons of his shirt to run her hands over his shoulders as they were definitely undone now. She took a few deep breaths, enjoying the way his own chest was rising and falling too. If he hadn't pulled away, she'd have started to undo a lot more than the top few buttons of his shirt.

Daniel pressed a kiss to her forehead.

"I've got to go."

"I know," she said, still catching her breath. "Go save Amy." She pushed gently against his shoulders.

"Can't move just yet," he winced. "Give me a second."

Bex giggled, biting her lip and he rolled his eyes at her. "Why's that then?"

"Not funny."

"Very funny."

"Bex."

His forearm was still resting on the wall above her head and his coat was practically blocking her from view of any passer-by. It made her feel safe and protected, completely boxed in by this man she found highly intoxicating. She tried not to analyse what that meant because she knew if she looked too closely at it, like well applied prosthetics, it would start to make her feel a bit uneasy.

"I honestly have no idea what you could be referring to." She pressed her hips into him and he dropped his chin to his chest, swearing slightly.

"Bex," he said again, his voice hoarse.

"I'd love to help you with your problem." She waited for him to meet her eyes before she continued. His breathing was still laboured and his eyes were black. "All you have to do," she said in a sultry voice as she trailed one hand to the top of his trousers, "is think really hard of your grandad." She grinned as she leant away from him, dropping her hands to her sides.

Horror crossed his face before a low chuckle left his lips. He leant into the wall more, his laughing getting louder and Bex joined in, grinning at him as he shook his head.

"That was evil."

"I said I wanted to help."

"Yes, you did."

"What did your filthy mind think I meant?"

Laughter bubbled out of him, his shoulders shaking and he slowly pulled himself away from the wall.

Bex decided to take mercy on him and change the subject. "I need to meet this Bry. No one seems to like him."

Daniel frowned. "Who else doesn't like him?"

"Well...she didn't *actually* say it out loud but I don't think Lizzie does."

He ran a hand over his jaw. "Interesting. I got the vibe Matt didn't like him either."

"Really?"

"Caught them arguing in the hallway on New Year's Eve."

"Matt and Lottie's boyfriend?" Bex's eyebrows shot up. "It takes a lot for Matt to argue with someone."

Daniel raised his own eyebrows at that.

"Oh come on, Daniel. You know he isn't naturally argumentative."

"He broke Charles's jaw and gave Lizzie a bloody nose."

"He gets hot headed when he's protecting the people he cares about. And he was aiming at Charles, not Lizzie, he would never have hurt her! Think about it, when have you seen Matt really argue with anyone? Think about last time. Did you ever know him to be in a fight? I'd say he's more laid back than you and Charles!"

"You have a point."

"Wonder what this Bry guy did to piss him off."

"The guy seems okay. I don't think he's quite right for Lottie but he's not Felix." He pulled a pained expression. "As long as he doesn't hurt her he's good in my eyes."

"That's a low bar you're setting."

Daniel sighed. "Lottie isn't known for making good relationship decisions. Do you remember Anna?"

"The girl who stole your mum's money?"

"Yeah. Found out after that she'd stolen from Lottie too and Lottie had carried on going out with her. Then there was Tom, then Connor - I liked him but not his need to smoke weed all the time - and then Felix."

"Have you asked her about her dating life this time?"

Daniel shook his head. "No. I hope she's had some good relationships, I really do. She deserves them."

She studied his eyes and saw they were slightly shuttered. Pain was seeping through from behind the strength he was trying to portray and it caused her chest to pinch painfully. There was a lot of emotion under those eyes. "You're a good brother, Daniel."

He looked away and she saw the guilt deepen in his expression.

"This time, I intend to be better."

"Have you ever thought about telling her what happened? With Helen?"

"I can't. There's still a risk it might get back to Amy."

"It might help her, knowing her brother went through a similar thing."

"I know." He let out a long breath. "But I can't. I just can't. If Amy found out…" He looked away again, tugging his bottom lip under his teeth. She reached forward, turning his head back towards her.

"You don't have to tell anyone you don't want to."

He took a slow, steadying breath. "Does that make me selfish?"

"Daniel Williams, selfish is not a word I'd ever associate with you."

His eyes softened. The look he was giving her changed and it made her stomach somersault.

"Thank you."

CHAPTER THIRTEEN

The house was full of noise when Daniel got back from work. It sounded like people were talking in the living room and he could hear music coming from somewhere. It made everything feel that bit warmer.

"Hello?" he called, shrugging out of his coat and placing it neatly on one of the hooks by the door. Unlike most of his siblings, Daniel had inherited his father's tidiness. He liked to keep things as organised as he could, which was rather counterproductive as Amy loved to keep things as messy as possible. He glanced at four pairs of her shoes scattered at the bottom of the stairs, one lone trainer a few steps up, and a duvet she had presumably dragged from her bedroom abandoned over the bannister.

He had literally cleaned this morning, how the hell had she managed to create this much mess already?

The question made him smile. He cleaned as a way to organise himself, to ground himself or to switch off when his head got too full of work. He didn't need Amy to be tidy. Her mess had never bothered him and without it, he knew his home would look more like a show piece than an actual place where people lived.

It had been a week since his date with Bex, and Daniel still didn't know quite what to think of their last date. He had tried not to analyse what she had said about where she wanted their relationship to be but the words had whirled around in his head the moment he'd had any time to himself. They were responsible for why he had been cleaning this morning.

It confused him.

When he had remembered, all his feelings had come back at once. Like a tornado striking him in the chest. It didn't feel like it had been thirteen years and he'd hoped it had been the same for Bex...

But he tried not to think about that too much.

Instead, he'd tried to focus on how she had made him feel on the date, on the walk, during that kiss.

Those were the things he should be focusing on.

She wanted to date and he wanted to date her, so if she wished to start things from the beginning, that's simply what they would do.

His phone buzzed in his pocket and he smiled, knowing full well who would have texted him. Besides, being with Bex made him happy, that's all he should focus on at the moment.

"Hello?" he called again, slipping off his shoes.

"Hey Daniel, we're in here!" came Lottie's voice from down the hall.

He walked down the corridor into the living room to find Lottie, Bry, Amy and a man he didn't recognise, all crowded together. The living room was fairly small. There were two cornflower blue sofas pressed together in a 'L' shape that took up most of the space, a small rug in the middle, a television tucked into the corner and the rest of the room was taken up by bookshelves. Currently, the books were ordered by colour - Amy had been busy.

"Hello," he said, pausing in the doorway to look at them. Amy was sat on the floor, paints spread out around her and he could see blots of colour on her tights and on the carpet - *fantastic*. She turned her head up to grin at him and the brief annoyance he had felt over the state of their living room faded.

He was a pushover when it came to Amy Williams.

"Hi Dad."

"Hi Daniel!" Lottie waved enthusiastically from the sofa. "Bry had the day off so he came with me to pick up Amy, and we bumped into Sam!" She had her legs curled up underneath her and for a second, Daniel's eyes paused on the small bowl in her hand. Were those tomatoes? Why was she eating tomatoes?

The sight of them almost made him question whether she was feeling well. Lottie wasn't usually the biggest fan of 'healthy' snacks.

Bry was sat next to her. He was muscular, not anywhere near Matt's physique but still quite obviously loved sports, his eyes cat-like and his hair a dark brown that fell in waves down to his shoulders.

Daniel still wasn't sure about him - especially after Bex had told him the previous week that Lizzie wasn't too fond of him either – but he smiled at him anyway.

The man Lottie had named as Sam stood up, brushing his hands down his thighs. He had short, red hair and a slight beard covering his chin. Everything about him was very square, from his shoulders to his jaw and, as he met his gaze, Daniel couldn't help but think there was something really familiar about his brown eyes.

"Hello Daniel, sorry to ambush you, I wondered if I could have a word?" He offered his hand and Daniel shook it, his eyes flicking between him and Lottie. Had Lottie invited a *stranger* into his house?

"I thought you two knew each other?" Lottie said, sitting up slightly straighter and looking between the two.

"We do, kind of. It's been a while," Sam said, with a short nod and a convincing smile.

Daniel relaxed somewhat. He was fairly used to not recognising people. Having worked in A&E for most of his adult life, he had passed hundreds of faces and sometimes he could be looking at a patient he had seen before and he would still have no idea who they were until his eyes flicked over their notes and it would all come flooding back. Still, there was something in his gut telling him that he had never met this man.

Inwardly he groaned. He was probably going to try and sell him something. Such a classic Lottie thing to do, to invite the salesman at the door in for tea and biscuits. Outwardly, however, he tried to relax his stance and continue smiling at the man opposite him.

"How can I help?"

"In private, if that's okay?"

"You definitely said he was an old friend," Lottie said, looking uncertainly between Sam and Daniel. "You said you knew him!"

Bry reached over and placed a comforting hand on her knee.

"Like I said, it's been a while." Sam's smile had started to look forced, like it was straining at the edges but his stance seemed relaxed enough.

Daniel eyed him. "Okay, sure, let's go in the kitchen."

"Thanks for the tea, Lottie," Sam said, putting down one of the blue mugs Daniel had bought Amy last time they had gone to Brighton.

Lottie didn't say a word, she was now watching Sam like a hawk, her expression wary.

Daniel wasn't sure why but he felt nervous as they walked out of the living room, his palms feeling itchy as Sam followed behind. There was something in his gut flaring and he tried his best to ignore it, blaming it on exhaustion. Tiredness was creeping across his shoulders, making his eyes feel heavy. It had been an especially hard day and he knew his body would ache as a reminder tomorrow.

"Right then." He rubbed his hands together, turning around to face the other man the moment the kitchen door shut behind them. "How can I help?"

Sam brushed a hand up the back of his head and his gaze dropped to the floor. Recognition flooded through Daniel but he still had no idea where this man was from. There wasn't even the slightest hint of a memory.

"You've got a lovely house."

"Thank you."

There was an awkward pause between them. The clock on top of the microwave ticked ominously and Daniel shifted on the spot.

"Look, I just want you to know this isn't exactly easy for me." Sam's brown eyes flicked up to meet him. "And I know we've never met. It was shitty of me to use your sister like that but I saw an opportunity and I took it."

Daniel felt his stomach tighten.

This wasn't the way a talk with a self-assured salesman would go. Sam seemed nervous and hesitant. His eyes skirting around the room and he kept playing with a chunky black ring he had on his right hand, sliding it back and forth across his little finger.

Daniel folded his arms across his chest. Was this man about to ask him to prescribe something? It had happened before. He'd been followed from the hospital and had needed to jump in a taxi to avoid the man following him home.

"I wanted to come and say I'm sorry. First and foremost, I'm really sorry."

"Sorry? For what?"

"I...I knew Helen."

"Oh," Daniel sighed, his body sagged slightly and he leant back against the worktop. "That's okay. Thank you." He smiled. "How did you know her?"

Sam still looked incredibly uncomfortable and he winced at

Daniel's comment.

"Well, I- I knew her quite well." He looked up uncertainly. "Very well."

Ah.

There was a beat of loaded silence.

Daniel tilted his head, observing Sam. His words didn't hurt as much as he would have expected them to. His chest tightened and he felt something dark move in his torso but it wasn't painful. It was just a dull ache from an old wound.

"You had an affair?"

Sam winced. "Yes."

Daniel turned away from him, reaching up into one of the cupboards to get a glass. "I don't really see the point in you coming to tell me that."

"No, no, of course not. And I'm so sorry, I didn't know if you were aware that-"

"That my wife cheated on me. Yes. I did know." He moved to the sink and began filling his glass up with water. The hiss of the tap was a welcome break through the tense patch of silence.

The first time he had found out, it had hurt.

It had felt like a knife had been pushed through his stomach and up through his lungs. Stereotypically, it had been on a day he had finished work on time. Amy was just five months old and she'd not been sleeping well. He wanted to get home to help Helen out, knowing she'd been exhausted the last couple of days. He'd grabbed a bottle of wine and her favourite box of shortbread biscuits, and practically ran home to surprise her.

Over the years he'd tried so hard to block out the memory of walking into the living room to find his wife and some other man tangled up on the sofa. He'd tried to drink it away, he'd tried to work it away, and he'd tried to bury it away, pushing it underneath the surface of his memory as if it had never happened.

But it had.

Helen had screamed. The nameless man had looked terrified.

Daniel had stared. He hadn't muttered a word. He hadn't shouted like people did in films, he hadn't tried to fight the naked man in his living room, he didn't even drop the wine. He had just looked between the two of them, his heart feeling like it had splintered inside of his chest. He'd picked up the baby monitor from the side and had gone and sat in the nursery they'd made out of the spare room upstairs. He'd sat in there for hours. Even when Amy had woken up, he'd simply stayed in there, shushing her back to sleep and praying no one would ever come to find them.

She'd said it was a one-time thing. She'd promised it was a lapse of judgement.

She'd say she was lonely, that she missed working, that she felt useless and unattractive.

She'd said he'd made her feel like that.

So, he'd agreed that she would go back to work and he would stay home with Amy. He'd quit his job. He'd become a full-time dad, and at first Helen had seemed so much happier. Her face had been brighter, her hugs more welcoming and their relationship had got back on track.

Until one night her friend had brought her back from a night out. He'd laughed as Helen had stumbled through the door, catching her before she hit the wall and thanked the woman he vaguely recognised for bringing her home. The woman had gripped his arm whilst Helen had been slumped against him, his wife's head resting in the nook of his neck. Her friend's eyes had been so sympathetic he had known it straight away, he'd felt it like a needle in the arm, the stab of worry. *She was with someone,* the woman had mouthed before making her apologies and leaving as quickly as she could.

That had hurt too. All of the trust and the care he'd begun building back up inside of him, the happiness he'd felt that they'd overcome a huge hurdle in their relationship and seemed stronger because of it, felt laughable.

He felt like a joke.

That time she'd broken down and told him it was all part of the fact she felt he loved Amy so much more than her. Being at work made her feel separate from their family unit, she felt like she was struggling. Floundering. Not enough.

So, he'd forgiven her and she'd agreed to go to counselling.

And then, three days after Amy had turned one, they'd moved to London for Helen's promotion.

It had felt like a new start.

Until her nights at work got longer and longer, and she had started to come home smelling of alcohol and men's aftershave. He'd ignored it. Boxed it away. She'd told him he was being paranoid and controlling. She'd told him he was always trying to put her down. He'd asked her if she was still going to counselling and she'd snap at him.

A familiar pain rippled down his back and he shifted his weight to the other foot.

"Look, Sam, if this is your idea of coming to clear your conscience then I'm frankly not interested. My wife told me about the affairs." He reached forward and turned off the tap. "And we worked through it. It's common after having a baby and having no time for one another." Or at least that's what he told himself. That's what he had said over, and over again as he'd waited for her to come home and simply stared at their bedroom ceiling.

"We were having an affair before Amy."

Daniel flinched.

Hurt balled up inside of his lungs and he breathed out hard.

He hadn't known she'd had affairs prior to Amy. He hadn't even suspected- he pushed the pain in his chest down as it threatened to rise. He took a long drink of water before he turned around to face Sam.

"I'm sorry-"

"I really don't see the point in you coming to tell me this." He put his glass down on the side. "Unless your intention was simply to ruin my day."

Anguish crossed Sam's face. He rubbed a hand over the back of his head again, brushing his palm back and forth across his short hair like he had an itch. His brown eyes moved to the door and then back towards Daniel. "Look, this is really awkward for me-"

Daniel's expression hardened. "Oh, I'm sorry, how inconsiderate of me."

"Daniel, I-"

"You had an affair with my wife," he cut across sharply, cold anger now fully behind every word. "Thank you so much for coming to dig up painful memories for me. Bloody kind of you. Now, please leave."

"It's more complicated than that-"

"I really don't need to hear it. I don't need your apology. I don't need to forgive you. Just get out of my house." Daniel moved towards him, holding up a hand so to guide Sam into the hallway.

"She has my eyes!"

Daniel stopped, throwing the man a bewildered look. "Excuse me?"

Sam swallowed and jutted out his chin. "Amy has my eyes."

Daniel froze. Shock, anger and outrage pulsing him through him so strongly that his hands curled into fists. The words from Sam's mouth seemed unreal, made-up, as if they hadn't actually been said.

He couldn't be suggesting-

He wasn't actually trying to say-

"What the hell is that meant to mean?" he spat.

Sam's shoulders slumped. "You know what I'm trying to say. And I'm sorry, man, I really am. My mum saw you two at the premiere the other night and she rang me straight away-"

Irene.

Daniel's mind bounced back to the way she had been looking at Amy, the way her eyes had so keenly run over the pair of them.

"What are you implying?"

"You know what I'm implying," Sam said quietly.

Daniel could feel his body shaking. He felt anger but his words felt like they were getting weaker and weaker.

No.

No, no, no.

"Amy is my daughter," he said firmly, taking a few steps towards him. "She is *mine*."

Sam's eyes were filled with pity. Pity that threatened to gut Daniel before spearing him through the chest. "She looks just like me, Daniel. Red hair, brown eyes-"

"That doesn't mean anything!"

"She's the spitting image of my niece. Look," he went to grab for his phone and Daniel nearly choked.

"Do you expect me to look at that?!" he shouted. His eyes flicked to the door, conscious of the fact the television might not drown out their conversation.

He couldn't have Amy hear this.

He wouldn't have Amy hear this.

"Maybe not. But you need to. You need to believe me."

"I don't need to believe anything. I *don't* believe you."

"Then you're being deliberately stupid!" Sam snapped. "You and Helen weren't even trying for a kid when she got pregnant."

How did he know that?

Daniel's stomach dropped and he felt panic begin to well and truly fill any part of his body it could get its greedy little hands on. He reached for the back of the nearest kitchen chair, leaning on it because he couldn't trust his body not to fall.

"You don't know-"

"Helen told me that she was pregnant. She didn't tell me it was mine."

It.

Amy wasn't an *it.* She wasn't an object. She was his daughter.

"If you weren't even trying, I'm guessing..." Sam faltered. His poisonous words finally coming to a stop as he put his tongue between his teeth.

Daniel glared at him, his hand gripping onto the back of the chair so tightly his knuckles were as white as bone.

He wouldn't dare.

"I'm guessing," Sam said, "that you wore protection. Helen said you weren't trying so I am guessing..." He looked up as if waiting for Daniel to confirm what he was saying. Daniel simply stared at him coldly. "We never did. We didn't bother with it. We were young, being stupid, kept thinking as long as I pulled out before *the deed* we would be okay. I can't imagine you'd be that naïve." He looked up at him sheepishly.

Naïve.

The word made Daniel's teeth grit together tightly as waves of pain threatened to suffocate him.

He had been *pretty* naïve.

It wasn't just the word that dug fresh needles of pain into Daniel's back though, it was the way that Sam had said it.

The exact same way that Helen had told him he was *boring.*

"It just makes sense for Amy to be mine," Sam finished.

Daniel felt like he was going to be sick. He felt as if someone was standing on his chest and slowly crushing him.

"Get out of my house," he managed to say. The words pulled along his throat like barbed wire.

"I want to see her."

"You just did. For however many hours that I wasn't aware of!" he snarled.

"Properly. I want to see her properly. I want to be part of her life."

Daniel's anger was wound up so tightly within him he could barely register the panic Sam's words were bulldozing into him. But it was there. Beating away in his chest like an extra pulse.

"You don't get to make that decision. For all I know you're some randomer off the street."

"Don't deny you can see it. I could see you trying to work out where you knew me from. It's her. We look alike."

"I don't have a clue what you're bloody talking about."

"Look, I'm sorry I was sleeping with Helen-"

"Are you?" Daniel snapped. "Are you really? Because as of yet, I've heard nothing to convince me of that."

"Come on- "

He straightened up, using his rage as a sturdier spine than his own. "You've come in here, told me you had an affair with my wife, told me you're the father to my daughter, the girl I've loved and raised for the last eight years," he began to strike off the points on his fingers, "told me that, not only were you having an affair with my wife, you weren't even being careful about it, and told me you knew of Helen's pregnancy. Maybe your curiosity over whose child it was, should have reared its head then." He took a breath. "Did that sound very apologetic to you?"

Sam's mouth thinned. "If you're not going to be reasonable about this then I'll just have to take this higher."

The panic that had been beating inside of Daniel's chest flooded through him entirely. He felt cold. Sweat trickled down the back of his neck and his words got stuck in his mouth. "What is that supposed to mean?"

"I want visiting rights. I want my daughter. My life...it hasn't been easy. I did some stupid shit in my twenties but I'm trying to turn it around. I'm being a better person. And when Mum told me about Amy...I just knew it was my calling. That this is the reason I had been getting my life on track. That this is the reason that I fought so hard to be better. And I really liked Helen. I feel like I owe it to her. I owe it to Amy. She deserves to have a parent, don't you think?"

Crunch. Daniel felt as if his ribs had just been snapped.

"She's got one."

"A real one."

There was a beat of silence.

"I am a real one," Daniel said but his voice was hoarse and jarred.

"Maybe one who isn't working all the time."

The statement hit him like a bullet. He took a step back as a familiar guilt coursed through his body. This time it was woven with fear. Utter, harrowing fear.

"I work to provide for my daughter."

"Look, that was a dickish comment, I'm sorry, but that little girl in there is my daughter and I want to be part of her life. Can't you understand that?"

"Can't you understand why I might be hesitant to let a man whose morals are so low they'd sleep with a married woman, come in and demand to see my daughter?"

"It wasn't just me! Maybe you should have taken better care of your marriage!" Sam snapped.

The comment was a kick to an old wound. He'd thought the same thing. Over, and over again. Helen had always told him it was his fault.

The boring Williams brother.

And now, realising that Helen had been cheating on him way before they'd had a baby was confirming just that.

It was confirming everything that Helen had ever said about him.

"I'm going to get in contact with some lawyers so I suggest you should do the same," Sam said softly. "I'm sorry, Daniel, I wanted to do this as civilly as possible. I really did."

"You don't even know if you're right!"

Sam patted his chest. "I do though. I really do. And so do you. Deep down. Surely you must have been curious."

"Protection isn't always effective."

Sam's eyes crinkled in sympathy. "Is that what you told yourself? Even when she grew up and looked nothing like you?"

Daniel felt utterly helpless. It felt like the walls around him were closing in and his heart was starting to struggle inside his chest.

He'd never felt this alone. He'd never felt this terrified.

"She's eight-years-old, Sam. You can't expect to swan in now and start playing Dad."

"I'm not planning on playing. Amy deserves to know who her real dad is. That is just basic fact. I deserve to have time with my daughter." He turned, leaving Daniel standing between the fridge and the table, unable to move as he tried his hardest to come up with something to say. Just as Sam put his hand on the door handle he turned to look at him. "I am truly sorry for sleeping with Helen. I should have been stronger." He tried to laugh. "But, I mean, she could be quite persuasive when she wanted to be, right?"

Daniel stared at him. His anger had gone. It had been crushed under the sheer tidal wave of panic, hurt and fear that had flooded through his body. He felt exhausted, completely drained of any kind of strength. Sam's comment should have stung but it didn't. It was just another scar Sam had stepped on.

"Please leave," he managed to say, forcing the words out of his mouth. "Just go."

"Okay. I'll send a DNA test through so you can see for yourself Amy isn't yours. If you get me a cheek sample so I could-"

"Get out!" Daniel shouted, pushing himself forward. "Just get out."

Daniel waited, watching Sam's pitying gaze as he turned and left the kitchen. His whole body stilled. He was unable to breathe, unable to blink, unable to think about anything until he heard the sound of the front door shutting echo down the corridor and into the kitchen.

Like a puppet master had cut the string from above his head he stumbled, grabbing hold of the table as his whole body began to shake.

No.

No, no, no.

Not Amy. They couldn't take Amy.

"Daniel, who was-?" Lottie paused in the doorway, her brown eyes widening in horror as she took him in.

Her brown eyes.

Her blonde curls.

He'd always thought that's where Amy had got them from. He'd always thought she looked more similar to Lottie than to him. But now he saw that Lottie's eyes were a fraction lighter, more round, and the curls in her hair were shaped differently, falling in a more concise format.

Had he been blind?

Had he known?

Had Helen known?

When he'd been getting up in the middle night as Amy had screamed, as he'd lain on the floor playing with her, as Helen had accused him of loving Amy more than her, had she known Amy wasn't his?

"Dad!" He heard Amy's voice and his eyes widened in panic, his hands slipping against the table and he almost fell to the floor.

"Just a second, darling!" Lottie said, leaning out of the kitchen. "Bry, grab Amy for me. Sweetie, your dad's smashed a glass in here, need to take care of it." Lottie jumped into the room and shut the door behind her. Quickly, she turned the key in the lock before stepping towards Daniel.

"What's wrong? What's happened?"

He was going to lose her. He was going to lose the person he loved most in the world.

The sound of brakes screeched through his head and pain quickly followed it, rippling down his neck. The iron taste of blood was on his tongue and the muscles in his lower left leg cramped, like they had when they'd convulsed in pain after the car had driven over his ankle.

Was that the way his life was always going to have panned out? Was he always destined to lose his daughter? Was it simply mapped out in front of him?

Was it just a case of whether he was alive or not to see it?

"He's…" He tried his hardest to breathe, to calm himself down, but his heart was racing so fast it hurt.

"I'm so sorry, Daniel. I should never have let him. I'm so sorry. He seemed so genuine. Who was he?" She stepped forward and placed a small hand on Daniel's upper arm.

"He…fuck!"

Lottie flinched. "What is it?"

"He thinks he's Amy's dad."

Silence pulsed around the kitchen. The sound of the television next door filtered through the wall and they heard Bry laugh loudly at something. The sound jarred within the four walls of the kitchen.

"What the hell did you just say?" The words hissed out of Lottie's mouth, and her grip tightened to the point of pain.

"I'm…I think he's right, Lottie."

"Shut up!" she said darkly, her eyes sparking. "Don't say that."

His whole body began to tremble again and he stared towards the living room, imagining exactly what Amy was doing at this precise moment. Imagining her still painting on the floor, spilling a bit of red onto the carpet and trying to strategically cover it with her foot. He imagined her smile as she heard Bry laugh and her eyes flicking to the television curiously. "Amy's not mine."

CHAPTER FOURTEEN

Bex knew it wasn't her right or even her place to be, but she was livid. She was furious. There were a billion different emotions all stirring up inside of her, but each one of them had a streak of red and an aftertaste of anger. She tried to stop her hands shaking, calmly placing them under her thighs as they sat just at a diagonal to one another on the old worn blue sofa, their knees gently brushing.

She'd known there was something wrong. The brief spark in his eyes as Daniel had opened the door had been swiftly overshadowed by something much more troublesome. The grey in his eyes had become more prominent and the frown between his eyebrows had remained on his forehead all evening.

They'd eaten together, Amy sat on the chair next to her telling her all about the painting she had to do as it was her form's turn to decorate the music room that year. Judging by her comments, Amy clearly didn't like doing art when it was set by someone else. She liked freestyle.

While Daniel had been cleaning up, Bex had followed Amy into the living room and Amy had showed her the way she was now restacking the bookshelves in terms of the size of the books.

Talking to Amy was easy. She was delighted that Bex was back in the house and stuck to her side nearly all night. Her brown eyes followed her as she moved and when it had come to going to bed she had insisted her dad stayed downstairs with her instead of putting her to bed.

"Leo and I are going to have a long chat anyway, Dad, so really, it's for the best if you stay downstairs," Amy had said, practically pushing Daniel back into the room and sounding a lot older than she was.

"Who's Leo?" Bex had asked, amusement dancing through her voice as they heard of the creak of the stairs and the closing of Amy's door above.

"Her imaginary friend. He's been around since she could talk. They have many *conversations*." Daniel had rolled his eyes. "Don't know whether I should be concerned her imaginary friend is an older boy."

"Is that what she's said?" Bex said, laughing at Daniel's discomfort.

"Yeah. Very tall and older. That's all I've got."

"Well, my imaginary friend was an elephant when I grew up so I wouldn't be too concerned." That's when she had turned to him and quite bluntly said, "So, what's wrong?"

He had told her everything and Bex found herself humming with rage as the shadow behind Daniel's eyes had got darker.

"So, that's the gist," Daniel said, calmly.

He folded and unfolded his hands in his lap.

Bex tried her hardest to breathe in and out, to settle her insides before she spoke.

"Bastard!" she eventually spat out. "Utter fucking bastard. Who the hell does he think is? Firstly, who just walks into a stranger's house and tells them *oh by the way I had an affair with your wife?* Especially when that wife died! Like, have some respect! And then he just tries to claim he's the father of your kid. I mean surely, if he was really that interested, he'd have been around before now. He knew she was bloody pregnant. Why didn't he ask? Or was the truth of it that he didn't bloody care? I mean, come on! The guy is clearly a moron!"

Her eyes collided with Daniel's and she winced.

Shit

That had been far too harsh. Her emotions had got the better of her and she had spoken without thinking. Her mouth went dry and she tried to quickly think about something to say that could be slightly more sympathetic and less passionate.

Daniel snorted, his face cracking out into a smile as he laughed. It got louder and louder, his chest shaking and his face reddening. Bex threw him an apologetic smile.

"Sorry."

"God, Bex, you have such a poetic way with words."

"Was that a bit much?"

"No." He shook his head and wiped a tear from the side of his eye. "It was actually quite good. I don't think I've laughed since it happened."

"This was two nights ago?"

He nodded. "Sorry I didn't tell you right away, I worked late again yesterday and I didn't want to tell you over the phone."

"That wasn't why I asking." She nudged his knee with her own. "I was asking because I don't like the idea of you going two days without laughing."

"Unfortunately, with my job, it's sometimes a regular thing." He looked at her, affection behind his eyes but his words made her feel sadder than he realised. They hit something sharp inside of her.

Daniel deserved to laugh every day.

She inwardly shook herself. "Look, we don't know for certain Sam is telling the truth! He is so stupid and emotionally challenged that there is a good chance Amy is *not* related to him. She's smart."

"She takes after Helen."

"You're smart." Her words came out clipped. "Amy's kind, witty, good natured. She's *your* daughter, Daniel. Don't stop believing that until you have a piece of paper confirming otherwise. And even then, being someone's biological father doesn't make them a dad. Look at... Craig!"

Daniel's face pinched.

"Exactly," Bex said, squeezing his knee.

"Just have to hope Amy feels the same way I suppose."

"Don't go there! You know Amy will not abandon you for some strange man who came to say hello one afternoon!"

Daniel refused to meet her gaze. "I can't blame her if she wants to know her real father."

Something heavy twisted in Bex's torso. A memory shook itself from within the cage she had put it in and her hands grew slightly clammy. "You *are* her real father. I envy the relationship you two have. It's special."

He looked at her, his eyes sharpening with interest. "You...you didn't have that kind of relationship with your dad?"

A familiar fear licked up her spine and she felt her barriers threaten to close on the small space she had left for Daniel over the last couple of weeks. She dug her nails into her palms and resisted.

"We did. Until he let us down."

Daniel tilted his head ever so slightly. "He let you down?"

She could tell he was trying to be delicate, hyper aware of how defensive she had gotten in the past when he'd asked her questions about her family. His care was obvious in the way he was simply mirroring her words instead of asking her a direct question. The fact he was even thinking about her feelings at a time like this made her sit up straighter and push away the automatic defensiveness threatening to rise inside of her.

"He did. In a big way. And one day, I'll explain it to you. But tonight, we are talking about you."

He held her gaze before nodding ever so slightly. "Okay. Whenever you're ready."

"Thank you." The tension around her torso eased slightly and she smiled.

Daniel returned it. "Sorry if tonight wasn't exactly the kind of date you were expecting."

"I was fed pasta, given wine, got to play with Amy's glitter pens and spend time with a really handsome man. Seems like a brilliant date to me."

"Should I be worried?" Daniel said sitting up, a playful smile on his lips. "You just said there's been another man in the house."

Bex smiled, shaking her head and leaning forward to run her fingers through his hair. She had wanted to do it all night but had resisted being affectionate in front of Amy. Daniel's hair had an irresistibly soft quality to it.

"I had fun."

"Thanks for coming over on a week night." Before she dropped her hand he took it gently by the wrist and pressed a kiss into her palm.

She liked it when he did that.

The small gesture was so affectionate that it made her heart race and her chest lift every time he did it.

She stretched, hearing a click in her shoulders as she reached high above her head. "It's fine. My body can function on a little sleep once in a while."

When she dropped her arms and looked at him once more he was now staring intently in front of him, his cheeks slightly pink. She noted the hand around his glass of wine was tense.

"What?" she asked.

He smiled to himself, shaking his head and continuing to stare at the blank television screen. "Nothing."

"Daniel, what is it?"

He put his glass down on the side and turned his head to look at her again. "Sometimes you really have no idea how distracting you can be."

Her heart raced at the look he was giving her, inwardly doing a small victory dance, but on the outside she simply raised an eyebrow.

"Really? Stretching? That's what did it for you?"

"Absolutely," he said, seriously, inching closer to her on the sofa.

"Was it my clicking bones? Is this some weird medical thing?" she teased, letting her hand rest on the inside of his thigh. "Or was it my scrunched up yawning face? Or was it the yawning sound?" His hand was on her neck and he was pulling her close to him. Her pulse had tripled and she felt heat streak up her spine as she realised just how dark his eyes were. "Or was it the fact I'm clearly tired? Or how high I could reach my arms into the air?" Her breath faltered as he brushed his mouth against hers.

"Are you done?" he whispered.

"Might be, why?"

"I won't kiss you until you're done."

She swallowed, pretending to think about what he had said. His thumb brushed against her jawline and she blinked rapidly, trying not to show just how much he was affecting her. "I think I'm done, don't you?"

"I think so too," he said before he pulled her into a kiss.

CHAPTER FIFTEEN

Bex opened the door and smiled, trapping the phone between her shoulder and her ear and gesturing for the man in front of her to come in. He shook the rain from his coat and wiped a hand through his thick, ebony hair.

"Lizzie, I've got to go, Marco is here to fix the window." She nodded. "Yep, will do. See you tomorrow, love you!"

Ending the call, she dropped her mobile onto the sofa.

"Thank you, thank you, thank you!" she said gleefully, opening her arms wide and embracing the tall man excitedly. Despite the fact it was clearly rainy and cold outside, he was still warm.

He laughed as she deliberately held the hug for longer than was needed, trying to pull some of the warmth of him into her bones – she had only got back to the flat thirty minutes ago and the heating had still not properly kicked in.

"Anything for you."

Marco was half Italian, half English, looked like a model and, at six foot five, towered above everyone. His body was firm and toned, and his face smooth and clean shaven. It did mean he came across as rather intimidating most of the time, especially as his eyes were so dark that they were nearly impossible to read.

When he stood next to her brother the pair of them were like something out of a catalogue. Whenever they went on holiday, women presumed they were on a lads' trip and would hit on the pair of them. Even as they flashed their wedding rings, a few would persist.

What happens on holiday stays on holiday.

And then they'd have to awkwardly point out that their spouse was sitting right next to them as a last resort.

"Which window is it?" Marco's Italian accent was pretty much non-existent now but the slight shadow of it made his voice more musical than most.

"Bedroom, it just keeps swinging open and it's bloody freezing."

"I can tell. Can you get off me now?"

"But I'm cold."

"Then put on a jumper!" He gently prised her off him, shaking his head affectionately.

Bex led him into her room where the skylight in the middle of the room was swinging back and forth, letting as much cold air into her flat as it could at one time. Occasionally it would stick to the frame but otherwise it looked as if it were having a merry old time playing in the wind.

Marco's dad had been a builder. He'd taught him simple DIY tasks ever since he was old enough to hold a spanner and had hoped he would go into the family business. Luckily for Bex he had been far more interested in a pursing a law career, otherwise he wouldn't have met Jason, her older brother.

"Coffee?"

"Yes please." He shook his head at the window. "Bex, honestly, when are you going to move out of here? I have to fix things at least twice a month. You could move in with us for a while if you needed to?"

"I like it! It's cosy."

"Mmmm." The word vibrated on his lips. "Cosy is not the word I'd use for somewhere where you're having to go to bed with three duvets." His eyes flicked to the bed.

"Always so observant."

"Thank you," he said dryly.

She left him to get started and when she returned with their drinks he was already sorting through the toolkit Bex had managed to convince the landlord to let her keep a couple of years ago. She sat down on the floor next to him, her back pressed to the wall. Because she lived in a converted attic it meant the windows were positioned very low. The walls were vertical until around hip height, before they sloped diagonally inwards. It did mean Marco didn't need any form of ladder as he worked but he was also tilted at a weird angle.

"So, how's life?"

"Good," he said, giving her a side eye. "Busy as always. You?"

"Okay. Can't complain."

"Can't complain? It's January. All you do is complain in January."

"It's only a few days away from February, January will be over soon." She smiled to herself but Marco's keen eyes seemed to catch it without even looking at her.

"*Cara?*" he said, suspiciously.

"What?" Bex asked innocently. She liked it when he spoke in Italian, even if they were just short terms of endearment or, more often than not, swear words.

"You know what. What's the smile for?"

She crossed and then re-crossed her ankles, stretching her legs out in front of her. Was she ready for this? Was she ready to explain it to them? She hadn't last time after all. She hadn't said a word.

But this time…this time she wanted that to be different. After all, she felt like she had been dating him the entire time anyway. Her brain was still muddled with the timelines but her emotions were still exactly the same as they had been. Even if Daniel's feelings weren't quite where hers were just yet.

Her stomach tried to dip uncertainly but she stopped it.

She trusted Daniel. She really did. She could feel it in her bones and she needed to start showing that trust.

She'd had nearly three years of evidence that Daniel wasn't going to hurt her.

"I'm kind of dating someone."

Marco blinked and then turned to look back at the window, looking bored. "Great."

"What?"

He sighed, deliberately focusing on the task in front of him rather than look at her. "Bex, you have a habit of picking really shit guys."

"They've not always been bad!"

"Mmmm." He pushed his hair back from his face and fixed her with his cold, dark stare. "I beg to differ."

Bex shifted uncomfortably and took a long sip of her coffee. Marco did the same, his eyes never leaving her face. He had this eerie way of staring at people. When Jason and Marco had first met - completing their training contracts at the same law firm - she remembered it was one of the things Jason would moan about. The fact that the other trainee had a spooky stare and a bad attitude. Then had come the competitiveness, as each had raced to be seen as better than the other. Jason's rants about Marco had got longer and more agitated. He was spending longer nights in the office, refusing to go home before Marco did. Jason began to talk of nothing else.

She'd started to recognise her brother clearly had a crush way before he had. He simply thought he hated the guy.

"He is different."

"Never heard that one before." Marco smirked into his own cup of coffee before placing it down on the floor and continuing to work on the window. After a couple of seconds, he said, "Go on, what's his name?"

"Daniel. He's a doctor."

Surprise flickered across his profile. "This one actually has a job!"

"Yes, Marco," Bex bit back.

"And a sensible one at that. How old?"

"Thirty-eight."

"Rents or owns?"

"Owns." She gestured at her own room. "Not that that would matter, would it?"

"Hair colour?"

"Brown."

"What kind of doctor?"

"A&E specialist. What is with the twenty questions?"

Marco smirked. "I'm waiting for the catch." He raised his eyebrows. "Come on, Bex, there must be something. You never pick normal guys."

"Daniel isn't normal," Bex snapped before she could stop herself. She swallowed, using her coffee as a distraction as she felt Marco's gaze rack up its intensity by a few knots. "He's wonderful. Normal guys suck."

"You sound like a teenager," Marco said, shaking his head disapprovingly but only for a few seconds before he reached down and squeezed her shoulder. "Okay, I believe you. Maybe this guy is different."

"He is. And his daughter-"

Marco groaned. "Right, that's more like it."

"He's thirty-eight, Marco. Having a child is hardly out of the ordinary!"

"How many kids has he got? By how many women? Where's the psycho ex-wife who wants to kill you? He is divorced right?" At Bex's expression, his eyes narrowed. "He is *divorced*, yes?"

A flare of protectiveness sparked through her body. "He's not divorced, no."

"*Figlio di puttana!* Bex-"

"He's widowed. And he's got one daughter and she's amazing."

Marco's eyes widened and his cheeks paled. Silence tapped slowly between them and Bex raised her eyebrows as Marco shifted on the spot. Eventually he dropped down to his knee and squeezed Bex's leg.

"Shit," he hissed. "Sorry, *cara*, I just...got a bit carried away."

"It's okay," Bex said. "You didn't know."

"I shouldn't have jumped to such a conclusion either. Mama would be appalled at me."

Bex grinned. "She'd hit you over the back of the head with a spatula again."

"That she would!" he said with a grin. Fondness filled his eyes as she laughed. "I'll always be protective of you, you know that?"

"I know. It's okay." She reached over and squeezed the hand he had on her leg.

Seeming satisfied Marco stood back up, turning his attention back to the window.

"So...this Daniel. Are we going to get to meet him?"

"Actually I wanted to talk to Jason and you about him. He's in a bit of trouble."

"Oh?" The easiness in Marco's expression fell again but she saw him trying his best to fight the automatic suspicion her words had brought. Whenever her previous boyfriends needed her brother's help it was usually with trying to get out of something not so legal.

"Legal advice. A man has literally just walked into his life and claimed Amy, Daniel's daughter, is their child and wants to have visiting rights."

The suspicion on Marco's face faded and instead, his eyebrows shot up. "That doesn't sound fun."

"No."

"Is he getting a paternity test done?"

"Yeah." She sighed. "I just really hope it comes back that Daniel is Amy's dad. Then this will all go away."

"His ex-wife cheated on him?"

Bex ran a finger around the rim of her mug, not wanting to divulge too much of Daniel's history even to Marco. It felt too personal. Too painful to share. And she knew Daniel didn't want anyone's pity. He hadn't even told his own family the majority of what Helen had done. They had known she had cheated. That couldn't be covered up when she had died in a car accident on her way to see a man she was having an affair with, but they didn't know about the other affairs. They hadn't known there was more than one until Sam had showed up.

"Yeah. Quite a bit. She was... manipulative."

There was a short silence.

"Well, happy to help if he needs. I'm sure Jay would say the same."

Only Marco ever called Jason, Jay. Bex had tried it once and Jason had burst out laughing whilst Marco had given her a steady look and shaken his head. It felt wrong in her mouth anyway. Jason had always been Jason. Neither she nor Kyle, her younger brother, had ever shortened it.

Neither had their parents.

Not Jason, not our Jason, it's impossible. It's your fault. You've poisoned him.

The words still rang loudly in her head and they hadn't even been directed at her. They'd been directed at Kyle. Still, she would never be able to push them out of her memory.

The doorbell rang loudly through the flat. Bex frowned, pushing herself off the floor.

"Not expecting anyone?" Marco guessed.

"No, probably just the wrong flat." She walked back into the main room and clicked on the intercom. "Hello?"

"Hey, um, I'm here to pick up Ryan's stuff?"

She let go off the intercom and pinched the bridge of her nose, breath hissing out of her mouth. "For God's sake!" she snapped.

Ryan hadn't texted her to even arrange a date, let alone to tell her he was sending someone around. Taking another deep breath, she pressed the intercom. "Come on up."

She heard the person lightly chuckle over the static.

Luckily, the first time she had believed Ryan was coming over to collect his stuff she had boxed it up. It was still shoved under her kitchen table. There was a light knock at the door.

"Coming," she grumbled.

Opening the door, she tried her hardest not to glare at the man on the other side of it.

Still, he surveyed her expression and then calmly said, "He didn't tell you I was coming, did he?"

"No, he did not."

He winced. "Sorry, Ryan can be such an idiot sometimes."

Bex smiled. "That he can be."

"I promise he told me he had called."

"That's alright," she said, looking up at him. "Lucky I was in."

"Yeah, lucky." He frowned ever so slightly as he took her in, his brown eyes running over her. "Sorry, do I know you from somewhere?"

Bex shrugged. "Maybe we met at one of Ryan's parties?"

The man shook his head. "Don't think so."

Bex looked him up and down. He had dark red hair and a slight ginger stubble to his cheeks. His eyes were a rich brown and he had quite handsome features. "Sorry, I have no clue. Come on in. It's only the one box."

"Thanks." He walked in just as Marco stuck his head out of the bedroom door. A smile crossed his lips.

"Are you Daniel?"

The man's expression changed for a microsecond. Something seemed to flicker behind his eyes as he glanced between the two of them. "Um, no. I'm Sam. I'm here to pick up Ryan's stuff."

"Ah, right." He glanced at Bex before disappearing back into her room.

She rolled her eyes. Marco didn't like Ryan or anything associated with him. He had never met the man but he had heard enough.

Marco's appearance seemed to have made Sam nervous. He was shifting his weight from shoe to shoe now and his head was turning this way and that as he looked around her flat.

"I'm just using your bathroom, *cara*," Marco called, coming out her bedroom again. He'd unbuttoned a few buttons from his shirt and his hair looked messy.

How the hell was he not cold?

"Okay, still need to push the button twice to flush."

Marco rolled his eyes. "And yet you still refuse to leave this flat.

You know you want to live with me."

"Hmmm," she said, trying to do a good impression of himself. He raised his eyebrows before walking away and Bex turned her attention back to the box. She folded down the flaps before pulling it out from underneath the table. There wasn't that much in it. Just a few t-shirts, pairs of socks and a disgusting hoody that Bex had *never* worn. She'd never understood the love for people to wear their other half's clothing. She wore hoodies after a workout to keep warm before she rushed home, never as an actual fashion choice.

She bent to pick up the box and turned to see that Sam had stopped looking around the room. Instead, he was looking at her and he didn't even blush as she caught him staring. The corner of his mouth lifted ever so slightly.

"I think I know where I know you from, are you friends with Lottie Williams?"

Got that from my arse, did you?

"She's a friend! How do you know her?"

"Work."

"Ah, small world. You have good taste in friends." She paused. "Well, some."

Sam laughed. "Ryan's never been the most sensible of men."

"No."

He sighed. "But he's been there for me recently so I can't talk about him too badly. My father passed away about a year ago."

"Oh god," Bex said, wincing. "I'm so sorry."

Sam smiled sadly. "That's okay. Gave me a lot to think about. Weirdly, I think it was good for me." He let out a huge sigh. "Anyway, not sure why I'm revealing that to a complete stranger. You must have one of those faces."

Bex smiled. "I'm a makeup artist. I'm used to people telling me their secrets."

"Sounds like a fun job."

"I enjoy it." She smiled forcefully. She did enjoy it. She loved her job. But she very much doubted that's what Sam meant. She could tell from the smile on his mouth that by *fun* he had meant *easy*.

"What kind of hours do you do?"

His interest surprised her.

"I get into work officially around 4.00 a.m."

"Ouch," he shuddered. "Doesn't sound so fun after all."

"It's a lot more work than people give it a credit for."

He nodded. "Sounds like it."

They stood awkwardly before Bex offered him the box. "Here. Promise I haven't filled it with glitter or anything."

Sam laughed. "Do people do that?"

She had definitely done that before. "Who knows?"

He walked towards the front door and she quickly skated around him to open it. "Be careful going down those stairs. They're steep."

He hesitated, looking down before he turned on the spot, a small smile on his face. "Sorry, I know this is probably really inappropriate, but would you like to grab some dinner sometime? You know, when I'm not carrying your ex's things?"

Bex blinked in surprise.

Wow.

Clearly Ryan hadn't been *that* much of a good friend.

"Thanks, but I'm seeing someone."

"Ah," Sam said, nodding behind her to the bedroom. "Sorry, shit, should have guessed."

Not wanting to get into a long explanation as to why the man in her bedroom was not her boyfriend, Bex simply nodded. The grin on her face, however, was all for Daniel.

"Exactly."

Much to her surprise, her answer seemed to pull a smile onto Sam's face. It unnerved her. "Well, as long as he's keeping you on your toes. You seem like the kind of girl who wouldn't be able to stand a boring boyfriend."

Bex blinked a couple of times.

What a weird-

"What a weird thing to say." Bex voiced her thoughts out loud.

Sam shrugged and smiled again. This time, Bex realised exactly why it had looked so odd. The smile didn't reach his eyes. It didn't even skim them.

"Just saying." He then tipped his head to her and turned to walk down the stairs.

She watched him carefully, something uneasy beginning to truly churn in her stomach. A minute ago she had been enjoying this man's company, thinking he was actually a nice friend of Ryan's. But now, she felt like she'd missed something. A sign she was meant to be looking out for.

Or a warning that she had completed ignored.

"I didn't like him."

Bex jumped, clasping a hand to her chest. "Jesus Christ, Marco!" she snapped, finding her brother-in-law just behind her.

CHAPTER SIXTEEN

"You look shattered, my dear."

"Thanks Aminah," Daniel laughed, washing his hands as thoroughly as he could in the sink.

"You've been very odd recently."

"Please stop, all this flattery will go to my head." He glanced over his shoulder at her and saw her hazel eyes watching him curiously.

Aminah had been one of Daniel's oldest friends. They'd worked together since he'd started practising in London. She was in her late fifties, had soft hazel eyes and a soft smile. Aminah wore a different coloured headscarf each week, and whilst being one of the warmest people he knew, she also took no nonsense. It was her who people turned to if they had a patient getting out of hand. Her voice had an authority to it that no other could match. She often worked the same shifts as him and they got on well. Sometimes he felt like she had taken on the role of his carer. When Helen had passed away, she'd been beside him constantly, trying to physically pry any extra work she could from his hands.

He was going to miss her.

She was going to start training to be a GP next year so she could have a job which meant she could spend more time with her future grandchildren. Her daughter had got married last year and she was hedging her bets that it was only a matter of time before they'd be along soon.

She placed her clipboard down on the side and rubbed her hands together. "What's going on? One second you've got this cloud over your head, and the next you're smiling like the cat who has got the cream."

He shrugged. "Family drama."

"And?" Her keen eyes narrowed.

"Just...stressful."

"Yes, but the smile?"

He felt a blush colour his neck and he moved away from the sink, shaking his hands dry. "I...err...think I've met someone."

Instead of smiling, Aminah narrowed her eyes even more. If she did it again, they'd be shut. "Think?"

"Well, I-"

"Daniel, a man just came in and wanted me to deliver this to you." Tully, a South African doctor in her mid-twenties walked into the small corridor where they were stood and placed it on the side by the sink. "I didn't think you'd want me to leave it in the staffroom." She was frowning and as Daniel dried his hands and reached to take it, he felt his stomach drop.

All three of them knew what that was.

Something in his stomach curled in pain.

"Right, um, thanks Tully." He forced himself to meet her gaze and smile. He was grateful that she hadn't left it in the staffroom but he was still embarrassed she had even seen it. He pushed the corners of his lips up even higher.

Tully went bright red and dropped her own eyes to the floor. "You're welcome." Her voice suddenly seemed to have risen five octaves and she shuffled backwards out the door she had come in.

Daniel didn't have time to think about how weird that was before his focus was back on the box in his hand.

Paternity test.

Silence bounced between them, the sound of the hospital becoming white noise as he stared at the box. It felt heavy in his grip even though he knew it couldn't be. He turned it over, the words and instructions merging into one as he tried to think of something to say.

He cleared his throat. "I should probably explain-"

"I hope whoever you're seeing thinks you're as amazing as little Dr Tully Hawkins does," Aminah cut across him quickly. She nodded at the box. "That's none of my business. Teasing you about junior doctors fancying you, on the other hand, definitely is." Her eyes were soft and sympathetic, and Daniel felt a rush of warmth towards his friend.

He silently thanked her, hoping it showed in his face, before registering exactly what she had just said.

"Tully is twenty-six. I'm sure she does not think about me in the slightest."

Aminah laughed. It was a musical one that danced but was never really that loud. "You're so blind sometimes, Daniel. It's cute."

"No, I'm not."

"She goes bright red every time she sees you, and don't get me started on that fake girly voice she puts on. She's South African! Her voice is naturally beautiful, she needs to stop shape shifting it around you!"

Daniel shook his head at her. "Thank you for the distraction, but you're wrong."

"About South African accents or her fancying you?"

A bark of laughter left his lips. "About her fancying me." He winced as he said the word *fancying*. That was not a term a man in his thirties should use. He turned away from Aminah's gentle teasing and stared down at the thing in his right hand. Swallowing, he put it in his pocket.

"Right, best get moving. I've been washing my hands for five minutes now," he said, overly cheerily.

"You can refuse you know," she said, gently. "You don't have to do that test."

He looked at her, his chest tightening a fraction. "Honestly?"

"There's no lawyer's note with it. There's no gun to your head. You don't have to do that."

He looked at her, knowing from her expression he wasn't hiding his worry or his sadness very well. "I think for Amy's sake, I do."

January fell into February, the sky got lighter and the tension behind people's eyes lessened fractionally. People were feeling more optimistic, already talking of spring and warmer weather despite it still being just as cold and rainy as the start of the year. February simply made these things seem more possible in people's minds.

Daniel had a rare day off. He had taken Amy to school and was now sitting reading a book on the sofa with his feet up on the table in front of him. It had been a long week and tiredness buzzed around his temples. He'd spoken to Bex that morning. She'd had a short break between *Jack and Jill* and *Elevenses* - she was helping out on the other show that morning due to staff sickness - and they'd discussed their evening plans.

He missed her.

A lot.

Whilst his memories of their past life felt very recent, in reality it had been a long time since he had actually been touched affectionately or looked at with loving warmth. Bex did both of those things and it hacked away at the solid rock he hadn't even realised had built up in his chest. It was the small things. The way she kissed his cheek when she was passing or ran her hands through his hair when they were watching television. The way she folded her knees on top of his thighs or kissed his neck when she rested against his shoulder. The way she straightened his tie, or stroked a hand down his back when he was talking about anything to do with Sam. The other day she'd offered to give him a neck massage because work had left his upper body aching. He'd refused although he'd appreciated the offer. With Amy in the house, they hadn't yet gone any further than kissing and he'd been worried that if he'd let her rub her hands into his skin he'd end up pulling her down on top of him. He couldn't risk Amy coming in and seeing. Her ability to move around the house as quietly as a shadow was worrying. And there was the fact that he potentially had a paternity case on his hands. He could hardly risk Amy witnessing Bex and him having sex and repeating that to anyone.

Since Helen, he hadn't risked bringing anyone home. He had kissed two people, been on three dates, and that was it. Amy was more important. He never wanted to put her in a position where there was a strange person in her house or she potentially saw her dad at his worst.

Her dad.

That was why his nerves were on edge.

That was why he couldn't concentrate on the book in front of him.

That was why he had rung Bex this morning even though he'd known she'd have been at work.

It was like someone had rung a clock somewhere and he knew

when the last bell sung, he was going to be in for a whole lot of pain. Today was the day he was due to receive the paternity test results. He rubbed his hand around the back of his neck and closed the book in his hands.

Sam hadn't reached out to him since he'd been to his house. Instead, he had simply sent him the paternity test. It wasn't even as if Sam would ever know if he had done it or not, but he had planted the seed in Daniel's head and with the test so easily at his disposal, he had to follow through.

Getting Amy to do the cheek swap was fairly easy. She'd been excited, thinking she was doing something fun involving his job.

He hadn't had the heart to tell her the truth.

Not yet.

His phone rang.

Withheld Number.

Usually he would ignore it but for the sake of a few minutes of distraction, he clicked answer and put the phone to his ear.

"Hello?"

"Hello, is that Daniel Williams?"

"Speaking," he said quickly, sitting up and swinging his feet down so they rested on the floor.

"Hello, this is Jason from Dunwoody Lawyers."

"Lawyers?"

His stomach dropped and he felt a tightness begin to grow in his chest.

Had Sam *already* gone to a lawyer? Why hadn't he told him?

The laugh down the phone was warm. "Don't sound too scared. I'm on your side."

Daniel frowned, his body relaxing somewhat. "Oh, is this a 'have you had an accident' call?"

There was a pause. "No, I don't deal with that kind of law. Or that type of scam if that's what you're implying."

The man's tone felt like a telling off.

"Sorry." Daniel stood up from the sofa.

"My name's Jason Wright, Marco told me about your issue with another man stating he's your child's biological father."

Marco?

Daniel didn't know a Marco.

However, just last week Charles had insisted Daniel use his

lawyers if he needed one.

"They are on the pay roll anyway. You should use them. Even if they don't deal in family law, they'll know someone who knows someone who does."

Maybe Charles had gone that step further and just contacted them himself.

It would be the kind of thing Charles would do.

"Oh thanks, I appreciate the call."

"No problem. So, talk me through what's happened so far?"

Daniel explained about Sam turning up at his house. Jason was silent, listening carefully to everything Daniel was saying. Occasionally he heard the scratching of a pen against paper but that was it.

"And then I sent off the paternity test two days ago-"

This time Jason did interrupt. "What paternity test?"

"The one Sam dropped off at my work."

"Oh, wow. So this guy thinks he can firstly come into your house under false pretences and then turn up at your work presenting you with a paternity test?"

For the first time, Daniel felt a true flicker of hope flare through him. "Yes."

"Sounds like harassment to me."

"And me!" came a chorus of voices in the background.

"Two seconds, Daniel." He heard Jason pull the phone away from his mouth. "Guys, my case. Not yours!"

In response there was a deep, male laugh and the sound of a female tutting loudly.

"Have you told him yet that paternity tests don't count in court unless they are done by a third party?" called the female voice.

"Demi, I know how to do my job. You made me a partner, remember?"

"How could I forget? Still debating whether that was a good decision." Her tone was teasing.

The phone rustled as Jason put it back to his ear. "Hello Daniel? Did you hear absolutely every word of that?"

"Sort of."

Jason sighed. "Well, like my colleague said, the paternity test wouldn't be considered as evidence until it is done by a third-party member."

Daniel turned to look at the ledge just above the fireplace. There were four photos. One of his whole family, crammed onto a sofa for Christmas. Daniel had been twenty-four. It had been the Christmas before he had met Helen. His smile was wide and he had his arm around Maria, his other around Charles. The only thing he didn't like about the photo was Charles's expression. He was smiling but his eyes were burnt out with tiredness and pain. It had been the first Christmas after Lizzie had broken off their relationship. Charles's face was pale and the shadows of a hangover were clear under his eyes. Daniel had never realised just how unwell he looked. He should probably take that photo down.

The other photos were of Amy and him. Amy as a toddler, balancing her weight on his feet as he held her hands. Amy on her first day of school, her school uniform practically shining from the amount of times Patricia had insisted on washing, ironing and polishing the buttons on it. Amy had insisted Daniel be in the photo too, refusing to smile until he stood next to her. The last one was the most recent. It was from the previous summer. Amy and he had Mr Whippy ice creams in their hands and were knocking them together as if they were pints at a pub.

Pain balled in his chest.

"Daniel?"

He took a shaky breath. "The paternity test may not be legal in court but...it will still tell me right? There's no chance of it being wrong?"

Jason clicked his tongue, clearly debating how best to answer. "I won't bullshit you. There is always a chance of tests being wrong. Human error. Mix-ups. Anything could go wrong. But otherwise, no. The paternity test will tell you if you're Amy's biological father."

Daniel's eyes were trapped by the last photo. The smile on his face and the equally as big smile on Amy's. His heart pulled hard.

She's mine.

She has to be mine.

"But, what I will also tell you is this. You have parental responsibility. Therefore, no matter what this Sam throws at you, at the moment, you're in the winning spot."

"What do you mean?" He felt like he couldn't get the words out fast enough.

"You are her parent. You've been looking after her for the last eight years. You have parental responsibility by marriage as you were married to her biological mother. To me, this man would be an idiot to try and take you to court. You're a doctor-" Daniel frowned, he didn't remember having told Jason that, "-you own your own home-" Maybe Charles had told him all of this? "And you are Amy's best interest."

Daniel used his free hand to grip his forehead, rubbing his fingers against his temples. "You think?"

"I know. And maybe Sam knows too. It's why he sent you a paternity test. Hoping you'll bend before it goes to court. He probably sent it to your work to intimidate you. To get people asking questions. After all, he knows where you live so why didn't he just send it to your home?"

Daniel swallowed. "You make a good point."

"It's my job to. Now, have you checked her birth certificate?"

Daniel blinked a couple of times. "No. I hadn't even...well, it hadn't come to mind."

"Check it. If he does try and take you to court, and you have the birth certificate to prove you're the father, he's literally trying to sail a sinking ship."

"I hadn't thought of that," Daniel said, the hope in his chest gaining legs.

"Once again, it's my job to," Jason laughed. "On a personal note though, I'm sorry you're going through this."

"Thanks." He let out a long breath. "And thanks for all your help, Jason. Sorry to have taken up your time. I really appreciate you doing this."

There was a beat of silence down the phone. "...You're welcome, Daniel. I can't do anything until Sam actually starts legal proceedings, but if you need me, just call. We could always put a restraining order in place even if he doesn't take you to court."

"You make it sound easy."

Jason laughed again. His warmth was almost infectious even down the phone. Daniel could feel it injecting him with a semblance of confidence. "I try."

"I'll let you go."

"Ring me if you need to."

"I will do."

He tossed the phone on the sofa and quickly made his way up the stairs to the makeshift study. It was a small room, right next to his bedroom, which he had fully intended to make into a study when they had moved in. Now it was full of cardboard boxes, a broken computer monitor and some of Amy's old baby things which he still hadn't taken to the attic. It was the one room in the house that was messy. Stuff was casually thrown here and there, and a layer of dust firmly settled over the top of it all like snow. He had no clue where to start looking for Amy's birth certificate, the last time he had needed it was when he had been entering her for schools and that had been in the aftermath of Helen's death.

It had been a blur.

He had felt numb.

He hadn't really been concentrating.

It had been hard. Despite everything, Helen's death had hit him. She'd been his wife and the first woman he'd ever loved. Looking back, he could see how toxic their marriage had become. He could see he had been holding onto it like someone holding onto a stack of papers in a storm.

And when she had died… he'd been so angry.

Furious.

The kind of anger that turns blue hot, searing at his edges and making him want to find an empty room and yell as loudly as he could.

Angry that he had to pretend he was devastated.

Angry that he wasn't devastated.

Angry that he didn't feel more upset.

Angry that he did feel upset.

Angry that she had left Amy.

Angry that Helen had turned into a woman he didn't recognise when he had thought she was his forever.

Angry that he stayed long enough to see her become an echo of her former self.

Angry that he had to make a speech at her funeral after everyone had discovered she'd been cheating on him.

Angry that he couldn't keep that a secret. That his wife had died on her way to see someone else in the middle of the night.

Angry for the bruises on Amy's scalp. Helen had left their three-year-old asleep at home, he'd been on a night shift – having returned to work as a locum doctor as they'd been struggling financially the previous year - and she'd fallen out of her crib and banged her head.

At the funeral, the pity mixed in everyone's looks for multitudes of different reasons had eaten away at him and fed the anger even more so in the pit of his stomach.

The months after the funeral were like a watercolour in his head. Nothing really added up.

Except for Amy.

She had been the one thing he could cling on to. The one person who brought him comfort in just the touch of her hand or a small smile on her mouth.

He began to search, not caring as dust landed on his suit trousers or as it flecked into his hair. His hands grew tired as he tore through box after box, pushing items this way and that, and only occasionally pausing when he spotted photos or old pieces of Amy's school work.

Eventually, he stumbled on a promising looking folder.

Amy was written across the top in Patricia's swirly handwriting. She had helped him get Amy's things ready for school applications – he'd been a bit clueless as to what to do.

The folder struggled to open, paper jammed into it so tightly that the metal binders struggled to keep them all in place. He was lucky. On the third page was the birth certificate.

He smiled.

He'd never actually looked at it before.

Amy had come and everything had happened so quickly that it hadn't interested him to look out for a piece of paper. He couldn't even remember talking about it with Helen.

As his eyes crossed the document he sat back, resting his back against one of the overcrowded bookshelves.

The document was simply a piece of paper in his hand. Unlike a marriage certificate it was all typed, the letters all neatly spaced out rather than in his unreadable scrawl or Helen's curled writing. It noted Amy's full name – Amy Victoria Williams - when she was born, where she was born. Then there were details about Helen; her full name, her maiden name, etc. He smiled, chuckling inwardly at how odd it was that he was finding reading about Amy comforting.

His eyes flicked down to the bottom and that slight joy halted in its place.

The hope in his chest buckled under a new pain it hadn't been expecting.

His eyes crossed the paper over, and over again, searching for the mistake, searching for the thing he hadn't spotted.

Where was his name?

His eyes moved faster, refusing to believe what he was reading.

Father: Unknown.

Unknown.

Soon the word was burning into his irises, causing his vision to blur as he crumpled the piece of paper into his palm. The sound beat around the room, greedily eaten up by the atmosphere and Daniel slammed his head back into the bookshelf with such force that he felt pain surge through his skull. A few books fell from above and hit him hard.

Unknown.

He gritted his teeth and felt tears already streaming down his face.

Unknown.

Helen had known.

Through the long nights, through the illnesses, through the tantrums, Helen had known. When he had given up his job to be a full-time dad so Helen could go back to work, when he had run out at 4 a.m. because she'd had pregnancy cravings for olives, when he had caught her cheating and had sat with Amy because she was the only thing in the world to him that felt right. She had known the entire time.

The sound of post falling on the mat by the front door filtered up through the house.

He didn't need to go downstairs to know what it would contain.

The paternity results would be there, and they'd be the final nail in the coffin he'd fallen into.

CHAPTER SEVENTEEN

"Kyle, there's three other people at this table."

"Darling brother, I need my carbs. You know this. And don't pretend like Marco didn't make another tray of roasties because he knows I like to eat." Kyle flapped his hand dramatically and continued helping himself to the potatoes from the bowl. They were the perfect kind of golden yellow that roast potatoes needed to be, crisp around the edges and almost shimmering in the dining room light.

Bex laughed at the dry look Jason threw their younger brother. "That's not an invitation to eat the entire first batch."

Kyle sighed. "I am a dancer. I need my energy."

"You're not dancing right now."

"Bex, tell him how one's metabolism works."

"Stop hogging the potatoes and I might."

Kyle handed over the bowl, pouting ever so slightly. "I can't believe I have to put up with this kind of bullying, Marco tell them it's disgraceful."

"It's disgraceful," Marco said, in the most deadpan voice anyone could have mustered.

Bex and Jason snorted with laughter. Kyle pretended to look annoyed for a couple of seconds before his face broke out in a grin. He shrugged. "I like my food."

Kyle worked in the West End. He loved to dance and he could tap better than anyone Bex had ever seen. He had a round face, bright eyes and was a lot bigger than 'traditional' dancers, however, his fitness was top-level. He still regularly did the beep test just for his own amusement and reached level 15 on most occasions. Kyle was also extremely flamboyant. Currently, he had his blonde hair swept back into a bun, he was wearing smoky eyeshadow and his nails were painted all different colours. Bex honestly didn't see why he insisted on painting his nails each Sunday just to have to take it off again for a Monday evening performance, but that was just Kyle.

They were sat around Jason and Marco's dinner table. They tried to get together at least once a month but it was hard. Jason and Marco were often shattered at the weekend due to their long hours and often mentally exhausting cases, Bex occasionally worked weekends if she got a job at a wedding or a television special, and the only day Kyle didn't work was a Sunday, which usually meant he woke up hungover.

"So," Jason said, reaching for the jug of tap water in the centre of the table. "Who got the phone call from Dad on New Year's Day?"

Bex and Kyle both raised their hands and threw smiles at each other.

"I got two phone calls. Didn't answer either of them, *obviously*," Bex said, drawing out the last word and widening her eyes to add an extra bit of emphasis.

Kyle looked up. "Ooo, I got four! Does this make me the favourite?"

Jason shook his head from across the table. "I got six, so no."

"You've always been the favourite though so, it doesn't count. Now I'm winning between Bex and me."

"How many of those calls did you answer?" Bex said, addressing her older brother.

Jason looked down at his plate. His blue eyes flitted over his food and Bex noted the way his fingers curled tighter around his cutlery. There was another beat of silence.

"Jason?" she said carefully.

Marco answered for him, his voice gentle. "All six of them."

"Jason!" Bex said, failing to take the accusation out of her tone. "Why did you do that to yourself?"

Sometimes Bex didn't feel like the middle sibling. She often felt like the oldest.

At seventeen, she'd been forced into that position.

She shut down the memory just like she always did when it began and focused on Jason.

He shrugged, pulling at the sleeve of his jumper.

"What did he say?"

"The usual, that he was sorry."

"That he was sorry?"

"Yep." Jason now toyed with a piece of meat at the end of his fork, pushing it around his plate. "But then, as always, he started trying to make excuses for Mum. Said we just have to understand it was the way she was brought up. That we could all be a family again if we just pretended it hadn't happened. That it was down to me to make that bridge."

"What a load of flaming bullshit." Kyle rolled his eyes. "I'd rather walk into a pub after a football game where the home team had lost, dressed in drag inspired by the opposition, than try and *make friends* with Mum."

"I like football," Marco said, raising his eyebrows at Kyle. "Liking football doesn't automatically make you homophobic."

"Well, hopefully you'd be in there to protect me then, darling."

Marco smirked, rolling his eyes. Jason remained more subdued. He put down his fork and moved back in his chair, bringing his right hand up to play with his opposite sleeve.

"He wants you to pretend like nothing happened?" she asked softly.

"Yep."

"You know what that means though Jason, right?"

He looked up at her, his eyes hard. "Yes, Rebecca, I know what that means. I'm not going to do it."

Silence fell across the table and Bex sat back in her chair, throwing her brother a concerned look. Kyle squeezed her knee affectionately under the table, shooting her a small smile.

Opposite them, Marco reached across and put his arm around Jason's shoulders comfortingly. He whispered something in Italian in Jason's ear and some of the darkness lifted from her brother's expression. Jason threw Bex an apologetic look.

"Sorry."

A small smile crossed her face and she shook her head, dismissing his apology because it wasn't needed.

Kyle groaned theatrically beside her.

"Marco, how many times, you're making my expectations in men way too high. And you're not helping me with my bad boy detox. I start to think that maybe they will end up like you and actually be a kitten underneath it all."

Marco gave Kyle a cold stare as he let go of Jason and picked up his steak knife. "I am not a kitten."

"Yes you are," Kyle said, ignoring Marco's glare. "You're as soppy as they come when it comes to Jason. You're a kitten." He turned to Bex nodding. "Isn't he?"

Bex felt Marco's glower turn in her direction.

"A little bit," Bex teased, trying not to laugh.

"I'm not a kitten," he repeated sternly.

"Sometimes you are," Jason said, turning to look at him with a proper smile now on his face.

Marco raised an eyebrow in the typical way Marco always did, and stared pointedly at her brother. "You think so?" His voice was soft but his expression was anything but.

Jason chewed on his food as he stared right back at him. Bex inwardly laughed as she recognised her brother was trying to play it cool but a blush snaked its way up his face and pinked his cheeks. Marco smirked before leaning towards him. "Call me a kitten again."

"Eurgh, stop it now," Kyle said, stabbing a potato. "You'll make me vomit."

He caught Bex's eye and winked, his mascara making his eyelashes cast shadows across his face.

Jason broke from Marco's gaze first, his cheeks still scarlet. Marco chuckled under his breath and Kyle theatrically rolled his eyes again. "Next topic, please!"

A grin crossed Jason's face. "I spoke to Daniel this week."

Bex's stomach clenched nervously and she swallowed hard, taken off guard. Daniel hadn't told her that he had spoken to Jason and she hadn't actually expected things to have moved that quickly.

She hadn't even had the opportunity to tell Jason about Daniel properly. He'd been quite upset when he had rung her the day after Marco had come to fix her window. He'd insisted the next time they met he'd needed to know everything about her new 'serious' relationship.

She realised with an unfamiliar jolt that the reason she was feeling anxious about Jason's next words was because she desperately wanted Jason to like Daniel. She wanted him to approve.

She wanted them to get along.

"Oh?"

"Yeah." Jason chewed thoughtfully. "I was...surprised."

"Why?"

Marco chuckled to himself in response and Bex's gaze flicked between the two of them.

"Sorry, am I missing something?" Kyle said, turning to look at Bex. "Have you finally left Mr Steroids?"

Jason snorted with laughter whilst Bex fixed him with an irritated stare.

"Yes, Kyle." She turned back to look at her brother. "Why were you surprised? And why's Marco smirking?"

"I'm smirking because of the reason he, and I, were surprised."

"Right..." Bex said cautiously. "Well?"

"It might have had something to do with the fact that he actually said the words *thank* and *you*."

Bex rolled her eyes. "My exes haven't been that bad!"

Kyle patted her hand patronisingly. "Oh, babe, they have."

"You can't talk until you've actually had a proper relationship."

Kyle batted his eyes at her. "Excuse me, I'm thirty, flirty and thriving. I have plenty of time for *proper relationships*."

"I wouldn't say any of your relationships fall into the 'proper' category, Bex," Marco said dryly before pointing a finger at Kyle. "And you're not thirty anymore."

"Hey!" Bex and Kyle said at the exact same time.

Marco's lips twitched into a smile.

"Anyway," Jason said, reaching for his wine glass, "he seemed nice, Bex. I'm impressed." He took a long sip of wine, holding her gaze. "And then I may have googled him."

"Jason!"

He grinned. "Daniel Williams. An A&E doctor! Very impressive. And related to Charles Williams?"

"Holy shit! What!" Kyle yelled, throwing his cutlery dramatically onto the table and ignoring the look Marco threw him. "You're dating Charles Williams' brother?"

"Oh, yeah, I guess." Bex winced. Sometimes she found it hard to distinguish between Charles, the English teacher, and Charles, the celebrity. She forgot that to other people he wasn't just the tall, friendly husband - now boyfriend - of her best friend. He was actually *a name*.

"Have you met Charles?" Kyle asked excitedly, his food forgotten as he turned to face Bex. He was practically bouncing in his seat.

"I spent New Year's at his family's home."

"And you didn't tell us!" Kyle smacked Bex hard across the arm. "OW!"

"You could have invited me!"

Bex laughed, enjoying the look of outrage on her younger brother's face. "I didn't even think. Charles is just," she shrugged, "Charles to me."

"*Charles is just Charles to me.* You know, him and his ex-girlfriend came to see *Wicked* once and I almost had a heart attack when I caught his gaze during the bows. That man's eyes should be illegal."

"Kyle!" Jason laughed. "Leave it."

"He's single now, why didn't you go for him?"

"Kyle!"

"Daniel is way more…" Bex trailed off, resisting the blush threatening to spread up her neck. Wine always made her skin more prone to showing how she was truly feeling. She looked between all three men before looking down, catching Jason's grin as she did so. How to describe what Daniel meant to her in an adjective? It was impossible. "Charles is not single," she finished.

"Oooo insider gossip, do tell?"

"No."

"What! Why?"

"Because you couldn't keep a secret even if we paid you a million pounds," Jason said from across the table.

"That's not true! Marco-"

"It's true," Marco said, simply.

Jason and Bex laughed as Kyle stuck his tongue out at him. Then he turned his attention back to Bex, his eyes glinting. "If this Daniel is related to Charles, is he drop dead gorgeous then?"

Bex smiled. "Well, I obviously think so."

"Jason does too," Marco added, coldly.

"Oh, leave it!" Jason said, running a hand through his hair.

"You were looking at photographs of Charles and him at different premieres for far longer than you needed to"

Jason flushed red. "No, I wasn't."

Kyle whipped out his phone from under the table. "There's pictures of the two of them on a red carpet?"

"Yes," Marco said, sounding not too pleased.

"Marco, don't get jealous. Jason and I just have very good taste," Bex said, smiling at him cheekily.

"I never get jealous," he said flatly but then his lip twitched. "But that was smooth, well done." He leant back in his chair and surveyed her. "Are you happy, *cara*?"

"Yes." She raised her eyebrows at him playfully. "Slightly sexually frustrated at the moment because I haven't been able to have him yet, but otherwise all good."

Jason spat his food back onto his plate and Kyle spluttered half of his wine down his front.

Marco smirked. "That was mean."

Bex laughed, her eyes dancing as Jason threw her a disgusted look and Kyle began laughing so hard he smacked his hand down twice on the table.

She turned back to her plate and conversation moved on to Kyle's latest auditions and what he had got up to in the early hours of the morning after a show. His stories went from simply forgetting to get the last train home, to ending up in Regent's Park Zoo as he got lost and climbed over the wrong fence, to jumping naked into the Serpentine with his fellow ensemble members in January. His phone lay forgotten beside him and a small part of her was glad he hadn't start flashing around photos of Daniel at a premiere. That wasn't *her* Daniel.

She smiled, looking between the three of them. Her brothers were everything to her. She'd had to protect them for so long that it still felt weird to see them as happy adults in their own right. Part of her knew and missed that they didn't need her protection anymore, yet another part believed that they still did.

Her mind flicked back to Daniel. She would have to ask him why he hadn't brought up the fact her brother had been in touch.

And then she would suggest they meet in person.

The idea excited her in a nervous, good way.

She felt so secure in their relationship the idea of introducing him to her family no longer seemed scary.

Daniel wasn't going to hurt her.

Daniel was never going to hurt her.

She pierced a potato with her fork, her appetite virtually non-existent as she toyed with the idea in her head. The significance of it was not lost on her. She knew what it meant.

And she knew what she wanted to do about it.

When she could next get Daniel alone, she was going to tell him what she had been going to tell him all those years ago.

She was going to tell him that she loved him. That she would stand by his side through this case. She would fight for him and for Amy.

Nerves fluttered in her stomach but another part of her felt excited.

Last time, she'd been terrified when she had realised she was in love with him. At first, she hadn't recognised the feeling for what it was because she had thought she'd been in love with boyfriends in the past. But it was nothing compared to this. She had refused to tell him. Refused to let herself be that vulnerable with someone who could hurt her.

Who could crush her.

She'd never been that vulnerable with anyone.

Her parents had shown her how much it hurt when you let a loved one trample all over you.

Her ex boyfriends had shown her that men couldn't really be trusted: promises were worth nothing from their mouths. She liked their company enough but she had never fully trusted any of them with her feelings. And those she had even fractionally, had hurt her.

But Daniel was different.

He was so *good*. Her mind cast over the last time they'd been together. She'd picked up Amy from school and he'd walked in the door just over an hour after they'd got home. The look he'd thrown her as he found Amy applying a whole lot of Bex's expensive makeup to Bex's face appallingly had made her chest tighten and something delicious shoot up her spine. Those grey-blue eyes had been fixed on her with such warmth it had pinned her to the spot. Desire had punched her sharply in her core.

That night she had hoped she could get him naked but by the time she had taken off all of Amy's badly applied makeup, and then reapplied her own, Daniel had been fast asleep. She had crawled in bed next to him instead, letting him sleep after his long day. At some point in the night he must have woken up as the next morning, they were the other way around. His chest was to her back and she was in his arms, his nose pressed into the back of her neck. His smell had been everywhere and she had felt tightly cocooned by the warmth of him. Despite hearing Amy pottering around downstairs, the urge to spin over and pin him down had been so great she'd barely restrained herself.

She pressed her knees together at the memory.

Right now, all she wanted was him. The amount of times she had nearly reached for his belt when they'd been kissing was ridiculous. She'd had to grip his hair even tighter to stop herself. It was driving her crazy. She needed to either book a hotel *fast* or find someone to put a lock on his bedroom door because it was starting to feel like some sick form of torture.

Something tapped her foot and she looked up to see Marco watching her. There was a small smirk on his face like he knew exactly what she had been imagining. She blushed and his smirk grew into a grin. Laughing silently he shook his head at her and she shrugged, rolling her eyes, before forcing herself to refocus on her siblings' conversation.

CHAPTER EIGHTEEN

Daniel practically sprinted from his car and up the set of ridiculously steep stairs to Bex's flat. The buzzer on the door had been broken and the door was propped open by a discarded trainer so he had managed to get into the building without even alerting Bex that he was there. He knocked, trying his hardest to catch his breath and praying that she was in.

"Who is it?"

"Me," he called and after a couple of seconds the door was flung open. "How was your brother-?" His words were cut off as Bex pulled him by his collar into her flat and kissed him. Hard.

"Bex," he said, laughing as he kissed her back, enjoying the fact he had found her in grey jogging bottoms, a white crop top and her hair up in a messy bun. She looked casual, relaxed, and he liked that side of her just as much as he liked her dressed up. He placed his hands on her hips so as not to touch her bare skin, but reading his mind she placed her hands on top of his and moved them upwards.

"You're my boyfriend," she teased. "Touch whatever you want."

His blood ran molten at her words and his brain practically blacked out.

She pushed him back against the wall and began kissing him harder.

"Wait," he said quickly, laughing as Bex was not deterred by him pulling his mouth away and simply moved her lips to his neck instead. "Bex, wait. I've got to go-shit." He closed his eyes as her mouth hit a particularly sensitive spot on his throat and her hands moved to the belt buckle of his trousers. "Bex," he tried again. "I've got to go. I was only meant to be here for ten minutes to say hello on my way to Rickmansworth."

"Ten minutes is plenty of time, I can be quick. Just don't fall asleep on me again, okay?"

He laughed again as her mouth moved back up towards his jaw and then up towards his ear. He opened his mouth to protest but his words came out muddled and wrong as she stroked her hand over his trousers.

"I don't have time," he groaned.

"Trust me, you don't even have to do much. I've taught myself how to do this practically all by myself."

She had started undoing his shirt but her words acted as trigger. Swiftly, he moved his hands to grip her wrists and tipped his head forward, back off the wall, so he could look at her properly. "Bex, wait," he said, his breathing coming out fast. He noted the spark of mischief it caused to flare in Bex's eyes and a smile crossed his lips. He shook his head. "I'm about to go and see Sam. I can't be late."

She stared at him for a couple of seconds, her cheeks flushed and her eyes bright, before her body slumped and she pouted dramatically. "Have I told you how much I hate that man?"

Daniel laughed again and pulled her into a hug, holding her close to him and taking a deep sniff of her hair.

"You've changed your shampoo," he said, detecting a strong smell of coconut in her hair.

"Oh," Bex giggled into his neck. "No, babe, this is dry shampoo. It's what us girls use when we aren't expecting our gorgeous boyfriends to come around." She pulled away and tugged at the bottom of his blazer, "Especially when they are dressed in another fucking incredible suit."

"I thought I should dress up to meet the devil."

"You mean this wasn't just for your pit stop to see me?"

"I'll take note that you appreciate the suits." He couldn't help but run his hand over the bare skin of her waist, enjoying her sharp inhale of breath as he did so.

"I love the suits," she said, but her cheeks suddenly reddened at her words and she looked away.

Bex was blushing.

Nibbling on her lower lip and definitely blushing. It was a rare sight.

"You okay?"

"Fine," she said shrilly. "I wouldn't usually let anyone catch me dead in these kinds of clothes. Even last time I don't think you saw me in anything resembling lazy wear."

"You never have to put on a show around me, Bex. You can wear whatever you want."

"Except for right now. Because right now I want to be naked."

He swallowed, laughing again as he had to look away this time. "You are so evil sometimes."

"I know." She brought him into another hug, turning her nose into the crook of his neck. "How are you feeling about today?" Her words tickled his throat.

"Not great. Partly why when I realised I had a bit of spare time I so desperately wanted to come and see you." He squeezed her gently.

"You don't know if he's her biological father yet."

He appreciated the fact she used the clinical term but even so, the sentence caused a sharp blade of pain to enter his spine.

The moment he had picked up the letter a few days ago he had known he wasn't Amy's biological father. It was something in the weight of it. Something in the way it smelled and felt his hands.

But, even after having mentally prepared for the worst, it had still destroyed him.

Opening up the slip of the paper, trying to understand all the different words and jargon in front of him, about strands and how many of his strands matched Amy's, his brain had flicked between pain, hurt and despair.

What hadn't helped was the rush of hope that had filled his chest when he'd seen the probability of him being Amy's dad was 35%.

And then he'd read on.

If he'd been Amy's biological dad it would have been closer to 100%. It wasn't meant to be a fifty-fifty split down the middle between Helen and him. It was meant to be 100% for both.

In short.

Not Amy's dad.

He'd stopped shaking about an hour later. He'd blinked as if he'd just woken up and found himself in a lump by the front door. His cheeks had been wet, his body tired and his mind racing.

"I know." He breathed Bex's scent in again, finding comfort in every single particle of her. He felt her run a hand down his back, exactly along the line where his scar was beneath his layers of clothes and the small action caused his heart to swell. He pressed a long kiss to the side of her head. "But I need to tell him. I need to see what he's going to do next."

"Why?"

"Because if I just ignored it he would come to find me. And then Amy might get hurt. If...if he is Amy's dad, he deserves to know."

He felt her shrug in his grip. "So damn noble."

He laughed, stroking his hand down her back affectionately.

"Do...do you think he is?" she whispered.

Daniel sighed and they finally let go of each other. Bex's face was filled with concern and she was watching him so carefully he felt something tug deeply in his chest.

What he would do to in that moment to cup her face and tell her how much he still loved her.

He swallowed away the thought, letting their conversation from their first date ring back through his head, clinging onto the words she had said so as not to let himself get carried away.

It hadn't been the same for her.

She hadn't remembered like he had.

But she was acting so...

"Daniel, you okay?"

He blinked. "Sorry, got carried away. What was the-oh, right, do I think Amy is his?" Saying the words felt like pushing razor blades out through his mouth, but the next word was harder. "Yes."

"Yes?"

"Yes. The more I think about it the more he looks like her. And if truth be told we weren't trying for a baby at the time. Helen wanted to focus on her career and she didn't believe in taking medication that messed with her hormones and I respected that, I didn't mind, I thought Amy was just meant to be." He brushed a hand through his hair and looked away, feeling the familiar pain build up behind his eyes. He sniffed sharply. "So, if they were...and he wasn't...yeah, it makes sense."

He felt Bex squeeze his side affectionately and he turned his head back to look at her. "It's going to be okay, Daniel." She pressed a kiss to his nose. "Now, get going. Otherwise you'll be late. Ring me when you're done."

Unable to resist, he cupped her face in his palms and pressed a long, slow kiss to her lips. He wasn't brave enough to communicate how he was feeling but he was as sure as hell going to try and tell her by any other means possible. When he pulled back, she blinked a couple of times as if to steady herself. A surge of confidence ran up his spine and his mind flicked back to what she had said earlier. His eyes tracked hers and a small flicker of hesitation sparked in his gut.

"What is it?" she said, her eyes darker and wider. She was breathing hard from just their innocent kiss and his eyes were captured momentarily by the sight of her mouth.

"Bex, just so you know, when we have sex there is no way I'm going to let you do any of it by yourself." He stepped into her, dipping his head to her ear and lowering his voice. "And it won't be a five-minute quickie up against a wall. It might have been a while since we were together but I remember exactly where you like to be touched, exactly where you like to be held, and exactly where you liked to be kissed. And I intend on savouring every single second of it." He pulled away, his eyes meeting hers. "Okay?"

She stared at him for a moment, her mouth partly open and her eyes nearly the darkest he had ever seen them. Her nostrils flared and she stepped back quickly, pushing his hands away from her and glowering at him. "Get out now, Daniel Williams, or I will not be responsible for my actions."

Daniel laughed. "I'm going, I'm going." He held up his hands and moved back towards the door, inwardly marvelling at the fact that he could have this kind of an effect on the beautiful woman in front of him. He reached for the door handle. "Talk to you later?"

"Get out!"

CHAPTER NINETEEN

It was a slow drive out of west London. By the time Daniel had left Bex's there were cars everywhere, buses so full that their windows were simply planes of steam and the noise from all of the traffic had left him with a dull headache around his right temple. He let out a small sigh of a relief as he left the busy city centre and started driving along longer, wider roads with higher speed limits.

As he relaxed his mind began to wonder.

He'd enjoyed work a lot over the past few days, enjoyed the distraction of the people, the cases and the other doctors. However, occasionally, he'd caught Aminah watching him with a slice of concern in her eye that she couldn't hide, and the events of the last few days would come rushing back, striking him right in the chest. It was a physical reaction as well as an emotional one. His shoulders tightened, his breath stuck and pain would build behind his eyes.

Seeing Bex had helped. Calling Bex the moment he had come back to life after reading that he wasn't Amy's father had helped.

She had helped.

Just her voice and the way she spoke to him helped. She'd even let him blather on about work to her for a good thirty minutes on the phone the previous night. He'd needed to talk about something other than Amy, he'd needed to distract himself and she had listened. She hadn't interrupted. She'd just listened, even though it had been late and she needed to get up early the next day for work.

He tried to cling onto that feeling of warmth as he drove out of London but it was being shadowed. Like something was chasing after it, bound to extinguish it yet he couldn't even make out what it was yet.

Daniel had a simple plan for tonight. He was going to tell Sam the results of the DNA test. He was going to do talk to him reasonably. He would request Sam do a DNA test and if, *if*, he turned out to be Amy's father, Daniel would find a way to tell Amy and see if she wanted to see him.

His hands tightened around the steering wheel and he made himself take four slow and steady breaths, concentrating on the directions the sat nav were giving him and trying to ignore the hole that had been ripped through him since he'd discovered he wasn't Amy's father.

Unfortunately, unlike his brother, he wasn't a good actor.

Amy had been able to tell something was wrong.

When he'd dropped her off at school that morning she'd made him kneel down and she'd hugged him hard, her small arms wrapping tightly around his neck. She didn't usually like hugs when he was dropping her off at school, she was already at the age where that might seem uncool, but, in the corridor of her primary school she'd clung to him. It was still fairly early, no one had been around as Daniel had to drop her off at breakfast club, which started an hour before school did but still, he'd felt a lump form in his throat at the gesture.

"What was that for?" he'd said as she had pulled away, his eyes careful to assess her face in case she was hiding something that she was upset about.

Amy had simply shrugged. "You've been weird this week."

"Have I?"

"Yeah. When you getting to Nanma's?"

"This evening, way past when you'll have gone to bed."

She grinned like he had issued a challenge, and he didn't have the heart to fight her on it.

"Okay, bye Dad."

"Have a good day. I love you, Amy."

"Dad!" She'd rolled her eyes and he'd stuck his tongue at her. But, before she had walked into the hall where breakfast club was held, she'd looked over her shoulder and yelled, "I love you too, Dad."

Part of him suspected she somehow knew he needed to hear that.

The drive to Rickmansworth was relatively easy once he was out of London. It was just late enough that it was past rush hour but too early for him to catch everyone coming back from restaurants and pubs after their fun Friday night.

The sky was a dark purple, the clouds so low they were practically skimming people's rooftops, and although the rain had eased away by the time he got out of his car he could still smell it in the air.

Sam's home looked like something out of a fairy tale and Daniel immediately resented it.

It was a small cottage. Red brick, with small windows that had flower gardens hanging from their rims and outdoor white panels that were thrown upon and adorned with swirls. Honeysuckle ran up from the bottom of the house to the second storey windows, reaching up as if aiming for the sky and in the darkness the house glowed like a home in a postcard. The warmth of it was tangible even from the outside.

Daniel flexed his hands as he tried to suppress the nerves rushing through him.

Before he got to the door, it opened. Sam stood there, wearing a pale blue jumper and jeans with startling bright trainers. He scratched his head as he watched Daniel walk up to him.

"Thanks for ringing. Hoped you'd spot it."

Sam had written it down on the back of the paternity test. A further punch in the stomach when Daniel had seen it at the hospital.

Feeling sick, Daniel nodded, pressing his lips closer together.

This was weird.

This whole thing was weird.

He walked up to the door and felt any bit of confidence Bex had injected into him falter. Why had he agreed to do this? Wouldn't it have been easier to wait for Sam to come to him?

Easier, yes.

Better, no.

Realising he wasn't going to respond, Sam stepped to the side and let Daniel walk into his home. It was as warm as it looked, the heat immediately engulfed him like he'd looked into a hot oven and sweat prickled along the back of his neck. He could hear the television was on down the hall but the house still somehow felt quiet. Even his own footsteps felt too loud in the hallway.

"Come through, can I get you a drink?"

"No, I'm fine, thanks," Daniel said. His voice sounded robotic and clipped. He knew he wasn't giving off the best impression but his defences were up.

They walked through into the living room. It was fairly empty. There was a sofa along one wall with a multi-coloured throw placed over the back, a television larger than his placed on a small unit by the wall, and a singular guitar in the corner of the room. The wall, however, was decorated with photos of Sam and his family from all ages. Daniel recognised Irene in most of the photos. His eyes narrowed in on her and he felt his mouth turn down into a frown.

She had been the one to ruin all of this.

She had been the one who had come after him.

Pain curled up his back in the diagonal line he'd come to recognise so well and he tried his hardest not to flinch.

"Would you like to sit?"

"No," Daniel said simply. He turned to face the other man, crossing his arms in front of his chest.

"Suit yourself." Sam reached across and clicked the remote. The television flicked to black and a heavy silence filled the room.

Daniel didn't know what to do with his body, he wasn't sure where to put his hands or how to stand or where to stand. He felt awkward and too tall for the room. He also felt like he was already on the wrong foot, and they'd barely even begun to talk. He tightened his folded arms.

"Did you do the test?" Sam asked, finally.

"Yes."

Sam shifted his weight slightly on the spot. His face had reddened and he looked just as uncomfortable as Daniel. "And?"

"I'm not Amy's biological father."

He nodded, a grunt in his throat. "Sorry."

Daniel fixed him with a cold stare. "Well, I wouldn't have known had you not let yourself into my house."

"I didn't let myself in-"

"No, you convinced my little sister you were an old friend."

"I said of the family's. I was *technically* a friend of Helen's."

Daniel locked eyes with him, his lips a fine line. Anger spiked deep inside his chest. "Is that really where you want to take this conversation?" He let a pause ring out around the room before adding, "Again?"

Sam sighed, before turning to the sofa and sitting down on it.

"Honestly, Daniel, I'm not here to cause you any pain. I simply want to get to know my daughter."

"Why?"

Sam's eyebrows shot up. "What do you mean, why?"

"Why now? Why walk into her life now? Why bother?"

"Because it's the right thing to do. I thought you'd see that. Being a medical man."

"I don't see what my job has to do with it."

Sam rubbed his hands along his thighs. "Look, I lost my dad about a year ago. It was really hard for me and when Mum showed me the picture of you and Amy...it was Dad's birthday. Mum's friends took her to the premiere to distract her. I thought it was a sign. A sign that now I had my life together, this was my next purpose. I needed to be there for my daughter."

Daniel looked away, hating the fact that despite everything he felt a flicker of sympathy for the man. Once upon a time, he'd lost his mum to cancer. It had ripped him open on the inside, especially as she had been so young. Luckily because of Lizzie, Maria was now alive. He knew other people weren't so lucky.

"You don't need to be there for Amy. She has a family. She has a network."

"But she doesn't have a dad."

"What the hell do you think I am?" Daniel snapped, unable to keep his voice under control. He dropped his arms to his sides and turned away, trying to focus and not let his pain get the better of him. Anger coiled tightly inside his torso and so did fear. He tried his hardest to hear Jason's words run through his mind, to hear his firm tone as he told Daniel about parental responsibility and Amy's best interests. But it was like listening to a radio in a neighbouring car - the words were muffled and he couldn't turn up the volume. "You don't even know if she's your daughter."

"She looks like me."

"You still don't know for a fact."

"Wouldn't you rather it be me? Rather that than some other stranger Helen slept with?"

Daniel turned back around. "I don't know you, Sam. The only person I wanted that test to say was Amy's dad was me. And it didn't. And please don't kid yourself that you were something special. My wife had many affairs."

"Why didn't you stop her?"

Daniel shot him an incredulous look. "Have you invented something to stop people cheating? Because maybe you should pursue investing in that rather than trying to take my daughter from me. It'll be a lot more profitable for you."

Sam rubbed his hands over his temples and looked across the room. "Look Daniel, I get this must be hard for you-"

"I really don't think you do. I've been Amy's dad for eight years. Nine if you include when Helen was pregnant. And to go from wishing her a Happy New Year's Day on January 1st to knowing she isn't actually *mine* a month later is a hard pill to swallow. Where were you after a 12-hour shift in hospital when Amy needed help with her homework? Where were you when I had to run around ragged to get childcare sorted as I needed to go to work? Where were you when she had the chicken pox and cried nearly every night?" Daniel glared at him and Sam continued to avoid his eye, shifting uncomfortably. "I'll tell you where you weren't. You weren't with Amy."

"That's not fair."

"None of this is fair!" Daniel barked. He breathed in slowly, trying to regain his composure. "Look, I wanted to see you to talk about you...you being more of a fixture in Amy's life. Only if you turn out to be her dad. I managed to get her to do another cheek swab so you can have it and send off your sample too. If she turns out to be your biological daughter," the pain in his chest was worsening, "well, we can go from there."

Sam looked up at him. Something flickered behind his eyes and he looked down, playing with the ring around his little finger. "That's very nice of you but...well, I've changed my mind to be honest with you. I want Amy. I want to be a proper dad. I want her to know me and have me in her life. I want to be *everything* that you just said." He stood up. "I want to be there."

"Like I said, if it turns out you are her biological father then I'm prepared to let you be a part of-"

"I will be seeking full custody."

The two words hit Daniel like a train. He took a step back, staring at the man in front of him. It felt like the anger had just been winded. All he felt was pain. Pure, desperate, pain.

"What?" he whispered, his words sounding as if from the throat of a stabbed man. "Why?"

"I'm her dad."

"What about her family? You didn't ever say full custody. You never said that!" He stared at Sam's set expression. "What about me?"

"I'm not going to be unreasonable. You're still her family, but you aren't her dad. You can visit on weekends. I'll make sure to get you visiting rights."

"You can't do this." His stomach jolted, staring at the man in front of him. *You can visit on weekends.* The words played on a loop inside his head. He didn't even get every weekend off. His job didn't work like that. He didn't know why that was the thing standing out in his mind but it was.

"You can't ignore the fact that you're a doctor. Your shifts are unpredictable. That's not stable for a child-"

"It has worked so far!" Daniel snapped.

"It's not stable for a child. Different shifts, different time patterns, different people putting her to bed every night-"

"I am a single dad, I can't afford not to work!"

Sam raised an eyebrow. "We both know that's not true."

"Excuse me?"

"Charles Williams is your brother. If you asked him I'm-"

"I'm not taking handouts from my brother," Daniel hissed. "That thought has never even crossed my mind."

"That's because you put your pride above your daughter. It would have been better for her."

Daniel stared at him. "It's got nothing to do with pride!"

"You'd have been there for her! You wouldn't keep having to move her around to different people when you need childcare. It would be more stable for her to be in one place, you can't deny that!"

"She is in one place. She's with me."

There was a long beat of silence. It drummed through the room and made Daniel's ribs rattle. The two men glowered at each other.

"Daniel, think of all the other things too."

"What things?"

"You're Charles Williams's brother."

He gritted his teeth. "And like I said-"

"Not that. I mean...I can only imagine what kind of lifestyle he exposes Amy to. Drugs, alcohol-"

"My brother has never touched drugs in his life. And a second ago you were telling me I should take his money and sit at home all day, so I don't think you have that low of an opinion of him either."

Sam ignored him. "He's an actor. They've all done drugs."

"You don't know my brother."

"And then there's your sister!" Sam's eyes rounded dramatically and he tilted his head to the side in disdain.

"Which one?" Daniel snarled.

"Which one do you think? Lottie, of course. I was still in Tring when she went doolally."

Daniel flinched. "Is that how you speak about people with mental health issues?"

"She was crazy! I remember seeing her once try and step out in front of traffic, laughing her head off and telling your mum to stop panicking as none of this was real."

"It was a misunderstanding."

Sam took a step towards him. "She dresses like a nutcase, lets persuasive strangers into the house and…" He let out a long slow breath. "Look, I have no real issue with it, one of my best friend's is gay, actually, but having Amy exposed to someone bisexual that early on could be confusing-

"I really wouldn't go there," Daniel growled. "I don't think who my sister chooses to date should be a part of this." He had to physically plant his heels into the floor to stop himself stepping forward and hitting him.

"Probably not seeing as that American she's dating now has no clue how to act around children. He just looked confused every time Amy asked him something and kept asking her if she liked PE."

"I doubt that scarred her for life."

"Lottie's isn't a perfect role model, Daniel."

"Amy likes her."

"Amy probably likes eating pizza for every meal but that doesn't mean you should let her."

Daniel took a step forward, his eyes blazing with so much fury he could feel they were almost beginning to smart. He curled his hands into fists by his side. "Once again, Sam, you're not her parent."

Sam refused to look away. Instead, he gritted his teeth. "And then there's your girlfriend."

"My girlfriend?"

On the outside he remained cold and angry, but inside he was trying his hardest to remember when Sam would have discovered he had a girlfriend.

"Bex Wright?" Sam held his gaze for a few more moments before he shook his head, a laugh on his lips.

Daniel's nostrils flared. "What about her?"

"You do know how to pick them don't you, Daniel?"

Daniel didn't say anything. He wasn't sure if he could. He simply watched Sam as he got his phone out of his pocket and texted someone.

"Do you mind-?"

Daniel's phone beeped in his pocket and Sam nodded towards it.

"I know Ryan. Bex's ex. I went over to her flat to pick up his stuff the other evening. I had no idea about the connection until I recognised her from Mum's pictures. I just sent you a couple of photos I took."

"Of her flat? Fascinating."

Sam held his gaze. "No." He paused with a sympathetic slant to his mouth that didn't look earnest. "She had a man in her room."

Daniel felt the pain like a bullet. It pierced through his chest and wave, after wave, of poisonous bile flooded into his lungs. His jaw tightened and he pressed his tongue to the bottom of his mouth, trying his hardest not to let his feelings flash across his face.

Sam looked away. "I am sorry, Daniel."

"I don't believe you."

"I just sent you a photo."

"There will be an explanation."

"Fucking hell!" Sam snapped, anger flashed across his own face. "Be a bloody man and stand up for your fucking self!"

"Photo evidence-"

"He was in her bedroom! He looked like he'd just walked off a catwalk for Christ's sake! I even asked her if he was her boyfriend and she said yes. Wake up, Daniel!" He slammed his right fist into the palm of his left hand. "Do you really think Amy should be around that? A woman who just sleeps with as many men as she can, hops from one to the other? She was with Ryan a second ago. She was flirting with me at one point! And you have her on the 'safe adult' list to pick Amy up from school!"

It felt like a dagger. Sharp, pointed, set in the deepest part of his chest and slowly being dragged across his heart.

He could hear Bex's voice in his head. He could hear her shouting about the hypocrisy of men. He could literally visualise what she would say if she was here yet he didn't open his mouth to defend her.

He couldn't.

It felt like cement was so slowly pouring into his throat.

First Amy.

Now Bex.

He was losing everything.

Screech.

Brakes.

Headlights.

Just like he had lost it all before.

Maybe it was meant to be.

His heart was beating so fast he could hear it in his ears.

"And let me guess, you let her look after Amy on her own too?"

Daniel said nothing, he still found it impossible to move away. Instead he dropped his gaze and that was confirmation enough for Sam.

"And you've been dating, what? A month? And you allow her to look after your daughter? You're completely blinded, Daniel. A gorgeous woman walks into your life and you've lost all sense of reality. I mean I'll give you credit for your taste."

"Shut up," Daniel snarled.

"She's hot. But she's playing you. Daniel, you're a nice guy. She…she doesn't seem like the type to be with nice men."

Boring men.

The words echoed around his head, old insecurities sitting back up as they were shaken and disturbed. He tried his hardest to push them away. Tried his hardest to hold on to the way Bex had looked at him just hours before, the way she had touched him, the way she had made him feel. But the memory was getting blurred. Her words of affection were turning into words of spite. Helen's colder tone overlaying Bex's loud one.

"Do you leave her with Amy?"

Daniel took a few seconds to respond. "She looks after Amy, yes. From time to time."

"She could be anyone!"

"She's not." The words felt foreign and weird within his mouth. "She's Bex. I knew her before we started dating. I trust her."

"Before you started dating?" Sam fixed him with a suspicious stare. "How long before? Did she cheat on Ryan?"

"You, of all people, can hardly be outraged about cheating."

"I wasn't the one who did the cheating!"

"Bex didn't cheat on Ryan." He swallowed hard. "And she hasn't cheated on me. She wouldn't do that."

Looking exasperated Sam opened his mouth to say something, but then he simply closed it and shook his head. "Fine. Just hand me more ammo then."

"Excuse me?"

"Can't you see, I'm literally listing all the things I'm going to throw at you. The long hours, the irresponsible guardians, the inability to be at home when Amy needs you, the random women you bring into your house-"

"Before Bex I hadn't dated anyone since Helen."

Sam locked eyes with him. "Seriously?"

"Seriously."

"Not even a casual thing?"

Daniel scrutinized him. "If you're asking me if I brought women back to the house I shared with my daughter for a one night stand then I can assure you, again, the answer is no."

Sam muttered something under his breath that Daniel didn't catch but he could guess from the tone it was an insult.

"Sam, you're not getting custody over my daughter. I have already spoken to lawyers about it and they have reassured me not to worry."

Sam's expression hardened. "Have you had the time to tell them everything I just told you? All the reasons you aren't a fit parent?"

The insult was simply another punch to the throat. He didn't say anything. Instead he squeezed his back molars together as hard as he could, desperately fighting back the abuse he wanted to shout at the top of his lungs at the man opposite him. Sam squared out his shoulders as if preparing for a fight. "Don't jump the gun yet then, hey? I want to be there for Amy. I am her best chance and you will see that once I gather all up all my evidence."

"Like how you don't like my girlfriend?"

Sam narrowed his gaze. "You've known her a month or so and she's cheating on you. If you allow me to use her as evidence then you deserve to lose. I was in her flat, the man literally came out of her bedroom. All scruffy haired and shirt undone. I've sent you the photos. Man to man, Daniel, I can see you're a good person. I don't want you to be taken the micky out of again. Why'd you let women do this to you?"

Daniel stared at him. He could feel heat running up and down his body and even though anger was at the forefront of his mind, he could tell other emotions were very close behind. He could practically taste them in his mouth and he knew he needed to get out of there.

"I need to go."

Sam muttered something in annoyance before adding, "Fine. Suit yourself."

"I guess I'll see you soon."

"Seems so."

Daniel let himself out, not looking back or closing the door behind him.

It had started to rain again.

He drove four streets away before pulling into a small avenue and cutting the engine. The sound of the radio died and all he could hear was the slight patter of rain as it danced on his car's windscreen. He pressed his head to the steering wheel, feeling his body tremble and welcoming the cold feeling of rubber against his forehead.

He couldn't think. He could barely breathe.

Amy. His head kept repeating her name over, and over, and over again. He felt the sting of tears in his eyes bite down hard. *My Amy.*

After five minutes he sat back in his seat, a weird, cold sense of numbness settling in his chest as he slowly pulled out his phone. He hesitated.

He shouldn't even check. He shouldn't even look.

Reluctantly, he clicked onto Sam's message.

Sam had sent him four photo attachments. They were still fuzzy, blurred out and waiting to be downloaded. His thumb hovered over the screen.

He trusted Bex.

He believed her.

He knew her.

...But did he? Maybe this time things were different. Maybe something had happened in this lifetime and not the last? Maybe he'd missed a step? Sam's words rung through his head and then so did Bex's. Her reluctance to go straight back into a relationship with him. Her insistence they took things slowly. Before he knew it, he'd clicked the screen and the photo shot open.

There was a man peering out of Bex's room, a small smile on his face. From his jawline alone anyone could tell he was muscular. He had the kind of face Daniel expected to see on aftershave adverts.

The kind of man who Bex would go for.

Even after one photo, he'd seen enough.

Daniel closed his eyes and let his phone slip from his hand into the gap between his and the passenger's seat.

The hurt was sudden. It overloaded his senses and he squeezed his eyes even tighter together, trying to ignore the rage that was stuck between his teeth.

Again.

He'd let it happen again.

He hissed as pain shot up his back, playing along his scar. His body felt as if it were on fire. His face crumpled and he felt his torso tighten sharply as if it had just been scrunched into someone's hand.

Why'd you let women do this to you?

Sam's words sounded loudly in his head.

He was risking losing Amy for her. He'd put her above the need to protect his little girl. He hadn't even thought of the risks or the consequences.

Sam was right. What was he doing letting a stranger look after her? Letting her pick her up from school? What the hell had gotten into him?

Something pulled in his chest.

He knew exactly what had gotten into him.

Bex.

The woman who had never wanted to introduce him to her family.

The woman who kept her history guarded from him even though he had told her all his secrets.

His mind ran back over the memories of their relationship last time. The way they had hidden it from everyone. How many times had he told her he loved her only for her to look the other way, or smile kindly at him? They'd been together for nearly three years and she had never uttered the 'L' word. Surely, he should have realised that was a sign sooner? Surely, he was clever enough to realise that meant something?

He'd been right on New Year's Eve. He'd been so bang on the

money and then he'd let his lust- his love for this woman get in the way of his reasoning.

Bex would never love him the way he loved her.

And he would not risk Amy for anyone.

Bex wasn't Helen, but she'd hurt him in a different way.

Maybe even more severely because she had built him up, made him believe he was actually worth something again, only to flatten him with her shoe.

When he'd arrived at her door this evening, had she really been excited to see him or had she been thinking of someone else? Someone with black hair and a stern expression.

Stop it! He told himself firmly. *Just stop it.*

But his mind had photographed the picture Sam had sent him and stuck it at the forefront of his brain.

He couldn't unsee it.

He groaned as his words played back in his head. When she had told him to *Get out* had she been secretly laughing at him? Had his version of flirting been hilarious? Helen had always said he was awful when it came to seduction. At first she'd teased him about it, saying she found his shyness endearing. When he had tried again, later on in their relationship, she had just laughed and patted him on the head. Maybe Bex had just wanted him to leave to stop embarrassing himself.

Something in his gut was screaming at him that his thoughts weren't true. Something inside of his chest was desperately trying to block every single question that ran through his head. Even a small part of his brain was trying to show evidence to the contrary, flashing him images of Bex's blackened eyes, her stuttered breathing and her flushed neck, but he pushed them aside.

He needed to be sensible.

He needed to stop being so bloody emotional.

He needed to put Amy first.

Bex had to go.

CHAPTER TWENTY

Bex folded up the letter she had been writing for the last two days and tucked it under the small pot on her kitchen table, running her fingers over the edges before standing up and feeling nerves dance up and down her body. It was nearly word for word what she had written last time.

She loved him.

She had then and she did now.

She was going to tell him what she had wanted to really say when walking back from *Alfonso's*. Before she chickened out and grouped him with all the other men she had known in her life. Before she had doubted him for a hot second.

She was going to ask him if they could go back to how they had been last time, practically living with each other. She was even going to ask if she could move in with him. After all, he had wanted her to before.

"God, I'm nervous," she said out loud, shaking her hands out in front of her like she had just washed them.

They'd barely spoken since he had last been to her house the previous night, but he had texted her and asked if he could come around in the late afternoon as Amy was at a birthday party.

She'd asked him how it had gone with Sam but he hadn't really answered, avoiding her questions easily and she thought maybe he was waiting to talk to her in person about it.

The buzzer to her front door sounded and she jumped, quickly running over to it and letting Daniel in. She opened the door to her flat, unable to simply sit still and wait for him to knock, and waited to see his head appear as he walked up the staircase. As she spotted him she felt her stomach dip and her chest tighten.

Why had she doubted him?

He was different.

With him, everything was easy.

Everything was safe.

She didn't have to be as cold with him, she didn't have to be so abrasive. She could let her walls down and be herself. He would look after her just as she wanted to look after him.

Daniel looked impeccable. As always.

Smart suit, great hair and when his eyes found hers she saw them smile. Then she saw them drop and take in her outfit. She noted the nervous dip of his Adam's apple and the fact when his eyes met hers again, they were laced with desire.

"Come in," Bex said, stepping to the side.

Without saying anything he nodded, his side brushing her front as he passed and she felt her insides clench even more. His words from the previous evening rung through her mind and she felt her skin flush.

There was something electric and heavy in the atmosphere. It was unmissable and as the door shut and Daniel turned to face Bex she saw he was using every bit of self-control he could not to reach for her. His jaw was locked, his eyebrows narrowed and his nostrils flared.

Fuck that.

She took two confident strides forwards and captured his mouth against hers, pouring everything single thing she was feeling into the way her lips moved against his, the way she ran her hands up through his hair and pulled her hips into his. Daniel groaned, the noise causing butterflies to scatter within her torso and his hands gripped her waist. He held her to him, his mouth instantly becoming demanding. He took complete control of the kiss, pushing her back until her back hit the wall as his hands flew over her body, cupping, pressing and tormenting where he could. She whimpered and Daniel's kiss intensified. It was like nothing she had felt ever before. It was strong, and powerful, and she was fully turned on by it. She tried to pull him even closer to her, hitching her leg up and wrapping it over his hip. His answering groan sent charged sparks up her spine.

Daniel had had his moments before. She had managed to install some level of confidence in him and he'd been the one, after all, to initiate the kiss in the study on the evening of Lizzie's thirtieth. But this was something else. She could taste it on his lips and slowly, she started to taste his pain.

The hurt.

"Daniel, wait," she gasped, gently placing her hands on his shoulders and pushing him away fractionally.

He was breathing hard, his mouth swollen and without looking at her he let his forehead rest against hers. She cupped his cheeks, running her thumbs across his skin. Her leg slowly dropped to the floor. "What's wrong?"

The moment the question left her lips, he pulled away, turning and striding a couple of feet away. She could see the tension rippling through his body and the absence of an answer beat down between them.

"Did something happen with Amy?" she whispered. "What did Sam say? Have you told her?"

"No," he bit out. "No, I haven't." She saw him flex his hand by his side. "This is over, Bex."

The words didn't register straight away. They bounced around the room, taking their time before they reached her. And when they finally did, even then she couldn't quite understand them.

"What's over?" she said, trying to keep her voice calm as a weird sort of desperation danced up inside of her. "The case? Has Sam dropped the case?"

His silence sunk into her skin, coating over her heightened emotions and turning them to lead. He couldn't mean-

No.

He *couldn't* mean them.

"I can't do this anymore." He cleared his throat, his shoulders rising and falling. "I can't do whatever *this* is with you anymore."

"Excuse me?"

"We're over."

Her eyes darted to the letter she'd stuffed beneath the pot in the centre of the kitchen table, icy shock filling her body at the same as hot humiliation coursed through her. Even the white edge of the paper looked as if it was mocking her. Her eyes returned to the back of Daniel's head and she felt the agony of his words rip through her all at once.

"At least turn around and face me if you're going to say that," she barked, pushing herself up away from the wall and biting back the tears threatening to spill out of her eyes.

He turned slowly and she flinched as she realised his face was completely blank. Like someone had taken a photo of him daydreaming and it had frozen. He almost didn't look real.

"Why?"

"Bex, I don't want to-"

"Tell me why." When he didn't respond, she continued, "That wasn't a question, Daniel. Tell me why."

She studied his face, silently begging for some sort of emotion to crack through the mask he was wearing, to be able to see what he was really thinking, but there was nothing.

"The truth of the matter…" He took a sharp breath. "The truth of the matter is that I've always cared about you way more than you ever cared about me and I can't do it anymore, Bex. We were in a relationship before and I was so sucked into it I failed to see the truth. I failed to see you weren't as invested in it as me as I was too blinded by how badly I loved you."

Bex's eyes once again darted to the note on the kitchen table. Her throat felt like it was closing in on itself and she felt her eyes prick painfully. A thousand splinters sunk into her skin.

When she didn't answer, Daniel continued, pinching his nose and closing his eyes.

"You couldn't say it last time. Not even after two and a half years. I should have realised - I should have…I shouldn't have accepted it. I should have stood up for myself." He looked her straight in the eyes. "Bex, let's be honest. This was never going to be a forever relationship. A forever relationship can't be lopsided. It just can't. I've done that before. I've been there." He gestured at her. "And I don't blame you, Bex. Honestly. I don't. But you deserve someone who you love entirely. Who you love to bits. And that's not me."

"Where the hell has this come from?" Bex snapped, her anger flaring up inside of her. She took a few steps towards him.

"We don't work. Last time showed that."

"Last time, I thought we were pretty happy."

"Were we?"

She flinched and for a second she saw a flash of concern behind

Daniel's eyes. He straightened up and it was gone.

"We hid everything. We didn't tell anyone we were together. We had to make Amy lie for us." He ran his hands through his hair. "I made my daughter lie for me."

"That was just because of Lizzie and Charles! You know that!"

He shook his head ever so slowly. "Do I?"

"Yes, you do! We talked about this. We talked about this before, you can't just go back and rehash the argument. That's not fair!"

"It is fair when I realise I was being blind. Everything I said on New Year's Eve still stands. Everything I said is still true. New Year's Eve...the drink got the better of me, you were there and I forgot how much this didn't work-"

"So this was all some drunken mistake?" she snarled, barely able to make him out now due to the group of tears she refused to let go off. "A six-week drunken mistake?"

"We don't make sense. I'm not your type."

"I think it's up to me to decide that."

"Bex, stop making this difficult-"

"Don't tell me to stop doing anything!" She walked up to him, anger building up inside her to such an extent she could practically taste its acid. "So what was today, Daniel? You were coming over to screw me and then break up with me?"

His face paled. "Bex, that wasn't what I was trying to do."

"Oh, did I misread that?" She jerked her hand behind her, pointing a finger at the wall. "Did I get that wrong? Was that not what that just was?"

"I...I don't know what that was."

"That was you kissing me. That was you pushing me up against a wall. That was you convincing me you were following through on what you said *yesterday*. Yesterday, when you stood in this room and I thought things were great between us. I thought things were even better than last time."

"Bex, please-" Some sort of emotion was finally breaking through his mask but it wasn't enough to balm any of the hurt he had just plunged through her bloodstream.

"You came in wanting to dump me but thought you'd just get *some* in the interim?"

"You know I don't think like that!" he snapped.

The sentence rung out between them and Bex felt a tear slip down the side of her face. She wiped it away furiously.

"Do I? Do I know that? Because five minutes ago I thought I knew the conversation we had on New Year's Eve was over. Done. Complete. I thought you wanted to be with me. I thought these last six weeks were brilliant. I thought that on Valentine's day you were taking Amy and me out to that Chinese on the water by Regent's Park. I thought I was about to have sex with someone I...I really cared about."

He struggled to keep his calm expression and she saw pain flicker behind his eyes again. "I guess I woke up, Bex."

The statement slammed into her, clamping down hard against her chest and stabbing through her heart. She felt the pain as easily as if it were real. As if someone really had slipped a knife between her ribs.

Those words. They were nearly everything she had ever feared about being vulnerable with someone.

Them deciding she wasn't enough.

Then deciding she wasn't worth it.

Them letting her down.

Them hurting her.

Daniel was hurting her.

He sighed. "We can't ignore the facts."

"What facts?"

"When we all remembered I...I didn't wake up with this feeling like you were an ex I was fond of from a few years ago. I woke up feeling the exact same I did on the morning I died. The exact same emotions. They were all suddenly there, lying in my chest. I never wanted to take this slow. I never wanted to start again. I wanted to be with you. Properly. That's how it felt to me."

"Why didn't you just bloody say that?"

"And have you run from me again? And have you do that sympathetic tilt with your head and that small, awkward smile? And have you pity me again?" He turned away from her, not giving her the chance to respond and she felt her face crumble in on itself. She pressed the back of her hand to her mouth to stop herself sobbing. She'd been on the verge of screaming at him that it had been like that for her too but his words had silenced her.

That's what he thought of her then?

That she didn't let him in because she was some cold-hearted bitch?

"If you really felt all of that when you remembered, why didn't you call me?" she hissed, managing to push back the sob in her mouth.

"It was *because* I felt all those things, Bex," he said, his voice sounded disappointed as if she should have been able to figure that out on her own.

With his back to her, her eyes were pulled to the letter again. She wanted to grab it, thrust into his face and tell him that's exactly how it had been for her. Exactly the same. That tonight she had been planning to tell him that. To literally bare her soul to him.

But his words were ringing in her head.

The fact he still believed he had loved her more than she had loved him.

The fact he didn't realise how much bigger this all was for her.

The fact he thought so little of her.

It was pulling her barriers up, forming ice around her emotions and she felt rooted to the spot, unable to voice anything.

"I know there's someone else, Bex."

For a second, his words almost made her laugh until he turned and she took in his entire expression. There was a dark hurt beneath his features.

A hurt that didn't need to bloody be there.

A cold laugh let her lips. "You really think that little of me?"

"I've seen pictures." He ran a hand along the back of his neck. "And I get it, we weren't technically in a relationship-"

"I thought we were," she said, slamming his sentence down. "I called you my boyfriend, I stayed over at your house, I looked after Amy. I'm pretty sure we were in a relationship!"

He looked away. "Bex, please-"

"What pictures?"

"I have photos of someone in your room."

"So?"

"It's recent. A man in your bedroom, Bex."

"And you believe them, do you?"

"Yes."

"Photos can be doctored. Photos can be old."

He honestly thought she would do that to him? Especially after everything he had told her about Helen?

After everything he'd confided in her?

"That's true but these weren't. Bex, it's okay."

"How can you say that?" she said, her voice catching in her throat. "How can you say it's okay? If someone showed me pictures of you, naked, entwined with another woman, I wouldn't be okay. The difference between us though is that I wouldn't believe them." Her eyes crashed into his. "I wouldn't believe them because I trust you."

"Because you know me," he said, very gently. "I would never do that to you."

Anger flared in her chest. "And I would never cheat on you! I wouldn't do that!"

"There's no point-"

"What are you trying to say? That you're more moral than me? That you have better standards? I would never cheat on you, what part of that do you not fucking understand?" She stepped forward and Daniel flinched.

It was such a small movement but it hurt far more than anything else had that evening. She stared at him in shock, tears falling from her eyes as her face slackened and she forgot all about trying to hold them back. Daniel straightened up, looking away and clearing his throat. His hands went to the collar of his shirt, flattening the sides even though they were already flat.

Silence danced around them and Bex suddenly felt very, very cold. It crept inside of her bones and made her want to shake.

"You think I'd…" She swallowed, her hand half way to her mouth. "You know what, you've just shown me just how little you think of me."

Daniel looked down at the floor. "It was just a reflex."

"Get out." She walked past him, forcing herself not to reach for him, not to hold him. She wanted to. God, everything in her soul wanted to reach forward and pull him into her arms. She'd seen the ghosts in his eyes. She'd seen the shame on his face. He hadn't been able to hide that from her. He hadn't been able to box that behind a mask. Her body ached to hold him, to tell him it was okay and that she understood, but the weight of everything he had said that evening was strapped to her back and her need to not be anywhere near him crushed her sympathy.

Her fingers reached for the letter on the table and she took it out, pushing back the sobs that raced up her throat.

She'd told him everything in that letter.

She'd given him everything.

Every single piece of her.

"What's that?"

She turned to face him, feeling more tears stream down her face but refusing to wipe them away.

"It's a letter."

"Was it for me?"

"Yes. Like last time. It was going to be yours. It was really rather important." Her voice was emotionless. "Well, I thought it was anyway. I thought it...I thought it might mean something. Unfortunately you just proved me wrong...or you proved me right. Whichever way you might choose to look at it." Her lips trembled as she said the last sentence and holding his gaze, she tore the paper down the middle, then into quarters, then into eighths, before letting the pieces flutter to the floor like ash from a fire.

Daniel swallowed, looking between her hands, and her face and then away, as if he couldn't stand the sight.

"I asked you to get out, Daniel."

He brushed his hand behind his neck and closed his eyes as if he were momentarily in pain. "I...okay."

She watched him walk towards the door, every step feeling like a blow to her chest and she kept her lips pressed together to stop herself shouting after him, to stop herself begging for him to change his mind.

She would never lower herself to that.

"Daniel," she managed to say just as his hand skirted the door handle.

"Yes?" He looked over his shoulder at her and she saw there was a slight shine to his eyes too.

"I'm not Lizzie."

He frowned. "I know you're not."

She didn't take a step forward in case her legs betrayed her, so instead she jutted out her chin, trying to hold onto a fraction of the strong Bex she knew she could be around everyone else. The one she had moved aside just for him, just so she could show him the real her. "What I mean by that is that I love my best friend, I really do, but I'm not her."

His frown deepened. "I know."

"I don't think you do." She swallowed. "I want you to know I'm not going to be sitting here, waiting around, keeping myself available for a Williams boy to decide I'm good enough for him. I'm not going to pine after you for the next thirteen years hoping you realise what a bloody mistake you've made. I won't be that girl. I'm not Lizzie."

Daniel's face paled. "That's not what this is, I never said you weren't good enough-"

"Didn't you?" she laughed cruelly. "Think back over what you said when you get home because that's exactly what you did." She nodded at the door. "Now, get out."

She wanted him to stay. She didn't care how much it went against all her values, she wanted him to refuse to leave, turn around and tell her he'd made a mistake. She wanted him to sweep her into his arms, to take back control, to kiss her hard and apologise.

God, she was weak.

He had been an absolute arsehole but all she wanted was him to say 'sorry'. She knew she would have forgiven him too.

Weak, cold-hearted bitch.

She dropped her eyes as he left, unable to look to see if his eyes had sought hers one last time. The door shut loudly in the silence.

With a crumbled sob, she covered her face and sat down heavily on the kitchen chair. Every emotion she had trapped inside poured out of her in tears and in words that made no sense. She let out a scream and buried her head into her arms.

She'd never felt pain like this. Not when she'd caught previous boyfriends cheating on her, not when she'd been knocked unconscious the first time she had skied down a black slope, and not when she had broken her arm rock climbing with Marco. It was a different kind of pain to anything she had ever experienced. It stabbed, poisoned, gutted and broke.

The only thing comparable was how she had felt when she'd had Daniel's head in her lap and seen the last smile on his lips as he bled out into the streets of London.

But even that hadn't quite been...this.

Because this pain Daniel had inflicted himself.

And that's when she came to a horrifying realisation. A realisation she hated herself for. She might have never said that she loved Daniel out loud, but it hadn't protected her. She'd always thought it would. Thought it would prevent her from getting hurt or making her vulnerable.

Just because she hadn't said it out loud didn't make her safe.

It didn't protect her at all.

She glanced at her phone next to the kitchen sink.

She couldn't ring Lizzie, which was the one person she wanted to ring more than anyone right now. She'd be with Charles and she didn't want to create an awkwardness there.

She couldn't ring Jason, because he might drop Daniel's case and despite everything...she just couldn't bring herself to do that.

She couldn't ring Kyle because he would ring Jason.

She reached across and flicked through the numbers of some of her closest friends but none of them felt right. None of them would understand anyway. Letting out a yell of frustration she shoved her phone into her jeans and marched into the bedroom.

She needed to change. She needed to let out some of the upset and hurt balling up inside of her. Grabbing some workout clothes from her drawers, she began to strip herself of the clothes she had picked out specifically for this afternoon and pulled on her navy leggings and matching sports bra.

She needed to get this fucking feeling inside of her out. She needed it gone.

Before it crippled her.

CHAPTER TWENTY-ONE

Bex walked along the streets of London, not caring that she was getting her newly washed trainers dirty or that she wasn't wearing enough layers to keep her arms warm. Her blonde hair was tied back in a high ponytail, the curls she had tonged through it around lunchtime were slightly misshapen and out of place. She'd walked to her gym and right past it. She'd seen the lights and the welcoming smile of the receptionist but she couldn't bring herself to walk in.

What if someone tried to talk to her and she opened her mouth for just sobs to come out?

Not that she thought she could cry anymore. Her face felt dry with it, her skin practically cracking anytime she moved. She tried to focus on the sound of her feet, one in front of the other melodically and mechanically propelling her forward, but her mind always drifted.

Back to him.

Before she knew where she was she was outside of Lizzie's building. The three-story house felt so much like a part of her home that she felt her chest rise ever so slightly.

But Lizzie wasn't there.

Her floor was dark, no lights shining out from the windows and for a second she considered just letting herself in anyway. Lizzie wouldn't be there, she'd be with Charles, but maybe her flat could offer some sort of comfort to-

Movement downstairs caught her attention. A figure in the window and before she knew it, she was crossing the street and letting herself in with the key Peggy had given her a long time ago.

The door to Matt's flat was black. It had the golden number nine

on the front and scuff marks along the bottom. Bex stared at it, ringing her hands together as she contemplated whether she really wanted to bother him.

He was one of her best friends but would he get this? Would he understand?

He didn't believe in love, he didn't believe in long lasting relationships.

Would he even care?

Their relationship was built up around their love of fitness and having a laugh with one another. Would he be able to cope with a crying Bex on his doorstep? Maybe part of the reason he kept his relationships short and sweet was because he didn't want to ever get to the stage where a woman would cry in front of him.

Taking a deep breath, she knocked.

"Coming!"

A couple of seconds later Matt opened the door and the moment Bex clocked him she knew she'd made the right choice. Even just seeing him felt like a relief. His face, however, dropped at the sight of her.

"Fuck, Bex, what's happened?"

His words acted like a trigger and suddenly Bex was crying again, burying her head in her hands as Matt pulled her into a hug, his whole body encompassing her easily as if she was small and dainty, rather than 5ft 11 and strong.

She was pulled inside and ushered quickly into the kitchen/living room. Bex looked up to see an alarmed looking woman staring at her from the sofa.

"Oh god, you've got a date. Of course, you've got a date. It's a Saturday. I'll go-" Bex said, her words somewhat watery from the sobs in her throat. She wiped her hands aggressively across her face and tried to turn around but Matt manhandled her into a chair, firmly placing his hands on her shoulders.

"Sit still."

He walked over into the living room. Awkward trepidation danced up Bex's back as she saw him sit down next to the woman and discuss something with her in a low voice. The woman had poker straight, black hair but the ends were dyed pink. Her skin was very pale and as Bex watched, she looked over her shoulder and threw Bex a dirty look.

Shit.

"Matt, honestly, I don't want to intrude." She began to stand but Matt stood too.

"Sit down, now." He turned to look at the woman and without lowering his voice this time said, "I'm going to look after my friend. As you can see she is clearly upset. I'm sorry, Rey, we will just have to rearrange." He spoke slowly and concisely, and then rose his eyebrows at the end as if challenging her to fight him on the subject.

Bex shrank down more in her seat, turning her face away from the pair of them.

"We will talk about this later," Rey said, her voice soft but cold. Bex heard her stand up and move towards her. She paused by the table. "I hope you feel better soon."

"Thanks," Bex said, gulping slightly and meeting Rey's cold gaze. When she had left, Bex turned towards Matt. "I'm so sorry-"

"Stop, you're starting to sound like Lizzie. Would Rey have had a problem if you're weren't attractive? No. If you were one of my male friends? Probably not. If you were my sister? No, she would have thought it was sweet. I don't need that kind of bullshit from someone I've met only three times."

Bex blinked back tears. "I think you threw a compliment in there. That was really sweet of you." She could feel more sobs clambering up her throat, making it harder and harder for her to speak.

"Oh dear God, I'm going to need some alcohol for this clearly." The side of Matt's mouth twitched upwards. "Right, come sit on the sofa and I'll get you a triple gin and tonic."

"Okay," she whispered. "Thank you."

Something was chucked at her and she grabbed it instinctively. It was a red hoody with 'Loughborough' written across the front.

"And put that on, you're shivering."

She threw him a grateful smile, pulling it over her head and welcoming the warmth she didn't know she had needed.

Maybe hoodies weren't so bad.

"Daniel broke up with me," she whispered, needing to get the words out.

Matt stopped, his arm suspended in mid-air as he reached for the gin bottle above the fridge. His eyes widened. "What did you just say?"

"Daniel broke up with me," she hiccupped.

"Okay." He breathed out slowly, placing his hands on his hips. "Quadruple gin and tonic, for the both of us."

Please open your eyes. Please, Please, Please.

Bex stared down at the man by her knees. His eyes were shut. Amy was screaming. The boy to the side of him was beginning to start CPR, slamming his hands on top of Daniel's ribcage.

He had to wake up.

He had to.

Blue flashing lights were approaching, Bex could feel the flicker of them piercing her eyes and her heart felt as if it were tearing in two. The pain was unbelievable. The smile had gone from Daniel's face.

Please, *she pleaded.* Please, wake up. I wish you'd wake up.

The blonde head of the boy opposite her snapped up as if he'd heard her thoughts. As if he had read her mind. His green eyes met hers. Those green eyes that were so familiar.

Why were they so familiar?

"Dad!" Amy shouted again and Bex looked down.

Daniel wasn't waking up. Daniel wasn't stirring.

As the boy leant over him, pinching Daniel's nose and pressing his mouth over his, he didn't flicker.

He still felt so warm.

But Daniel was dead.

"BEX!"

Bex jerked awake. Her body felt like it had fallen into the mattress and she yelled out, shoving the man on top of her away. Panic rose like bile in her throat and she screamed, punching upwards towards the man's throat.

He managed to grab her arms, yanking them back down just as her brain put together where she was and who he was.

Matt's green eyes pierced through the darkness.

"Matt! Oh my God, I'm so sorry." The moment she said his name he relaxed, letting go of her hands just in time for her to sit up and pull him into a hug. She caught the fear in his eyes seconds before she buried her head into his shoulder and burst into tears.

He held her tightly, rocking her ever so slightly until her sobs quietened.

"Bex, you were properly shouting," he said, his voice wavering.

She was still shaking, she could feel her whole body trembling and she curled her fingers into his t-shirt, burying her head further into him and welcoming his embrace. It had been so long since she'd had that dream that it had felt like she had been experiencing it for the first time. Her heart hammered in her chest painfully.

Slowly, her breathing began to return to normal. Instead of the sound of blood in her ears, she could hear rain against the window drumming through the room, and she could see light coming in from the hallway.

Matt had insisted she slept in his bed whilst he slept on the sofa. She'd tried to argue but he hadn't given her a choice.

"I...I dream of Daniel dying."

Matt didn't even stiffen. He simply ran a hand down the back of her head calmly.

"Like he did before?"

"Yeah. I dream of the car crash. It used to be every night until we...until we started dating and it went away. That was the first time I dreamt about it since New Year."

Matt's chest moved ever so slightly. "You didn't wake me up screaming on New Year's Day."

"Maybe, because it's been a while since I've dreamt it, it was more extreme." She swallowed. "I don't know." Her face was still wet and she could feel her eyes were burning. "I did have it on New Year's Eve. It was why I went downstairs that night."

"Shit," he hissed softly. "I thought you were just drunk. You should have said," Matt said, laying her back down in the bed. For a second she thought he was just going to leave, thinking a hug and a small chat was enough to calm her down. He walked out of the door only to return with a glass of water. He handed it to her before getting in the other side of the bed. "Drink some of that."

She tentatively sipped it, only realising just how thirsty she was when the first drop hit her throat. After she'd drank almost half of it she turned and put it on the bedside table as Matt shuffled down under the covers. He was wearing a black t-shirt with boxers, and with anyone else it would have probably been a weird awkward move to make, but it was Matt.

"Now come on," Matt wrapped his left arm around her shoulders and pulled her into him, letting her rest her head on his chest. It was such a nice gesture that Bex had to close her eyes to fight back even more tears. She didn't know when she'd become so emotional but right now, it seemed to be that every little thing was heightened and every little nice thing Matt did was making her want to cry.

"Matt," she whispered ever so softly.

"Yeah?"

"Why can't we fancy each other?"

Matt snorted, his body shaking with laughter and Bex felt a smile cross her face too. Their chuckles patted out into the air around them before falling away, leaving them both in a more comfortable silence.

"Do you need me to distract you? I could sing if you want?"

"Don't you dare! I've heard you at karaoke, I do not need you singing me to sleep. I'll probably have more nightmares."

"Shattering my Hollywood dreams there, Bex."

"Anytime, sugar."

She shuffled her head closer into him.

"I thought you'd be shit at this."

"At what? Cuddling?" He sounded vaguely offended.

"No, at comforting me. I worried you might not be able to handle a crying woman."

He stroked his hand over her shoulders. "I have a little sister, Bex."

"I know. But Lizzie likes to hide everything."

"She does." He sighed sadly. "But when Charles wasn't around this time, she couldn't hide how she felt about losing Leo."

Bex winced inwardly. God, she hadn't even thought about that. Of course Matt had experience with helping emotional women. She squeezed him gently.

"Do you think I'm insane?" she whispered, closing her eyes again.

"Only a little bit," he teased.

"You're lucky."

"Why'd you say that?"

"Not believing in love. Keeping yourself safe. The alternative fucking hurts." She laughed at her last sentence but he didn't respond. Instead he ran his hand over her hair twice before letting it rest between her shoulder blades. She practically felt words buzzing in his chest. "Matt?" She opened her eyes and looked up at him. He was staring at the ceiling, his jaw tight and his mouth pursed as if he were about to ask a question. Even in the darkness, she saw something move behind his green eyes.

Finally, he opened his mouth. "I...I do believe in love, Bex. And believe it or not I have been heartbroken before."

"That's not what you have ever said before," she said, not able to stop her tone from being mildly indignant.

He sighed. "I know. Just, it's easier that way. To pretend. To just switch it off. It makes everything...easier."

"Who hurt you?" She sat up now, resting her weight on her elbow so she could look at him without straining her neck. "Want me to kill them?"

He laughed, the hand that been wrapped around her coming up to push his hair out of his face.

"No. No, I'd never want that." His chest rose and fell. He didn't look at her but his next words were soft and unsteady. "If I tell you a story, you have to promise not to tell anyone."

"Scout's honour."

"I'm serious, Bex. Not even Lizzie." His eyes met hers.

Bex frowned at that but she nodded. "Okay."

He patted his stomach, indicated for her to lie down again and she obeyed. "Seems only fair when you're being so open with me." He coughed and she had a feeling he was biding his time, already regretting opening his mouth. She waited patiently. It felt like when she saw a stray cat on the side of the road and she'd crouch, patiently waiting for it to come to her for affection. She knew if she pushed Matt he'd close up, just like the cat would always run away.

"You know I drink that fancy coffee?"

Bex sighed dramatically and she felt Matt laugh. "You being open lasted long."

"It's part of the story."

"The fact you buy overpriced coffee?"

"Yes."

"Sure."

His voice lowered. "It was her favourite."

The statement felt heavy with loaded meaning and Bex tried her hardest not to tense or show her sharpened curiosity. She kept her ear pressed against Matt's chest and waited for him to continue, glad he couldn't see just how wide her eyes were.

"It was from up the road. One of those independent coffee shops and she loved getting coffees there. Whenever she came over, she'd always go via there, pick up two coffees and come and see me. She loved it. Said it was the best in the world. I can't really taste the difference between coffee- it's just coffee – but it was sweet that she would always get me one anyway. So, this girl and I...we were close. We became really good friends. She was like a constant bundle of energy in my life and I...well I don't know if I was falling for her or if I just really cared about her, but I knew I wanted something more. I knew I wanted to do something about it. But I couldn't make my move."

"Why not?"

He paused. "We...we worked together. It was awkward. But, one night, we were here and she was baking."

"She was baking inside your flat?" She lifted her head ever so slightly off him.

"Bex."

"Sorry, I'll shut up. Just seems a bit weird-"

"Bex."

"Fine, fine." She heard him grunt as she dropped her head back down.

"It wasn't that weird for her. She always did that kind of stuff. And she loved baking. She said it was stress management. It helped her think over things and she liked baking in my flat...for whatever reason. I didn't mind. I liked the fact this place smelt like a home when I would come in after she'd been making something or other." Bex frowned again. Why didn't this woman bake in her own home? "Anyway, she'd just had a really bad date. She was trying to internet date and it was making her sad. The constant weirdos, the ghosting, the users. She was feeling down about herself and I'd been to the pub with a few friends after work and I just...just told her she had nothing to worry about."

"What does that mean?"

He sucked in a breath, "I told her exactly what I thought. I was tipsy. I was feeling brave and flirtatious. Forgetting every reason why we shouldn't be together."

"What did you say?"

"I just...paid her a few compliments."

"Like?"

Matt prodded her in between the shoulder blades. "Stop being so nosey."

"I'm trying to paint a picture!"

"I...I just told the truth, basically-"

"That she was the most beautiful thing you'd ever seen?"

"Right, that's it. Story over." He shifted as it to prise her from his chest but she protested.

"No, no, sorry! Don't stop!"

"Will you be quiet?"

"Yes." She nodded to emphasise her point.

Matt sighed. "So, I said some nice things and then I kissed her. And she kissed me back. And we really couldn't stop. It was just that. Just kissing, but it was...great. I didn't even want to rush into trying to get her into bed. I wanted to take my time kissing her. Weird, I know."

Bex felt something slip in her stomach. "I don't think it's weird at all."

"Well, I didn't want to rush her. She knew of my inability to commit to anyone so now I'd finally kissed her, and we finally admitted we liked each other more than friends, I didn't want to panic her or scare her away. She stayed the night but all we did was kiss. The next morning, I woke up and she was snuggled in next to me and I genuinely had this feeling as if...as if this was it. She was it. I knew she was the perfect one for me. She woke up and we talked for a while, kissed a bit more, but I wanted to do something special for her so I ran out to get her favourite coffee and some food from the shop down the road. When I came back she was half way out the door." Even Matt couldn't hide the pain laced behind the last few words. His breath was still shallow and in her peripheral vision she could see his free hand was curled into the duvet.

"She wouldn't even look at me. Just said *God, I feel like I've just woken up. That was a huge mistake, wasn't it? What were we thinking?*" He paused and Bex squeezed him gently. "I tried to stop her but her words...the fact she was so dead set on it being a mistake. I felt stupid. I felt so embarrassed and humiliated. Felt like an idiot for not sticking with my gut about falling for people. So, I let her go. Never saw her again."

"She quit her job!" Bex said, unable to stay lying down. She sat up and stared down at Matt.

"Yeah," he said quickly.

"She didn't have to give notice or anything?"

"Bex, that really isn't what's important here."

"No...sorry." She swallowed. "What did you do?"

"Nothing. Wasn't really anything I could do. But, from then on, I bought that bloody expensive coffee stuff. It had all changed in those moments between me leaving and me returning to the flat. Fifteen minutes tops. Something changed in that fifteen minutes and if I had just had her favourite coffee in the flat already, maybe things would be different."

"You can't think like that."

"Well, I do." His lips twitched into a forced smile. "Better to think it was the coffee's fault rather than something to do with me."

Bex smiled down sadly at her friend, running her hand over his forearm affectionately. "How long ago was this?"

"About..." He blew out some air between his cheeks. "Three, maybe four years."

"Why didn't you go after her?"

He shrugged. "Pride. Humiliation. Fear. To name a few reasons."

"And you've kept buying the fancy coffee ever since?"

"Yep." His green eyes met hers. "So, yeah, I may not be the best person to help you handle these situations but I do get it. I wasn't in a relationship with her but we were really good friends. It felt like a break up when she left. And I knew I could have loved her. I know we could have been… something."

Bex lay back down, putting her arms around him and holding him tightly. She felt him laugh, the noise vibrating near her ear.

"I'm fine, Bex. It was a long time ago."

"She has no idea what's she missing."

Matt didn't answer. Bex felt tiredness beginning to creep back over her. Her head was beginning to pulse with an incoming hungover and she knew she needed to sleep to push it away. She let her eyes close.

"Thanks for the distraction, Matt."

"You're welcome." He hesitated. "Please don't tell anyone, Bex." The vulnerability in his voice woke her ever so slightly.

"Of course not. Your secret is safe with me, I promise. I won't let anyone else find out you aren't as anti-love as you make yourself out to be."

He chuckled and Bex felt a sad wave flow through her.

"Why is it always so hard?" she whispered.

He didn't reply for a very long time. Bex thought he might have gone to sleep and as her own eyes began to shut she just about heard his response.

"You only have to get it right once, Bex. Everyone can get something right once."

The next morning Bex woke to the smell of coffee and toast. She stretched out against Matt's warm bed and blinked heavily. The day before had played havoc on her face. She could feel how dry it was, like paper stretched over her skull. Crying plus alcohol plus the night time interruption also meant her head was pounding. She groaned, crossing her arms above her forehead and trying to will herself to sit up.

Finally, she swung her legs out of bed and made her way to the kitchen.

"What are you cooking?" she asked from the doorway.

He looked up at her, fresh and alert, his scruffy hair slicked back from a shower. He looked disgustingly well. "Scrambled eggs, avocado and tuna steak, want some?"

"Tuna steak? In the morning?" She pulled a face. "I thought I could smell toast."

Matt laughed and pointed in the corner. "There's also toast."

"How are you this chipper?" she said, dragging her feet over to the other side of the kitchen.

"I've been awake for a while. Needed a run."

"A run!" She shook her head. "You're worse than me."

"Far worse." He winked at her, knowing all too well it would wind her up and step on her competitive side. In any other circumstance, she would have said something witty and scathing back but right now, she just didn't have the energy.

Both of their phones started to ring. Bex's was on the table where she had left it the night before and Matt's was in his pocket.

Lizzie.

"Hey hun, what's up?" Bex said at the exact same time Matt answered his own.

"Hey mate."

Bex walked away from him, into the living room section of the room.

"Hey!" Lizzie's voice was bright and enthusiastic, and despite everything Bex couldn't help but smile.

"You okay?"

"Yeah," Lizzie stalled. "Umm…" She laughed and Bex heard Charles laugh somewhere in the background.

"You're being weird. What's up?"

"I… er I have some news."

"What news?" Bex rubbed her temples, trying to ease some of the tension pulsing inside of her head.

"I might be the teeniest tiniest bit engaged?" Lizzie phrased it as if it were a question, sounding almost nervous with disbelief as she finished the sentence.

Bex's face broke into a smile. It hurt her tear-stained skin but she didn't care. She didn't care in the slightest.

She shrieked down the phone at the exact same time she heard Matt say, "Fuck off, mate! That's amazing!"

CHAPTER TWENTY-TWO

Charles ran his hand through his hair, pulling slightly at the edges. One arm was thrown around Amy, her head resting on his chest as she slept and the other kept going back to his hair.

Daniel knew he was stressed. He could see it in the dark cloud behind his brother's eyes. And it had diminished the smile that had been ever present at the corner of Charles's mouth for the last few months. The smile that refused to go away and was purely for Lizzie. Daniel was surprised that when he'd first seen it that evening he'd felt a deep guttural stir of jealousy.

It had been nearly three weeks since Bex and him had broken up. Well.

Two weeks and five days.

It was a Friday night and he was sat in Charles's living room. The television was on but neither of them were paying any attention to it and rain was beating down against the windows.

The moment he had left Bex's flat, Daniel had felt like his entire body had been drained of energy. Like something had punctured him in the side and every ounce of his being had slowly dripped out.

He still felt shattered, his mind running back over, and over, what he had said and how he could have phrased it better. He remembered everything in so much detail. The hurt in her voice, the way her hands had trembled as she'd held that piece of paper, the horror in her eyes when he had flinched away from her.

He remembered the slight chip on the kitchen table, and the fact she'd had four coats hanging on the back of the door. He remembered the fact the entire flat smelt like fresh linen mixed with her irresistible perfume. He remembered the way she had fitted into him, like the missing part of a puzzle.

And every memory burnt. It stung like alcohol on a wound.

He'd done the right thing.

He'd had to break up with her for Amy's sake and his own.

She would find someone else.

Yes, she had been upset but it wouldn't be forever.

Not for her anyway.

He tried to tell himself this but every time he thought it, his mind went back to that letter. The one between her hands had felt heavy with significance.

"I just...I don't understand."

He'd only just told Charles about the break-up properly. He hadn't wanted to tell him after he had announced his engagement so he had waited till three days ago when Charles had agreed to look after Amy for him. Charles's face had slackened and he'd immediately told him to come around the next night that he was free. Apparently Lizzie hadn't known either.

"What part don't you understand?"

"Well, you haven't actually said why you broke up with her?"

Daniel shrugged. "We weren't right for each other."

Daniel wasn't about to share with Charles the exact reasons why he had really broken up with Bex. He wouldn't do that to her. It would just mean it was more awkward if they ever had to meet in a group setting. What had happened between Bex and him was their business.

"But you were."

"Charles, no one thought we were right for each other." Daniel's mouth quirked into a smile. "I'm the boring Williams brother, remember? And Bex is...*Bex.*" He ran a hand over the nape of his neck and looked away, unable to be the subject of his brother's stare for much longer.

"Did she used to call you that?"

"Who Bex?" His head snapped back around immediately, defensiveness stiffening his posture. "No, course not. She would never-"

"I meant Helen."

The look his brother was giving him suggested he already knew the answer. Daniel didn't respond, instead he looked down at his hands.

"You never talk about her."

"Should I have to?"

Charles pursed his lips. "Yes. When she's still in your head, feeding you rubbish. Yes."

"She's not in my head, Charles."

"Then why did you just talk about you and Bex like that?"

"Just leave it. I'm not in the mood to talk about it."

"Well, I am," Charles snapped. "You've got this part of your history completely buried away from all of us and now it's not only come to bite you in the arse in terms of Amy, but it's also making you make ridiculous decisions."

"Ridiculous decisions?!" Daniel said sharply, as they heard the front door open and voices enter the house.

For a second Daniel felt hope fill his chest and it confused the hell out of him. He shouldn't want to see Bex. He shouldn't want to see her for a very long time.

It was just a reflex, he told himself.

An out of date reflex.

His hope deflated as he overheard the voices in the hallway.

If Bex had been out there, he would have already been able to hear her. She was never one to be quiet. Right now, he could only hear Lizzie, Jenni and Kristina.

He glanced at the door into the hallway. "Does Lizzie hate me?"

Charles snorted. "A little."

The door opened and four women walked in, stopping dead when they saw who was in the living room.

Daniel swallowed, his heart thumping hard in his chest as his eyes immediately locked onto Bex. Her hard stare back was practically glacial.

He stood up and felt four sets of eyes follow him.

He'd never experienced this. He'd never been *the bad guy*. The one that women glared at or spoke about when he walked in a room.

"Hello," he said cautiously.

"Come on, Bex, let's go upstairs," Jenni said quickly, grabbing Bex by the wrist.

"I'm fine."

Charles stood up quickly, dislodging Amy but she simply slumped down into the space he had vacated, still fast asleep.

"I did text you," he said to Lizzie, before he turned his head to Bex. "I'm so sorry, I didn't want you to have to come face to face with him."

With him.

Even his own brother thought he was the bad guy.

"I didn't check my phone," Lizzie answered, her glare still fixed on Daniel.

Bex's eyes flicked briefly between the two men. She jutted her chin and drew her shoulders back and down. "You're sorry, Charles?" She moved her gaze away from him and instead pinned Daniel with a glare he could feel in his gut. "So you've gone around telling everyone just how you dumped me then? So much so that everyone is feeling *sorry* for me."

"It's not like that," Daniel said, stepping forward but Lizzie immediately sidestepped to practically block Bex from view. She was too short to block her completely though but the gesture was still there. Her fury was still spilling out of her and Daniel felt it tear at him.

Lizzie had never been angry at him.

Not once.

"He hasn't told me anything," Charles said quickly.

"So he hasn't told you that he thinks I cheated on him?"

Charles flicked Daniel a dark look. "No."

"Excuse me?" Lizzie hissed, looking back at Bex before turned back to glower at Daniel.

Daniel's eyes flicked to Bex's.

He'd expected to be dragged through the dirt. He'd expected her to confide in them already but judging by Lizzie's reaction she clearly hadn't told them much.

He inspected her eyes. All cold fury. He saw the barriers were back up, the firmness in the blues irises and the steel behind her pupils omnipresent. It made him feel hollow.

"Come on, Bex," Jenni said, her voice laced with kindness and this time Bex let her lead her from the room.

The moment she left Daniel put a hand to his forehead and he felt his shoulders slump. He felt everyone's gazes on him but he ignored them, instead trying to process the strong reaction his emotions had sparked when he had seen her. Even from that brief minute, he felt tired.

"You are the most irritating person in the world, do you know that?" Lizzie said. He looked up as she folded her arms across her chest, her eyes sparkling with frustrated tears. She walked up to him and he straightened up.

"Lizzie, I'm sorry."

She ran her dark green eyes over his face.

"I hate you but I love you all at the same time, so I'm just going to do this." She leant down, grabbed his glass of red wine off the side table and threw it in his face.

The cold alcohol hit him and he winced, feeling the drink soak into his shirt and tasting fragments of it against his lips.

"Lizzie!" Charles said, but he could hear a laugh in his brother's voice.

Kristina openly snorted.

"And then I'm going to do this," she snapped, and Daniel almost stumbled as she pulled him into a tight hug.

"You'll get red wine on yourself," he said softly but she hugged him tighter. He caught Charles's eye over Lizzie's shoulder as he returned her embrace and saw him shaking his head, amusement playing across his lips.

When Lizzie pulled away, she wiped a hand across her face in frustration, her eyes turning back into a glare.

"You look tired," she snapped, accusatively.

"I haven't been sleeping well."

"You look knackered."

"I've been stressed."

She hesitated, her lip trembling ever so slightly. "You look sad."

He took a breath, "Lizzie, I-"

"You look sad, you fucking idiot."

He smiled ever so slightly at her annoyed tone.

She ducked her head. "I'll pay for another shirt."

"It's okay." He shrugged. "I've got about five identical ones."

She sniffed as if his comment annoyed her.

"Is…" He almost swallowed his question back as Lizzie looked at him again, her eyes cold once more, but he had to know. "How is she?"

"Men," Kristina snapped angrily but he didn't look at her. He kept his eyes on Lizzie's.

He could see she was weighing up how much to tell him, how

much to reveal. "She's quiet," she said softly, sadness seeping into her features and her words had as much weight as boulder being slammed into him.

Bex was quiet.

She'll get better. She'll be fine.

He inwardly repeated the words over, and over, but he still felt a heaviness on his shoulders that wasn't there before. He looked up and met Charles's gaze. "We'll go."

Charles nodded. "Okay."

He picked Amy up in his arms, but as he turned towards the living room door Charles gripped his forearm. "You say Helen isn't in your head, Daniel, but Bex wouldn't cheat. It's not in her nature and I know you know that." Their eyes met but Daniel didn't say anything. He kept his lips locked together.

Outside, he welcomed the cold air and the way it rattled through his hair but he couldn't get rid of the lump of guilt in his chest. He couldn't stop seeing Bex's face, all cold, hard edges, and hearing Lizzie's words run through his mind.

She's quiet.

"Daniel!"

He heard Lizzie call his name just as he lowered Amy into the backseat of the car. She was running across the tarmac of the drive and she almost crashed into him when she reached him. She grabbed his forearm.

"I know you're going through something awful right now, I know the idea of losing Amy is scaring you senseless, but please don't push away everyone who loves you. That man is not going to take Amy away from you. We won't let that happen. In the mean time you can't go cutting everyone off because of it. You can't let it change you."

Daniel cleared his throat. "Lizzie, that's not-"

"Trust me." Her eyes turned pleading. "Just trust me, it makes it one hundred times worse. Let them in. Let them in even if it terrifies you." She reached up on her tiptoes and kissed him on the cheek.

She'd got it wrong.

That wasn't what he was doing.

He wasn't just pushing her away because of the court case. There were just a lot of issues it had helped shine a light on.

"Lizzie, honestly, it's not like that."

She lowered herself down onto her heels, placing a hand on

Daniel's chest over his red wine stain. "You know she'd have never cheated on you."

Daniel swallowed, keeping Lizzie's gaze but not responding.

"She's my best friend, Daniel. I know she would have never, ever, do something like that, let alone to you. I don't care what you believe. You will figure out you're wrong."

He didn't turn the radio on as he drove home. Instead he watched the branches sway in the wind and noted just how many houses were still glowing with warm evening light. He noted that the ground was wet from the earlier rain and there were far more cars on the road than he had expected. Red lines formed in front of him and he patiently waited, tapping the wheel as he tried his hardest to keep distracting himself. To think of anything else but what Lizzie had said and how Bex was doing.

"Dad?"

"Hey, sleepy head," he said, throwing Amy a look over his shoulder.

She was sat up, staring out the window, worrying at her lip. He hadn't even noticed she had woken up.

"Why does everyone think you're an idiot?"

He stilled, his hands pausing. "Amy, what have I told you about eavesdropping? I thought you were asleep."

She didn't answer, instead she simply stared out of the window.

He sighed. "They think I am an idiot because I am no longer dating Bex. You already knew that though."

She hiccupped and Daniel winced.

He knew how much Amy had come to care about Bex.

"What did she cheat on?"

Daniel's back stiffened.

No.

He wasn't going there. Not with Amy. "It was for a test we were both doing," he said quickly.

He heard her ran her hand up and down the window sill. "I miss her."

"Sweetheart, I'm sorry. It's for the best though. It means I can spend some more time with you." He turned his head very briefly to smile at her but concern grew in his gut as she saw she was screwing her face up, pressing her nose against the glass as she tried not to cry. "Amy, I'm sorry," he said earnestly.

"Why did Aunt Lizzie say you were going to lose me?" whispered Amy. She spoke so quietly that the words only just made it to him.

Daniel's gut crunched. He stared at the road ahead, willing for the last few minutes to vanish as if they had never existed.

"Amy," he felt a growl in his voice, "how many times have I told you not to eavesdrop?"

"What did she mean?!" Amy yelled.

"You shouldn't have been listening!" he shouted. The sound bounced around the car and then fell heavily. Amy began to cry and Daniel winced.

Anger, guilt and fear crawled up his chest.

"Shit," he whispered, not caring if she heard or not.

He pulled over sharply, hearing a honk from the car behind him but barely even registering it.

"I'm sorry I shouted," he said, trying to settle his breathing.

She didn't respond so he turned around in his seat to look at her. Amy had pulled her knees up to her chest and she had her eyes pressed shut, her forehead still up against the window.

"Amy?"

She still didn't respond so Daniel got out of the car, walked around to the back and got in the opposite side to her. Leaning across he carefully undid her seatbelt and pulled her into him. To his relief, she didn't resist. Instead she placed her head on his chest and her body began to shake as she cried harder.

"Amy, there is something I need to tell you, okay?"

She hiccupped. "That you're giving me up?"

"No." He almost laughed, pulling her head back so he could smooth her frizzy hair out of her face. "Never," he said more firmly when he caught her gaze. "I love you so much, sweetheart."

Her lip began to tremble. "What's going on?"

"I need to tell you something and I understand it's going to confuse you, and you'll have a lot of questions, and even as an adult I might not have the answers."

"But you know everything," she said softly.

He sighed. "Not everything." He pressed a kiss to her forehead, inhaling her cinnamon smell. "Not nearly enough, sweetheart."

PART TWO

CHAPTER TWENTY-THREE

"I heard you Helen," Daniel said, coldly. *"I literally just heard you make plans with your colleague at work."*

Helen had her arms crossed over her chest, her brown eyes glued to him as he paced back and forth across their bedroom and he could feel the resentment vibrating off her. It settled on his skin and he itched to scratch it away.

She was making him feel like she had just caught him making plans to have sex with his colleague before work.

"Why don't you ever trust me, Daniel? Why can't you trust me? This relationship is never going to work if you don't trust me!"

"Trust you?" Daniel shouted. *"Trust you! All I have done is-"*

"Stop getting worked up, you're going to wake Amy up!" She ran her hands through her brown hair. It fell in waves down to her shoulders and recently she'd had a blonde streak dyed through it on the right-hand side. *"And I can't deal with her right now with you acting like a child as well."*

"Helen," he said, trying to keep his voice as calm as he could and ignore the hurt balling up inside of his chest. *"I picked up the phone to call Mum and heard you telling Aaron that you'd see him tomorrow morning before your boss-"*

"Which I will! We work together! We are good friends. Am I not allowed to have friends anymore? Do you realise how controlling you're being Daniel? Do you realise how manipulative you are?" Her hands were shaking and she was ringing them back and forth in front of her. She reached behind her to the bedside table for her brown mug and took a swig from it.

Daniel watched the movement, trying his hardest to unpick her words from his skin, to stop them making him doubt himself.

He knew what she had said.

He knew what he had heard.

And he knew that his wife was cheating on him. Again.

Deep, deep down, in an emotional hole he didn't want to explore, he felt like part of him had always known that she was going to cheat on him again.

Still it hurt. It stung. He felt gutted. He had given up his career, he'd moved, he'd taken on the sole responsibility of Amy in order for it to be easier for Helen, and it still wasn't enough.

"*You said*, Can't wait to see you tomorrow, handsome. Bright and early, *and he said*, I will be thinking about you all night. *Helen, I know.*"

"*It's for an exam, Daniel. We are planning an exam together. He will be stressed thinking about it all night. And I'm allowed to call him handsome. I don't get upset when you call people sweetheart.*"

"I call our daughter sweetheart!" *He pinched the bridge of his nose tightly.* "What exam exactly are you planning? You work at a research facility."

"*I meant a test. Like an experiment. An experiment!*" *She hiccupped momentarily.* "*I can't believe you'd listen to my phone call, Daniel, that is a real breach of privacy. We need to talk about your paranoia. It's a real red flag.*"

He looked away, gritting his teeth together in frustration. Every lie she told. Every way she tried to get around it. He knew her tricks by now and yet it still hurt. He still looked at her and tried to see the person he'd met at university. He still tried to hold onto the idea that she would come back. That his Helen would find her way back to him.

But then she would do things like this.

And the bad times had really started to outweigh the good recently.

"Aaron was talking about sex, Helen. It was obvious."

"He wasn't."

"I was listening!"

"You're making it up. You misheard." *Helen's voice faltered ever so slightly and her eyes flicked across the room nervously.*

"I'm not."

He watched her reach for her mug again. It was trembling in her grip so much it clinked against her teeth.

"What's in the mug?"

"Tea," *she said defensively.*

He met her gaze and then looked away. They both knew it wasn't tea but that was a battle he didn't want to take on right now.

"He complimented your body."

"A man is allowed to compliment me, Daniel! Maybe we need to get you help, maybe we need to discuss this with a professional."

"He complimented your naked body. In detail. He said your heavy breathing was turning him on." *Daniel couldn't even look at her. He remembered hearing*

Aaron saying it. He'd remembered the shock vibrating through him as he heard his wife reply in agreement. Pain had kept the phone trapped to his ear, kept him listening as the two had begun to describe exactly what they were going to do to one another. Humiliation had crowded his shoulders.

"I didn't...I didn't..." Her voice dropped and her eyes began to well up. He saw her eyes flick around in confusion. "I don't remember."

"Maybe that's because you're drunk," he snapped.

"Daniel," she whispered, her defensiveness crumbling, "I'm sick. I'm sorry. I have a problem, I just-"

"Leave it, Helen," Daniel said, running his hand across the back of his neck and turning away from her, unable to look at her sorrowful expression. "I need to go to bed. I need to think."

"No, please," she said, desperately, grabbing onto his arm. "You know I am not a bad person. You know I'd never cheat on you. It was just a drunken phone call, Daniel, I promise. I will set him right in the morning, I will tell him-"

Daniel pulled his arm away from her. "I literally heard him say how much he had enjoyed sleeping with you the other night. I'm guessing that was the night you told me you were going to go see your sister?" He raised his eyebrow at her. "When I had to cancel going out for dinner for Patricia's birthday because your sister really needed your help. I'm guessing it was then."

He saw the switch in Helen's expression. Her expression went from pleading, desperate, and upset to hardened anger within a split second. He swallowed, taking a step away without making it obvious that's what he was doing. He knew that switch. He'd seen it so many times before. And it was his signal to be careful and to shut up.

"Don't talk to me like that," she snapped.

"I'm going to bed. Amy will be up at 5 and I need to get up with her."

She let out a frustrated yell from between her teeth. "You're obsessed with that bloody little girl. Obsessed! It's not normal Daniel!"

"The agreement was that you work and I look after Amy," he said, trying to keep his tone calm. "I just said I need to go to bed so I can keep my end of the agreement. Now I need to go-"

"Can't we talk about this? Like reasonable adults?"

"What is there to talk about?" Daniel shouted, his voice rising despite every alarm bell inside of him telling him to stay calm. "That you've cheated on me, again? That you're screwing someone else behind my back, again?" He stared at her, his eyes close to brimming over. He wasn't sure if his tears were out of hurt or anger. "Tell me, Helen, do I have to get tested again? Please tell me you at least wore protection with this one."

She slapped him. Hard. The sound vibrated around the room and Daniel closed his eyes briefly, feeling his brain rattle inside his skull.

"Sorry," he said bitterly, opening his eyes to look at her.

She shook her head, a few tears staining her cheeks. "Bet you'll bloody love it, being back in a hospital! Back to where you want to be really. You'll go for the test and never leave."

So, that was a yes then. He needed to send off for another bloody test.

He didn't bother to point out that he wouldn't need to go to hospital, instead he took a deep breath and tried to remind himself that this wasn't Helen. He pictured them at university together, the day they had bought ice creams and hers had spilled down her arm when they had jumped to get out of the way of a cyclist. He'd let her have his and she'd looked at him like he was her hero. He always tried to go back to that moment. To remind himself that Helen wasn't well. She had an alcohol problem and she was severely stressed. Her job put a lot of pressure on her. He needed to remember that.

"I'm going to bed before either of us say something we regret."

"See! You can't even fight for me! You can't even argue with me! Where's the passion, Daniel? Where's the anger that I slept with someone else? Why don't you care?"

"Trust me, I care!"

She shook her head at him, a sneer crossing her face. "You did this, this is your fault! I feel so stifled in this house just seeing you every night! You're always shattered, you're always dozing off! Do you know how boring that is to come home to?"

He stared at her, the dull throb in his skull too familiar to even notice. "Helen, I'm going to bed." He walked over to the chest of drawers, opening the top one and unbuttoning his shirt.

"The boring Williams brother. Always were. I don't know why I didn't see it when I first came to your house. I should have gone for Charles really." Daniel's hands curled around the drawer he'd opened, ignoring the stabs of pain she was delivering and keeping his back to her. She'd said that before. Many times. Didn't mean he'd learnt how to ignore it, however.

The baby monitor beside the bed blinked to life as a cry echoed through the room. He turned his head to look at it, the sound breaking through the strained atmosphere. The sound, to his surprise, gave him some sort of relief.

Amy.

The only thing in their relationship they'd got completely right.

"I'll go," he said, shoving his shirt in the wash bag and reaching for a soft, grey t-shirt from the open drawer.

Helen switched again. Her expression softening, her anger dispersing like it had never been there.

"Don't. Just leave her, Daniel. Just this once, leave her, stay with me." She wrapped her arms around him, pressing her head into his back. "I need you."

"No, you don't," he sighed, his voice tiresome as he moved his hands to unpick her fingers from his torso. He felt the brush of her mouth on the back of his shoulder. "I feel like we haven't been together in months. Just turn off the monitor and stay with me." Her hands were back on his torso, sliding down towards the waistband of his trousers. "Please, Daniel. I feel rotten about all of this. Make me feel better."

He pulled away from her. "Helen, I'm going to go and check on Amy."

"But what about me?"

"I'll come back afterwards," he said, coldly.

"She's just crying for attention!" she snapped, anger threading its way back into her tone.

"Yes, probably. But I want to check on her." He gripped the t-shirt in his hand. "She's our daughter. I just need to check on her." He attempted a smile. "I'll be back after, okay?"

"Don't you dare walk out of that door!" she snarled and Daniel realised he was too late. Angry Helen was back. "Don't you dare choose her above me!"

He ignored her, reaching for his phone off the side and picking up the baby monitor. The safest thing to do was not to say anything. To remain calm.

"Daniel!" Helen shouted again just as Amy's own screams increased. "Daniel! Come back here now!" Her voice had turned nearly into a screech.

His hand just touched the door handle when his knees buckled and he fell into it, head butting it hard as white pain seared down his back. Before he had time to think, he was on the floor. Within a second Helen was next to him, kneeling in front of him and cradling his head.

"I'm so sorry. I'm so sorry, Daniel. I didn't mean to, I didn't mean-"

"What did you do?" He winced, trying to turn his head but Helen's hands tightened and stopped him from moving. Stopped him from seeing.

"It was you. You got me so mad. The belt was suddenly in my hand and I wanted you to stop walking away and it just happened. I'm sorry, Daniel. I'm so sorry. It just happened."

He could feel his back was wet, he knew whatever she'd done was deep and a wave of dizziness washed over him, causing him to drop the baby monitor and lean into the door again.

"Helen, let go off me."

"I'll get help. I promise. I need it. I'll go and get therapy."

"You're already having therapy," he grunted, reaching for the baby monitor but at her silence his eyes flicked up to meet hers. Her eyes were wide and she was worrying at her bottom lip. "You are having therapy, aren't you?"

"I...I...the doctor never referred me."

"What do you mean the doctor never referred you? We're paying for it, it's a private thing. You didn't need a doctor's referral."

Helen bit down on her bottom lip. "Therapy is expensive and I just wasn't sure if I really needed it."

He stared at her. "You were the one who said you did. To help...to help with your need to always be looking for something better and feeling like your life isn't enough." Daniel pulled himself up the wall and to his feet, staring at her as more pain seared through his back. Amy was still screaming. The sound was drilling into his brain. "You've been going to therapy for two hours every Sunday for the past year..." His eyes searched her face.

"I...I'm so sorry, Daniel."

"What have you been doing?"

"Just...taking a break mostly. Just having some time to myself. I work five days a week, Daniel."

He would have given her time to herself. If she had just asked he would have given it to her but the fact she hadn't, the fact she had kept it quiet and done it repeatedly every week, whilst he'd been exhausted, taking care of Amy continually...

Anger pulsed through him. He grabbed at the door handle and Helen threw herself at him.

"No, please! Please don't go! I didn't mean to lie!" She was on her knees in front of him, her arms wrapped around his hips.

His back was beginning to throb. "I need to go to Amy!"

"You love her so much more than you ever loved me, I can't bear it!"

"You know that's not true," he said, his patience was wearing thin but he didn't want to snap at her again. Not after the pain he could feel down his back.

"Please, Daniel." Her hands moved to front of his trousers again. "I can make you feel better, I can make you forget all of this." She was too drunk to even manage the buckle on his belt. Her hands were shaking and for a second he had to fight the bullet of sympathy he felt for her run through him.

He'd loved her so much once.

He'd thought she was everything.

"Helen," he said, grit in his throat, "right now I never want you to touch me again."

She pressed her head into his stomach, her hands falling to his knees as she *sobbed. He could feel her tears on his skin and he looked upwards at the ceiling, trying his hardest not to anger her again.*

"Helen, I need to see Amy," he said, as softly as he could. "I'll be back, I promise-Fuck!"

She bit him. Hard. Her teeth sinking into the skin of his stomach and clinging on.

He pulled away from her, stumbling back against the door and bolting out of it.

She didn't scream. She didn't do anything. She simply stared at him like she was in a day dream and he caught her blank gaze as their bedroom door swing shut.

Pushing open the door to Amy's room, he slammed it behind him, taking a few steady breaths as the realisation of what had just happened hit him. He stumbled back, grabbing a chair and slotting it underneath the door handle, his breath harsh and ragged whilst his heart thumped hard.

After a couple of seconds of waiting, staring at the door handle and pleading with the universe that it wouldn't move, he straightened up, feeling his back protest. He knew it was bleeding. Quite heavily judging by the droplets on the floor. He'd dropped his t-shirt at some point so he reached for an old dressing gown he'd left in the nursery, throwing it over him so that when he picked up Amy she wouldn't feel it.

Amy.

He turned to look at her. She was standing up in her crib and definitely not screaming.

"So, you did just want attention then?" he said with a sigh.

She grinned as if understanding what he said before clapping her hands together and warbling a bunch of sounds that made no sense. She stumbled, falling back onto her bum as she let go of the side but her smile stayed on her face.

"Daddy!" she said loudly, holding up her hands to him.

Daniel walked over and picked her up, letting her wrap her little arms around his neck and he breathed in her baby smell that was still part of her even as an eighteen-month- old. It was comforting.

"I love you so much, Amy," he whispered, feeling desperation and fear beginning to build behind his eyes. He felt them prick with tears and he shut his eyes, squeezing Amy even tighter.

"Love, love," she said softly back.

This was never what he had wanted his life to be.

He had never planned for this.

But without it there would be no Amy and he wouldn't have wished her away if Helen had struck him with a hundred belts.

His wife had struck him.

The realisation hit him properly between the ribs and his body felt suddenly exhausted.

She'd been angry before. She'd broken plates and glasses before. She'd even once broken a chair.

But she had never hit him.

She'd never bitten him either.

She'd slapped him before, of course, but women did that right? That happened on television shows and in movies all the time.

But then again, he'd never seen his mum slap his dad. He'd never witnessed Patricia slap Simon.

Another wave of dizziness washed over him and he quickly walked back to the sofa, sitting down and wincing as he felt the fabric of the dressing gown press into the wound.

God, it felt deep.

He was going to have to try and sort it out himself later.

Amy had settled somewhat. Screaming seemed to have tired her out and he could feel her body relaxing against him, her little head tucking itself in as one hand went to his ear and she squeezed it gently.

"Love, love," she repeated softly.

"Love, love," Daniel said gently, stroking his hand across her fiery curls. He blinked away the memory, feeling the edges of it curl into his brain and pain surged down his scar. Now nine-year-old Amy was fast asleep in her bed. Holding her toy giraffe by its neck, her breathing soft and slow. Daniel forced himself not to cry, blinking back the sharp sting of tears.

The custody trial was next week. Over the last few months it had been revealed that Sam was Amy's biological father and Sam had immediately begun court proceedings. Stress and worry was now a constant companion of Daniel's. Her last birthday had been hard. He had tried to make it as special as possible but with the court case coming up he'd almost felt like it was the start of the end.

Please don't take her away. Please don't take her away from me.

He thought he heard a soft whistle of laughter by his ear but his head was too full to focus on it. Instead, he simply sat on the edge of his daughter's bed and made a wish.

CHAPTER TWENTY-FOUR

Bex was feeling fairly okay for someone who had been woken twice in the night from nightmares and who had been at work since 3 a.m. She had drunk about six litres of water and had done a quick Pilates workout during Jack and Jill's first and second segment on air. Now, she was sat just behind the cameras, watching her friends do what they did best. Working at Lightswitch Studios had so many perks but the early mornings coupled with interrupted sleep caused her brain to fuzz. Now, sat in the studio, the bright lights were making her eyes ache but at least they were keeping her awake.

Jack and Jill, the presenters she was tasked with looking after, were so laid back that normally Bex could get away with staying in their dressing rooms for most of their filming. She'd be radioed if there was an emergency or Jill would text her if she felt Jack had managed to rub off all his makeup within the first fifteen minutes. But today, she needed the distraction. She didn't need to be alone in a room with her own thoughts.

It was her own fault. She'd been on a date the night before, which had gone semi-okay except for the fact she hadn't realised Daniel Williams was still very much taking up space in her mind. Everything Tyler had done she had compared it to him.

Every. Single. Thing.

It had been months since she had even seen him and yet it had felt like he'd almost been on the date with her.

Tyler wasn't as tall as Daniel.

Tyler's hair wasn't as thick as Daniel's.

Tyler's eyes weren't as interesting.

Tyler didn't always listen.

Tyler drank beer in a weird way.

Literally, her brain had picked him apart, not leaving anything in its place. She found issues in nearly everything he did. Issues she would never have even thought of before.

At the end of the date he had gone to kiss her and she had let him, hoping the touch of his mouth would maybe spark some life back into her.

She had felt absolutely nothing.

Not even a stirring of excitement. Not even a slight kick in her stomach.

Nothing.

Nada.

And his mouth had felt weird, like she couldn't fit hers to it properly.

It had irritated her so much she'd kissed him back harder than she probably should have done and Tyler had taken that as an invitation to be more handsy.

Bex had put an end to it eventually. Part of her had been tempted to go home with him, just to see if sex would make the feelings go away. But the thought of it had made her chest clench. It was the first real emotion she had felt since he had pressed his lips to hers and she'd known it would have been a bad idea.

How was she still like this?

It had been months.

She had bid Tyler goodbye and walked away from a man who she had really thought she could have had fun with. He was funny, laid back and worked at the smoothie place next to her gym. For once she had broken her own rule - he was a few years younger than her. But younger meant less chance he would want something serious and she knew she didn't want anything serious.

Serious meant pain.

Serious meant hurt.

Bex had walked home, enjoying the light evening sky and the smell of bonfires in the air, and trying her hardest to wipe Daniel from her mind. Just when she had been getting somewhere, Jason had rung her to ask her once again why she had not brought Daniel to a Sunday dinner. She had smiled, and lied, and told him that he was just far too busy. Jason had sounded more put out than usual by her answer, but she insisted they were going to have a great Sunday without her bringing her boyfriend. She had even taken the Monday off for it as it had been Marco's birthday the week before and they were having a mini belated celebration. It was also the weekend of Lizzie's hen do. She would need Monday to recover from both.

She still hadn't told Jason the truth about Daniel and her.

Too afraid that it might in some way impact the case.

She didn't know how Daniel hadn't told him by now if she was honest, but maybe he was thinking the same thing?

A tap on her shoulder made her jump. She turned to see Lizzie standing behind her, her eyes bright and her lips tugged forcefully downwards as if she was trying to stop herself from speaking. She gestured behind her and Bex quickly followed her out of the studio.

"Hun, it's 7 in the morning. You realise you don't have to be in at this time, right? Is this because of Neil? Has Tyrone still not hired a bloody replacement?"

Neil's leaving had hit Lizzie squarely in the chest. Bex had seen the lights in her best friend's eyes dim ever so slightly, her shoulders slump and Bex understood why.

How could Neil value their friendship if he hadn't even bothered to tell Lizzie he was leaving? He also had then dropped the bombshell that he had a job in Australia for six months. He'd gone on and on about how excited he was to be going and said nothing about missing his life in England.

At his leaving do, Bex had had decided to drop in to have a word. She was prepared to grab him and give him an earful when she had spotted him by the bar. As usual, he was surrounded by friends. That hadn't surprised her.

No, what had surprised her was the fact she could see the sadness in Neil's eyes. A sadness he was covering with cocky smirks and gloating. He had visibly paled when she had told him Lizzie wasn't coming.

Something was going on with him but she hadn't been able to connect the dots. Nor had she really wanted to, except to try and ease the new shadow on Lizzie's shoulder or the fresh bags under her eyes. Tyrone had failed to hire someone new, instead insisting he was just waiting on the right candidate if Lizzie could just work a little longer and a little more for the time being.

"He's interviewing people today," Lizzie said, on a yawn. "Look, I really need to tell you something. It's about the news this morning."

Lizzie's expression was hard to read. Her eyes were shining and yet she was clearly trying her hardest to keep her face straight and serious. Laughter kept slipping through though. Not as a sound but in the way her eyes would crease or her lips would twitch.

Bex raised her eyebrows. "And you came in early just to tell me?"

"No-"

"Lizzie, why aren't you home with your fiancé?"

To Bex's surprise, Lizzie's face twitched again. She looked as if she had just managed to hold back a sneeze and she turned away from Bex, shielding her face before turning back.

"Look, let's go into a dressing room."

"Okay."

Bex led Lizzie into Jill's dressing room, switching on the light and admiring just how tidy Jill kept everything inside of her room. It was pristine. Even the furniture was placed around the room in tight right angles. It was why Bex often hung out in Jack's dressing room when the show was going on - she wasn't afraid to sit down in there.

"What is it?"

"The newspapers have found out that Charles is in a new relationship," Lizzie said the words so quickly they toppled out of her mouth all in one go, her hands flapping in front of her.

"Shit," Bex said, taking a steadying breath. "That's really shit. Are you okay?"

But there was something once again in Lizzie's expression that wasn't making any sense. She didn't look scared. She didn't look worried. And that was very un-Lizzie-like for this kind of scenario.

"I'm fine. I'm absolutely dandy."

"Dandy?" Bex repeated slowly, eyeing her friend up and down. "Lizzie, are you alright?"

Lizzie took her phone out of her pocket, pressing her lips firmly together and humming an answer as her face grew redder and redder.

"What's going on?" Bex asked cautiously.

"I mean, I guess it was bound to happen sooner or later, right?"

Maybe Lizzie was having a nervous breakdown. Maybe this really was too much for her to handle.

Bex's mind cast back to Charles's pained expression in the car on New Year's Eve and her heart tugged sharply in her chest.

"Lizzie-"

"They were bound to find out. Bound to try and rip the relationship apart-"

"Lizzie-"

"And I mean quite frankly, I'm appalled. I'm hurt. I'm shocked." Her tone of voice was still making no sense but worry was beginning to truly grow in Bex's chest. And it was hand in hand with frustration.

Yes, it was shit if the newspapers found out but it wasn't the end of the bloody world. It didn't change anything.

Not really.

"Lizzie, you're not planning anything right? If the truth is out, the truth is out. You're not going to do something stupid are you?"

Lizzie froze, her hand stretched out midway towards Bex as she offered her the phone.

"What do you mean by that?" Her confusing, muddled expression fell from her face and she pulled the phone back to her chest.

Annoyance flickered through Bex. "I mean, are you planning on having any adventures to Primrose Hill to try and fix this?"

"No. I would never do that!"

"Would you not?"

"No, Bex!" she snapped.

"Don't act so defensive! Why do you think Charles doesn't want the newspapers finding out about the two of you? He thinks you'll regret it. He doesn't want you exposed to any of the bad stuff that comes with his job."

"Bad stuff?" Lizzie snapped. "The bad stuff is him being away all the time, him travelling all over the world and being absolutely knackered when he comes home, him being linked with every female actress he shakes hands with. Who cares if we add our relationship in the newspapers into the mix?"

"He does!"

Lizzie's hand dropped to her side. "Charles thinks I'd want to do it again? That I'd reverse our lives?"

Bex's gaze flickered across her best friend's face and she felt a sting of regret buzz into her body.

Okay, maybe she had been a bit harsh.

"He doesn't want to lose you again. That's all it is."

"But he said this? He told you this?"

Bex swallowed. "Yes."

Lizzie's face dropped and for a few seconds she looked very, very lost. "Why didn't he say something? We are getting married in two weeks. Does he really think I'd give that up?"

Bex sighed. "You did last time."

"I don't want to lose him." Lizzie's eyes flicked to Bex. "I never want to be without him again."

There was an awkward silence between them. It lingered heavily in the tidy room, making it feel somewhat dirty and messy.

"Well, then." Bex shoved Lizzie's arm playfully. "Instead of coming into work early in the morning, why don't you spend the time in bed with him?" She winked at her. "Awake or asleep."

The responding smile along Lizzie's lips was slight but it was there. "He was working today too. He was up before me."

"Ah, so it wasn't just because you wanted to see my beautiful face over his?"

Lizzie's smile grew timidly. "I mean, that was obviously the *main* reason." She nibbled at her lip and looked away.

Bex nudged her arm again. "He did say this in December. Things could have changed since then."

"He's still so scared of the newspapers finding out about us. I always...I kind of always thought it was just a PR thing. Like he can't be seen with a nobody on his arm...OW!"

"You're not a nobody."

"Bex! Don't pinch me!" Lizzie rubbed her arm frantically. "That hurt!"

"Don't say you're a nobody then. So, hang on, the newspapers don't know about you?" Bex said, frowning. "That's not what you were going to show me?"

"Not exactly," Lizzie said, rocking back on her feet. "I mean, they do have a picture of me." Once again the weird smile was back on her face. Bex noted how at some point during the conversation Lizzie had tied her hair up without Bex even noticing.

"Go on," Bex held out her hand. "Show me what you were going to show me. Have the papps at least used a good photo? Am I in it? What does Charles think?"

"Charles thinks it's hilarious."

"Hilarious?" Bex frowned.

Lizzie's lips twitched again as she handed Bex her phone.

Bex stared at the screen in front of her. It took a few seconds for her brain to realise what she was reading and slowly, her whole mouth opened as her eyes clocked the photos. Before she knew it, she was shaking, her eyes nearly streaming with tears as she also heard Lizzie fighting back laughter too. The tension around them eased and soon Lizzie was beside her, reading the article over her shoulder as Bex tried to stop herself choking on her own laughter.

The title read, **Charles Williams Finds Love In Childhood Best Friend.**

But the best friend in question was not Lizzie.

It was Matt.

Every single photo was of Charles and Matt. Charles and Matt sneaking away after the premiere, Charles and Matt in the front of the car on New Year's Eve, Matt picking Charles up from his radio show, Charles and Matt jogging around Regent's Park together, Charles looking as if he was collapsing with laughter at something Matt had said as the latter looked on grinning and rolling his eyes, Charles and Matt standing extremely close together clearly trying to hold their conversations in whispers and finally, Charles and Matt smiling at one another as they came out of Tring train station.

"I mean," Bex said, trying to catch her breath, "I've always had my suspicions."

Both women snorted with laughter, Lizzie leaning back against the wall in order not to fall to the ground as her whole body shook with it.

"What makes it even funnier is that in some of these photos, I was there too! They've cut me out so it looks like the pair of them are alone."

"This is gold. I mean this is pure gold!" Bex said, flicking her eyes across the page. "Wait till they make the connection that he was the one who punched Charles last September."

Lizzie's eyes rounded. "I hadn't even thought of that!"

"They'll make it out to be some unrequited love or something like that. Passion overcoming Matt and he had to lash out."

"Charles rang me up in fits of laughter. He keeps sending me different screenshots of new articles."

"Patricia must be going mental."

Lizzie shook her head, smiling. "She's actually not that cross. Apparently Matt is good looking enough for this to be okay."

"Oh, well, as long as he's good looking then what's the harm? Right?"

"Stop!" Lizzie said, shaking her head and starting to laugh again. One arm was wrapped around her stomach like she was in pain. "I haven't managed to reach Matt yet. He's away in Singapore at the moment so it's right in the middle of his working day."

"I would love to be there when he finds out. I want to be literally stood by him when the first person sends him a 'I'm so happy for you' text."

Lizzie's phone buzzed in Bex's hand and a text message from Charles flashed across the top.

According to sources, I've loved him since I was six. Please forgive me Lizzie, clearly we were never meant to be if I was in love with your brother before I'd even met him. I just couldn't resist those dark green eyes Xx

It was followed by a stream of 'crying with laughter' yellow faces.

Bex shook her head. "Charles is a fully-grown adult. Tell him he needs to use less emojis when he texts." She handed the phone back to Lizzie, shaking her head as she saw the smile on Lizzie's face grow.

"Isn't it brilliant though?" Lizzie said, taking a breath and wiping a tear away from her eye.

"It's hilarious," Bex agreed. To her annoyance she felt an urge to text Daniel. To ask if he had seen. To hear his laugh down the phone. Instead her fingers danced uselessly against her thigh. She saw Lizzie texting Charles back and a roll of jealousy thundered through her like nothing she had ever felt.

She wanted to be the one texting a Williams boy.

She wanted to be the one grinning like an idiot anytime she saw a text from him.

"Bex?" Lizzie asked softly.

Bex quickly blinked, realising she'd been staring a fraction too long.

"Sorry. Zoned out. Couldn't stop thinking about those pictures."

Lizzie grinned. "Which one's your favourite? I'm going to get it framed for Matt's room."

"The laughing one. Especially as Matt always takes the piss out of Charles's laugh."

"I should have realised he was just flirting."

"Yeah, I mean, wasn't it obvious?"

They grinned, Lizzie shaking her head and wiping away the last of her tears. She shifted off the wall and placed her phone in her back pocket. "Well, I thought you'd enjoy that."

"I did. Best bit of this entire week!"

Lizzie winced. "Guessing the date didn't go well then?"

Bex shrugged. "It was okay. Nothing special. Not that you care." She raised her eyebrows at her. Recently, Lizzie had been getting more and more persistent about Bex contacting Daniel. She had kept asking her to talk to him but Bex had refused.

She wasn't about to crawl after someone who didn't want her.

"I might disapprove but doesn't mean I can't ask." Lizzie crossed her arms over her chest. "I do think Daniel and you should talk-"

Bex cut her off, "That's not going to happen, Lizzie."

"But the trial will be over soon. Then you can figure all of this stuff out!"

"It wasn't the trial that was the problem, Lizzie. He thought I cheated on him, he didn't trust me and he believed he cared more about me than the other way around." Bex had finally told Lizzie the entire story of the night Daniel had broken up with her when Neil had sent Lizzie an e-mail, *an e-mail,* saying he couldn't come to her wedding. It had been the final straw for Lizzie. She had cried, heartbroken over the fact a friendship she had truly valued had come to an end. Bex had been trying to distract her so that Lizzie wouldn't feel so upset and had blurted out what Daniel had said to her that night. Apparently, bonding over painful situations did, in fact, help.

However, it had also given Lizzie this weird sort of energy to fix Bex and Daniel's relationship.

"Yeah, but he was just being an idiot. He was just in a panic over losing Amy."

"You don't know that."

"I know Daniel. So do you."

"Exactly. And I know everything he said he genuinely believed. Anyway, I'm fine. It's in the past. I've moved on."

Lizzie scoffed.

Bex raised her eyebrows "What's that meant to mean?" Lizzie didn't say anything, she looked down at her feet and clicked her toes together. "Lizzie, I asked you a question."

"You've not been yourself since you two broke up. You're like Matt. When you're upset you work out more and I've barely been able to see you outside of work because you're always at the gym or at the box or whatever it is you call it. You've been sleeping less, you haven't gone on any dates apart from last night and you just seem...different."

"Different how?" Bex arched her eyebrow, regarding Lizzie with a cold look.

She shook her head at her. "Don't do that. Don't get defensive. I know it must *horrify* you that a man has actually affected you but you can't try and say you're over Daniel when you're clearly not."

"I am over him, it was a short lived relationship and he showed-"

"It wasn't that short lived, Bex. You dated for three years last time-"

"Two years and eight months."

Lizzie raised her eyebrows at her interruption, her mouth thinning and she pressed her lips together.

The silence between them stretched.

Lizzie turned to face her properly, leaning her shoulder against the wall. "What was it like when you remembered? Really, Bex? None of that bullshit you've been saying."

Bex studied her hands. She had painted her nails a light coral colour the week before to make her feel more summery but, she realised, she hadn't even bothered to go over them last night before the date. Something hard formed in her chest. To others that would mean nothing. It could simply be put down to forgetfulness and not being bothered about how her nails looked. But Bex was bothered. She liked putting on makeup, she liked painting her nails, she liked wearing nice clothes. The fact she hadn't cared enough about her date with Tyler to even realise some of the polish was chipped showed her that she hadn't really been giving it a chance from the start. She hadn't really cared about it.

"Bex?"

"It was like nothing had changed. It felt like the morning he died."

"Why didn't you tell him that?"

"Because it's not what men want to hear, men run away from commitment, just like your brother."

Lizzie shook her head gently. "But Daniel isn't Matt. Daniel isn't *just another guy*. He's Daniel. And he went through the exact same thing you did. He remembered too."

"And he didn't call me! He didn't even answer my call when I caved and rang him! Our first conversation was on New Year's Eve. And then, just when I decide I am going to come clean, that I am going to be vulnerable with him, he breaks up with me because apparently I never loved him as much as he loved me."

"Did you ever tell him you loved him?"

She stared ahead, running her nail along the inside of her thumb. "Not in words."

"Maybe you should tell him?"

"Tell him now? After everything he's done? I was prepared to be vulnerable with him, Lizzie, but I'm not prepared to be an idiot."

"You wouldn't be being an idiot, you'd be taking a chance."

Bex shook her head, looking away and feeling something cold and sharp harden inside her.

"He's a mess."

Bex felt her body stiffen but she tried her hardest to keep any kind of concern from entering her expression. "Is he?" She shrugged to emphasise just how *unbothered* she was about this news.

"Yes, Bex. Daniel is usually cool as a cucumber. Sharp as a whistle. Even after Helen died he didn't look as if he lost the plot once. Now, his hair's a mess, he looks tired all the time, and sometimes he isn't even clean shaven. Daniel! Not clean shaven!"

"He's just worried about the case."

"Yes, of course he is, but wouldn't it be nice if he had someone to help him with that."

"I gave him Jason for Christ's sake! What else do you want me to do?" Bex glared angrily at Lizzie, her defensiveness rising as her friend's words got to her.

"Jason?" Lizzie frowned.

"My brother?"

"What's your brother-? Oh, my, God!" Lizzie sucked in a harsh breath between her teeth. "Your brother is Daniel's lawyer!"

"Obviously!" Bex snapped.

"Obviously? Bex, I've never met your brother! How am I meant to keep up? I've spoken to him, what, twice on the phone?"

Bex shifted on the spot uncomfortably. "You see him nearly every other year."

"You flash his pixelated face at me on the phone whenever you spend Christmas with me! How the hell am I meant to put the two together? Daniel hasn't even put those two things together!"

Bex frowned. "What? Why not?"

"He thinks it's one of Charles's lawyer's lawyer friends! Even Charles thinks that! He mentioned it to his lawyer and he thinks they just got to work! No one has even questioned it! Bex, Daniel has no idea Jason is helping him because of you!"

Bex stared at Lizzie. Her eyes running over her agitated green eyes and across her frustrated expression. She could see Lizzie was grinding down on her teeth between sentences and she noticed her body was pushed forward as if she was about to run into her.

Shit.

Had no one put the two together?

Why hadn't Jason said something?

"I thought Jason would have mentioned it?"

"You can't blame this on your brother."

"I know." She clapped her hands together. "Well, it worked out for the best-"

"No, it didn't-"

"Have you heard from Neil?" Bex asked, desperate to change the subject.

Lizzie's expression dropped. "No."

"So, he's definitely still not coming to the wedding? So, I can still keep looking forward to it?"

"I guess." She shrugged. Bex winced at her downcast expression.

Gently, she tucked Lizzie under the chin. "Sorry, that was a low blow from me. I panicked. I just don't want to talk about Daniel, okay?"

Lizzie nodded. "Fine. Are you at least coming to the trial next week?"

"I'm going to try."

Lizzie eyed her suspiciously, disappointment flickering behind her eyes. "Okay. I guess that'll do. For now."

CHAPTER TWENTY-FIVE

Bex had her sunglasses pulled down over her eyes and was cradling the coffee Marco had just handed her.

"So, good night?"

"Great night, amazing night, fun night, but not so fun morning," Bex winced, pointing at her head. She felt as if there was a monkey inside it jumping up and down, and every part of her body hurt to move. "I think hangovers are worse in the summer. In the summer you feel bad about hiding under a blanket all day. It's too warm to just put on your dressing gown and slouch around the house. You feel gross about having a McDonalds. Whereas in the winter, that's all acceptable."

"I don't have a problem with any of those things at any time of the year," Kyle said, searching through his handbag in the seat beside her. He finally found what he was looking for and took out a white and blue packet of painkillers. "Take these. My friend Olivia needs them for her back and they work like a dream."

"Why do you have them then?" Marco asked, raising an eyebrow at him.

"Don't ask," Kyle said with a sweet smile. "Don't want to bother your pretty face with the sordid details of my life."

"That's never stopped you before," Marco said coldly, straightening up and turning back around to continue chopping up the vegetables.

Bex laughed at Kyle's look of mock outrage. "I am an angel." He placed a hand to his chest and Bex noticed today he was wearing golden sparkly nail varnish. His was far better than her own. They'd gotten worse over the week and she hadn't even bothered adding a fresh coat for Lizzie's hen do the previous night.

What is wrong with me?

The night had been fun. Bex had organised a ton of games that were very 'Lizzie' friendly before Lizzie's secondary school friend, Yasmin, had insisted they go out for a proper 'clubbing' experience in London. Bex hadn't minded but she knew it wasn't really Lizzie's scene. Bex, knowing clubs, picked one in Soho. It was underneath one of the West End theatres and she knew it well because Kyle had taken her there a few times before. She had told Yasmin it was the hippest place to be. However, once they got inside the club Yasmin had quickly realised she'd been lied to at the exact same time as Lizzie's face had broken out into a wide grin. The whole place was a shrine to the nineties and noughties. Busted, Spice Girls, S Club 7 and Britney Spears blasted from the speakers and soon Yasmin's pinched expression had fallen from her face. They'd all jumped around, dancing and screaming for the entire night. By the end of it Bex and Yasmin had even been holding one another up as they were both wearing extremely high heels.

Now, even with her extensive fitness regime, Bex's calves were killing her and her throat ached almost as much as her head.

She took the pills Kyle gave her and threw him a smile.

He reached over and took her sunglasses off her face just as Jason walked in, a huge grin on his face. He was wearing a black t-shirt that emphasised his physique and had leather bands over each of his wrists. Bex's eyes flicked to them, something pinching in her chest at the sight.

"You okay, Jason?" she asked, her hungover brain forcing the words out before she had time to think about whether she should ask.

Jason threw a glance over his shoulder. "Yeah, why?"

She took a sip of her coffee and narrowed her gaze at him. "You sure?"

"Yes."

She glanced between Jason and Marco's backs. "Are you two okay?"

Marco turned around, placing his hands on his hips. "I think it's a bit rich, *cara,* that you're asking us about our relationship when you won't even let us meet yours."

"You have met him!"

"At work doesn't count," Jason said. "And Marco hasn't actually met him yet. I don't usually introduce my clients to my husband on the way out of every meeting." He walked over to the side and pulled open one of the cabinets above the sink.

"How professional of you," Bex grumbled. She watched him, her eyes focusing on Jason's wrists. Why was he wearing those things? He didn't need to hide anything around them. When she looked up she realised Marco had caught her. She blinked, squinting at him in case her hungover brain was playing tricks on her.

Nope, that was definitely a smile on his mouth.

"Right, I'm getting a drink. Who else wants one?" Kyle said, jumping up.

"No," Bex said, shaking her head and gripping her mug tighter in her hand. "Not for me."

"Yes for you," Jason said. "You're going to need one."

She frowned at him. "What? Why?"

He smiled. "We kind of have guests."

That explained the bands.

Bex straightened up, even the ache in her head slipped ever so slightly. "Guests? Who?" She stared at him, her eyes trying her hardest to interpret the expression on her brother's face but her mind was too fuzzy. Kyle handed her a gin and tonic and didn't meet her gaze. Anxiety began to build in her core.

He wouldn't invite *them*.

Surely not. Not with Marco here too.

"Kyle?"

"It wasn't my idea," he said, raising his eyebrows at her and holding his hands up in surrender.

Bex's stomach dropped, her skin going cold. She slammed her mug down on the table. "Jason, please tell me you wouldn't be that stupid!"

Jason paled just before the doorbell rang. It sounded so ominous and final. Bex felt her stomach turn as if she was about to be sick. "It's Mum and Dad, isn't it?"

"I'll get it," he said, walking around the table and towards the hallway.

Bex leapt off her chair and grabbed him by the front of his t-shirt. "Don't you dare let them in. What did they say to you? What did they say to make you forgive them? What the hell were you thinking?" She knew her voice was ringing loudly but her hungover brain couldn't dial down her panic, it couldn't make her rationalise what Jason had done. How could he do this?

Her older brother was so clever in so many ways and yet so naive in others. He was easily manipulated, too gentle for his own good and cared too much about other people and what they thought of him. She'd protected him since she was seventeen. She wasn't going to let him just throw that away because their parents had sweet talked him around on the phone.

"Bex-" Marco said, walking towards them.

"I'm not letting them hurt you again, I won't have it, Jason!"

She felt Marco behind her. His hands gripped her biceps, slowly pulling her away from her brother who looked slightly shell shocked.

His eyes flicked from Bex to Marco. "You were right."

"I'm always right, Jay," Marco said, a trace of a laugh in his voice.

"What do you mean? What's going on?" Bex snapped, struggling to get out of Marco's grip but his hands tightened around her and held her back to his chest.

"I'll get the door," Jason said, staring at her with something close to sadness on his face.

"I'm coming!" Kyle said, happily.

"No!" Bex kicked out but Marco held her still and barely flinched. "Get off me, Marco! Now! Or I will throw you!"

"*Cara*," he said, lowering his mouth to her ear, "do you honestly believe I'd ever let them back into Jason's life?"

His words acted as a trigger. She sighed, her whole body relaxing enough for Marco to let her go, take her by the shoulders and turn her around to face him. When their eyes met, he raised his eyebrows. "I will never let your parents near your brother again. The wedding was their last chance." His eyes crossed her face. "It's my job to protect him now, not yours."

"I'm his sister!"

"Yes, his younger sister. And I will love you forever for everything you have done but you need to start living your life and stop trying to protect everyone around you from the outside world." His eyes searched hers. "And you have to let go of the past. You have to let go of what they did."

"I'll never forgive them."

"That is fine, but don't let it poison you either."

"What are you talking about?"

He studied her. "I told Jason as much."

"You told him what?"

"I told him that I think the reason you're not letting us meet Daniel is because he's serious. He's a real thing. And if we meet him, it just confirms that. And after what you parents did, as much as you may want it, you are terrified of letting something important in again. You're also terrified of letting anyone near your brothers in case they hurt them and turn out to be a nasty person."

She froze, staring at him. Her heart pounding in her chest. "What did Jason say?"

"He didn't believe you were still that hung up about your parents. He didn't believe it had hit you that hard. He didn't believe you were still protecting them."

"It only hit me because-"

"Because of your brothers. I know." He reached out and cupped her cheek. "But like I said, I'm Jason's protector now. Not you. And Kyle...well, Kyle is stronger than all of us I think." He pulled a face. "But don't tell him I said that. But if he ever needed it I would be there in a flash. You, my love, need to start living your own life and repairing your own heartbreak. I can take it from here."

"I'm not heartbroken," she snapped.

"Your parents let you down. Of course, you're heartbroken." He dropped his hand and let a proper smile spread across his face. "Now, try not to kill your brother too much."

"What do you mean-?"

"FUCK! NO!" came a shout from the hallway.

"Kyle! Child!" Jason's voice barked.

Kyle came flying into the kitchen. "Absolutely not. You don't both get hot men! That's not fair. That's completely not fair. One of you needs someone I can look at without drooling. Are you kidding me?" He fanned himself dramatically and then looked back down the hallway. "And with a little girl, sweet baby Jesus! You're trying to kill me. You stopped me from Googling him that time. I was not prepared for this! I will not stand for it!"

"Kyle," Marco muttered, rolling his eyes. "Stop being so dramatic." He pushed past him into the hallway and Bex followed, staring at Kyle in confusion as he glared at her.

"Bex!"

Bex's head spun so fast she felt her neck pinch sharply as she locked eyes with the small girl with red, curly hair and brown eyes who had yelled her name.

"Amy!" she said, her mood lifting and then her eyes flicked up to the man behind her. Tall, dark-haired, and looking impeccable in a dark blue shirt and trousers. His eyes were fixed on her and she watched as he took a deep breath in. "Daniel."

"Hi Bex," he said, a confused smile spreading across his mouth. The line between his eyes was back and she noticed he had a slight stubble to his jawline.

Very un-Daniel like.

She broke his gaze to duck down as Amy pelted up to her. She hugged her tightly, pulling her into her chest and only letting go once Amy did. When she looked back up, Daniel was still staring at her and she felt a sharp prickle of awareness dance across her neck.

Apparently, another cure for a hangover was seeing your ex who you were still deeply attracted to. As Bex's headache started to ease away, she was reminded of the fact she was wearing a grey hoodie and black leggings.

Very un-Bex like.

She stood up. "Sorry, Jason didn't tell me we were expecting guests otherwise I'd have changed."

"You look great," he said, without thought or hesitation and she saw him wince at his own words so slightly that no one else would have even noticed it.

"You have to say that," she replied, trying to make her voice as jovial and relaxed as possible. Confusion flickered behind his eyes and before he said anything stupid, she strode forwards and flung her arms around Daniel's neck. Leaning into his body, she pressed a kiss to his cheek. His body was tense against hers but his arms automatically came up to return the hug.

"Go with it," she hissed in his ear before pulling away and moving to the side, circling one arm around his waist and squeezing into his side. "Nice surprise, Jason."

Daniel looked at her, then he looked at Jason, and then he looked at her and his eyes widened. He held his breath for a second before turning back to look at Jason.

"You're related?"

Jason laughed. "Of course!" He frowned at Daniel. "You didn't know?"

"No," Daniel swallowed, glancing at Bex again. "I thought this was all down to Charles."

"Charles?" Jason asked.

"Well, I asked him for legal help and I just presumed he'd got you to help. When you kept mentioning *the sis* I thought you meant my older sister. I thought Patricia must be dealing with it all. That's why I looked so confused all the time when you mentioned getting together. She doesn't do Sunday lunches or family get-togethers. It's not really her thing."

"Sorry," Jason laughed. "I should have been clearer. You must have thought I was absolutely crazy."

Daniel smiled. "Well, the best people are."

"Dad gets told he's crazy a lot too," Amy said, raising her eyebrows at her dad.

"Yes thanks, Amy," he said, shaking his head slightly at her.

Amy's eyes flicked to Bex. "Stupid kind of crazy. A bit of an idiot in fact."

Bex couldn't help but smile as Daniel gave his daughter a pointed look. "Thank you," he said sternly.

"God, I love her," Kyle said, happily moving to sit beside Amy on the floor. "Can I keep her?"

There was a charged silence in the hallway. Jason opened his mouth to talk but didn't actually say anything and Marco glared at Kyle. Kyle looked none the wiser, flicking his eyes between all of them.

Daniel's laugh broke through the atmosphere. "There's actually a bit of a queue at the moment."

Bex squeezed his side and liked the small smile he threw her. "A queue you're winning, of course."

Something in his eyes softened as he looked at her.

She quickly let go of him, taking a slight step away, not enjoying the jump of nerves flooding through her body or the way her heart had just picked up speed again. When she looked up she noted Marco was watching her.

"Right, let me introduce you," she said quickly, rubbing her hands together. "The loud one sitting on the floor is my younger brother, Kyle."

Kyle waved. "I won't come and shake your hand as I'll probably never let go. You are far too beautiful to be a straight man."

"Kyle!" Jason said, shaking his head at him.

"Stop flirting with my boyfriend, little brother."

Amy laughed and Daniel's neck flushed red.

"Aww, he blushes!" Kyle said, sticking his bottom lip out in a pout.

Before Bex could apologise for her brother, Daniel spoke, "Well, it's not every day you get called beautiful," There was a slight laugh threaded through his voice. "Don't think anyone's ever called me that before."

Bex felt a slight jolt in her stomach. Had she never told him that? Well, it wasn't a traditional compliment to make to a man but she was surprised she hadn't told *him*.

"Bex, how could you not remind this man of his beauty every day?"

"Kyle, Amy is right beside you!" Jason said, sternly.

"And her beauty is of another world," Kyle said as Amy continued to giggle, her eyes slightly wary of him but her cheeks flushed with laughter.

"I'm Marco," Marco said, clearly bored of waiting for Bex to introduce him. He stepped forward and focused his gaze fully on Daniel, squaring out his chin and lowering his voice. Jason and Bex exchanged glances, Jason's eyes dancing with amusement and Bex's with annoyance.

"Hi," Daniel said, his voice uncertain. He glanced at Bex and there was something behind his expression that she couldn't read. Probably terror if he had any sense, Marco was giving off *I'm the boss of the Mafia* type vibes. "I'm Daniel."

The corner of Marco's mouth quirked up. "I know."

Daniel's gaze hardened uncharacteristically. No, that definitely wasn't fear behind his gaze. His mouth pressed together.

Woah. What the hell?

"I'm Bex's brother-in-law," Marco said, letting go off his hand. "Jason's husband."

Daniel blinked a couple of times, his expression breaking. His nostrils flared and she saw his hand flinch by his side. "Oh right. Nice to meet you."

What was going on inside his head? The emotions behind his eyes seemed to be on some sort of rollercoaster, switching back and forth and back and forth. Bex wondered if everyone else was picking up on this but no one else was looking at Daniel as intensely as she was. Something sick twisted in her gut. Surely he wasn't freaked out by her brothers' sexualities. Surely that wasn't it.

Daniel was not like that, right? He was *not* like that.

Her inner voice sounded like it was begging.

She felt someone's gaze on her though and she looked down to see Amy watching her, a small smile on her face. She seemed to turn and whisper something to the side Kyle wasn't sitting and Bex could have sworn she heard a soft laugh whistle around them.

Bloody hangover making her imagine things.

She inwardly shook her head. "And everyone, this is Daniel and Amy. Right, seeing as you tricked my boyfriend into coming today, I'm going to have a quick word with him if that's okay?"

"Fine," Jason said, smiling. He slapped Daniel on the shoulder jovially. "What can we get you to drink?"

"Whatever you're all having."

"Finally, someone who will drink strawberry daiquiris with me!" Kyle said, clapping his hands together and standing up.

"I don't think that's what he meant," Marco said dryly.

A genuine smile crossed Daniel's mouth. "I mean I wouldn't say no. It's been a while since I've had one."

Kyle grinned widely. "Coming on up! Come on Princess Merida," he held his hand out for Amy to hold, "let's go make daiquiris."

"Amy, you can stay with your dad if you want," Bex said quickly.

Amy shook her head, grinning at her. "I'm going to go make dakeys."

"Yeah Bex," Kyle said, deliberately sounding like a bad imitation of a teenager. "We're going to go make dakeys!"

"How exactly are you going to make those?" Marco called after them.

"With your blender of course."

"Do not touch my blender," Marco barked, quickly following as Kyle grabbed Amy around the waist, lifted her up, and began to run.

"We're the fun kind of chaos," Jason said, smiling between Daniel and Bex. "I promise."

"Don't worry, I will fully warn Daniel about it now he's been thrown into the lion's den." She deliberately moved her eyes to the kitchen before looking back at her brother. "Now if you could give us a minute."

Jason got the message and walked away. When his back had disappeared through the door to the kitchen, she grabbed Daniel by the hand and pulled him through the nearest door and into the toilet.

CHAPTER TWENTY-SIX

Daniel couldn't comprehend what was happening. His brain felt it had been put through Marco's blender and his insides were wound so tight that they were beginning to ache.

Jason and Bex were siblings. They were related.

Charles had never got him a lawyer.

Bex had.

And he'd stood in Bex's flat, a mere few days after talking to Jason, and told her she didn't care about him.

He could feel something dark curling in the pit of his stomach.

God, he'd gone over and over that evening ever since it had happened. In the last few months he'd been so tempted to ring Bex that he'd had to delete her number from his phone. It had happened gradually. The doubt, the small voice in his head that told him he'd made a mistake. He'd pushed it away, repeating to himself that he had done what was right, but as his nightmares had begun to get worse a small part of him believed the universe was telling him otherwise.

He'd had to ignore the fact he knew Amy was lying whenever she came home from seeing Lizzie and told him she hadn't seen Bex. He could tell when Amy had seen Bex. It was in the way she walked, in the way she smiled and usually, in the way her nails were painted or her hair was done a different way. It was also obvious by the fact his daughter felt the need to tell him *she hadn't seen* Bex. He'd never asked, she'd just add it on the end of a story, *And Bex wasn't there so don't worry.* Which meant Bex had been there. Amy was a good secret keeper but she wasn't subtle.

He'd kept reassuring himself he'd just done what was the best for the both of them but now...he glanced up. Bex had her back pressed against the toilet door, her head thrown back against it and her eyes shut. There was an awkward silence growing around them and, with it, a weird sense of frustration began to build in his chest.

Why hadn't she said anything?

Why hadn't she told him?

Before he could say anything though, her eyes snapped open.

"If you have a problem with my brothers being gay you need to spit it out now and then leave."

He stared at her, shock shooting through him like electricity. "What? Where did you get that idea?"

She slumped back against the door, not answering his question but he saw the relief in her expression. She placed a hand to her chest, kneading the heel of her palm into her sternum.

Instead of waiting another second for Bex to finish having her moment, he stepped forward into her space. Her body stiffened.

"Why didn't you tell me about Jason?"

"I thought you knew."

"How would I know?"

"Our surnames?"

"Bex, I work with a Dr Wright. Amy has a teacher who is Mrs Wright. Isn't there a famous musical actor called Harry Wright?"

"Don't mention him in front of Kyle. He loves the guy but Harry always beats him for roles."

"My point is it's not a unique surname."

Bex looked down. "I thought Jason might say."

"Why didn't *you* tell me?"

"When? After you told me I didn't care about you?" she snapped, staring him straight in the eye.

He closed his eyes briefly. "I should never have said that."

"No, you shouldn't have, but you did and here we are!"

Their eyes met angrily.

Daniel knew he had no right to be angry, he knew it was his fault but that didn't take away from the fact that angry was what he was. It was building up around every other emotion, boxing them in as if to protect them.

"If you'd have just told me!"

"Then what? Suddenly you'd realise I cared about you." She

pushed herself off the door and stabbed a finger into his chest. He barely felt it, instead he was too focused on her hard gaze. "How about all the other little things I did? Day to day things? Ordinary things? Like waiting to walk you home from the hospital, like leaving a cup of coffee by your bed when I got up for work, like picking Amy up from school, like never making a bad remark about Helen, despite the fact I've never hated someone more in my life."

"That was last time Bex."

"Last time, this time, they all blend into one. They're all the same."

Daniel stared at her, his heartbeat in his throat as his frustration grew. "That's not what you said after *Alfonso's*."

"Because I didn't know how you felt! I panicked and I pretended not to care as much as I did."

"Why?!" Daniel snapped.

Bex stilled, and Daniel heard the blender in the kitchen switch on.

"We have to be quiet," she whispered.

"Why?" Daniel said, lowering his voice and taking a step forward. She pressed her back firmly against the door.

"Because we have to pretend we are in a relationship. My brother is a professional but just in case it could impact you or Amy in any way, I haven't told them we broke up."

Daniel ran his eyes across her face. Her words felt like knifes in his gut. She'd been protecting him. This whole bloody time she had been protecting him. "I meant why didn't you tell me how you really felt?"

"You didn't tell me!"

"I was going along with what you said. I was following your lead. I wasn't prepared to make another fool out of myself by telling you my feelings first."

Silence settled between them, both of them breathing hard into it and unable to tear their eyes away from each other.

"You never made a fool out of yourself, Daniel."

"When you next tell someone you love them, and then they smile and kiss you in response, then get back to me on whether you feel like a fool or not."

Something passed behind her eyes. A shadow or an acknowledgment. He wasn't sure which and it was gone before he could focus on it properly. "It wasn't like that, I never thought of you as a fool."

"I felt like one!"

"Then why the hell did you stay with me?"

"Because I thought you were *it*." He closed his eyes to break himself out of her gaze. Embarrassment curled at the base of his spine and regret pulsed through him. Why had he just said that? He let out a long breath. "So, this whole time you felt…"

"Exactly how I did the day you died."

Unable to stop himself, he dropped his head to hers, forehead to forehead, and felt her warm skin against his. He could smell a strawberry shampoo on her hair that wasn't hers and she wasn't wearing her usual perfume. Memories flickered through his mind of when she'd used to stay at his, forgetting to bring stuff with her and having to borrow his shower gel and go without her perfume. One Christmas, he'd bought Bex her own versions to keep at his house. She'd given him the most dazzling smile, like he'd handed her a dream holiday to Barbados and not just some toiletries. He wondered who the strawberry shampoo belonged to and his jaw tightened.

No.

He wasn't going to go there.

Not when he'd just come face to face with Marco in the hallway and discovered the man Sam had caught in Bex's bedroom was not only her relation but also gay.

He'd been such an idiot.

He heard her take a shaky breath and he opened his eyes, taking in just how close they were before his gaze was slowly pulled down to her mouth.

"It didn't even feel like a memory," she said softly. "It just felt like it always had."

Pain coursed through him. That's exactly what it had been like. *Exactly.*

"Bex," he said, his voice strained. "Why didn't you tell me?" He couldn't tear his gaze away from her mouth, it was so close and the amount of emotions firing through him right now was making him want to throw caution to the wind and kiss her. Even with her brothers in a room nearby, even with his daughter making strawberry daiquiris with basically a stranger across the hall, even though he had just realised what an imbecile he had been, he wanted to take his time and kiss Bex slowly. Or hurriedly. His brain couldn't quite make up its mind.

"We better go," she whispered.

"Why didn't you tell me, Bex?"

Her eyes flicked up and he took his forehead off hers so he could look into them properly.

Something bitter formed behind her expression. "Because I was too scared that you were just like every other man and you'd hurt me." He knew what was coming next. He could tell by the way her throat dipped and she jutted her jaw upwards towards him. He didn't try and stop her, he knew he deserved to hear what she was about to say. "It's a pity you proved me right."

Okay, it could have been worse. It could have been far worse. Daniel had been surprisingly good at acting as her boyfriend. He'd slipped back into the role and been attentive but distant enough so not to be inappropriate. Her feelings were still a kaleidoscopic mess but she was keeping on top of them. Amy, on the other hand, had just been giving them odd looks all day. Odd looks coupled with a smile as if she was in on some big joke.

To Bex's surprise, she had started to enjoy the day. After the initial awkwardness, and the incident in the toilet, she found herself relaxing as she realised just how well Jason and Daniel got on. Her brother acted like himself in Daniel's company, making jokes and never hiding any of his own traits - she'd seen him do enough of that over the years. He'd often try and appear more masculine around people who made him uncomfortable, often lowering his voice or trying to talk about football or cars. With Daniel, there was none of that.

Marco was suspicious. She could tell by the way his eyes flicked between the two of them and the weird manner in which he asked Daniel questions. But then again, Marco was always cold to people he'd only just met. He came across hard and intimidating, often glaring people away before they had a chance to approach. It was why Jason and him had gotten off on such a wrong foot. However, as everyone drank more and more, Marco began to relax, visibly brightening when he said something under his breath in Italian and Daniel replied.

She hadn't known Daniel spoke Italian.

When she said this out loud he had flushed and said he was good at hearing it but not so good at speaking the language. He'd had an Italian exchange student at school and they had stayed in touch.

Kyle, meanwhile, had made it his mission to not only adopt Amy but make Daniel go as bright red as possible by paying him as many compliments as he could think of. Even Daniel's ears had begun to change colour at one stage.

Bex had laughed at his awkwardness, and when he had caught her eye she had shrugged, "Nothing I haven't told you before."

And for a second they hadn't been acting. She'd felt it in the swoop of her stomach as he'd stared at her and she'd stared back at him.

God, it had felt easy. Leaning into his side on the sofa, one of his arms casually around her shoulders.

She had looked away first, forcing herself to remember all of the things he had said in her flat and pressing her nails into the palm of her free hand - her other one was on Daniel's thigh - before being distracted by Amy asking her if she could show her a magic trick. As she let the young girl show her what she'd learned to do with a pack of cards in the last hour of Kyle's company, she felt the same swoop in her stomach again, coupled with the skin at the back of her neck goosebumping and she had a pretty good idea it was because of a particular someone looking at her.

This was dangerous.

Pretending to be together was dangerous.

"Why do you have a dance mat?" Amy asked curiously, pointing across the room at the bookshelf.

Everybody turned.

"How on earth did you spot that?" Jason said, the smile that had been present on his face all day lifting even higher.

"I'm observant," Amy said, with a modest shrug that made everybody laugh.

"You have a dance mat!" Kyle shrieked, jumping up. "And you didn't tell me?"

"And that is why we stuffed it in the bookshelf," Marco added dryly. "It was a drunken purchase and one we wish not to focus on."

Despite Marco's words, Kyle was across the room, pulling the blue folded up mat from out between two rather heavy looking books. "We are so playing."

"No."

"We are, aren't we Amy?"

Amy giggled the way she always did when Kyle talked to her. "I do love dancing."

"See Marco, she does love dancing. Are you going to deprive a little girl of her love of dancing?"

Marco gave him a long look. "Fine. But if you get carried away, it's being thrown in the bin."

Kyle set up the dance mat, plugging it into the games console neatly tucked under the television and grabbing Amy by the hand. "This is going to be so much fun."

Amy nodded her head in agreement, glancing back at Daniel to see if he was watching. Bex followed her gaze and saw a fond smile on Daniel's face. He was relaxed, not bothered in the slightest that Kyle had taken Amy under his wing or was about to start dancing with her in the middle of the living room. She let her eyes run momentarily over his face, taking in the curve of his jaw, the length of his nose and the small shadow beneath his cheekbone. There was freckle just in front of his ear and she blamed the alcohol for her sudden need to want to lick it.

It was nice pretending.

Pretending to be with him, pretending to still have him.

She knew it had torn open a scar that hadn't yet healed but part of her thought it was worth it. For this comfort.

He didn't turn his head but she saw him register her attention. His chest rose and fell with more weight to it and his eyes darted ever so slightly to the side before returning to look at Amy and Kyle. The blush along his throat gave the game away though.

But Bex didn't stop looking.

It was like she couldn't.

This man had been everything, he had been what she thought she had wanted.

Until he had hurt her more than anyone else ever had.

The last thought finally made her look away, finally made her remember that this was all fake and she tried to concentrate on what Amy and Kyle were doing instead.

Three games later and it was obvious that despite how much Kyle loved Amy, he was just as over competitive when it came to sports as Bex and Jason were. He had won all three rounds but he wasn't a bad winner. Instead he kept telling Amy how fabulous she was as they did it, his feet moving speedily across the mat as he clapped his hands enthusiastically.

At the end of the third round she dropped down to the floor, grinning her head off but out of breath.

"I can't go on," she said, slapping a hand to her head.

The room paused, staring at her until Jason began to laugh and Marco grunted in annoyance.

"Jesus, Kyle, she's spent a day in your company and look how much you're rubbing off on her."

"I love it!" Kyle said excitedly, reaching down to pick Amy up under the arms and spin her around. "I'm getting a mini me. Amy Williams, your Uncle Kyle is going to make sure he takes good care of you forever."

Something hard lodged in Bex's throat and she felt Daniel tense beside her.

This wasn't fair.

What were they doing?

This wasn't fair on Amy, this wasn't fair on Kyle.

Bex and Daniel looked at each at the same time, the same dilemma playing across their faces but then Amy was folding herself up onto Daniel's lap and the moment they had was broken.

What the hell were they going to do?

Bex felt Marco's keen eyes boring into the side of her but she chose to ignore it, scared if she looked back he would see everything written across her face.

"Right Marco, your turn."

"No."

"Yes! Your turn."

"No."

"Why not? Scared you're going to lose?"

"You're a professional dancer, of course I am going to lose."

"But you're Italian. Isn't it in your blood to be good at dancing?"

"I think that's a Spanish stereotype, actually," Jason said.

"Okay, fine, but Italians have good rhythm too. Think of Enrique Igl-"

"He's Spanish, Kyle," Marco grunted.

"Look, you have more rhythm than us mere English mortals do. And you're gay so you must know how to dance. Jason is the only exception to that rule."

"Hey!" Jason said, sitting up.

"Don't make me remind you of your first dance!" He looked at Daniel. "We have a video of that somewhere, Jason made an absolute mockery out of himself."

"Kyle," Marco said dangerously but Kyle's smile grew wider.

"Oh, I do love it when you get all grumbly and protective, Marco, I really do, but even you can't deny Jason can't dance."

"I can't," Jason added, taking a sip of whiskey. "I really am rather sh-"

"Language!" Kyle gasped, pointing at Amy.

"Rubbish, I'm rather rubbish."

Bex tried her hardest not to laugh at the thunderous expression Marco was giving Kyle and she felt Daniel's chest vibrate next to her. They shared a look.

"So, Marco? Up for the challenge."

"I am not dancing with you."

"Fine, you versus Bex. How about it?"

Marco's eyes slid towards her. "Bex, I would consider."

"Homophobe," Kyle huffed, shaking his blonde hair out behind him before putting it back into a bun.

"I think he's just a bad loser," Bex said, arching her eyebrows at him. "Just because I am not a professional dancer doesn't mean I won't beat you."

"Maybe, but as Kyle pointed out, you're just a mere English mortal too."

"Game on!" Bex stood up and Amy cheered her enthusiastically.

She stood on the mat. Marco on her left and as the game started she focused on slamming her feet down hard on the corresponding buttons. It was hard work, often because the back button didn't seem to want to play fair, but she managed to twist her body around and work it out. Jason was dying with laughter, filming them both on his phone as their angry, formidable expressions clashed with the bright, happy pop song coming from the television. Kyle was cheering them both on and she could hear Amy's continual clapping from just behind her.

Bex won by twelve points. Her triumphant smile and her subsequent jiggle on the spot made Marco's scowl darken.

"Aw, Marco, don't be a sore loser."

"Shut up. I'm going to get another drink."

"Don't want a round two?"

"No," he snapped. He walked past her towards the kitchen.

"Jason, maybe you need to go kiss him better."

"Rebecca," Marco growled over his shoulder as Jason caught Bex's eye and tried not to laugh out loud. "I'm warning you."

"Dad should have a go."

Everyone turned to see Amy sitting beside Daniel, a big grin on her face as Daniel turned his head and gave her a hard look.

"No, Amy," he said quickly.

"You should!" she insisted.

"Yes, please do!" Kyle joined in enthusiastically. "I bet you'd be marvellous."

"I highly doubt that."

"What's the harm?" Bex said, unable to stop herself. His eyes met hers and she saw something behind them click into place as his gaze pinned her to the spot.

"Fine."

"Wahoo!" Kyle cheered, reaching across the back of the sofa to high-five Amy before running around to help pick a song for Daniel and Bex to dance to.

"You're going down, Dr Williams."

He chuckled, rolling up his sleeves as he came to stand next to her. She tried to forget the things that very movement did to her but her eyes followed his fingers as he tucked in the navy material by his elbows. "You're forgetting one thing, Miss Wright."

"What's that?"

He looked up with a smile. "I have a nine-year-old daughter."

And then the music started.

Bex had never expected Daniel to be good. She had never expected him to actually know what he was doing. His feet moved fast, his body had rhythm and he smiled throughout, adding an extra hip swing here or there just for the fun of it and to Kyle's great delight.

It was toe-curling attractive.

She'd never needed Daniel to want to work out like she did. She had never needed him to like exercise. But she hadn't realised quite how much she had needed to see him do it. His skin flushed pink, his eyes were bright, and the slight cocky tilt to his mouth was damn distracting.

Too distracting.

"Bex! You lost by nearly half!" Kyle said, pointing accusatively at the screen.

"I think she was too busy staring at Daniel," laughed Jason.

"No, I wasn't. Beginners luck," she snapped, glancing at Daniel. He was grinning at her, his hands on his hips and he looked relaxed. She liked that look.

"Don't be a poor loser, Bex," Marco added, now seated back in his armchair with another drink in his hand.

She would have flipped a finger at him if Amy hadn't been in the room.

"Round two?" she said, looking at Daniel.

"Best of three?"

"Fine."

"Is *this* the part where you take me down then?" He raised his eyebrow. "Because it didn't feel like much of a challenge last time."

Bex glared at him, trying her hardest to resist the smile at the back of her mouth that wanted to burst forward. She heard Kyle wolf whistle and even Marco's deep laughter travelled across the room.

"You're going to regret that."

"Looking forward to it."

The game started up again, and Bex didn't let her eyes stray from the screen this time. Kyle had made it a level more difficult and Bex felt her heart rate start to pick up as her feet flew across the ground. She was aware of Daniel's presence next to her but she didn't let it get in her head. She refused to.

She won.

"See?"

"Well played," he admitted. "Well played."

"Round three for the win."

They both grinned at the exact same time and Bex felt her stomach dip ever so slightly before she slammed it away and turned back towards the television.

Right.

She needed to win this. She could not let Daniel beat her.

She wouldn't let anyone beat her but especially not Daniel.

He didn't even do sports.

Kyle was messing about with the controls, putting the game up to the maximum difficulty and choosing a song he liked enough to go with it. Daniel leaned over and his fingers gently brushed the inside of Bex's wrist. She tensed as the action sent electric spirals skating over her skin.

"If I win I can take you out to dinner," he whispered low in her ear but as her eyebrows skyrocketed, he quickly added, "to apologise."

Just to apologise?

That is what she wanted to say, that is what she wanted to flirt suggestively back, but she forced the words away, biting them back as if they had never been there.

Kyle's gin and tonics were clearly messing with her.

"And if I win?"

Daniel smiled but said nothing, stepping away as Kyle picked a song.

"I don't plan on letting you win," he said, appearing to talk to no-one but his voice was quiet enough that she could hear him.

Her chest tightened and she felt a flush begin to crawl up her skin. His eyes were still fixed forwards, staring at the television, but she saw the determined slant to his mouth.

"And go!" Kyle screamed.

Bex's feet flew across the floor.

She hadn't agreed to it.

She hadn't actually said anything.

Yet, alongside her usual competitiveness was a sudden flare of angry determination.

She was going to win.

She wasn't going to let him take her out to dinner to apologise.

He didn't get to get out of what he had done that easily.

She slammed her feet down, pounding the floor to the beat with as much strength as she could muster. She glanced to her left and to her horror, Daniel's points were ahead of hers. Whereas she had cardiovascular fitness on her side, his coordination and timing were on point.

She heard Jason whoop loudly in the background and a familiar competitive heat trickled up the back of her neck which had nothing to do with his proposal. It had everything to do with the fact that Bex Wright didn't lose.

An idea sparked in her mind. Flicking her hair over one shoulder as she danced her feet across the floor, she allowed herself to take two seconds to glance at him.

"You're so ridiculously attractive right now," she said, not bothering to lower her voice.

Daniel slipped, his foot brushing past the left pad and cutting his rhythm like sharpened scissors. He had just enough time to throw her a look of outrage before he quickly began to tap again.

"Low blow."

"Just saying how I'm feeling."

"Sure."

"What? Your competitiveness is actually a huge turn on."

He slipped again, stumbling slightly and Bex heard Marco chuckle behind her. "Not fair, *cara.*"

"I'm just telling the truth. I mean, the man's showing me just how well he can dance. What girl could resist. Those hip movements keep reminding me of-" Her speech broke off as Daniel shoved her and she stumbled to the right. "You bastard!" she snapped.

Daniel threw a smirk at her as he continued to dance.

"Amy's behind you!" Kyle shouted loudly. "My darling girl can't hear such petty language."

Bex jumped back on the mat as quickly as she could, keeping her arm up, ready to shove him if he came near her again. He did the same and soon their forearms were locked against each other, each trying to shove the other whilst keeping their place. The moves got faster and faster. The arrows pointing in all different directions as the climax of the song approached and both of them were now missing nearly every point as the other tried to jog them.

"You're ruining my high score," Daniel grunted.

"You're ruining my winning streak!"

The song came to a finish and they both had to slam their left and right foot down at the same time on the final beat. With their arms locked in a battle between them, leaning their weight against each other, Bex slammed her feet down slightly too passionately and in a second, her feet were gone from beneath her. Falling to the floor her left leg swiped underneath Daniel's and he fell too, hitting the floor with an 'oomph.'

It felt like the whole room held its breath as they both groaned, their bodies a jumble of body parts linked together.

A jokey American voice sang out across the room, declaring that player 1 was the winner whilst playful music tinkled in the background.

"Player 1, hey?" Daniel said from the ground. His voice broke the shocked atmosphere. Jason spluttered with laughter, trying his hardest not to spit his drink up everywhere, whilst Amy burst out laughing and Kyle cheered, drumming his hands on his knees. Even Marco was chuckling under his breath.

Bex sat up, trying to detangle her legs from him. "You totally cheated."

"Only because you cheated first," Daniel said, sitting up too.

He had a large grin across his face and his eyes were shining with amusement but that's not what grabbed Bex's attention. It was the line of red just above his eyebrow.

Her skin went cold and Daniel's cheerful expression dropped as he saw hers.

"Bex's, what's wrong?"

"You're hurt." She pointed at his head. "You're hurt, oh, my God." She pulled herself forward, nearly falling over her knees in order to get to him.

"Bex, I'm fine." He reached up and wiped the back of his hand across his eyebrow. "I must have just hit it on the table when I fell."

His words did nothing to calm her. She had done that. She had hurt him. The tips of her fingers were tingling and her chest was so tight it hurt to breathe.

"I hurt you," she whispered, her eyes flashing across his face as she reached forward, wanting to cup his face, wanting to look at what she had done but at the same time her hand hesitated.

What if he didn't want her to touch him?

What if he didn't want her near him?

Overwhelming panic was beginning to fill in her chest and she saw Daniel's eyes clock it.

"Bex," he said softly, leaning forward and taking her outstretched hand, pressing her palm gently to his cheek. "I'm fine. It was an accident."

"I promise, I would never-"

"I know," he said, seriously. "Trust me, I know. It's just a scratch."

Everyone was watching them. Bex could feel all their sharp eyes running over them, analysing them, trying to put the pieces together.

It came as a shock but she realised she didn't care.

She didn't care that they were all watching.

She didn't care that they didn't understand.

All she cared about was Daniel and the fact *he had* to know she would never, ever hurt him. She sat up higher on her knees, leant forward and pressed a long kiss to his forehead before dropping her mouth to his eyebrow. She kissed it gently.

"Sorry."

She moved to sit back down again, but before she could move her hand from his cheek, he took it in his own, turned his head and pressed a kiss to her palm.

His eyes never left hers.

The jolt that ran through her caused her stomach to flip.

She sat back, her skin still tingling where his lips had touched it and her eyes never leaving his.

"Well done," she said, shakily. "Good game."

His mouth pulled into a smile. "Thanks."

They continued to stare at each other, Bex feeling heat rising higher and higher in her cheeks but she refused to look away. She could feel the tension beating down on them and she didn't know where it had come from or why it had appeared but she knew it was messing with her plans and her emotions. She knew it was causing havoc inside her brain, havoc that she would have to address later but not now.

"It's getting hot in here, so take off all your clothes-"

"Kyle!" Marco snapped. "Is this really the time?"

Kyle ignored him and carried on singing. "I am getting so hot, I'm going to take my clothes off! Amy, sing with me!"

Daniel burst out laughing and Bex followed suit.

CHAPTER TWENTY-SEVEN

One bed.

Shit.

Jason had insisted Daniel stayed. It had gotten so late that he didn't want Daniel and Amy getting a taxi across London and, as Jason had said, they had the room to spare anyway. Kyle was in the spare room, Amy was on the sofa bed in the study and now Bex was stood in the room she'd adopted as her own when she stayed at her brother's house.

Except now, Daniel was meant to be sleeping in there with her. When she had walked into the room and seen the clothes Jason had laid out on the duvet for Daniel the reality of the situation hit her. The smile that had been on her face since she had watched Daniel pick Amy up from the sofa to put her to bed slipped.

Shit.

Shit. Shit. Shit.

What was she going to do?

He was still in the study, helping Amy get sorted for bed, so it meant she had minutes before he came in.

She could pretend to be asleep. She could jump into bed right now and just shut her eyes. She glanced at the bag she had brought and winced. It was July, and 'her' room in Jason and Marco's house had one tiny window above the wardrobe. She'd packed the lightest pyjamas she could which also happened to be the exact same pyjamas she'd been wearing the night of the New Year's Eve party.

She *could not* wear that.

She sat down heavily on the bed.

Or could she? She could wear that and literally put a barrier of pillows in the middle of the bed. Or she could run and ask Jason for another top of his and some jogging bottoms. She could wear her hoodie to bed? Or keep her leggings on and wear a t-shirt?

Her palms felt sweaty.

Tonight had been too close to being real. The looks they had shared, the moments they'd had. It had minimised the last few months, erasing them as if they hadn't happened and she was back again in February.

Like Daniel hadn't broken her heart.

Like he hadn't shown her his true colours.

Shit.

What the hell was she going-?

There was a tentative knock on the door.

"Come in," she whispered.

Daniel pushed the door open slowly, slipping into the room and then looking around in confusion. "Want me to turn on the light?"

"Oh, shit, yeah, good idea. I'll do it." She reached for the lamp on the bedside table closest to her and winced as a soft warm glow filled the room. The orange light spread its hands up the wall and filled the room in a gentle hue but it did nothing to calm her nerves.

She heard Daniel's footsteps and felt the soft dip of the mattress as he sat down next to her. His cologne smelled great and the soft brush of his side against hers caused the emotions she was trying her best to bury to start flapping hard in her stomach again.

"Before you say anything, I just want to say thank you," he said, firmly, not even bothering to lower his voice into a whisper. "Thank you for absolutely everything you've done."

"You really don't have to thank me."

"No, I do. This whole time you've put me first and I really didn't deserve that."

"Well," she said, sniffing sharply. "You were a bit of a bastard."

They shared a short laugh, glancing at one another. "I can't disagree." He leant across and squeezed her hand gently. "I'm going to go sleep downstairs. I won't take up any more of your evening but thank you for pretending, for going along with this. I understand it must have been hard."

It really hadn't been.

Pretending to be with him again had been surprisingly easy. It was the dealing with the wallop of emotion that came with that pretence that was hard.

"No," she said quickly, finally turning her head to look at him properly. "No, don't. My brothers will catch you and I don't want them to think anything weird is going on."

Daniel frowned. "Bex, I'd offer to sleep with Amy but I can't. I...um," he ran a hand over the back of his neck.

"You're still having the nightmares."

His grey eyes met hers. "Yes."

The unspoken question and answer hung in the air and for a second, Bex considered ignoring it. She didn't. "Same."

The word lingered between them.

She sighed. "Come on, let's get ready for bed." She gestured through to a door to the right. "There's a toilet through there. Extractor fan makes a racket so don't jump when you turn the light on."

He insisted she go first and Bex was relieved he had his back to her when she came out, letting her sneak to the bed in just her chemise without any further embarrassment. She took advantage and dove under the covers, watching him as he walked into the toilet before staring up at the bedroom ceiling.

Who the hell was Daniel Williams turning her into?

Since when did she dive under covers so men didn't have to see how little she was wearing? Since when did she feel awkward asking a man to spend the night with her? Since when did she want to help her ex this much?

She shifted uncomfortably, hoping the movement would shake her head a little bit at least. Instead, it made the most prominent question rear up.

What am I doing?

She heard the door to the toilet open and Daniel walked into the bedroom wearing a grey t-shirt and shorts that were far too big for him. As he slowly moved to the other side of the bed and got in, Bex leant away and turned off the light. The darkness sunk into their surroundings and silence filled the air as they both stared at the ceiling.

The bed was just wide enough that they didn't have to be constantly touching but Bex felt like she was stood next to a static wall. Every nerve ending on her side nearest him was standing on end and she felt a low dip in her stomach as he let out a long breath.

He could feel it too.

She knew he could.

There was no way she could be feeling this much between them on her own.

Unsaid words passed before her eyes and she forced herself to close them, telling herself to go sleep.

The memory of his cut eyebrow came to the forefront of her mind and she inhaled sharply. It had been nothing. A scratch that had just looked worse than it was but the sight of it had filled her with fear. And at the same time, with a stab of shame.

"I…" Her voice sounded croaky, as if she hadn't used it for weeks not minutes. "I'm sorry about the night in my flat. When you flinched I shouldn't have got angry with you. That was bad of me."

She heard Daniel swear under his breath and he turned on his side to look at her. "Really? After everything I said to you that night, *you* want to apologise?"

"It's played on my mind quite a bit." She stared up at the ceiling, focusing on the little white lines she could make out in the darkness.

"Consider it forgotten. Completely and utterly."

For some reason his words didn't soothe her guilt. "It was awful of me to react that way."

"It was my fault, I'd made you feel-"

"No." She finally looked at him. "That was on me. I take full responsibility for that. No matter what, I shouldn't have reacted like that. Your reaction *was not* your fault. Never think that."

He stared at her, his brow dipping as if in bewilderment before he looked away. "It's completely forgotten."

"Okay," she said, swallowing to try and push the lump in her throat away. It remained where it was, guilt still coating her insides as she remembered the way she had reacted. "I wanted to hold you. I wanted to hug you."

"Bex." She felt him reach down and hold her hand, bringing it up to kiss her knuckles. "It's forgotten."

His touch was like medicine. Her insides relaxed and she felt a swoop of relief rush over her. She turned her head to look at him and his words from New Year's Eve echoed in her head. She had always needed his touch to reassure her and he had always needed her words… yet she had never given them to him.

Had she really been that selfish?

"Two seconds," Daniel said, dropping her hand and moving to get out of bed. He walked over to his trousers and reached into the pocket before coming back.

Lying back in bed, Bex could see he had his mobile in his hand. He clicked the screen for a couple of beats, the white light illuminating his face in the darkness, before handing it to her.

Bex's eyes widened.

No man had ever simply handed her his phone before. If any of her ex-boyfriends had it was under strict instructions not to press anything else or go through their messages.

That probably said something about her poor choices in men. "What is it?"

"You'll see," he said. He lay back on the bed, placed his hands behind his head and stared up at the ceiling. His eyes looked heavy but his jaw was set with purpose. She waited a second before looking down at the phone in her hands.

Her eyes widened and she sat up, pulling the phone closer to her. It was a photo.

A photo of Marco sticking his head out of her bedroom and Bex speaking to him, a small smile on her face. Marco's hair was ruffled and by the way he was positioned it wasn't obvious if he was wearing a shirt or not. All the camera could see was his neck.

Pieces of a jigsaw she hadn't been trying to put together clicked sharply.

"That fucker," she hissed.

"Not quite the reaction I was expecting," Daniel said, but there was no laughter behind his words.

"Sam. Your Sam. The Sam trying to take Amy is also the Sam who is Ryan's friend. He came to pick up his stuff. He seemed nice…" She trailed off, remembering the way he'd flirted with her, stared at her, tried to charm her. He'd known who she was. He had been testing her. "That bastard."

This time Daniel did laugh.

"No, I'm being serious. He tried to ask me out." She turned to look down at Daniel and saw his lips thin. "He tried to ask me on a date yet he clearly knew who I was."

Daniel's eyes flicked to hers. "The night I went to see him, the day before we broke up, he showed me that photo and told me he would tell the courts I allowed Amy to be looked after by someone I'd just met. Someone who was sleeping around behind my back. Everything he kept saying made me feel so incredibly stupid. He told me I was a fool for going out with someone who was evidently cheating on me. Especially after Helen. He kept saying he would use it against me. It's not an excuse but it's...it's an explanation."

Bex stared at him, her heart softening in the darkness and a sense of understanding settling inside her chest.

"Daniel," she whispered softly. "You absolute idiot."

"It's fine. Honestly...well, no, it's not fine. But it's my fault. Don't feel sorry for me, I was stupid and overreacted. I was really, really stupid and *I* take full responsibility for that." He swallowed. "Nearly had a heart attack when I saw Marco today."

Bex laughed, handing him back his phone and he turned to put it on the bedside table next to him. "I did wonder what was going on inside your head." She shuffled down and lay on her side, propping her head up with her hand. Daniel mirrored her. "You looked pained."

Understanding settled in his expression. "That's why you thought I had an issue with them being gay."

Bex winced. "Yeah, I read that wrong."

"I mean, you didn't know I'd seen that photo so I don't blame you." His eyes tracked across her face. "You've got a nice family, Bex."

She grinned. "I know. Even if Kyle is a bit much."

"Hey, if I'm ever in a bad mood I know where to go. The guy could probably make Eeyore feel good about himself."

"Eeyore? Really? That was the first example you could come up with?"

"I have Amy, I have an excuse!"

She winked. "Sure, sure."

He smiled at her affectionately and she felt her stomach swoop again. Somehow they'd edged closer together and she realised she hadn't given a second thought to what she was wearing now. Even in just her chemise, her skin felt warm under Daniel's gaze.

"How come...how come you never introduced us last time?" Bex's face dropped and she saw Daniel wince. "Sorry, sorry, none of my business. Ignore me." He dropped back onto his back but Bex didn't move. Instead she drew a circle with her index finger against the mattress, letting her finger go round, and round, and round. Marco's words rung in her head.

"I'm protective of my brothers. I don't know if you remember but I was going to introduce you."

"I remember," he said softly. "I remember it all."

She didn't dare look up, she didn't dare meet his gaze. "I'm not protective because I'm scared of what people will think, I'm scared if my opinion of said people will be completely wrong. I'm scared to see that side of people. I'm scared in case they hurt them and no one," she stabbed her finger down into the sheet, "no one is allowed to do that."

"You think people might judge them because they are gay?"

Something about the way he was looking at her made her answer truthfully.

"My parents did."

Daniel sucked in a breath sharply. He turned very slowly, not propping himself up this time and Bex took it as an invitation to lay down, resting her head on the pillow opposite and easily making his features out now her eyes had got used to the dark.

"They didn't approve?"

"No, they didn't."

He waited for her to continue. She could see his eyes were wide and alert but the distance between them reminded Bex that he wasn't the person she had once hoped he would be. Despite everything, Daniel was not the one she would share this story with.

As if reading her mind he nodded. "I get it."

"Once upon a time I was going to tell you."

"I know," he said, and his expression appeared rather calm given what she had just said. "It's fine. We'll go to sleep."

"I'm sorry."

"No," he shook his head, bringing one arm under his pillow and still lying on his side, facing her. "No apologies. It's fine."

She eyed him. "You sure?"

He edged closer so he was roughly a few inches away.

Why did this feel so strange?

Her eyes widened in shock as, with his free hand, he leant forward and brushed a few hairs out of her face. Keeping his eyes on hers, he slowly dropped his hand to hold her jaw. "You never have to tell me anything you don't want to. I'm sorry I pushed you before."

"You never pushed me. I get it, we were together. You should tell the person you're with…everything."

"Only when they make you feel safe."

She sucked in a sharp breath at his words. They caused her skin to tingle unexpectedly and she felt the heat around them rise.

She could only manage to whisper his name, her brain too busy trying to put everything together to do much else.

He smiled and then moved his body closer still. She felt his warm breath against her skin, it smelt of mint. He held her gaze as he skated his thumb over her lower lip and Bex felt deliciously trapped by it all, unable to move but also not wanting to.

"After I'm finished making sure that no one can take Amy away from me, I'm going to make sure I do everything in my power to fix what I broke with you." He only had to move his head a fraction to press a long kiss to her forehead. It filled her with warmth. "I'm not going to force that story out of you, Bex. One day, you will tell me readily because I'm going to be the man you trust with everything."

Bex felt momentarily paralysed by his words. Her whole body shivered and she still could feel the shadow of his lips on her forehead.

Daniel smiled ever so softly. "Good night, Bex." And then he turned over and Bex was left staring at his back.

She rolled over and stared at the ceiling, thinking her skin was too alive and her blood to fired up to get any sleep.

She must have done though because the next thing she knew she was waking up, partially on top of him. One of her arms was stretched across him and her right leg half looped over his hip. Her nose was buried into the side of his neck and his right arm was holding her to him. She knew she was doing a shit job of pretending she was still asleep.

Almost as shit as he was.

CHAPTER TWENTY-EIGHT

The courtroom was really cold. Unlike what they showed on the television, it was relatively boring and small. The walls were white, not wooden, people were sat on black chairs, not long brown pews, and there was no ominous jury looking on from the left.

If it wasn't for the fact it was *this* case, Bex would have been disappointed with the normality of it all.

She hadn't even been sure if she was going to come, only making the decision at the very last minute to cancel her Crossfit class and grab a train over to St Albans. She'd had about five missed calls from Lizzie and a very angry text she hadn't looked at properly. She hadn't told Lizzie about the weekend yet. She hadn't told anyone.

Despite her sprint, she was still a few minutes late so she slipped in at the back. She hadn't expected Marco to be sat right beside the doors. He had grabbed her hand and pulled her into the chair next to him.

"Nice to see you," he whispered in her ear, his expression stern and cold.

"Hello," she replied, staring straight ahead.

"Where have you been?"

"At work."

"Couldn't take some time off to be with Daniel on the morning of his trial?"

"Jason keeps telling us this is an easy win."

"Yes, but Daniel is still convinced things might go wrong."

"Well, he needs to calm down then."

She felt Marco studying her. His cold gaze bore into the side of her face and she forced herself not to meet it.

"*Cara*, what's happened? You look tired."

"I'm always tired. I have unusual working hours."

"You don't look like yourself." He lowered his voice. "You're not together anymore, are you?"

Bex balled her hands in her lap before quickly unfurling them in case the movement gave her away. "We're fine."

"That's not what I asked."

But then they had to stop talking as a hush fell over the crowd and Daniel, Jason, Sam and two people Bex didn't recognise walked in. One was clearly Sam's lawyer. She was short with curly brown hair and glasses, and the other was a taller with greying hair and almost perfect posture. He had an air of authority about him.

"That's Judge Varma, Demi say he's a good guy," Marco whispered, following her gaze.

She hoped that was truly the case. She went to narrow her gaze at Sam, now knowing exactly who he was, but her eyes snagged on Daniel.

He was putting on a good front, she'd give him that, but she could see the cracks in his armour as easily as if she were staring at a broken mirror.

Daniel's hair had been combed back but he hadn't had it cut. It was still just a fraction too long to control so he didn't appear as squeaky clean as usual. Other than on Sunday – post the dancefloor game -she'd only ever seen him with messy hair in the morning, when she'd been tucked into the side of him or he'd been making coffee before he got in the shower. Even from where she was sitting, she could see he had dark circles under his eyes and his clothes were ever so slightly too big for him. She hadn't realised the other day that he'd lost weight but now she saw it emphasised his high cheekbones and strong jaw. It made him look even more defined and chiselled, but it meant he'd lost some of his youthfulness too.

Bex snapped her gaze to Sam, feeling her anger bristle out of her.

Sam might not be an outright villain but he'd done this. This was all his fault because of his sudden need to be a father to a child he didn't know.

She hated him for it. She scanned the audience, pausing when she saw the white hair and the sickly green coat of Irene Copperton. She was at the front, her hands clasped in front of her. She even had the cheek to keep glancing at Amy who was sat next to Lottie three rows back. The young girl was by the aisle and kept leaning out to look at her dad, trying to catch his attention.

Jason and Daniel had sat down, Jason just in front of Daniel at a separate table, but he had turned his seat to the side, placed a comforting hand on Daniel's shoulder and was saying something quietly to him. His blue eyes were confident.

Thank you, Jason. Thank you.

She felt someone's hand curl around hers, unpeeling her fingers from their tight position. She had balled her hands into fists again without even realising it.

"He's going to be okay, *cara.*"

"You promise?" she whispered softly, flicking her gaze to Marco and realising her view had become slightly distorted. It looked as if she was looking at everything through glass. The tears in her eyes didn't even have the confidence to sting.

Marco's cool gaze studied her expression again. "I promise."

Daniel was trying his hardest to suppress the feeling of hope he had in the bottom of his chest. If all things went well, today was the day the Judge would rule he could continue to have full custody over Amy. The Judge seemed to like him. At first he'd been rather intimidating; his eyes were cold and his mouth set in a permanent grimace. When he had heard Daniel had agreed with the mediator that Sam could have visitation rights as long as Amy wanted to see him, things had changed however. Sam hadn't agreed to it, hence why things are progressed to the courtroom and Daniel was under the impression Judge Varma judged him for it. From then on, the Judge's eyes had always been that much softer when addressing Daniel and his voice that bit less harsh.

"We have one more witness we would like to bring forward, Your Honour."

The Judge nodded. "Very well, then."

Jason turned to face Daniel, ducking his head. "They are grasping at straws at the moment."

Daniel's lips twitched ever so slightly but he still didn't relax. He caught sight of Sam watching him from across the other side of the room. The man looked...apologetic. His expression was pained and his eyes were creased as if he was worrying about something. Everything about him seemed to be apologising but Daniel had no idea what he was apologising about. Well, other than the obvious but he hadn't seemed to be sorry about that so far. He heard a bitter laugh from the front row and just stopped himself from grinding his teeth.

Irene had been laughing a lot during this trial. It wasn't a gentle laugh or a genuine one. It was mocking and patronising.

Daniel sat up straighter, turning in his seat to see who Sam's lawyer could be calling forward.

The woman making her way up between the chairs was very pale. She walked with confidence and smiled genuinely at Daniel as she walked past where he was sat.

Swearing to tell the truth, the whole truth and nothing but the truth, she sat down, running a hand through her pixie cut.

"Who is she?" Daniel whispered to Jason, who had turned side on so he could still communicate with him.

Jason shook his head, pulling a bemused look.

"Please state your name for the court," Sam's lawyer said, standing up.

"Dr Elena Ossemann."

"Thank you Doctor, and thank you for agreeing to come today." She nodded.

"Dr Ossemann, what is your job role?"

"I'm a doctor of psychology. I work in the Child and Adolescent Mental Health Services situated in London and I lecture at Imperial University."

Daniel leant forward in his seat. Were they going to try and call him crazy? Had they tried to analyse Amy? Was her odd shoe wearing habit going to be dissected as a cry for help?

Despite his wishes, Amy was here. Lottie had insisted on bringing her when Amy had declared she wanted to come. He'd caught her eye as he had walked in and winked at her, liking the fact her gaze had been pinned solely on him and it hadn't wavered towards Sam. She had been clutching her toy giraffe in her hand.

"Now, Your Honour, you'll remember my client did put domestic violence as a reason as to why he believed Amy should no longer be in Dr Williams' care."

"Yes, Ms Tagnor, and it was dismissed by the mediator first and then by myself. There was no evidence and Amy declared you were being…" the Judge made a show of looking through his notes, "*the stupidest, stupid person I've ever met.*" There was a ripple of laughter around the room and Daniel saw a small smile even cross Dr Ossemann's face.

"Yes, Your Honour." Sam's lawyer's face tightened. Her name was Michelle Tagnor, she was referred to by her surname by everyone and her gaze had the ability to make him feel like he was in serious trouble. Jason had told him that he hadn't come across her before but his partner in the firm, Demi, had. Daniel liked Demi. She was a kind and determined woman who worked hard and was good at her job, and she always had time to ask him how he was. He wasn't even her client but since they had met she had sent an e-mail every Monday enquiring about his health and how he felt about the case. It was a small thing, but he'd noticed it.

"Do you still wish to proceed with your line of questioning, Ms Tagnor?" The Judge asked.

Daniel noticed a smile flash across Jason's face.

"Yes, Your Honour," Tagnor stammered. "Despite Amy Williams' statement, my client still has reason to believe that his child is at risk of being hurt if she remains in Dr Williams' care."

Daniel tried to ignore her words, tried to push them away but it was hard. A flare of anger stirred in his gut at not only the implication he would ever lay a finger on Amy, but also the way in which Tagnor addressed Amy as Sam's child. Since the start, she had simply referred to Daniel as if he were a stranger living in Amy's house.

"Dr Ossemann, in your experience, what is the most likely reason a child will be abused?"

The Judge frowned. "Ms Tagnor, please can you clarify how this line of questioning will help me to make my decision?"

"I believe this will assist Your Honour in providing a fuller picture to the court in respect of Amy ever being left in a position that could bring her harm."

Daniel opened his mouth but Jason lifted a hand centimetres off the table. It was a subtle reminder for him to stay quiet.

The Judge paused for a second before dipping his head. "Then you may proceed."

"Dr Ossemann, could you please answer my question?"

The doctor smiled nervously. "The most common reason why children are abused is because the abuser wants to establish some form of control, some form of power. The abuser may have low self-esteem or feel jealous over the love and attention their child receives. Furthermore, it is most probable that the abuser was abused themselves."

Daniel flicked a glance at Jason. He looked just as confused as Daniel felt.

Where was this going?

"So, if, for example Dr Williams was abused then he, himself, would be more likely to abuse his own child."

"Well...it depends from case to case, but it is more likely that a victim of abuse would become an abuser than someone who lived free of abuse."

Judge Varma turned to look at Daniel. "Dr Williams, were your parents in any way abusive?"

Daniel shook his head. "No. I had a very happy childhood."

He smiled and turned back to look between Dr Ossemann and Tagnor. "Continue."

"I wasn't actually referring to Dr Williams' childhood, Your Honour." Tagnor turned and something in her eyes, the way she held herself like she'd just won a point, made Daniel's back stiffen.

He glanced at Sam but the man was no longer looking at him. His shoulders were slumped and he looked...he looked guilty.

"On the 15th March 2010, Daniel Williams went to hospital due to complications with an open wound on his back which he had tried to clean himself. It was infected and had to be cleaned. It was obvious-" Daniel's blood ran cold, his heart thumping painfully inside his chest as Jason turned to look at him, "-that the wound-" his breath was getting tighter in his chest and he stared at Tagnor who was reading from an open folder with a small smile on her face. His head began to pulse, "-was from a belt of some sort."

No. No. No. No,

How had they found this out? How had they got hold of this information?

Daniel felt like he was going to be sick. He turned in his seat, desperate to get Lottie's attention to get Amy out of the room only to find Lottie was now sitting alone, her eyes shimmering at him and her hands shaking. Someone had already grabbed Amy. Daniel only felt the briefest sense of relief as he felt the eyes of everyone else watching him.

His parents.

Charles.

Lottie.

Patricia.

He hadn't told anyone. He'd refused to.

The only person he'd ever told was Bex.

He turned back in his seat, feeling his stomach turn sickeningly and Jason moved his chair a fraction closer to him.

"It's okay," he whispered softly.

But it wasn't.

It wasn't okay.

"Daniel Williams was in and out of hospital for the next year with different small injuries like this which he'd always tried to fix himself first. The police were called twice by neighbours who had reported hearing what sounded like a domestic incident from the family home. The police attended and found Dr Williams once with a black eye and the second time with only a broken lip but there was glass shattered across the kitchen floor. We believe that after Amy was born, Dr Williams started to become a victim of physical domestic abuse. Helen Williams abused him physically as well as emotionally by having multiple affairs and not attempting to hide in them any way. Furthermore-"

Daniel's head was racing. Humiliation crawled up his spine and he felt his lungs screaming for more air but it was getting harder and harder for him to open his mouth and inhale.

"At Helen Williams' funeral, we have many witness statements declaring Amy arrived with bruising to her forehead."

No.

His arms were shaking. Cold hands were pressing down on into his lungs, crushing them, and he felt as if his organs were beginning to shut down.

"We are worried this might have been caused by Dr Williams lashing out when it was discovered his wife died on her way to meet someone else."

He wanted to shout, he wanted to protest, he wanted to tell them that wasn't what had happened but he couldn't breathe.

Jason stood up quickly. "Your Honour, we wish to take a break."

Shame, embarrassment and fear crushed over Daniel. He could

barely make out one emotion from another as they churned inside of his gut. His body felt as if he was going through an emotional washing machine. He didn't hear the rest of the conversation, he didn't even lift his head, but suddenly he was being moved. Jason holding him up on one side and another figure on his left.

He was walking, being guided without even seeing where he was going, down a corridor, away from the courtroom and then into a smaller room to the side. It was cold. There were no windows and he collapsed into the leather sofa in the corner, his arms shaking and his chest tightening more and more. He felt as if he had a snake around his ribs. Every small breath was making it harder and harder to breathe.

Water was thrust into his hand and he heard murmured whispers as Jason spoke to whoever else was in the room with him.

They knew.

Everybody knew.

He had tried so hard to protect Amy from ever finding out, from ever knowing what her mother had done. He hadn't told anyone, fearful that it would accidentally come up in conversation or they'd be overheard. He hadn't ever wanted her to find out. To ever feel guilty.

How much had Amy heard? How much had she understood of what the lawyer was saying?

His back flickered with pain and he closed his eyes, his breathing getting tighter. Water spilled over his knee as he crushed the plastic cup in his hand.

He really couldn't breathe. Panic flooded through him as he realised his body was screaming for oxygen. He needed to tell someone he couldn't breathe but he couldn't open his eyes.

He couldn't find the words.

Pain shot up his arm and his heart hammered hard.

And then, something changed. Something in the room shifted.

He felt her presence first.

Then he felt her hand close around his forearm.

The perfume she always wore when she was going out to a formal occasion or a party drifted to him.

Surely if he could smell that he could breathe?

Why was none of this making sense?

He heard her third. Her voice was gentle and so familiar.

"Daniel…Daniel…look at me."

He opened his eyes and stared at her, not believing that she was squatted down in front of him.

He tried to mouth her name, but his breathing was becoming so strained and difficult he couldn't get his mouth around the word. The pain in his chest intensified and for the horrifying moment he thought he might be having a heart attack.

And then Bex leant forward and pressed her mouth against his.

She pulled away. Her mouth tingling even from that brief touch as she took his free hand in hers and ran her thumbs across his palm.

He was still staring at her but his breathing had slowed. The sweat across his brow gleamed but he no longer looked like he was about to faint.

"Daniel?" she whispered softly.

He licked his lips and frowned in confusion. "Bex?"

She'd seen on a television show once that to stop a person having a panic attack you should make them hold their breath. On this particular show, the man had kissed the woman. Bex had taken that bit of fictional advice and run with it, but at least it seemed to have worked. Daniel was no longer hyperventilating, or swaying slightly on the edge of the sofa, but he was still shockingly pale and there was a slight tremor to his body.

"I got Amy out," she said softly, knowing where his brain would be, "she didn't hear anything. Matt saw me jump up. He was closest. He grabbed her."

Daniel's torso slumped as if an invisible force holding him up had finally let him go.

"Thank you," he whispered, dropping his head into his hands, tears in his eyes.

"It's okay." She ran a hand over his hair, unable it seemed not to touch him, not to reassure him that she was there. "It was a total bastard thing for them to do."

Daniel sucked in a sharp breath. "How did they find out?"

"No idea," Jason said.

Bex turned to look at him and saw her brother's brow was furrowed and his arms folded tightly across his chest. Marco was stood by him, looking through the papers that had been on Jason's desk in the courtroom.

"They didn't disclose the information beforehand. Demi says they have pictures. They should have disclosed that," Marco said coldly. "They are playing a risky game."

"Will it work?" Daniel asked and Bex felt her heart tug sharply at the tone in his voice. He sounded so defeated.

"Shouldn't do," Marco said, shaking his head. "The judge has to dismiss this. All it does is open up doubt in his mind, but he can't make a decision based on this. Also this is just a theory. It's like saying that because Kyle got dropped on his head as a child, he's going to be a mass murderer because most murderers have falls and subsequent head trauma as children. Kyle gets on my nerves but I've never once been scared for my life in his company."

Jason threw him a look. "You need to stop listening to those true crime podcasts."

"I'm sorry I didn't say. I didn't think it was relevant," Daniel said, his voice strained.

"Why was Amy bruised?" Jason asked.

Bex glowered at him. "If you think, for one second-"

"I don't," Jason said calmly. "I don't think Daniel lay a finger on her but I need to know." His eyes met Daniel's. "Is there any truth behind the claim?"

"Helen left her alone on the night that she died. I'm guessing she thought she'd be fine. We'd…" he paused, taking a steady breath. "I'd been teaching her how to sleep in a proper bed. Helen put her in the crib that night. I'm not sure if she forgot Amy was now trying to sleep in a real bed or she just wanted to keep her in a safe space while she was gone. Amy woke up in the night and climbed out. She fell and bruised herself quite badly. The bruises looked particularly bad because there was no one there to look after her. I was at work - locum work to bring us in some more money - and when Helen was found she didn't have her driving licence on her. The car she was driving was registered to her mum, so no one knew Amy was by herself. I didn't until I walked in that morning. Helen left around 11 p.m. supposedly and I got home at 7. Thank God she just bruised her head."

Bex squeezed Daniel's hand before straightening up. "Boys, can we grab a minute alone?"

"Of course," Jason said, quickly straightening up. Marco stayed where he was, studying the pair of them but with a nudge from Jason, both men made for the door.

Bex watched them leave before turning back to look at Daniel. He had his eyes shut again and his free hand was now pressed to his forehead. She took the cup of water from his other hand and placed it down on the small coffee table before moving to sit beside him.

"Tell me how you're feeling."

He pressed the sides of his forehead harder. "I'm... I am feeling scared, terrified, embarrassed -"

"Embarrassed?" Bex exclaimed. "What the hell for?"

"For all of it. Now I know Amy didn't hear, all I can think about is how many people were in there. Everyone has always thought I was an idiot for staying with Helen after the cheating, now what the hell are they going to think?"

Bex reached over and took his chin, pulling his face around to look at her. "Ahh, you see, I think I can help you there as it's probably exactly how I felt when you told me," she said softly. "I felt angry, upset, and completely devastated that you had to go through that alone."

"You're different, Bex." He looked away.

"They are your family, Daniel. They love you. They aren't going to think anything bad about you. What about Lottie, huh? She went through a similar experience. Did you feel she was stupid or pathetic?"

"Of course not!" His eyes snapped to hers.

"Well, then. What do you have to feel humiliated about? You were a man stuck in a relationship, trying his hardest to keep it going for the sake of his daughter. That's an admirable thing."

He ran a hand over his face. "I didn't think you'd be here today."

It was Bex's turn to look away now. "I couldn't miss it."

"Thank you."

"Haven't done anything yet, you just wait until I go in there and fling Sam into a wall."

Daniel laughed. "I wouldn't put it past you."

There was a knock at the door and they looked around.

"They've asked if we are ready to go back in," Jason said, opening the door just a fraction. Marco was no longer with him. "I asked for a couple more minutes as I want to talk things through with Daniel."

Bex turned and squeezed Daniel's hand again. "It's going to be fine," she reassured him.

He didn't say anything but his eyes told her everything.

CHAPTER TWENTY-NINE

Angry Jason was quite a sight to see. Daniel hadn't realised until he had sat down and gathered himself that there was ice-cold rage pulsing from his lawyer's body. Judge Varma picked up on it instantly and Tagnor glanced warily across the room as Jason addressed the court. Daniel had to be questioned over Amy's bruising but he answered everything as truthfully and calmly as he could. Whenever Tagnor questioned him he noticed that Jason did not look at him. He stared at Tagnor instead, his gaze sharp and intense. Tagnor felt it too. She kept shrugging her shoulders and giving him wary looks. An equally intense gaze was piercing through her back.

Marco.

He had his eyes trained on the lawyer the way a lion might watch its prey.

Twenty minutes after they had come back from their break, Judge Varma addressed the court. At first he gave a brief outline of everything that had happened, stating each individual's arguments and counter arguments, and the laws he would rely on to make his decision. As he spoke Daniel's nerves began to grow. Jason had warned him that the final speech wasn't quick and dramatic like on television, but the longer he drew it out the more Daniel felt he could have done more. He could have said more. He could have proven himself more. He felt Jason's hand rest on his forearm as he continued to curl and uncurl his fingers. His right leg was jogging so hard on the spot that he was surprised the sound wasn't echoing around the room.

He couldn't lose her.

He just couldn't.

He'd die before he let that happen.

The fact Amy wasn't his child biologically had hurt him at first, but it hadn't changed how he felt towards her. It hadn't even marked it.

She was *his* daughter.

"Thank you to both parties for coming here today. Family matters are never easy, especially not when it they are put under a microscope within a courtroom and even more so when they involve children. Ms Tagnor, I cannot take on board any of your evidence regarding Dr Williams' abuse. I think Dr Ossemann's refusal to come back into the courtroom after the incident you caused should be seen as evidence enough of your poor conduct. I let you question Dr Williams about Amy's bruising as abuse is a serious matter. Something which I don't think you fully understand. Abuse is a serious issue and bringing it up in court, without prior-warning, wasn't very professional of you. I must say, however, I find it to be poor evidence. Just because Dr Williams was in an abusive relationship does not mean he will automatically abuse his child. Reports from her school show Amy to be a happy, healthy, well developed and an intelligent young woman." He moved his firm gaze away from Tagnor. The only sign that she was embarrassed was her red cheeks and her right hand was twitching. There was also a scowl behind her expression that she wasn't hiding well.

"In this case, I really have to rely on what I think would be in the child's best interests. Mr Copperton, you are Amy's biological father. You work from home, you have a well-paid job and you live near higher performing schools."

Daniel felt his spine begin to curve as anxious dread filled his lungs. His eyes flicked to Jason but his eyes were pinned on the judge.

"You have a mother close by who could help look after Amy and your finances show you could even afford to go part-time without it damaging your lifestyle at all."

He was going to lose.

Daniel felt his throat begin to clamp and sweat pooled where his neck met his blazer.

How could he compete with that? How could he-?

"However, since discovering Amy was not his biological child, Dr

Williams has fought to keep custody. He has not abandoned Amy, which, unfortunately, in my career I've seen a lot of people do when they realise they aren't biologically related to the child. Yes, as it has been stated his work involves long hours, stressful situations and unpredictable shift patterns. But it also is a job I highly respect and a job I don't think any of us can begin to understand the pressures of. Yet despite this, he still provides for the child. Despite this, Amy states herself that he's the best dad in the world." Daniel closed his eyes, feeling his mouth tremble and curling his hands into the wooden table beneath his nails. Jason's grip on his arm grew stronger. "Your line of questioning today caused Dr Williams to have a panic attack. Mr Wright informed us that none of his family knew of the abuse Daniel's ex-partner subjected him to as he never wanted the child to find out or blame herself. He never wanted her to resent her own genetics. Victims of abuse are encouraged to talk to people, to seek help. He sacrificed his own wellbeing for that of the child's. To go through such a thing alone must have been particularly hard." He paused and Daniel opened his eyes ever so slightly. He could hear his heartbeat was in his head. "I have come to my decision."

There was silence in the courtroom. Even Irene had stopped laughing. Jason's grip on his arm became almost painful.

"Mr Copperton, I'd like to congratulate you."

There was a collective intake of breath.

No.

Daniel was going to be sick. Tears pricked his eyes and he sat up, desperation urging him forward in his seat as his body felt like it was collapsing inward. His eyes met Judge Varma's and he felt a sound like an animal start to build in his chest.

Please don't.

Please.

She means everything to me.

Judge Varma smiled.

"Congratulate you on finding possibly the only person who might still allow you visiting rights after this. Especially after what your lawyer just put Dr Williams through. I think it's obvious to anyone in this room that it is in Amy's best interests if she stays with her dad." He took a breath. "And just to be clear, that is Dr Williams. Case dismissed."

Daniel sagged, his body folding down onto the table. He put his hands behind his head, pressing his fingers into the back of his skull and let out a long, shaky breath. His body felt exhausted, like it had run a million marathons and he felt tears scorch his cheeks. The animal noise that had been beating inside his chest settled and yet relief did not flood through him.

Feeling Jason's hand on his shoulder, he pushed a sob back between his teeth, wiped his face furiously and stood.

"Congratulations," Jason said, now stood next to him. He grinned widely before pulling him into a hug.

"I will never be able to repay you," he said, hugging the man he now considered a friend back just as hard. "Thank you so much."

Jason laughed, gripping Daniel's shoulders as he stepped away. "I'd say any time but let's hope you never have to go through that again."

"Let's hope!"

He looked around, desperately searching for Amy's face but amongst the crowd of people who now seemed to be towards the front of the court, he couldn't spot her. No one was allowed up to see them yet, not until they walked out of the courtroom. Daniel turned to grab his wallet off the side, desperate to find Amy as quickly as he could when a small body crashed into his legs, almost knocking him over. No one had bothered to try and grab her and he looked up to see one of the security guards quite obviously staring in the opposite direction. Daniel knelt down and pulled Amy into a proper hug.

"Hello sweetheart," he whispered into her ear.

Amy's grip was almost strong enough to hurt. She buried her head into his shoulder and he realised she was crying as his shoulder began to dampen. He squeezed her tighter, letting her take all the time she needed and realising just how much he needed to hold her too.

And then he felt it.

There. It. Was.

The wave of relief. The surge of happiness that fired through his blood. He pulled Amy even closer to him, his hand on the back of her head and he pressed kisses into her hair.

"I was really scared," she whispered, her voice trembling ever so slightly.

"Pfft, really?" he said, trying to make her laugh.

She didn't, so instead he ran a hand down the back of her head and whispered, "No one is ever going to take you away from me, Amy Williams. You're my daughter."

"You're my dad," she whispered.

He gripped her even harder. "Yes, I am. And I'm not going anywhere. Who else is going to make you Easter egg hunts in November?"

Her responding giggle sounded watery. "I love you, Dad."

"I love you too."

No one else approached them as he hugged her, letting her consume every part of his focus.

His biological daughter or not, she was his.

And she had been the best thing to ever happen to him.

He looked up finally when Amy's tears seemed to have subsided and smiled at his family. They hadn't left yet despite people trying to usher them outside. Maria and Lizzie were messes, tears streaming down their faces and their mouths trembling as if they were stood in their own personal earthquake. Charles looked exhausted, his eyes haunted as he looked at Daniel, and Lottie looked heartbroken, part of her face hidden as she had it pressed into his dad's chest. Patricia looked furious, her eyes glaring at Tagnor as she packed away her stuff. If looks could kill, Patricia's would.

He owed them all explanations.

He realised, with a slight sink of his heart, that one person wasn't in the crowd. He squeezed Amy tighter.

It was okay.

It made sense that he could have only one good thing at a time.

Bex left the courtroom, walking quickly through the corridors and hearing the sound of her shoes against the shiny floor bounce around her. She'd been sitting with Amy right to the last second, covering her ears whenever the judge had mentioned anything about abuse. Amy had objected until she had seen Bex's firm stare. As the decision had been made, she had urged the little girl to run up to Lottie and then sped from the room. As she got to the big wooden doors at the front she did a double take. Matt was only just coming back through them.

"You missed it. They went back in ages ago."

"Oh no, did I?" His voice sounded jovial and out of place.

"Yes."

"Did we win?"

"Yeah, he did."

Matt wiped his hands against his trousers and Bex noticed the slight black tint to his fingers. "Well, that's good then. Why are you leaving?"

"That's actually a question I was going to ask myself," said a stern voice behind her.

Matt flicked his gaze over her head. "Who are you?"

"Her brother-in-law," Marco said, coldly.

Bex folded her arms across her chest and turned to look at him. "I don't need a babysitter."

"Good because I'm not here to babysit." He turned to Matt. "Can we have a minute?"

Matt nodded, ducking around the pair of them and walking back towards the courtroom.

"Marco, stop being an arsehole."

Ignoring her, Marco grabbed her by the arm and manoeuvred her to the side. "I'm here to ask why you chose to leave the courtroom like the devil was after you when your boyfriend just won his case." His dark eyes flared at her.

Bex threw back her shoulders and squared up to him. In response, he simply raised an eyebrow.

"It's my business, Marco."

"You made it my business."

"I made it my brother's business."

"No." He shook his head. "You made it my business when I came and fixed your window and you told me all about your new boyfriend. You made it my business when that man walked into my house and you couldn't keep your eyes off him."

Bex scoffed and Marco raised his eyebrows even higher, a darkness entering his expression.

"*Cara*, you told me this guy was a good one."

"He is!"

"Then why do you look so tired? Why have you been avoiding us over the last few months? Why do you look like you've lost weight?"

"I've not lost weight!" Bex snapped, outraged. "I work out just as much as I always do. I'm lifting heavier, I'm capable of quicker times on the rower, I-"

"None of that means you haven't lost weight. You don't look like yourself. Is that because of this man?"

Bex pressed her lips together. "No man has that kind of power over me."

Marco tilted his head to the left, his eyes flicking over her expression. "No man until Daniel Williams."

"Not ever!" Bex shoved his shoulder and turned to leave. She got as far as the steps outside before Marco was beside her.

"What happened between the two of you?"

"I don't have to tell you!"

"You do when you're this upset, Bex! You do! I've never known you to let a man affect you like this."

"Daniel hasn't affected me! He doesn't have that kind of power. I don't care that much!"

"You clearly do-"

"I CLEARLY DON'T!" Bex yelled, slamming her feet into the floor and causing a few passing people to stop and stare at the pair of them. "I don't, Marco. That is why he dumped me. That is why it is over. Because I can't let anyone in. I can't trust anyone. He said he clearly cared about me more than I did him. And what was hilarious about the whole thing was it was on the night I was going to finally tell him that I loved him. I'd written it down. I was finally going to be brave. And then he broke up with me."

"You wrote it down?"

"Yes. It's ripped to pieces somewhere in my bedroom right now."

Marco raised an eyebrow. "So you kept it?"

"Don't try and over analyse that," she sneered.

"Why did he think you didn't care?"

She looked away.

"Why?" he snapped, stepping forward.

"Because I couldn't admit I loved him."

Their eyes met. Bex looked away as a small smile crossed Marco's lips. "Sounds familiar."

Bex knew that Marco had waited eighteen months for Jason to say it.

"Yeah, well, my guy didn't deem me worthy enough to wait around."

"*Cara*," Marco said softly, stepping forward and reaching out a hand to squeeze her forearm. "Trust me, that man is completely and utterly in love with you. I can tell that much. I know-"

"I'm going home," Bex said, shaking her head and feeling the sting of tears behind her eyes. "Congratulate Jason for me."

"Don't go, not now."

"I'm not going to let him hurt me again."

"I think that man would rather die than hurt you."

"If you think that then why have you looked angry this whole time? Any time you look at us, you look suspicious. You try and analyse us. You glower intensely."

Marco smirked. "You thought I was angry at him?"

"Yes! Who else would you be-?" She looked away, pulling her lower lip into her mouth and shaking her head. A huff of cold laughter escaped her lips. "You were angry at me?"

"Yes. I could see all the emotions that were written across Jason's face when we met, written across yours. Except you've had more years on your own, you've hardened that outer shell even more, you've decided to date more dickheads in the interim to help back up your twisted idea that love makes you weak whilst, at the same time, desiring it more than anything."

"I do not desire love more than anything!"

"Yes you do. You want someone to love you and take care of you. You've had to be the one to take care of everyone else your entire life and you want someone to do the same for you. But you know that comes with a cost and with every idiot you have dated you've simply proven to yourself that the cost isn't worth it, when you haven't actually been giving yourself a fair chance."

She didn't want that.

He was wrong.

She wasn't one of these people who needed *love*. She had love. She loved her friends, she loved Lizzie, she loved her brothers. She didn't *need* the big love. She didn't need anyone to take care of her. She'd managed since she was seventeen to take care of herself. Why would she need someone now?

"I'm taking you home," Marco said softly.

"I can take myself!"

"I know you can," he shrugged. "But I'm driving you anyway."

CHAPTER THIRTY

Daniel left the courthouse with a much lighter feeling in his chest than when he had entered. Amy was clinging onto his left hand and Lottie had slotted her arm through his right. His family had been...well, his family. They had hugged him, they had jumped up and down, they'd cheered and then they'd all, in their own way, told him they'd be there for him when he wanted to explain. Right now, however, he simply wanted to celebrate. To bask in the happiness that he had his daughter still with him and she was still legally his own.

Maria turned to ask him something when a loud noise erupted from their right. It sounded like a mixture of fireworks, shouting and metal pans being banged against kitchen sinks. White walls of light slammed into the side of Daniel's vision and he put up a hand, pulling Amy instinctively closer as Lottie flinched and slackened her hold on his arm. He squinted at the commotion, his eyes slowly sharpening to realise there were roughly fifteen photographers beside them, taking photos and snapping at them all like hungry dogs. The sound of their flashes was deafening and he could hear shouting.

Someone was shouting his name like they were on a loop.

Just ahead Charles and Lizzie sprung apart.

"Charles, is it true your brother has been accused of child abuse?"

"Is it true your brother was the victim of domestic abuse?"

"Is your niece about to be ripped away from your family?"

Luckily for him, most of the photographers were cornering Charles. His brother had pushed Lizzie behind him but Daniel could see their eager eyes trying to get a gauge on who she was. Daniel grabbed her arm and pulled her towards him.

"You okay?"

"Fine," she said, squeezing his arm affectionately.

"Shall we go inside?" Maria asked as more people walked down the steps from the courtroom, effectively pushing them towards the photographers.

"This is a family matter. We must ask you to please leave Charles alone!" Patricia said so loudly that although every word sounded very calm, she had in fact bellowed it. She had transformed from his concerned, older sister into her work self - there wasn't much difference between the two but he noted her sharper eyes and more powerful stance. She pushed through them all and stood next to Charles, who was trying his best to smile and yet keep the photographers away from them at the same time. "This is a private matter. We will not be taking any questions or be making any statements."

Her words made the photographers pause for a second. The win was fleeting as they begun taking photos seconds later and shouting even more loudly. Some of the questions were now being directed towards him.

"Dr Williams, we've heard from sources you were heavily abused in your past relationship, could Charles have been there for you more? Or did being a celebrity eat up his time?"

"Do you two get on?"

"Do you resent him for that?"

"Did your parents just focus on him?"

He glared at them, shaking his head in disgust before looking down at Amy. At least she was hidden from the cameras because she was squashed in amongst them all. "Come on," he called to her over the noise.

He turned to move towards the car park, still holding Lizzie's arm in one hand but their exit was blocked as some of the photographers began to come up the sides.

"Who are you?" one of them asked Lizzie.

"She's a family friend," Daniel said quickly, pushing Lizzie back again as he tried to figure out what to do.

"I have footage of you holding hands with Charles just seconds ago."

Lizzie shrank back.

"Is she wearing an engagement ring?"

"Leave her alone!" Charles snapped angrily across at them, but the panic in his voice heightened the crowd even more.

"That is enough, thank you," Patricia called, clapping her hands together but no one was listening.

"What's your name?"

"Who are you?"

"What are you doing here today?"

They were going to have to go back up the steps into the courtroom and get security. It seemed the only way to avoid this absolute mess. He kept Lizzie behind him, desperate to get her away from the prying eyes of the photographers.

"Matt! Help!" He heard Lottie yell, waving up at presumably where Matt stood a few feet away.

"Lizzie," he shouted over his shoulder, "we need to go back inside. I think it's the only safe place to be."

"I agree," Maria said, who was just beside him.

Lizzie's green eyes were wide and panicked, she was breathing fast and white lights were still making them all wince. Her eyes momentarily flicked behind him and for a second, her growing panic paused. Instead, Lizzie frowned as if confused. Before Daniel had time to turn around and look, something hard brushed his back. He flinched automatically before realising it was Matt. The man shouldered past Kenneth and down towards Charles.

"Oh god," he muttered. What the hell was he about to do?

Matt grabbed Charles by the collar, yanked him around to face him and then...

Daniel blinked.

For a second the photographers paused. Their mouths hanging open and their cameras poised in their hands.

Daniel blinked again.

No, he wasn't imagining things.

The cameras roared back to life, yells striking against the air and white flashes practically blinding them.

Matt was kissing Charles. Arms thrown around his neck, leaning into him, the whole chi-bang.

The photographers' attention was torn away from the rest of the group and the pair of them were surrounded.

Charles and Matt parted, and because Charles was so tall, Daniel could see his brother's eyebrows had practically disappeared into his hairline. Bewilderment was etched in every facial muscle as his eyes read, *what the fuck do you think you're doing?* Luckily no one else was taking notice of what they looked like without their lips locked together. Charles's eyes flicked over everyone to meet Lizzie's and Daniel felt her tense beside him. The flash of pain behind his brother's eyes was fleeting but he heard Lizzie's breath hitch.

"Lizzie!" Daniel said quickly, knowing what she was about to do before she did it. She slipped from his grip. "Don't be stupid! Dad, grab Lizzie!"

But as Daniel looked for his dad, he realised the man was too busy laughing to pay attention. He was howling with laughter, his hand pressed to his stomach and tears running down his face.

Lizzie forced her way between the two rows of photographers, pushed Matt to the side, grabbed Charles by the shirt, and pulled him into another kiss.

"Jesus Christ!" Patricia snapped, holding her head in her hands. Kenneth looked up, saw what was going on and burst into fits of laughter all over again. Amy was giggling too.

"What's going on?" Maria said, looking between them all. "I'm so confused."

"I'll explain later, let's leg it to the car while they are all distracted."

He gripped Amy's shoulders and began directing her towards the car park, Kenneth and Maria following close behind him. He turned his head to try and grab Lottie's attention but she was frozen to the spot, staring straight at Matt, who was just emerging from the crowd of photographers now surrounding Lizzie and Charles. Matt smiled sheepishly, shrugging his shoulders and Lottie began to laugh, shaking her head at him.

"Not quite what I meant by help!" she yelled before mimicking their father as her body folded with laughter. Matt burst out laughing too.

"Lottie!" Daniel yelled, trying to catch her attention, but she couldn't hear him over everything else.

He cast a look between them. Matt was with her, he told himself, he was sure she'd be fine.

Turning his attention back to getting Amy in his car, they hurried forward. Kenneth was still laughing. He had to stop every few metres to press his hands to his thighs as his laughter thundered through him. When they finally rounded the side of the building and could see the car park ahead, Daniel relaxed enough to turn to him and shake his head, a smile across his mouth.

"Dad, come on, it wasn't that funny."

"What was that about, Daniel?" Maria asked, her eyes wide.

"The newspaper released some stupid story that Charles and Matt were in a relationship last week. I think Matt saw the newspapers cornering Lizzie and tried to create a distraction."

His mum's confused expression changing into a grin. "Oh, he's always been a good boy that Matt. That was some distraction."

"Some distraction!" Kenneth wheezed, wiping away more tears. "Did you see Charles's face?"

Daniel had. But the expression that had really stuck in his mind was the one when his brother's eyes had landed on Lizzie. Charles had been hurting.

Lizzie had clearly seen that too.

And just like Lizzie always did, she had been determined to rid Charles of any pain.

"I like Matt," Amy declared.

"Me too," Daniel said on a nod.

He looked down at Amy but she was staring right ahead, a grin across her face and her shoulders were beginning to shake. He followed her gaze to find there was quite a commotion going on in the car park.

"What's now happening over there?" Maria said just as he was just about to ask the same thing.

They walked forward to see Tagnor screaming down her phone whilst Sam stood staring at his car in horror. The sun was still high in the sky, and as they all made their way closer he began to see why they were both so cross. Someone had covered their car windows with stickers. Big, red, smiley faces that looked like they belonged on the front of school notebooks. On top of that, sweets were stuck on the bonnet and someone had let down one of Sam's tyres.

"There's fucking super glue in my locks!" Tagnor was shouting down the phone. "I can't get my key in the fucking door!"

"Oh dear!" Maria said, her hands lifting to her throat. "Let's go check our car, Kenneth! This is awful!" She turned to squeeze

Daniel's arm. "We will meet you back at ours. You must come over! I'll text the others. We are going to celebrate this crazy day."

"Okay, Mum," Daniel said, smiling at her. He tried to look behind her at the commotion but she pulled his attention back to her.

"What?" he said, frowning at her expression.

"We are so proud of you. You know that, right?"

"Mum," he laughed. "Stop. I know."

She pulled him into a tight hug, her arms crushing him to her. Maria, like her sons, was tall. She was just over six foot and her arms had the strength of a boa constrictor.

"I love you too, Mum," he said, gently.

"And I love you. So very much." He felt her reach an arm out and pull Amy into their embrace. "The pair of you."

"Love you too, Nanma," Amy said.

When Maria pulled away, she had tears in her eyes. "I'm just really proud," she said, cupping his face. "Really proud. And I'm so sorry you couldn't tell-" Her breath hitched.

"Mum, it's fine," he said gently. "It was a long time ago."

Kenneth slapped him on the back affectionately and Daniel tried not to wince. "Not again though, okay, my son? You tell us next time."

"There won't be a next time, Kenneth," Maria said firmly. "Any woman who comes near him is going to have to go through a screening process carried out by me."

He laughed. "Thanks you two."

"We'll crack out the good stuff at ours," his dad said warmly.

He watched them go, waving at his mum who kept turning around to wave at them. He felt a lump form in his chest. It felt like something heavy had shifted from him. Despite not wanting them to ever find out, he was relieved they now knew. Relieved that he didn't have to tip-toe around the subject. He would have to inform them that they couldn't mention it in front of Amy, although he would need to somehow check how much she had heard at the end of the case, but that was the only request he had. Bex had been right. His family didn't think any less of them.

If anything they seemed to be blaming themselves for not having seen it.

"You too big for piggy backs?" he said, looking down at Amy.

"No!" she shrieked, lifting her hands up in the air. He bent down and easily slipped her onto his back, enjoying hearing her squeal with laughter as she had to grab his hair so she didn't slip off straight away.

He deliberately didn't look at Sam or his lawyer's cars again. He didn't feel quite right rubbing his happiness in their face.

"So," he said as Amy dug her heels almost painfully into his lower ribs. "What sweets did you use?"

"Haribo."

He smiled, shaking his head.

He'd guessed it.

From the very moment he'd seen that grin across her face, he'd known.

"Oh really?"

"Matt said they were the best for sticking."

He felt Amy freeze and he laughed as she groaned theatrically. "Sorry, Dad." She dropped her head against his and he felt the scratchiness of her hair against his cheek. "I was meant to be keep it a secret," she huffed, swinging her legs ever so gently.

"You're usually a better secret keeper than that."

She ran her hands through his hair, making it deliberately as messy as she could.

"Amy."

"I can never keep secrets from you."

He tried not to let her statement make him too happy.

"Where'd Matt get the stickers from?"

"There was a corner shop nearby selling them. We went in there first to get ice cream when you had to go to the toilet-"

"When I wha-oh." His mind ran back over what Bex had said. Matt had been the one to grab Amy first and lead her out of the courtroom. "So, you went for ice cream and ended up vandalising cars?"

She rested her arms back around his neck. "Are you mad?"

He deliberately waited a few seconds before responding but just as he was about to, Amy cut him off.

"Matt said they had done a really bad thing. He said they'd gone through stuff they shouldn't have."

"Did he now? And that makes it okay?"

Her arms tightened around his neck. "They were trying to take you away from me."

Daniel swallowed away the lump her last sentence formed in his throat and he reached up with one hand momentarily to squeeze where her hands met in front of his neck. "I am mad," he said, making his tone mock serious. "I'm mad you didn't wait for me to join in."

CHAPTER THIRTY-ONE

Please open your eyes. Please Please Please.

Blue flashing lights were approaching, Bex could feel the flicker of them piercing her eyes and her heart felt as if it were tearing in two. The pain was unbelievable. The smile had gone from Daniel's face.

Please, *she pleaded.* Please, wake up. I wish you'd wake up.

The boy opposite her snapped his head up as if he'd heard her. As if he had read her mind. His green eyes met hers.

But Daniel wasn't waking up. Daniel wasn't stirring.

"What did you just say?" The boy asked.

"I want him to wake up!" Bex yelled, not knowing why but she felt compelled to talk to him. He had his hands still firmly pressed on top of Daniel's chest, beating down with some force but Daniel wasn't responding.

"That's not what you said, Bex."

"What did I say then?"

"You have to be specific!"

"I said I wish he would wake up!" she snapped. "Are you trying to make fun of me?"

The boy simply smiled. "I'd never dream of it, Bex."

How did he know her name?

His smile broadened and recognition fired through her.

The boy looked just like Charles.

Bex woke, her heart banging hard against her chest and she tasted blood. Sitting up slowly, she pulled the covers away from her, feeling them clinging to her body and yet knowing she had to get up. She

318

had to move. She had to remind herself none of her dream was real.

Marco had driven her home and insisted on walking her back and seeing her into her flat. He'd hung around for far too long but she had finally persuaded him to leave and fallen asleep nearly the moment he had left. Her head was still ringing with tiredness but she knew she couldn't go back to sleep just yet. She walked into the kitchen, feeling the cold tiles calm her ever so slightly as she went to pour herself a glass of water.

A faint buzzing reached her ears. She looked up.

Who would be calling at this time of night?

She walked back through the living room into her bedroom, her phone screen flashing into the darkness.

Daniel - **1 missed call**

Her throat felt dry at the sight and she licked her lips, hesitating as she leant forward to pick it up. As her fingertips brushed it, the phone began to ring again.

Taking a steady breath, she answered it.

"Hello?"

There was a pause at the other end and then a huge sigh of relief. "Did you dream it too?"

Bex closed her eyes. Less than twenty-four hours ago she had sat next to Daniel, she had comforted him... she had kissed him.

Her barriers felt like they were crumbling.

She wanted to let him back in so desperately but at the same time she was desperately trying to find the key to keeping him locked out.

"Yes. I've dreamt it every night since you broke up with me. Well... except one."

"Except in your brother's house," his voice was low.

She sniffed. "It's horrible."

"I know. It feels real every time. I wake up aching as if I've actually hurt myself."

There was a short silence.

"We won by the way," he said, clearing his throat ever so slightly.

"I know I was there."

"You were?"

"Yeah, I left after the decision was made. Didn't feel it was my place to be there."

He laughed ever so slightly. "You're responsible, Bex. You gave me Jason."

"I'm sure you'd have won no matter what."

"We don't know that." He sighed. "I'm really sorry."

Bex swallowed, her heart beat starting to speed up.

"Why?" She settled down on her bed, her back against the wall and her legs curled up under her.

"For what I said that night."

Bex closed her eyes, trying to not let the memory sting as it flashed before her eyes.

"You've said that already, Daniel. It's okay."

"It's not." He coughed ever so slightly. "It's really not. And the other night I never apologised properly. So, I'm sorry." When she didn't respond, he continued. "Marco paid me a visit this evening."

"What?" Bex snapped, her eyes flying open.

She was going to kill him.

"He's really rather intimidating, isn't he?"

"God, Daniel, what did he do?"

Daniel paused, clicking his tongue slightly. She pressed the phone closer to her ear. "He gave me a letter."

"A letter?"

"A ripped up, sellotaped-back-together letter."

Bex felt her blood run cold. Her breathing suddenly felt like she was inhaling particles of ice and she could hear her heartbeat in her head.

Her letter.

The letter.

That's why Marco had been hanging around her flat. That's why he'd insisted on driving her home. His eyes had practically lit up when she had mentioned the letter. How had she not bloody noticed what he was searching for? How had she not realised?

Why hadn't she thrown that bloody thing away?

Embarrassment curled its way up her spine, heating the ice that was in her veins and turning it to lava.

"Did you read it then?" she snapped.

"No."

His answer surprised her. Her anger paused, as if not sure what to do with itself.

"Why not?"

"I would never read it unless you gave it to me."

"You weren't even tempted?"

He laughed. "Of course I was tempted, but it wouldn't have been right. As shown by your anger just a second ago."

So bloody noble. So annoyingly respectful.

Stupid, stupid man.

"I forgot how good your self-restraint is."

"Not good enough to resist calling you."

Bex couldn't stop the smile that crossed her face. She sank further down into her bed. "Are you...are you flirting with me?"

His chuckle was low and sent goosebumps racing up Bex's arms. "We both know I can't flirt."

"You're doing a pretty good job of it."

"Must be your influence."

"You're doing it again."

He laughed properly this time, and the sound caused her chest to swell with affection. After it settled they were quiet for a short while. Bex found comfort in hearing his breath down the phone, hearing that he was very much alive. She wondered if he was finding comfort in hers too.

"Do you want to tell me what was in that letter?" he asked softly.

The question threw her. The warm, content feeling that had been growing in her chest began to deflate and panic sat up in her stomach.

"Daniel, today...today didn't mean I've forgiven you."

"I get that."

"Right then...so you know I'm not going to just forgive and forget. We aren't just going to get back together."

"I haven't asked if we can."

Discomfort prickled up her skin and Bex lay back fully on the bed, staring at her ceiling.

"I haven't asked if we can," Daniel repeated, *"yet."*

"Yet?"

He gave a low chuckle. "Yes, yet."

"That is a very confident approach you're taking."

"Trust me, I'm faking all of it."

A laugh escaped her mouth before she could stop it. She quickly pushed it away, closing her lips and turning her head away from the mobile.

"I know you must have your walls up. I get it," he said softly.

"They are pretty rock solid."

"I know." He sighed gently. "And I'm not the strongest of guys."

Bex laughed - she really couldn't help herself. "I mean...."

"Didn't need to laugh quite that loudly," he said, his tone one of mock grumbling. "No, I'm not the strongest of guys, but I sure as hell know how to climb."

She shifted in her bed, frowning ever so slightly. "What?"

"I might not be able to knock down those walls, Bex, but you can be sure as hell that I'm going to find a way over them."

Emotion clutched at her chest. She felt her throat close and she shut her eyes briefly, not allowing herself to say what she wanted to.

"You once said you weren't like Lizzie. That you weren't going to wait around for a Williams boy."

"I remember."

"Well, I am. I am like Lizzie," his voice became stronger. "And I will wait, Bex. I will wait until you have forgiven me, I will wait until you are ready, I will wait even if I am waiting forever."

Bex blinked tears away from her eyes, her mouth dropping open ever so slightly. "You can't! You can't just..."

He waited for her to finish. When she didn't, he hesitantly began speaking, his voice low and intimate in her ear and for a brief second she could imagine him next to her, bed sheets crumpled around them, his long arm thrown across her body, pulling her into him and his breath tickling her ear. "I can wait, Bex. I will. Waiting...It's what you do when you realise you've found the person who makes you happier than anyone else. It's what you do when you realise the only reason I'm being brave right now, the only reason I'm being this strong is because of the person I am talking to. The one who made me believe I was...I was worth this. I once told you that I had never loved anyone as much as I loved you. Do you remember?"

"Of course I do."

"Well, I meant it. I always will."

She blinked back tears, trying to regain her composure and silence stretched between them. All she could hear was his breathing in her ear. It hurt and soothed her all at the same time.

"You said you woke up. When you broke up with me you compared it to a drunken mistake and said you woke up."

His breath hissed slightly. "That I did. I was wrong. I was so, so, so wrong, Bex. I was too caught up in thinking you'd cheated. I was focusing on the love thing. I'm so sorry."

On the love thing.

"It hurt."

"I'll spend however long it takes making it up to you."

"What if you can't, Daniel?"

He let out a long breath. "Then I guess I'll spend the rest of my life trying."

CHAPTER THIRTY-TWO

Despite being August, the day of the wedding was cool. The sky was white, the morning air fresh and thankfully the humidity had dropped over the last few days so Lizzie's hair was doing what Bex told it to do. Fortunately for Bex, she had only had a minor nightmare the night before and had managed to keep it a secret from the three other women she was sharing a bed with - Lizzie, Lottie and Jenni. They'd all piled into the huge king size bed that was reserved for Charles and Lizzie's wedding night, wearing matching pyjamas that Lottie had gone out to buy as a treat. They'd eaten pizza, drunk wine and planned to watch a dozen or so romantic comedies but in the end had just chatted until nearly midnight.

Kristina had refused to join their literal sleepover and pulled out the sofa bed. Lottie had managed to persuade her into the pyjamas, however, and she had been the one who helped Bex get Lizzie to bed at a reasonable hour.

So far, the day had gone without a glitch. No newspapers had managed to find out about the wedding and Lizzie had been the most relaxed bride Bex had ever come across - and her job meant she had done her fair share of wedding makeup

Now they were stood in a little room at the front of the church. It was colder inside, like the walls were blocking out any kind of warmth, and there was a smell in the air that Bex could never name but always associated with her grandad.

She wasn't the biggest fan of churches, but Kenneth and Maria were religious so, subsequently, a church had been chosen.

Lizzie grinned around at all her bridesmaids and Bex's heart could have burst for her. She looked beautiful. She was wearing a simple ivory dress with an illusion neckline. The dress pinched at her waist and then fanned out to the ground, which suited her smaller height and emphasised her slight curves. Her hair was down, hanging in soft waves, and her makeup was beautiful - if Bex could say so herself. She had kept it simple so Lizzie wouldn't feel self-conscious, but had made sure to emphasise her eyes and redden her cheeks. There was a small knock at the door and the four of them - Lizzie, Bex, Lottie and Amy - turned to see Matt walk in.

Bex smiled.

The man looked as handsome as she had ever seen him. His hair was still slightly scruffy but it looked like it had been styled that way for once, and the black suit he was - wait a second.

"Matt, what are you wearing?" Bex said quickly at the same time as Lizzie asked, "Where's your suit?"

He smiled. "I'm wearing a suit."

Lizzie shook her head. "Very funny. Why are you wearing a black suit?"

Matt was giving Lizzie away and, consequently, he was part of the bridal party so he had been given a blue suit to wear to match the bridesmaids' dresses.

Matt smiled. "There's been a change of plan."

"What do you mean?"

Bex risked a glance at her. Lizzie looked confused but not yet panicked.

Good.

Panicked bride was bad.

Confused bride was okay.

"I'm joining the groomsmen."

"Matt," Bex said, clicking her tongue, "this isn't funny."

"I'm not trying to be funny. Charles is my best friend."

Confusion narrowed Lizzie's eyes. "And I'm your sister. Who am I walking down the aisle with? Mum?"

"No." Matt shook his head. "Love Mum but we thought there was someone slightly more appropriate for the role."

Bex felt cold fear lick its way up her body.

Please don't be Craig.

She stared at Matt. He wouldn't be that stupid, surely? He

wouldn't think *that* was a good idea? But, then again, Craig had always pulled the wool over Matt's eyes. He hadn't been able to see how bad or toxic he was until much later than everyone else.

"Matt, please tell me it's not Craig," Lizzie snapped, voicing Bex's exact thoughts. Bex moved forward to hold her best friend's hand reassuringly.

The smile slipped from Matt's face. "No! How stupid do you think I am? No way."

"Then what's going-?"

"This was Charles's idea. Do you think he'd let me ask Craig to walk you down the aisle? I wouldn't want Craig walking you down the aisle!"

"What did Charles decide?"

"He decided who should walk you down the aisle."

"And who is that?" Lizzie asked, irritation threading through her words. "You're really starting to piss me off."

From behind them came a slow, smug, familiar voice. "Is that really how a bride should speak?"

Irritation flared in Bex's gut as a reflex.

They all turned around to see Neil Grayson was resting against the wall, his arms folded, and a sardonic grin on his face. He'd managed to slip into the room through a door at the back and Bex wanted to half strangle and half hug him.

He only had eyes for Lizzie though.

"Hey, Whiskers," he said fondly, his smirk lessening. "Missed you."

Silence filled the room. Bex looked between the pair of them. Lizzie looked shocked, her eyebrows pinching together. A ripple passed across her expression. Neil's smile dropped.

"Fuck's sake, don't cry you idiot."

"But you said, you said, you said you didn't care!" Lizzie had started to flap her hands in front of her face and before Bex could reach her, Neil was there first. He pulled her into a hug, placing his head on top of hers and holding her fiercely.

"You're such an idiot," he said with a small laugh.

"But you said!" Her voice was muffled now but Bex heard the indignation flare in her tone.

"Turns out your boyfriend knows how to read me better than you do. Apparently it's his job to study faces, who knew?"

Bex glanced at Matt. He was smiling from the door. "Smooth."

"Like I said, it was all Charles really."

"Who else would have the money to pay for my flights back from Australia?" Neil chipped in. "Charming put me in first class, suave bugger." He held Lizzie's shoulders and eased away from her very slowly. "You stopped being a mess yet?"

"Yep," Lizzie squeaked, completely unconvincingly. "I'm just so confused. You didn't even want to say goodbye at work. You just left!"

"You didn't come to my leaving do!"

"Yeah, because you were being a twat!"

"Children!" Bex snapped, clicking her fingers together. "Don't really have time for this right now, and Lizzie, Amy is still in the room."

"Neil said fuck a second ago!"

Bex winced and Lizzie paled, quickly dropping her gaze. "Sorry."

"I didn't leave Lightswitch for the job in Australia," Neil said gently. "I quit before that, but that's a story for another time when Blondie over here won't kill me for ruining your makeup, okay?" He sighed. "Just know I was gutted I couldn't come to your wedding. I couldn't afford the plane flight back. I looked constantly and I already had the job in Australia before you two had booked a date. I pretended not to care because it was easier. Your soon-to-be-husband is apparently very good at seeing through my rubbish."

Lizzie blinked furiously and her face began to crease again.

"Neil, I swear, if you've got her crying *again*."

"It's not my fault she's just so overwhelmed by her love for me!" Neil grinned, he turned back to Lizzie and dropped his voice into a hushed dramatic tone. "If you want to run away together you just say the word, Whiskers, we'll go. I can grab us a taxi. I knew it was me you really wanted all along."

"Shut up!" Lizzie said, shoving his shoulder, laughter spilling out from her. She turned to face Bex. "Did I ruin it?"

Yes. In a bloody nutshell, yes.

"No." She glanced at Matt. "Give me five minutes." She grabbed her emergency makeup bag from the side. "We can fix this."

"Will do," he said, leaving the room.

Despite how much she disliked Neil, she had to hand it to him, this was the best surprise Lizzie could have had. For whatever reason, she adored Neil and his leaving without a proper goodbye or seeming to care at all had hurt her. She eyed him out of the corner of her eye. Once upon a time, he had accused Charles of being a coward for not admitting his feelings for Lizzie. She had a sneaky suspicion this was a similar thing. Not in a romantic sense. There was not a romantic atom between the pair of them, but Bex was beginning to believe in terms of friendship, Neil adored Lizzie Cartwright and that terrified him.

Annoyingly, he looked good. The blue suit exaggerated his pointed shoulders and his boyish features. His side fringe flopped down in front of his face and his skin was ever so slightly tanned from the Australian sun.

"Take a picture, Blondie, it'll last longer." He grinned at her and Bex rolled her eyes.

And *that* was just one of the many reasons she didn't actually like him.

His cocky sense of self was irritating as hell.

"Do you give everyone nicknames?"

The side of his mouth rose. "You noticed?"

Bex let out a grunt of annoyance before turning back to Lizzie and finishing off fixing what Neil had ruined. She straightened up just as there was a knock at the door.

"Ladies, are you ready?" It was Lizzie's mum, Jean.

"Yeah!" Bex shouted back. She looked down at Lizzie. "Ready to get married? Again?"

Lizzie smiled. "Yeah, go on then."

Amy was to go first. She looked beautiful in her little blue dress and she was taking her role as bridesmaid very seriously. Bex didn't know who had schooled her on being a part of the bridal party, but she had brought a small bag with her to store everyone else's items inside and it matched her dress perfectly. She also had a timetable with a list of all her responsibilities on it. Bex had an inkling Patricia had been involved. Lottie and her would follow and Lizzie would walk up with Neil afterwards.

"You look beautiful," she said, grabbing Lizzie's arm one last time and giving it a squeeze.

"Thanks." Lizzie already looked as if she were on the brink of tears.

And then they were being ushered forward, shushed by an older lady with grey hair - who stopped shushing them when she caught sight of Bex's glare - and the music began to play.

Walking up the aisle didn't faze Bex, but to her surprise Lottie felt tense against her arm. The younger girl kept looking down at the floor, pulling ever so slightly at the dress as people turned to look at them. She also had her arms positioned weirdly, sticking out her elbows at an unnatural angle as she held a small bouquet of flowers in front of her. Bex had never known Lottie to ooze confidence but she had never been shy. Maybe it was all the extra attention? Or maybe it was wearing something that fitted one style for a change? She turned her head to whisper in her ear.

"Can you smell burning?"

"What?" Lottie hissed, looking up, alarmed.

"I don't think someone approves of me being in their church."

The younger woman laughed, scrunching up her nose hard and Bex could see she was trying her hardest not to cackle in the way Lottie usually did.

"I'm going up in flames with you. I've lain with a woman before, remember?"

"Jesus, are we going to make it to the altar?"

"Bex!" Lottie whispered, still trying not to laugh. "You can't swear in a church."

"I could have said something worse. I could have said-"

"Stop!"

The pair laughed.

Lottie shook her head but she'd visibly relaxed, her shoulders coming away from her ears and her arms sitting more naturally. They were only a few steps away from the altar now and Bex turned to look at the front. Her own confidence was given a swift kick as her eyes met Daniel's.

For a second Daniel lost his cool too, blinking as his eyes momentarily became heavy lidded and his mouth parted. Bex even felt Lottie tense again, clearly picking up on the tension that just that one look had produced.

Daniel looked incredible.

His hair was perfectly styled, his face fresh and clean shaven, and the suit he wore fitted him perfectly. He looked better than the last time she had seen him. Calmer, more awake, less stressed.

She could have done with him looking just slightly more haggard if she was honest.

Each of the groomsmen wore royal blue ties to match the bridesmaids' dresses. They stood out in comparison to their dark suits and Bex tried her best to focus on them rather than Daniel's face.

Bex and Lottie moved to the side. Charles was already grinning like an idiot, rocking back and forth on the soles of his feet and constantly being told by Daniel not to turn around. Matt was laughing at him and Duncan, his other groomsmen and close friend, was simply shaking his head at it all with a smile across his face. Charles looked excited and Bex felt her heart lift as she saw him fixing his shirt and trying not to take a sneak peek behind him at the same time.

"Was he the exact same last time?" Bex asked, turning to look at Lottie. She had a smile across her face that mirrored her own.

"Yeah. I sometimes wonder if Lizzie realises just how much my brother loves her."

Bex smiled. "Take it from the girl who had to sit there whilst she pined over him this time, she definitely doesn't. She certainly loves him just as much back, though."

Lottie nodded, a smile on her mouth. "I think that's their secret. They both think they're the lucky one."

The music changed and everyone who wasn't already standing, stood. With her height Bex was lucky. She could see Lizzie and Neil walking up the aisle from the moment they walked into the church. Neil kept turning to whisper things in her ear and Lizzie kept laughing, but her eyes were fixed ahead staring at Charles, and Bex felt emotion swell in her chest.

Surely these two could make even Matt believe that love existed?

She shot a look at him but he had joined Daniel in telling Charles not to turn around, a cheeky grin across his face as the groom got more and more agitated. Daniel and Matt acted as a team, winding Charles up with smiles on their faces. Matt's smile was larger, more animated while Daniel's was slight but it lit up his entire face.

There weren't many in the church with them. Charles and Lizzie had planned a small wedding with few guests and only people they trusted and really loved had been invited. However, Bex could see quite a few of their friends from work amongst the guests and even the presenters from *Elevenses* - the show Lizzie worked on - were sat with their families nearer the back.

Bex flicked her gaze back to Charles. Matt was now counting down on his fingers to when Charles could turn around, whilst Daniel seemed to be keeping up a continuous commentary of what Lizzie was doing. He had one hand on Charles's arm and his mouth was moving super quickly. Bex could just about lip read the words, *and she's walking, and she's walking.*

Bex laughed at their childishness and Daniel paused, catching her eye for just a second and smiling at her.

Without thinking, she grinned back.

His momentary distraction gave Charles an opening. He mouthed the words *fuck this* and he turned.

Nothing happened. Because of course it didn't. The music didn't stop, the lights didn't fade, time didn't halt but even for Bex it felt like the air in the church stilled for just a second.

Lizzie stopped walking and the look the pair of them gave each other made Bex drop her gaze. She felt like she'd walked in on some intimate moment that she shouldn't have been privy to. There was such naked emotion between the pair of them that just that look made Bex's eyes burn and her heart tug sharply in her chest.

A whisper of a laugh passed her ear.

Gathering herself, she looked back up.

Neil looked to be trying to instruct Lizzie on how to walk. He was ever so gently tugging on her arm but she was rooted to the spot. Catching her eye, he mouthed, *batshit crazy. The pair of them.*

Bex laughed, unable to stop herself and Neil gave her a triumphant grin.

Even though he was still a few feet from Lizzie, Charles reached out a hand towards her. "Come here, Cartwright."

Lizzie's stunned expression turned into a wide smile and then she stepped forward, almost tripping as she did so but Charles took a step forward and caught her arm.

Bex heard Lottie sniff behind her.

CHAPTER THIRTY-THREE

"So, what you're saying is you wouldn't sleep with me even if I was the last person on earth?"

"Yep," Bex nodded. "I'm never going to sleep with you. Even if there was a crisis and we were the last two people on earth, and we *had* to procreate to save the population, I would never, ever, sleep with you."

Neil looked thoughtful, resting his elbow on the table and cradling his chin in his palm. He sighed. "Your loss, I'm really good."

Bex snorted with laughter, nearly spraying her prosecco over the table and Neil made a deliberate unnecessary dodge as if she had just spat at him.

"Seventeen," he muttered under his breath as he theatrically brushed the sleeves of his blazer as if they had been dirtied by Bex's prosecco.

"It was good of you," Bex said, when she had recovered slightly. "To come today, I mean. It meant the world to her."

Neil grinned, and for once it didn't have a smug tilt to it. "I pretend she's an annoying pain in my arse, actually no, scratch that, she is an annoying pain in my arse but I love her." He shrugged. "I meant what I said. I was pretty gutted when she didn't come to my leaving party."

"Next time, don't be dick and tell Lizzie you care then. Just tell her the truth."

He put the back of his hand to his head dramatically. "That I care too much."

Bex laughed. "You're going to regret telling me that in the

morning."

"Maybe."

"What did you mean earlier? That you quit ages ago?"

He drummed his fingers on the table. "I handed in my notice in October, and it wasn't because I didn't care that I didn't tell Lizzie." He took a long sip of his drink. "I told Tyrone if he hired Craig that I would leave. He thought I was bluffing."

Bex stared at him, emotion swelling in her chest. "You did that? For Lizzie?"

Neil shrugged. "Course. Lizzie's dad was on her Banned List for a bloody good reason. Tyrone shouldn't have hired him. So, I quit. Couldn't figure out a way to tell Lizzie without her feeling guilty. So, I just…just put off telling anyone I was going until my notice was up. I got offered the job in Australia at the beginning of January. I didn't really know how to say goodbye." He pursed his lips and looked away. "I'm not good at goodbyes."

"So, you were an idiot and pretended you didn't care instead?"

"Something like that." He cleared his throat. "But don't tell Lizzie yet. I still haven't told her about the Craig thing. Charles knows but…I mean Lizzie feels guilty if someone else falls over in the same room as her. Let alone me quitting to try and help her."

"Never thought I'd say this but you're a good person, Neil."

He flashed her a smile. "Good enough to sleep with?"

She rolled her eyes. "Fuck's sake, let me pay you a compliment without being a dick about it."

He laughed, leaning back in his chair and crossing his ankle over his knee. "I'm pleased she found Charles again. Eighteen."

He'd been doing this since he had sat down. Counting out loud. She knew he was probably begging her to ask him why, which was why she was deliberately not saying anything.

"Same. It's enough to make anyone believe in soulmates."

He pulled a face. "Almost anyone."

Lizzie and Charles had disappeared about twenty minutes ago. Lizzie needed to change her shoes and Charles needed to swap his shirt. The last time Bex had caught Lizzie, she had been firmly in the happy drunk stage, hugging everyone, and grinning up at Charles with open affection every few seconds. Charles had spilled something on his collar…obviously…but had actually managed to keep the rest of himself fairly smart. He'd been carrying Lizzie's heels in his hand for thirty minutes but neither of them had been in a rush to get changed.

"Have you ever thought of how old this makes us?" Neil said.

"Excuse me?"

"Technically, we had a do-over of thirteen years. So, technically, I'm forty one and you're-"

"Don't say it!" She held up a finger in front of Neil's face. "Don't you dare!"

"Forty-six. Nearly fifty." She kicked him and he shouted rather loudly.

"I warned you not to say it."

"Yeah but you also kick like a horse and have heels on. Give a guy a chance. Nineteen."

"Kick like a horse?!" Bex said, sounding outraged while also trying not to laugh.

"It's a compliment. You kick hard."

Bex shook her head at him, hating that she was actually enjoying this man's company.

"So...talking of telling the truth, what's going on between you and the best man?"

Bex rolled her eyes. "There is nothing going on between Matt and me, for the hundredth time-"

Neil let out a bark of laughter. "I'm not blind, I can see exactly who Matt has got his eye on." He tapped his nose as Bex's forehead crumpled in confusion. "I see everything. Although he's hardly discreet. I meant-"

"Who does Matt have his eye on?" Bex said, sitting up and twisting to see if she could see him.

There were only around thirty people left in the ballroom. Lizzie and Charles had booked their reception at the Tring Manor Hotel. The ceilings arched above them, lined with hidden lights that made the room feel larger and grander, the floor beneath them was marble, polished so well that Bex could have probably used it as a mirror if push had come to shove, and the dance floor was in the top right corner of the room. The large, round tables they'd sat at to eat had been folded away so quickly that Bex hadn't even had time to grab the last bottle of wine left on the top table, and now there were small, square tables dotted around so people could sit and eat if they wanted to whilst others danced.

Through the windows Bex could see the sky was a dusky pink. A summer evening had rolled in, basking everything in a beautiful evening glow and making everything it touched seem that bit more beautiful. The French doors to the small private courtyard were open and there was a warm breeze gently coming through it. It made Bex think of holiday.

She finally spotted Matt in the corner. His arms were folded across his chest and he was leaning towards a beautiful girl with long black hair. There was a single beaded braid running down the back of it and her sari was the colour of fire. Bex tried to rack her brain. She was pretty sure the woman was a producer of some sort who had worked with Charles a lot. They had been introduced briefly but there had been so many people she had met that evening that she couldn't remember for sure who was who.

"She's beautiful," she said with a grin, turning back to look at Neil.

Neil flicked his eyes to where Bex had been looking and then back again. A small smirk played across his lips.

"Blind. Anyway, twenty. So, you and Daniel, hey?" The smirk turned into a smug grin. "Tell me, what do the Williams men have that make you women go crazy for them?"

"You're not funny," Bex said, putting her glass down on the table.

"Go on, entertain me."

"Well, if you are as good at spotting things as you say you are, you'd have noticed there is *nothing* going on between us."

"That isn't true."

"It is true!"

"Come on, Blondie. I saw you two up at the top. Couldn't keep your eyes off each other."

"I was looking at Lizzie, I wasn't looking at him."

"Are you having a lovers' tiff?" he said, his voice becoming all whiny as he pretended to pout.

"Since February? I wouldn't call that a tiff, would you?"

"I mean, if the argument has been that long, the makeup sex will be fantastic."

"Neil, just shut up," Bex said, not even having the energy to raise her voice. Talking about Daniel drained her. Every time she had glanced up and seen him today it felt like a zap to her energy. Looking at him made her feel sad.

"Twenty-one."

She let out a frustrated growl. "Okay, fine, I give in. What the fuck are you counting?"

Neil took a sip of his drink, deliberately making it as slow as possible as he looked at her over the rim. "I'm counting how many times dear Daniel has looked over here since I sat down."

Bex's back stiffened. "What?"

"Every couple of minutes or so, even seconds sometimes, he looks up and he looks away. Or he looks up, stares, and then looks away quickly as if he's just been caught. He doesn't realise that I've caught him every single time, however."

Bex felt a shiver run over her bare shoulders. "It doesn't mean anything."

"Twenty-two. Doesn't it?" Neil tilted his head.

"No."

"Well, then." He stood up, holding out a hand.

She raised her eyebrows and craned her neck back to look up at him. "What do you want? A high five?"

"Come and dance."

She snorted loudly. "Absolutely not."

"Come and dance and make Doc jealous."

"What is with the nicknames? And I don't want to make him jealous."

Neil leant down towards her. "Is that why you have been reapplying your makeup every half-hour on the dot? Is that why you laughed deliberately at whatever the photographer was saying every time you both had to be in the same photo?" He smiled sardonically at her look of surprise. "I'm observant but you may call me magical if you wish. Some people would class it as a superpower."

"I think you're just aiding my idea that you're secretly Satan."

"No secretly about it. Now, are you coming?"

Bex hesitated, her gaze flicking from his hand to his face and back again. She didn't want to make Daniel jealous. She didn't want to give him any more excuses to try and talk to her.

But didn't a small part of her want to show him what he had missed out on? What he could have had if he hadn't been so stupid? If he hadn't hurt her?

No.

She wasn't that cruel.

Not after the numerous moments they'd had at her brother's

house.

Not after the trial.

Not after the phone call.

She wasn't.

She didn't need to make him jealous, she was indifferent, she was above it all. It was history and she didn't need-

She took Neil's hand and stood up.

"Twenty-three."

A small laugh escaped her lips and Neil led them to the dance floor.

To her surprise, the git was actually a good dancer. He didn't care what anybody thought and as the band began to play The Killers the pair of them jumped around with big grins on their faces. She swore that someone could have even mistaken them for friends. If Lizzie walked in now she would probably have a heart attack. Once on the dance floor she could feel Daniel's gaze. It was like her body was suddenly super aware of it and she had to fight her natural reflex to turn and look him straight in the eye. Neil would occasionally grip her waist or grab her hand and spin her, and she'd feel a hot prickle across her neck, but she kept her focus on Neil and refused to look for him. Next, the band switched to playing Kelly Clarkson and Neil literally danced as if he was having his own show, strumming on an imaginary guitar and they both shouted the words at one another. When the song finished, they clapped loudly, putting their hands over their mouths and whooping for the band.

Neil was grabbing his side, out of breath, and as Bex watched him comically pretending to be in agony, she realised she could no longer feel Daniel watching them. She looked over to where she'd felt he had been sitting and noticed his empty chair. Something locked in her stomach.

It felt like she'd been dismissed.

Rolling back her shoulders she noticed Neil had stilled. He was staring at something just past her shoulder. Bex turned around and saw one of the most beautiful women she'd ever seen. She had short afro hair, that was darker toward the woman's scalp and turned a lighter brown around the edges. She had vivid, brown eyes that had a gold hue to them and was wearing a simple purple dress that made her dark skin shine. As she spotted the pair of them she held up a hand and waved by putting down her fingers one at a time. Her gaze moved to Bex and then back to Neil, her expression clearly stating *what a surprise*. She walked towards them effortlessly, like she was gliding, and Bex saw a few heads turn to glance at her.

"Sorry, didn't mean to interrupt."

"Lara, what are you doing here?" Neil said, his voice sounding nothing like how Bex had heard him speak before. She glanced at him and almost stumbled. He looked completely caught off guard. There wasn't a hint of smugness or superiority in his expression whatsoever. He kept blinking, and she watched his Adam's apple dip as he swallowed and tried to regain some composure.

"Lizzie rang me earlier and invited me." Lara shrugged but Bex could tell the smile on her face was a little forced. "But don't worry, I can keep myself entertained." Her brown eyes darted to Bex and Bex realised instantly what conclusion she must have jumped to.

"I'm Bex," she said quickly. "Love your dress. And please, please, feel free to take this moron away from me."

Lara laughed, holding out a hand for Bex to shake. Every move she made was pure elegance. "Nice to meet you, I'm Lara. Great bridesmaid's dress."

"Thanks, Lizzie left the decision making to me, thank God. That girl isn't the best when it comes to fashion."

Lara laughed again, the guard behind her eyes completely gone. "Oh, but she tries."

"You live with Neil, right?" Bex said, trying her hardest to rack her brain and remember what Lizzie had told her about Lara.

"I'm his landlady. Well, *was* his landlady before he moved to Australia."

"Neil!" A high pitched, female voice shrieked and something small shot across the dance floor and launched itself into Neil's legs, almost taking him clean off them.

Whatever it was brought Neil back to life. He laughed and bent over to pat the little girl on the back.

"Hey Kacey."

"I've missed you so so so so so much!" Kacey said. She let go of his leg only to stretch her arms up so Neil would pick her up. He did so immediately, without hesitation, and the smile he gave the little girl was full of affection.

"I saw you this morning."

"To see if I had kept the Toblerone you left in the cupboard from

Christmas," Lara said dryly, raising her eyebrows at him.

"Hey, those things are expensive."

Bex narrowed her eyes at Neil. To her horror, she was starting to be able to read him and she felt seeking a Toblerone had just been a very poor excuse.

"And I only saw you for a few seconds!" Kacey said, shaking her head at him before she grinned, throwing herself forward and wrapping her arms around his neck. "It's been forever."

"Cute kid," Bex said to Lara.

"She's a rascal." Lara glanced between Neil and Kacey, her brown eyes softening. "And for whatever reason, she adores him."

Bex pulled a face. "Too young to know the truth."

Lara laughed. "Isn't *that* the truth?"

"Excuse me?" Neil said, frowning comically at the pair of them. "Do you two mind?" He raised his eyebrows at Lara. "And if we are really going to start pointing fingers, why is Kacey here and up so late? It's past ten."

"She insisted on coming. She didn't want to stay at home with Guy."

Something flickered across Neil's expression. "Guy's still around then, is he?"

"Yes."

"How long have you two been going out now? Two, three months?"

"Ten actually."

"Right, right," Neil nodded, a slightly sombre expression passing over his face momentarily before he turned his attention back to Kacey and tickled her under her arms. "Yet this little one still prefers to spend the night with me instead!"

"It wasn't about you."

"Oh yes it was," Neil replied, but he wasn't looking at her, he was still teasing Kacey who was starting to shriek and wriggle in his arms so much so that Bex thought for a second he was going to drop her. "It's because I'm still the best."

"Neil," Lara said, rolling her eyes.

Someone tapped Bex on the shoulder and she turned to see a nervous looking server standing behind her. He was wearing the green hotel uniform and his face flushed scarlet as her eyes landed on him.

"Um...um....Miss Wright, the bride needs you in her room."

"Does she need me to go up there and tell her how wedding nights are meant to work?" Neil said delightedly from behind her. "Does Charming need a diagram?"

"Shut up, Neil," Bex and Lara said at the exact same time. Their eyes met.

"I like you," Bex stated with a grin.

Lara returned it. "Likewise."

CHAPTER THIRTY-FOUR

The bridal suite was on the top floor of the hotel. It had three huge floor-to-ceiling windows that looked out across the grounds and two en-suites. She only had to knock once before the door was flung open and she saw a red faced, harassed looking Lizzie on the other side of it.

"Hun, what's wrong?"

"What are you doing?" Lizzie snapped.

Bex frowned. "Am I in trouble?" Lizzie grabbed her by the arm and yanked her into the room with quite some strength for such a small person. "Lizzie?"

Lizzie didn't say anything. She simply turned and flounced back into the main part of the room and Bex had to hold back a laugh. Drunk, angry Lizzie was like a bloody toddler. Charles was resting on the huge bed, his tie undone and he was holding a bag of ice to his forehead.

"You okay?"

He rolled his eyes and smiled. "I tripped, banged my head." He tapped one of the wooden beams of the four-poster with his foot. "Went and got some ice."

"And tell her what you saw when you went and got your ice?" Lizzie snapped, folding her arms angrily and glaring at Bex.

She looked quite a picture. Half her dress was undone down the back so it fanned out and made her look like she had wings. She was wearing a blazer over her top half to cover her modesty although Bex didn't quite know why she had bothered if it was for her sake – she'd literally helped her pick out her wedding underwear. Lizzie had clearly tried to tie up her fucking gorgeous hair - stupid girl - and now part of it was in her classic ponytail and part of it was flopping down the side of her head. Her green eyes were furious but Bex couldn't quite take them seriously as Lizzie had clearly rubbed the right one so much that she had a mascara halo around it.

"Tell her, Charles!"

Charles sighed and spoke in a much calmer voice than Lizzie. "I saw Daniel. I went to get some ice from the machine and I saw my brother on his way to his room. And-"

"And what did you see?" Lizzie demanded dramatically.

Charles glanced at her and for a second it looked like he was trying not to laugh. He reset his face and turned back to Bex. "Daniel...Daniel didn't look so good. He was upset."

"Upset?"

"Yeah he seemed disheartened-"

"He was crying," Lizzie interjected suddenly.

"Lizzie," Charles said, his eyes widening at her and he gave a slight shake of his head.

"Red-eyed, snotty nose, the lot," Lizzie insisted.

"Over what?"

"You."

"What did I do?"

Lizzie sat down on the end of the bed, curling a hand around the top of Charles's foot. "Downstairs. You and Neil."

"We were dancing!"

"Yeah! But with Neil!"

"It was Neil's idea."

"And since when have you ever gone along with Neil's ideas? When has anyone in their right mind said, you know what would be great, you know what would be superb? If we *follow* Neil's advice."

"Daniel saw right through it, Bex. I don't think he understood why you'd want to do that to him," Charles said softly.

"Because he hurt me!" Bex snapped. She jabbed a finger in Lizzie's direction. "Come on, Lizzie. Some female support here would be quite nice."

"He's apologised!"

"And you think that's enough, do you? A nice apology? He accused me of cheating on him! He said I didn't love him as much as he loved me, he said he deserved better." She crossed her arms over her chest. "And what? He gets a bit upset with me dancing with a friend? Really? How much has he had to drink?"

Outrage and frustration balled up inside her at the same time as upset and grief. It was a potent cocktail of emotions.

"Which bloody room is he in?"

"What?" Lizzie asked, glancing at Charles. Something behind her eyes should have caught Bex's attention but she was too mad to properly analyse it.

"What room is he in? I'm going to go find the stupid idiot myself. He's being an utter moron. And he's being a dick. I can dance with whoever I like for fuck's sake!" she snapped, slamming her hands on her hips as the two stared at her. "So? What room is he in?"

"Five doors down the hall on the right," Charles said quickly, a small smile on his face.

"Bex, maybe you should calm down-," Lizzie interjected but Bex was turning, already walking out of the room and then marching down the corridor.

He didn't get to be upset about this.

He didn't get to be hurt.

That wasn't fair.

She banged her fist on the door.

There was no response.

So she banged again, this time louder.

"Daniel!" she shouted, just as the door opened and she stumbled forward into him. He was wearing a white t-shirt and black shorts, and Bex shook away the knowledge ringing in her head that it was the kind of thing he wore to bed.

She didn't want to think about him bed.

Nope.

Not right now.

No, she did *not*.

"Bex? What are you doing?"

She brushed past him.

His room was simple. Two double beds, a window, a kettle and two mugs - one had been drunk from - a television and a small desk. His suitcase was nowhere to be seen and his tie, shirt and trousers were thrown over the back of the desk chair. There was a singular lamp on in the corner.

"Where's Amy?" she said, realising she hadn't actually thought about the fact that his daughter might have been asleep in here.

"She's with Mum and Dad. They got a bigger room and agreed for all the children to have a big sleepover in there."

"Right." She turned to face him, folding her arms across her chest. "Sit down."

He held up his hands. "Okay." He sat down at the edge of the bed gingerly and looked up at her in confusion. "Bex, what's wrong?"

"I've just had a bloody earful from Lizzie and Charles!"

Daniel's eyebrows puckered in confusion. "Right...about?"

"And frankly, getting the bride and groom involved in our drama is a bit selfish of you, don't you think?"

"Bex, I'm a bit lost-"

"And surely, if there is one thing you know about me, if there is one thing ANYONE knows about me is that I am not interested in Neil bloody Grayson." She glared at him. "Well?"

He swallowed, squinting at her ever so slightly. "I-"

"Let me just tell you right now, I don't like it when men think they can dictate who I can or cannot dance with. Doesn't matter if we are dating or not. Especially when I am dancing to great songs and jumping around. I was hardly grinding on him. I wasn't having a waltz. Not that it would matter if I was." She took a breath. "But, anyway, you and I aren't dating, so frankly, you don't get a say in the matter anyway."

"I know."

Bex stared at him, feeling her momentum get slightly stuck in her throat. "Right, good, well then. That's good."

"Bex, I have no idea what you're talking about."

"What do you mean?"

"I never asked Charles or Lizzie to get involved with us. I just wished them goodnight about twenty minutes ago."

"No, you met Charles by the ice machine."

"No, I met *Lizzie* by the ice machine."

Bex stared at him. "What?"

"I saw Lizzie wandering down the corridor with her dress undone, nearly half-naked, searching for the ice machine. I ran over to give her my blazer. She was in a right tiff because Charles had hit his head on the bed. I don't think she even realised she was half dressed. I then accompanied her back to their bedroom so I could hand Charles his ice." He ran a hand along the back of his neck but a smile tugged at his mouth. "He was absolutely mortified that Lizzie had insisted I come just for a bruise on his head, and then Lizzie asked me what I was doing upstairs."

"What were you doing upstairs?"

"Saying goodnight to Amy. I told Lizzie I was going to have a shower and head to bed afterwards because it was late. That's when she asked where you were." He winced ever so slightly. "I think she was hoping you'd be with me."

Bex's mouth dropped open. "She told me you were crying your eyes out over the fact I was dancing with Neil!"

Daniel's mouth twitched. "Crying my eyes out?"

"Yeah! Her and Charles said you were practically sobbing in the middle of the corridor."

"Because you danced with Neil?" he said slowly. "And you believed them?"

Embarrassment flushed Bex's skin and she crossed her arms over her chest defensively. "Wow. Well, I've got to say I don't like what marriage has done to her. Lying to my face."

"Yes, this past ten hours seem to have completely transformed her," Daniel said, his lips turned up at the corners as he tried not to laugh. His sarcasm irked her.

"Hey, you were the one who spotted her half naked walking down the corridor. Would Lizzie Cartwright have ever done that? No. But Lizzie Williams…"

Daniel stood up. "Correction. Lizzie Cartwright would do anything for Charles. Even if it was just a bump to the head."

Bex huffed, looking away. "Fine, you have a point."

"Thank you." He smiled down at her and she felt her heart begin to do the double step. "Why did you dance with Neil tonight?"

"For the fun of it," she said quickly. Too quickly.

"Is that all it was?" he said knowingly.

"Daniel, if you wanted to dance with me, you should have just asked."

"I was planning on it." The intensity in his gaze was making Bex feel unsure of herself. She'd come in so certain and defiant. She'd been furious at him. Now she felt she had taken a wrong turning and she was acutely aware of the fact Daniel and her were alone, late at night, in his hotel room.

Something just a few months ago she'd have killed for.

His hair was ever so slightly damp and his skin looked fresh and newly washed. She could smell his aftershave in the air between them and the slight hint of the shower gel he'd used. She could see a few lingering droplets of water along his throat.

"Why didn't you ask then?"

He reached up and cupped her cheek. "Dad duty called. And I needed to step away for a second."

The brush of his skin against hers threatened to make her skin spark. "Why?"

He rolled his eyes. "Because despite the fact I agree with everything you just said," he lowered his voice and stepped closer to her, "I was the teeniest bit jealous."

She laughed. It sounded bright and at odds with the atmosphere, but it made him smile wider.

God, she loved that smile.

He lowered his voice again, his eyes looking into her own as if he could see directly into her thoughts. "Was that the intention, Bex? Were you trying to make me jealous?"

She swallowed, her chest feeling tight and her skin electric. His voice was so low and soft it felt like it was caressing her. She dug her nails into the palms of her hands.

Say no.

"Yes." She swallowed, completely trapped by his gaze. "I was trying to show you what you were missing."

His eyes darkened. "Trust me, I know what I'm missing."

Her heart was pounding hard in her chest, her palms were beginning to sweat and she pressed her knees together to try and ease the unbearable ache Daniel was stirring in her core.

This couldn't happen.

She could not be pulled back into him again.

Managing to rip her gaze away from him, she tried to steady her breathing.

Daniel dropped his hand. "You still don't trust me."

"How can I trust you?" she snapped, frustration seeping into every word and she stepped away from him, running her hands over her face. "You broke everything! I trusted you! I really trusted you. I thought you were never going to hurt me. I truly believed that." A lump of emotion formed in her throat. She knew what she had to do. "Do you still have the letter?"

"What?"

"The letter. My letter. Do you have it? On you."

She knew he would. She knew he wouldn't leave it lying around. He'd keep it somewhere safe.

He paused. "Yes. I hoped to give it back to you at some point tonight. It's your property, not mine." She stared at him for a couple of seconds and his gaze grew wary. "What?" he asked.

"You are disgustingly respectful sometimes, do you know that?"

A trace of laughter left his mouth but she could see the pain behind his expression was threatening to eclipse any good feeling inside of him.

He walked over to the cupboard, opened the door and reached inside. She heard the zip of a suitcase and a few moments later he was stood in front of her.

"Your letter."

She took a deep breath. "Actually, it's yours."

His eyebrows rose. "What?"

"Read it."

His eyes widened in shock. "Bex-"

"Read it," she repeated.

"I can't."

"Fine, I'll read it to you." She took it from him.

"You don't have to do this."

"I do," she sniffed, opening up the neatly sellotaped together pieces. It still felt heavy in her hand. "Then maybe you'll understand. Dear Daniel-"

"Bex," he whispered softly, reaching for her arm but she yanked it away and turned her back to him.

Dear Daniel,

You know I can't stand writing letters. My handwriting is worse than yours and you're a doctor, your profession is well known for its terrible handwriting, but here we are.

I can't remember exactly what I said last time, but I am going to try and remember it as best as I can. The night you died I had a letter - the letter I am trying to copy - in my pocket. I was going to give it to you on your birthday. I'd been fretting over it for weeks because I was terrified, but I knew it was time. I knew I couldn't keep it from you any longer.

Her voice faltered and she felt a flicker of alarm as her eyes scanned the next sentence. Her heart was beating hard in her chest and she felt every bone in her body telling her to run.

She didn't.

Instead, she kept reading.

I knew I had to tell you how much I loved you.

Even writing that was hard.

Because I did love you. With all my heart. I know I never said it but I hoped you could tell. In the way that I held you, in the way that I kissed you, in the way that I wouldn't let you say a bad thing about yourself, in the way that I knew you. Every part of you. And you knew me.

I let you in, Daniel.

I haven't let any man in. Not really.

I haven't trusted them enough but you...I feel safe with you. I trust you. I know you would never hurt me.

And that's why I'm sorry I lied. I'm sorry on our first date when you asked me how I was feeling I said it was a mix of emotions and implied I wanted to take things slowly.

I said it because I was scared.

I said it because suddenly I thought me being so open, and honest, and vulnerable was a bad idea.

I couldn't let you see that part of me.

I panicked and told myself off for previously being vulnerable with you.

But it was a lie.

Because ever since New Year's Eve, I've known I'm still utterly in love with you. Back in November, when we all remembered, the love I felt for you simply slammed back into me. Like the ability to breathe or think. I just knew I still loved you.

Just like I know that I am in love with you now and I'm not scared. I know you will never hurt me.

And I want to tell you the reason I've found this so hard too. I want to share my family history with you but I'd rather do that in person than over a letter. So, when I hand this to you, you're welcome to ask and maybe it'll help you understand a little bit as to why I have been so guarded.

I love you Daniel Williams.

Bex x

There was silence in the room as she finished. Hot tears streamed down her face and she noted that her hands were shaking as she folded the letter back up again. She tried to breathe a bit more calmly before mustering the courage to turn around and look at him.

He looked shell shocked. His eyes were wide open and he was staring at her.

"That..." He swallowed. "That is what you were going to give me the day I broke up with you."

"Yes," she said, sounding braver than she felt. "That was what I was going to tell you on the day you broke me."

CHAPTER THIRTY-FIVE

It was taking every bit of his willpower not to kiss her. It was making his body practically tremble as he tried his hardest to stop his feet pulling his body any closer to hers.

In every conceivable way, the most beautiful woman in the world had just told him she'd loved him.

The words he had been desperate to hear for so long had left her lips and acted like balm to a wound that he hadn't realised was still hurting.

She had loved him.

He hadn't been crazy.

It hadn't been one sided.

It hadn't been like Helen.

He tried to ignore the niggle of pain in his chest as logic tried to remind him it was past tense. That he had in fact blown her feelings for him to smithereens on the very night she was going to tell him she loved him. She'd just been braver with him and more vulnerable than she had ever been in their entire relationship. She had just opened up to him in a way she never had.

And he needed to be brave back.

He needed to show her that she could trust him.

And that wasn't by kissing the hell out of her.

He looked down at her. His eyes flicked across her beautiful face, to her round eyes, to her pink cheeks and then to her mouth. The mouth that had the power to break him apart with its words, but he also knew how right it felt to kiss it.

Dragging his eyes away from her lips he noted Bex's breathing had got shallower, her eyes just a fraction darker and he tried to not let excitement zip through him, tried to ignore the tight jolt in his gut, tried not to inhale any more of the delicious mix that was her perfume and *her*.

Fuck.

"Daniel?"

"It was the same for me," he said, letting out a long breath of air. His hands balled into fists at his side as he noted the slight drop to her posture.

"What was?"

"I was still utterly and completely in love with you from the moment I remembered everything." He swallowed, enjoying the way her expression softened and her mouth puckered.

Stop looking at her mouth.

He closed his eyes briefly and took a deep breath.

Be brave.

Be brave, be brave, be brave.

"Just as much as I am now."

Bex's breath caught. "Daniel-"

He opened his eyes quickly. "Don't worry. I don't expect you to say it back." He tried his hardest to smile. "For once I mean it. I'm not going to try and pressure you into that."

"You never tried to pressure me," she said, softly. "I've told you that."

He looked down at the ground. "I feel like I did."

"You've been away from me too long, Daniel. No one can pressure me into doing anything."

His eyes met hers and he held her gaze. She hadn't been wrong the other day on the phone. He had been flirting with her. He had been trying his hardest to make his interest apparent.

His interest.

Even his own inner monologue tried to downplay his bloody feelings for her.

He'd never been one to flirt but there was something about Bex. Something that gave him confidence. Something that made him believe her when she complimented him.

When she had called him handsome.

When she had called him sexy.

When she had called him irresistible.

"You have been away too long. Far too long."

His head dropped, unable to resist her any longer and he pressed his mouth against hers. Electricity ran through him at the feeling but he held himself back.

It was slight.

It was short.

He pulled away, his eyes scanning across her face. "Was that okay?"

She swallowed. "Do it again and I'll be able to give you a proper opinion."

He didn't need telling twice. He crushed his mouth to hers, briefly registering her groan of relief as fire sparked up his spine. He pushed her back, one arm wrapped tightly around her waist and the other on the back of her head. The letter fell to the floor and Bex's hands moved to the bottom of his t-shirt instead, pulling it over his head with determination. He pushed her up against the wall, feeling his heart beat hard as his hands pressed against hers hips and moved upwards, slowly over her body, savouring every curve, dip and part of her. She whimpered as he bit down on her bottom lip and traced his hands over her breasts.

God, that sound.

Did she have any idea what it did to him?

Her hands moved to the waistband of his shorts.

He moved his mouth to her neck, trailing open mouthed kisses down to her collar bone. "I think we need to make things slightly more even, darling."

She laughed breathily, closing her eyes as his kisses skimmed lower. "Good luck. This dress took three women to get me into. You think you could get it off by yourself?"

He moved his hands, skimming them over her torso, down to waist and then around her back, feeling the elaborate detailing on the back. "This isn't just a zip kind of a job?"

"This is a bridesmaid's dress." She paused, her breathing shallower, as his lips skated over a particularly sensitive spot on her collar bone. "It's never just a zip."

He forced himself to pull back, placing both hands on the wall beside her and waiting for her to open her eyes. Slowly, she blinked them open, a small pout on her lips that made him smile.

"You stopped?"

"I'm accepting the challenge to get you out of that dress. Turn around."

"You're biting off more than you can chew."

"Turn around."

"Alright, bossy."

She turned and he stared at the elaborate combinations of crosses and buttons up the back of her.

Okay, he thought, *this is going to be harder than I was expecting.*

He moved her hair out of the way and over her shoulder, pressing a kiss to the bare skin at the back of her neck and enjoying the way she inhaled sharply at his touch. Then, he focused on the job at hand. The detailing was…a lot. There seemed to be more effort put into the doing up of the dress than there was in the entire dress itself. He started methodically, moving each lace away from the other and undoing buttons as he went. It took far too long but every time his skin brushed hers, he felt sparks run up his arms and the tension around them continued to rise despite the innocence of his actions. When he was finished, he traced his thumb down her spine and enjoyed watching the shiver that followed it.

She turned around, taking him by surprise as she hauled his head down towards her and she kissed him roughly. He didn't complain, meeting her passion with his own.

"Aren't you a talented man," she whispered against him, pulling her own mouth back so she could kiss down his neck. Using the wall to support himself he closed his eyes as her mouth trailed along his throat. His heart was thudding so loudly he was surprised she couldn't hear it, but he didn't care. All he could think about was how good everything felt. He choked out another gasp as she ran her hand over the front of his shorts.

Six years.

It had been six years since he'd done anything remotely resembling this and if she carried on doing what she was doing, it was going to be over within six seconds. He grabbed her by the wrist and felt her laugh stroke his throat.

Not deterred she moved her other hand to the front of his shorts, her nails dancing across the waistband before she palmed him. "Fuck."

"What's wrong, handsome?" she said softly, humour threading in and out of her voice.

He removed his arm leaning against the wall and grabbed her other wrist. "You know what you're doing."

"Of course I do."

With a growl, he let go of her wrists and scrunched her dress up around her waist.

Her breath caught as his hand glided up the inside of her leg, fingers brushing against soft skin until they reached the apex of her thighs.

"Daniel," she hissed out between her teeth. He pressed a hot kiss to her mouth as his hand dipped beneath her knickers.

"Two can play at that game, darling."

She shuddered against him, dropping her head to his shoulder and curling her hands around his biceps as he touched her intimately. With his free hand he pulled the straps of her dress down, running his mouth along her newly exposed skin as he felt her hot breaths against his shoulder.

"Shit, shit, shit," she hissed, her teeth slightly grazing his skin as his thumb started to circle on a particularly sensitive point.

"Might have to break the promise of our first time not being up against a wall again," he grunted, loving the fact her breath was as unsteady as his.

"Our first time was up against a bookshelf. At least this is flat-shit!" she hissed, her hips bucking towards him. "Please, Daniel."

She said his name in such a way he felt like electricity had just set fire to something inside of his body.

"Do you have-because I didn't think that we'd-?"

"In my purse."

He stepped away from her, grabbed it off the floor and found a small packet from the inside. She'd managed to get herself out of her dress by the time he looked back up and he froze, his heart beating so hard against his ribs he thought it might crack a few of them. Her skin was flushed, her eyes were dark, and she stood only in her underwear, slowly sliding her heels off her feet. The warm orange glow of his bedside lamp barely touched her and he wished he'd had the foresight to turn on every single light in the entire room.

"You are so beautiful."

She gave him a coy smile, beckoning him with a curled finger. "I know." He grinned at that and stepped forward, pressing his chest up against hers and savouring the feeling of her skin against his. She lifted a hand up to cup his face, her eyes softening on his face. "Do you?"

"Do I what?"

"Know how beautiful you are."

He tried to turn his head away but her palm held him still. "Bex, you don't have to say that."

"I know I don't, but I like telling the truth." She smiled. "So here are two for you. First, I think you're the most beautiful man in the world." Her eyes darkened as they dropped to his mouth. "Second, all I want right now is you, hard and fast, up against this wall." She patted it as if it were a dog, a cheeky smile across her face which he saw for a split second before he crushed his mouth to hers, his heart beat ringing so loudly it was merely a blur in his ears. His hands moved to her knickers at the same time as she pulled down his shorts and soon they were naked, their skin burning against each other's. He pressed his thigh hard between hers, using his body to pin her against the wall and groaned as she sucked his earlobe into her mouth. He murmured her name, tasting the shadow of her perfume on her skin before quickly covering himself.

"You're sure?" he panted.

"Daniel, I've never wanted someone more in my life."

He hitched Bex's leg over his hip, thrusting into her with a sharp shout. His knees almost buckled with sweet relief and he gritted his teeth as pleasure whipped up his spine.

The last rational thought that streaked through his head was that he was in heaven, before Bex's nails dug into his skin, her moan vibrated across him and his hips moved. The delicious feel of her blacked out the ability for his mind to do anything other than focus on the woman in front of him.

CHAPTER THIRTY-SIX

Lying in bed together, Bex traced her hand across Daniel's chest, enjoying the sound of his heavy breathing and his heart thumping beneath her ear. Likewise his hand drew patterns between her shoulders and the feeling of his fingers against her skin kept the warm and fuzzy feeling she had in her belly alive. His body was warm against hers, there was the faintest taste of salt on his skin, and her own body felt gloriously exhausted.

She lifted her head ever so slightly and glanced at bridesmaid's dress on the floor over by the desk. "I'm actually quite impressed how well you managed that."

"Sorry?" Daniel said, choking back laughter.

"I meant the dress. I meant undoing the back of the dress." She laughed, turning over so her chest was pressed to his and she looked up into his grey-blue eyes. His laugh became a low chuckle.

"Why do they make them so complicated?"

"So the groomsmen can't have their wicked way with the bridesmaids. It's highly frowned upon." The smile on Daniel's face grew and Bex bit her lip in delight at the sight. She really loved that smile.

As they continued simply looking at one another, Bex felt an overwhelming urge press down against her shoulders. It tugged at the side of her brain, refusing to be dissolved by the post sex daze she was stuck in and becoming more and more unavoidable. She inched her way up his body and brushed her hand against his cheek. He reached up, taking it gently and planting a kiss in her palm.

"What are you thinking, darling?" he whispered.

Bex smiled at the term of endearment. It made her feel elegant. A far cry from the woman who had just demanded for him to have sex with her up against the wall.

Her eyes moved between his eyes. "I want to tell you."

His eyes sharpened in interest. "Tell me what?"

"Why. Why I find this all so hard."

He held her gaze and carefully nodded. "Whenever you're ready."

"It's messy," Bex said, taking a deep inhale of breath. "It's *really* messy."

"I can handle messy."

She repositioned herself, bringing her head down next to his on the pillow and he turned so he was facing her, his hand coming to rest on her hip and his thumb circling comfortingly against her skin.

"I want you to know," he said gently, "that you can stop whenever you want."

A small part of her knew that once she started, she really wouldn't want to. She looked down, biting her lip. A squeeze against her hip brought her attention back to Daniel's eyes.

"Bex, you don't have to tell me anything."

"I owe you."

He cocked his eyebrow up. "How exactly?"

"Well, the few orgasms just now were a good start."

Just before they had gotten into bed, Daniel had turned off the light but even in the darkness she could see his skin redden.

"Bex, be serious."

She smiled softly. "I want to tell you because…it's you. I just want to be able to explain a few things."

He nodded, his thumb still stroking small circles against her hip and waited for her to start.

"Growing up, my family was ordinary. Mum, Dad, Jason, me and Kyle. Perfectly ordinary, boringly so. We lived in Surrey, in a three-bedroom house. We were very lucky. Mum worked in London in some high-level position in a bank. I never actually understood what she did, and Dad was a geography teacher. He looked after us, picked us from school, made sure we did all our homework. All that kind of stuff. It probably comes as no surprise to you that Kyle practically came out of the womb in heels and makeup."

Daniel chuckled, the sound warm and genuine and it made the new tension creeping up her spine dip back ever so slightly.

"He always wanted me to play with his hair, wanted to bake cakes, not go to football, wanted to paint his nails and not play video games. He was so comfortably *him*. He came out to us at twelve and it wasn't really a surprise to anyone. My parents were fine with it. We were all happy." She took a deep breath.

"Jason has always been *the first-born* son to them. He was athletic, good-looking, had girls falling all over him, was smart, and my parents adored him. Mum especially. We all knew he was the favourite but it kind of became a fun joke. How many photos of Jason could Mum put on the fridge? How many certificates of Jason could Mum frame in one year? How many times could Mum bring a conversation back around to Jason?" She smiled.

"Jason hated it. Hated how Mum would make an effort to always come to his football games and yet would always blame work for why she couldn't make it to Kyle's musicals. One night, after his team had won the previous weekend in the county finals, our parents took us out to celebrate. Jason got angry that we weren't also celebrating the fact that Kyle had got the lead in a musical at school. Kyle never really let it get to him. He was kind of...above all of it. Dad and I always went to his shows, as did Jason, as did his many, many friends, so I think he was happy enough as it was. He loved Mum but they never were close. When Jason turned sixteen, something changed. He grew quiet. He didn't go out as much, simply studied in his room, and stopped telling Mum and Dad when his games were. At one point he actually begged me not to tell Mum he was still playing. I thought it was because he felt guilty he wasn't studying all of the time."

"He got into Loughborough University on a sports scholarship. Matt doesn't know this but he actually met my brother at university. I didn't make the connection until way later, too late to say something, but when there was an incident in first year, Matt stepped in and helped him. He was good to my brother. Even if Jason was painfully shy."

"I can't imagine Jason being shy," Daniel said softly.

"It's because he's got Marco," Bex whispered. "After what happened Jason slowly became himself again but Marco truly brought him back to us."

"Good man."

"He's one of the best," she whispered. "I just wish he had come into our lives sooner." She sighed. "It was the Christmas holidays when everything *happened*. Jason had just finished his first term of university and our parents had decided to go away for a bit of winter sun. They were due to fly back on Christmas day as it was cheapest way to get home and they planned to see us in the evening. The first day they went away, Jason told us he was gay. He burst into tears and we ran at him, practically tackled him to the ground and wouldn't let go for at least an hour. He didn't want to tell Mum and Dad. They had put too much pressure on him already. So, we agreed to keep it a secret. Three days later he introduced us to his university boyfriend, Lex. He was nice. Nerdy guy, blue hair, glasses. He made Jason happy and with our parents away, Jason was becoming more like his old self. More jokey, more relaxed, more happy. It was great."

She swallowed.

"It was Christmas morning and Kyle had woken up at the crack of dawn like he always used to do. We shared a room so it meant I was awake too. He was like a bloody puppy, bouncing around everywhere and wanting to open every single present before anyone even got up. Anyway, he was on my bed, we were circling the films we were going to watch that day in the Radio Times, and Jason and Lex were downstairs, making pancakes and planning some sort of surprise."

"We... we heard a scream and suddenly Mum was in our room. She grabbed Kyle and began shaking him hard. She was screaming at him, telling him it was all his fault. He hit his head against the wall and that's when I snapped to life. I jumped between them, shoving her away but she kept lunging for him like she was possessed. She was screaming that Kyle had poisoned her baby boy. That he had ruined his life. It turned out that she had caught Jason and Lex downstairs making breakfast. Dad did nothing. He just watched from the doorway, looking helpless. He didn't intervene, he was a complete coward." She curled her hand into the pillow, squeezing it hard. The memory of her dad's face just watching was one she would never be able to burn from her mind. He had been their guardian. The one always there. And he had just stood and watched as their mum had tried to attack Kyle.

"Mum just went crazy. Finally, Jason came upstairs and was pulling her off us. She backhanded him and his head snapped against the doorframe of my room and still Dad did nothing. Absolutely fucking nothing. She...she told him that he had broken their deal.

That she would be sending him off to therapy in January."

"What we didn't know is that Mum had caught Jason kissing a boy outside the cinema years before that. She had made him promise to never do it again. The boy had been from Jason's basketball team so Mum had banned him from playing any sports. Said the changing rooms were clearly *confusing* him too much."

"Bloody hell," Daniel breathed and she risked a glance at him. His jaw was tight and she saw the anger in his eyes. Anger for her brothers. It made her heart swell in her chest.

"Christmas was ruined after that. They had come home early to surprise us but none of us wanted anything to do with them. Dad came up later to try and talk us into coming down for some food, explaining Mum was just very traditional and wanted what was best for us. That she loved Jason too much for him to just throw his life away. He literally said that whilst Kyle was right next to me. Kyle, who had come out years ago. They ruined Christmas for him. I know we are all meant to grow up but Kyle...I think he was going to be one of those types of people who got crazy excited for Christmas forever. They destroyed that. He doesn't even own a Christmas jumper now." She stared ahead, not really seeing Daniel in front of her but remembering Kyle's crestfallen face as their dad had said those words. He'd had a line across his cheek where their mum had managed to scratch him but he still had been wearing his dark red eyeshadow with bright green eyeliner. He had still been wearing his snowman woolly jumper with its obnoxious flashing white lights. He'd still been wearing fluffy reindeer socks. She'd literally seen the spark die in his eyes.

"Anyway, I ignored Dad. I couldn't even look at him. Jason had locked himself in his own room for the entire day. Lex had left. I went to try and speak to Jason once Kyle had fallen asleep. At first he wouldn't open the door so I forced my way in and found him crying in bed. I just held him for a while. And that's-" her voice caught. "That's when I saw the little sign in his room, the one on the back of his door that said," she stopped, trying her hardest to swallow away the pain, the memory of it making her feel sick to her stomach about how blind she had been. "That said how many days it had been since he'd cut himself."

Daniel inhaled sharply and Bex felt tears burn down her cheeks. "Since Mum had found out when he was sixteen he'd been self-harming. Trying to stop himself from feeling the way he was feeling about boys. He'd managed to stop when he was at university. He said a few guys had seen the scars when he'd been coming out of the communal shower and had avoided him because of it. It's why he always wears long sleeved shirts even in the summer or if he has to wear a t-shirt, he will wear bands around his wrists. Once my parents had finally gone to bed, I told everyone to pack. Jason was in too much of a state to refuse and Kyle was still a bit shell shocked. I think he thought he was dreaming. I took charge. I got them in my car and we drove and drove and drove. My aunt, Dad's sister, had always loved us. In her eyes, we were as much her children as Dad's. She took us in and she didn't tell them. We stayed there, Jason went back to university, Kyle switched schools - Aunt Miriam was a teacher herself so we managed to trick the system a little - and I quit. Miriam told me I didn't have to, that I should finish school, but I wanted to work. I wanted to earn enough money to be able to rent a place. To be able to look after my brothers. We were all waiting for the day Mum and Dad figured out where we were and I knew Jason was terrified. So, I worked three jobs and saved up every last penny I could."

She stopped, bringing a hand up to wipe a few stray tears away from her eyes.

"Bex, I am so sorry."

"Don't be. I got my brothers out. I never spoke to my parents again. We escaped. We had Miriam. Thank God for Miriam. But...even after all of that I still put my brothers in danger."

"How?"

"My first boyfriend after that I met at the pub. We worked together. I told him my brothers were gay. When he came in with a few friends one day when I wasn't there, they cornered him. Jason's a strong guy but he couldn't hold off four men. My second boyfriend seemed fine with it. Treated them both nicely enough. He never stayed at mine, which I thought was odd. When I finally asked him about it he said it was because he didn't want to risk Jason or Kyle coming onto him in the night if they met in the bathroom or in the corridor."

"Someone thought a lot of themselves."

Bex laughed. "Yeah, he did." She looked at him softly. "Meanwhile you let my brothers take Amy off to make strawberry daiquiris within five minutes of meeting them properly. You just blush when Kyle compliments you."

Daniel smiled. "The guy makes me feel like a God."

Bex laughed, reaching out to touch his chin gently.

His eyes flicked across her face. "So, you're scared to love someone because they might hurt your family?"

"Kind of. Yes. But also...love is so hard to admit for me because my parents said they loved us. They promised. A love between a parent and their child should never be questionable. It should *never* be doubted. But both of them turned on my brothers in some way or another. They hurt them. My dad's love for Mum made him blind to her weaknesses. To her issues. He lost us that day despite not having raised a hand or said a bad word. And Mum only loved us if we obeyed her rules. Jason and Kyle were so badly affected by it I realised just how vulnerable love makes you. Just how breakable it makes you."

"And after that...well I threw myself into relationships. Looking for a love that would help make the pain go away. Only for guys to cheat, to lie, to belittle me, and to hurt Jason or Kyle. So, I made myself a promise. That I would never tell someone I loved them, that I would never give anyone that kind of power until I was beyond certain I was going to spend the rest of my life with them. Because the moment I did, I was an open target." She winced. "Does it kind of make sense or do you just think I'm crazy?"

He cupped her face with his hand and she felt her blood fizz as his thumb skated close to her mouth. "You're not crazy. I get it. I really do. I am so sorry you went through that, Bex."

"It wasn't really me. It was my brothers. I just learnt from it."

"Bex, it hurt you too. You don't have to deny that. Just because your mum's anger wasn't directed at you, doesn't mean it didn't hurt you. You are allowed to feel whatever you do feel. You took on something no seventeen-year-old should have to take on. You basically became their mother and took care of them."

"We had Miriam."

His mouth tilted ever so slightly. "I've never known you to be quite this modest."

"Hey," Bex said, pushing him as his comment caused her to smile. "I mean it. We owe her a lot." She caught his eye, taking in his raised eyebrows and the way his chin was slightly turned towards her. She shrugged self-consciously. "Okay, and I guess I did do some things."

"Some things," he huffed out the two words in mock annoyance. "Bex Wright, I'm in awe of you."

She nibbled her bottom lip. "Do you want to know the night I truly learnt how much loving someone could hurt?"

He hesitated. "Are you going to say your flat?" His voice sounded strained.

"No." She shook her head and took his hand from her face, kissing the tips of his fingers. "The night you died. It killed me."

Suddenly, Bex found herself rolled onto her back, Daniel above her, his hands braced either side of her head. She felt her eyes begin to swim with tears.

"When you stopped breathing and that kid was giving you CPR- "

"Kid?" Daniel frowned. "What kid?"

"There was a boy. Must have been thirteen at most. He got Amy and came over to help."

Daniel's forehead creased. "I don't remember any kid. Not with Amy."

"You were dying, Daniel," she said, a small smile on her face. "Your memory might not be that great." She reached up and traced her hand down to the side of his face. "My heart didn't just feel like it was breaking. It was like it was splintering and it hurt so much but at the same time I also felt numb. Like I was frozen on the inside."

He kissed her, lowering his mouth to hers and she wrapped one arm around his shoulders whilst placing her palm to his neck, feeling for his pulse with her fingers.

"I'm here," he whispered against her mouth, understanding what she was doing. "I'm here, Bex."

This time, they made love slowly. Daniel took his time with her, holding her down and making sure she was the centre of attention the entire time. He gauged her reactions, he changed his movements when he realised something wasn't doing it for her and spent time on the things that were. By the time she cried out against his mouth, her body splintering with pleasure, she was already shattered, having been tormented and pulled to and from the brink so many times that her words had become a mixture of begs and pleas. Sleep claimed her nearly straight away, her body melting into the mattress but not before she felt strong arms fold around her and a warm body next to hers.

"Thank you for telling me," he whispered to her and she smiled, pulling his arm tighter around her.

CHAPTER THIRTY-SEVEN

Bex woke to the sound of a trolley being pushed outside of their room. She opened her eyes slowly to see a fraction of sunlight falling through the curtains. It was a whitish colour, highlighting a small part of the room and looking out of place amongst the dark blues and the greys. Alongside the silence, it gave the impression it was still rather early. Bex turned on her side and smiled at the man next to her. His hair was a mess, his face peaceful and his chest rising and falling softly. He looked beautiful. All sharp lines and dark features. His eyelashes were ridiculously long and he looked younger than she had seen him in months. She traced a finger from his forehead, down to his nose, across his cupid's bow to his chin. Even in his sleep she saw a smile tug at his mouth.

"I love you," she whispered. "I'm so in love with you and it terrifies me."

And that was why she sat up slowly, that was why she crept out of the bed and grabbed her dress, pulling it on and reaching for the little belongings she had brought with her. And that was why she could only glance back at him once, tears in her eyes, as she swiftly left the room.

The breakfast room was quite busy despite being so early in the morning. Bex had showered and changed in her own bathroom before coming down. Even after fifteen minutes spent under hot water she still felt like she could smell Daniel's smell on her skin when she moved a certain way or walked slightly too fast. She had changed into skinny jeans and a loose blue shirt, put on some mascara and lip balm, and headed out as quickly as she could.

Guilt clawed at her chest.

She knew how he'd feel when he woke to find her not there. Falling asleep tucked into his arms had felt so familiar and she'd enjoyed the way she'd vaguely felt his hands stroking her hair until sleep had claimed her. Her brain kept coming up with images of him waking up, seeing him looking around in surprise, and seeing his eyes realise her clothes were no longer there. Tears pricked her eyes. If it were the other way around, she'd have been heartbroken.

Stop it.

She was protecting herself.

She was doing the right thing.

He'd had his chance. She couldn't risk giving him another. Not when she felt this strongly about him.

She looked around the breakfast room. Lizzie and Charles weren't there yet but she saw a few familiar faces. When she spotted Maria and Kenneth in the corner with Amy and her cousins, she decided to turn around.

She didn't need breakfast. She just needed to get home.

Just as she was about to walk out, someone slammed into her, knocking her shoulder painfully and causing her to drop her suitcase as they strode past her.

"Excuse me?" she snapped.

The man ignored her. Bex realised with a jolt that it was Bry. He looked angry, his shoulders up around his ears and his back strained.

"Bry?"

He continued to ignore her. She looked around for Lottie but she was nowhere to be seen. Following her gut, Bex went after him.

"Bry, what's wrong?"

Bry marched over to the buffet, people jumping out of his way as they automatically registered that something was wrong. His anger was a force of its own, vibrating off him in waves. Bex looked around desperately again. Where was Lottie? What had happened? What did Bry have to be mad about?

Bry grabbed a jug of orange juice off a long table and stormed over to a table closest to the floor-to-ceiling glass wall. Jean and Chris, Lizzie's mum and her partner, were sat eating breakfast. Matt was sat opposite them, laughing at something Chris had just said.

Before Bex could yell, Bry was behind Matt and he had dumped the contents of the jug over his head.

He jumped back in surprise, his chair making a loud screech against the shiny floors and toppling over as he looked around in shock, staring at Bry like he was a mad man. Everyone went silent. All eyes turned to their table as Bry grabbed Matt by the collar and slammed him into the window.

"You're a fucking bastard!" he shouted, his voice carrying across the entire room.

Matt simply stared at him, clearly not in any pain despite the other man holding him by the neck. His eyebrows puckered up in confusion.

"Bry, sweetie." Maria had stood up from the table where Kenneth and she were sat with the children. "Put Matt down. I'm sure there's been some mistake. What's wrong?"

Bex found herself walking forward, staring at the scene in utter confusion,

What the hell was going on?

"You are an interfering fucking arsehole!" Bry shouted. He dropped Matt but at the same shoved his shoulder hard. The sound it made as it smacked into the glass made a few onlookers flinch. "She broke up with me. *She* broke up with *me*. The fucking cheek of it."

Matt's face darkened. "About time."

Even the waiters had stopped doing their jobs now, they were all watching.

"You filled her head with utter fucking bullshit!"

"You were controlling her," Matt said, sounding bored. "That was obvious when I found her nearly passed out in the toilets because she hadn't eaten anything."

"I was trying to make her healthy! I was trying to help her!" He thumped the back of his hand into his palm. "And what the hell were you doing in the girl's toilets anyway? You fucking sleeze."

Matt sighed, shaking his head at Bry as if disappointed. He stepped around him, turning his back to the angry man as he picked up his chair from the floor.

"I'm going to go and wash this out," he said casually to his mum, gesturing to his ruined shirt and wet hair as if it were an everyday occurrence.

"What's the matter, dickhead? Not in the mood for a fight?"

Matt didn't say anything. He simply pushed the chair back under the table and turned to walk away.

"I'm surprised. I've heard from Lottie many a time how Matthew Cartwright loves a brawl. Very quick to anger, just like his father."

Matt stumbled to a stop, his eyes widening as Bry's voice echoed around the room.

"Matt," Bex whispered, stepping forward and reaching out a hand. He was still a few metres away but she could feel his pain from where she stood. She could see it. Something had sunk in his green eyes and his forehead creased in hurt confusion.

Matt was never one to have an expressive face. He was quite good at guarding things but that statement had struck him hard.

"I think it's time you went home," Jean snapped, standing up very slowly. "And don't you *dare* compare my son to that man again."

"I'm only repeating what I've heard," Bry sneered, his eyes fixed on Matt. "I'm only repeating what Lottie told me. You call me controlling but hey," Bry continued, "at least no girl with me has to worry about me hitting her."

Matt turned, an angry yell in his throat and Bex managed to fly towards him, just in time to grab him. "Don't!" she hissed, as he surged forward. "Don't! This is what he wants."

"How badly did you break your sister's nose?"

"You have no idea what you're talking about!" Bex snarled angrily. She tried to seep every bit of calm she had into Matt, but he was shaking, his breathing heavy and she could feel the tension in every part of his body she was touching.

"Didn't you get suspended from school for breaking someone's collar bone?"

"That was different!" Matt shouted. "That was for Charles!"

"Oh, your supposed best friend? Didn't you break his jaw in two places? Didn't you put him in hospital?" Bry shook his head. "If you ask me, he only invited you here out of courtesy. You're Lizzie's brother. That's it."

"That's why he was one Charles's best men, was it?" Bex snapped. "You're talking absolute shite, Bry!" She turned her head to Matt. He felt so tense beneath her arms he could have been a living statue. "Don't listen to him, Matt. You know how much you mean to Charles."

"Apparently you even look like your dad!"

"Well that's not true," said a strong Irish voice and Bex looked around to see Kenneth had stood up from his table. "And like you'd know, boy, you've been around for five seconds." He turned to his wife. "Darling, when we get home, can we have a good long chat with Lottie as to why she always picks such bad partners for herself?"

Maria glared at Bry, her pinched face glowering. "I think that sounds wonderful."

"Perfect."

"*I* wasn't the problem! *I* was trying to help! All I was doing was trying to get her to lose some fucking weight!" Bry shouted loudly.

Bex's stomach turned.

What did he just say?

Her mind flicked back to walking down the aisle with Lottie the day before. The way she had been looking around self-consciously. The way she kept adjusting her dress. They way she had been sticking her elbows out. Her mind went back to the night before that when Lizzie had ordered pizza for them all. Lottie had said she was too excited to eat.

Shit.

"She was collapsed in the bathroom!" Matt yelled.

"Oh fuck off!" Bry snapped, glaring at him with his sharp, little eyes. "She was fine! She was just a bit drunk. Everyone gets drunk at parties."

"She wasn't drunk! You've come along and made her think something's wrong with her!"

"I'm just thinking of her health! I'm trying to look after her! Or I was until the ugly fuck dumped me."

Matt surged forward again and Bex almost let him. She almost let go of him to fly at Bry herself. At the last second she slammed her heels into the floor and held tight under Matt's arms. There was no way in hell she was going to let Matt prove him right.

"I'm so glad she came to her senses and dumped your arse," Matt snarled.

Bry sniggered. "We'll see how long it lasts, shall we? She'll see I was just trying to help. She'll see I was just trying to make sure she could be proud of herself."

"She should be proud of herself already!" Matt shouted.

"Doesn't mean much coming from you though, does it?"

Suddenly Bry was bent over, his arm locked behind his back and he screamed in pain as the person behind him yanked his wrist higher up his back.

"Time for you to go now, I think. And to stop saying mean things to people," Jenni said, her voice squeaky as she appeared behind Bry's back. There was so much anger contorted in her face she was almost unrecognisable.

Jenni had Bry in an arm lock. Her cheeks flushed with embarrassment as she realised everyone was staring but she kept her grip firm. Bry could barely move against her strength.

"Get off me!"

"No."

"Get off me, woman!" he shouted, struggling in her grip.

"If you think you're a master of health and fitness then you should be able to throw a big girl like me off."

"That's my girlfriend!" Kristina cheered from a nearby table, throwing her hands up the air. "Oh and she's stronger and fitter than you because size doesn't equal health or fitness, bastard!"

"You'd know that if you knew the first thing about fitness," Bex said, letting her eyes travel over him in disgust. "Guessing all those muscles are from steroids then?"

"Fuck off, you slag!" He struggled again but Jenni simply swiped her leg under him and he dropped to his knees, crying out in pain as they hit the marble hard. And then she was pulling him up, as if he weighed nothing, and marching him out of the room as he howled in wounded pain.

There was a hushed moment of silence. It crept over everyone. They all stared at each other before someone politely coughed, and someone else picked up their fork, a waiter walked across the room and slowly, people returned to their breakfast.

Bex let go of Matt. His muscles were still locked together and she couldn't see the expression on his face but she could see Jean's as she stared at her son. She looked crestfallen.

Kenneth moved towards them, his own face one of concern.

"Matt," Bex said softly but he ignored her, turned and began heading for the door. She followed him, grabbing her abandoned luggage and managing to keep up with his step.

"I just need some fresh air, Bex," he said over his shoulder as he clocked she was still following him.

"Then I'll come."

"No," he bit out. "I'm fine. I don't need you to babysit me. I just need some fresh air."

"You're not fine!"

"Yes, I am!"

"What he said isn't true, Matt. No one thinks you're like Craig!"

They walked into the lobby and Bex slammed into Matt's back as he came to a stop. Lottie was at the front desk, a suitcase that had a slash down the middle of it just behind her and as she turned to look them, Bex saw just how tired her face looked. Her eyes were red and she tried her hardest to smile at them as they both stared at her.

Matt moved first. He stepped forward, shaking his head at her, disappointment in every single one of his features.

"You get yourself into these fucking situations, Lottie," he snapped. "Next time, I'm not going to be around to carry you out of your shit."

Lottie's face paled, her brown eyes widening in shock.

Bex's stomach twisted in torment. Bry had said some horrific things, and he had implied that they had come from Lottie, but still… Lottie looked broken. This was not the time to pick a fight with her. If Matt had been in the right headspace, he would have seen that.

"I didn't ask you to carry me out of this one."

"Oh, so I was just to leave you slumped in a bathroom stall, was I? Passed out on the floor?" His voice was filled with cold rage.

"Matt, why are you acting like this?"

Matt's eyes scanned across her face before dropping to her suitcase. Bex saw his gaze snag on the slash down the centre and his hand curled by his side. "Did he do that?"

"Yes." She swallowed. "He was just getting a bit upset about me leaving."

"A bit upset?" Matt said, practically spitting the words from his mouth. "That looks like it was done with a knife."

"He just needs to calm down. We are going to go for a walk in a few days to talk over things and see if we can-"

"Fucking hell!" Matt snapped, his voice rising. "You're just so fucking desperate for someone to love you, aren't you?"

She stared at him, her lip trembling. "I…I…"

"So desperate you'd settle for pretty much anyone. Are you that stupid you'd agree to go for a walk with him? After he did that!"

"Matt, stop!" Bex said, reaching forward but he shrugged her off.

371

"Don't talk to my like that," Lottie whispered, tears filling her eyes.

Matt took a step forward so there was mere inches between them. His body towered over hers. "You're desperate, you're lonely, you're a poor judge of character and you need to fucking grow up."

"Matt!" Bex snapped. "Stop it!"

Lottie stared at him, her lip trembling and her eyes glassy. "You utter bastard," she whispered.

"Don't worry, your boyfriend already told me exactly what you think of me." He held her gaze as her eyes turned fearful.

"What did he say?"

Matt turned to walk away but Lottie grabbed his arm. "Don't walk away from me. You've had your speech now I'm allowed some kind of an explanation." She dragged in a breath. "This isn't you, Matt. What happened?"

"How the hell would you know who I am?" he said darkly, lowering his voice. "*You* walked away before you got a chance to properly find out."

He unpicked her hands from his arm and stormed off towards the foyer entrance.

"Matt, what did Bry say?" Lottie called after him, angrily. She looked at Bex, her eyes turning desperate. "What did he say to him?" Her voice caught.

Bex shook her head ever so gently. She turned to walk after Matt but paused as she passed Lottie's suitcase. "Please don't go on that walk. And please don't leave early because of him."

"What?" Lottie asked, her eyes rounding.

"Charles has booked us all in for the weekend. Don't leave because of Bry. And don't go on that walk, and don't give him another chance. He doesn't deserve you, Lottie."

CHAPTER THIRTY-EIGHT

Bex couldn't find Matt anywhere. The car he had rented was still parked in the corner of the car park so he hadn't left, but he had disappeared.

The sunny, dry morning had turned so quickly it might as well never have been there. Rain hung low in the air, like a curtain that was refusing to fall properly. It brushed over her bare arms and threaded through her hair and, for once, Bex didn't care. She didn't care that it was the kind of weather that clung to her face, or messed with her clothes. She didn't care that it was causing her to shiver. She couldn't even register the cold when inside of her she felt like her emotions were close to boiling over. She was completely torn. Part of her was aching for Daniel, guilt eroding everything inside of her as she kept imagining him waking up alone, whilst another part of her worried for Matt and the effect Bry's words were going to have on him.

After twenty minutes of searching the grounds, she sent Matt a furious text and jumped in the next taxi that pulled up outside of the hotel, forcing her luggage into the boot before someone caught her. Part of her was afraid if she waited any longer she would see Daniel and be made to face what she had just done. She wanted to just get away so she could pull a blind over everything.

She apologised for the state of her wet clothes as she slid into the taxi driver's car before relaxing back into the leather, finding very little comfort in the plush seating.

Five minutes into the taxi ride her phone vibrated and she took it out, hoping to see Matt's name across the front.

Jason.

"Hey, now's not really a good time."

There was a pause. "And why would that be?"

"Marco!" Bex snapped. "Why are you using Jason's phone to ring me?"

"He's not, you're on loudspeaker," Jason replied casually.

Bex felt her body tense in suspicion. "And what have I done to deserve this double team?"

"Wanted to check on you. Wondered how the wedding went," Jason asked, sounding far too relaxed. She could hear a grin behind his voice and it pinched at her insides.

"The wedding was fine, I'm just leaving."

"Leaving?" Jason couldn't hide his surprise. "But it's 9 in the morning. I thought that place had a spa! I thought you could use it for the rest of the day! Didn't Charles book you all to have the weekend there?"

"He did. I just have a lot of work to do."

There was a loaded silence at the end of the phone line.

"What happened?" Marco asked, his tone serious.

"Nothing happened, I just need to work. You know I don't have a normal work week."

"Yeah and you got an all paid weekend at the Tring Manor, I highly doubt you booked any work," Jason replied. "Bex, Marco told me what happened at the courthouse. How long had you and Daniel been broken up for?"

She was too tired to lie but it still took some time before she could open her mouth.

"Since February," she whispered. "I'm so sorry, I just didn't want it to affect the case. I couldn't tell you!"

"Affect the case," Jason mumbled. "As if I'd be that unprofessional."

"You might have been as you were doing it for free."

"A promise is a promise, Bex."

"Why didn't you tell us you dated before?"

Bex winced. "It's complicated. Hang on, how did you know that?"

"Did he tell you about the letter?" Marco asked.

"He told me about the letter ages ago, Marco. Why do you think I have been avoiding your-? Wait, did you read the letter?" She sat up fast, her heart pounding. How else would they know they'd been together before?

"I had to sellotape it back together, of course I read it! Some of it made no sense whatsoever but I got the gist. It sounded like you'd been together before. Sounded like there had been an accident of some sort."

"Marco," Jason said, sounding cross. "You didn't tell me you read it without her permission."

"You think she would let me read it? Do you know your own sister?"

"Even Daniel didn't read it," Bex snapped.

There was a sharp silence at the end of the phone and Bex felt a new tension slip into her shoulders. "He didn't?" Marco asked softly.

"No, he didn't want to as I clearly didn't intend for him to see it."

"That...that's noble of him," Jason said, she could hear the smile in his voice and it made her wince.

What was Daniel doing right now? Would he be awake? Had he already realised? Was her side of the bed already cold?

She shut her eyes and pushed her head back against the seat.

She'd done so many things in her life that she didn't always approve of. Many, many things when it came to men. But this...this stung like no other.

"I told him anyway. I read the letter to him."

"That's amazing!" Jason said, excitedly. "That's brilliant! I'm so proud of you-"

"But you're running?" Marco said quickly. "You just said you're leaving. Why are you leaving?"

Bex opened her eyes to find her vision blurry. She quickly blinked the tears away and took a deep breath, staring across the green rolling hills of Tring. Even in the rain it was beautiful. "Because I can't trust him. He hurt me before. I...I do love him but I just can't risk it. He's already proven that."

"*Cara*, for fuck's sake-" Marco snapped, his tone turning angry.

Muffled conversation followed and there was a sudden beep along the phone. Bex took the brief interlude as extra time to try and stop the well that was overflowing inside of her. Even her ribs were beginning to ache with the load of it all. She heard footsteps and a door close.

"Bex?"

It was Jason. His voice soft and clear down the phone.

"Yes," she bit out, feeling her lower lip tremble and trapping it between her teeth.

"It's just me. Marco can get a bit...passionate about these things." He laughed ever so slightly.

"If he heard you, you're going to pay for that later."

Jason laughed again and the sound made Bex smile. "I...I told Daniel about what happened."

"I see." Jason said, knowing immediately what she was talking about.

"He'll understand. I know he will. He'll know why I can't do this."

"He might understand, Bex, but he might not forgive it. I'm guessing you slept together?"

Bex swallowed, nodding.

"Did you?"

"Sorry, yes. I mean yes." Bex said, quickly.

"After you told him you loved him and you told him about our past?"

"I didn't exactly tell him I loved him. I told him I used to."

Jason let out a sigh. "I ran."

Bex paused. "What?"

"I ran. The first time I told Marco I loved him. Got up the next morning, went for an actual physical jog. Was terrified. Literally could feel my body almost going into shock. When I got back to the house I had convinced myself I had to break up with him. Marco was in the kitchen, making himself some toast. He had made me coffee. He just looked up, cocked an eyebrow and said, *Are you done with your tantrum or do you need some more time?*"

Bex laughed, the sound slightly tear stained, and Jason joined in.

"Jason I can't go back," Bex said quickly as their laughter died down. "I'm not going back."

There was a small pause. Bex didn't mind. Pauses between her and Jason were never uncomfortable.

"You know what I think hurt us the most that day?" he asked quietly. "It wasn't that Mum went crazy. It wasn't everything that she was saying. It wasn't even her slaps or her scratches. It was Dad. The one who had always been with us. The one picking us up from school, the one looking after us when we were sick, the one coming to cheer us on at anything school related, even if it wasn't important. It was the fact he said nothing. He did nothing. He sided with Mum.

He chose her over all of us. He wasn't horrified by what I was but he didn't love me enough to stand up for me." He took a deep breath in. "It's why it doesn't surprise me that the man you've fallen for is the complete opposite."

Bex's heart picked up its pace inside of her chest, thumping against her rib cage as her jaw tightened.

"Marco talked to Daniel about the whole thing when he went to see him. Part of the reason he broke up with you is Sam threatened to use your relationship against him in court. He broke up with you because he needed to focus on his daughter, and he felt he was focusing too much on himself. He chose his daughter and her needs over his own. He didn't stop to analyse what he wanted or what was happening. Something threatened his daughter and it simply had to go."

"That's not the whole truth-"

"I said *part of the reason*. Daniel didn't try and dress himself up as a hero. He told Marco everything."

"Did he tell him he broke up with me because he believed I didn't love him as much as he loved me? Because he thought I was cheating on him with Marco?"

"Do you blame him? Sam sent him a photo of Marco in your bedroom, Bex! Given his past, do you really hold it against him that he jumped to that conclusion?"

"He should have spoken to me."

"He should have. But shouldn't that just be a lesson to learn rather than the moral of the story? And as for the love thing, Bex you close yourself off. Your walls are high." He let out a frustrated sigh. "Look, that may not matter. Even now that may not make you turn around but shall I tell you what stopped me from running from Marco for good? What finally made me own my feelings? It wasn't the realisation that I loved someone. It was the realisation that I had trusted them enough to let myself fall in love with them. Subconsciously, I realised, I must have trusted Marco and fallen for him way before I actually realised it." He paused. "And if that doesn't work, then how about this. What are you going to do in two years' time when you're at Lizzie and Charles's anniversary party and Daniel turns up with a woman on his arm?"

Pain knifed through Bex's ribs and she almost dropped the phone. "I'd be happy for him."

"Really? A woman with a pretty smile who puts her arm around his waist and cuddles into his side, knowing she bagged a good one. A good guy."

"I don't date good guys."

"No, you marry them."

Bex choked back on the sob that had just threatened to explode from her mouth.

No, you marry them.

"Bex, what if he died tomorrow? What would you do then? How would you feel knowing the last memory he had of you was you leaving his room?"

"He was asleep."

"Rebecca," Jason groaned. Hearing her name vibrate down the phone hit her squarely in the chest.

She didn't need to imagine Daniel dying.

She had seen it.

Over, and over again.

"Jason, I'm terrified," she whispered.

"Better to be terrified than to regret it later."

His statement halted her tears. She stared out of the window, the sign to Tring train station flying past the window and she felt something zip up her spine.

"Which are you going to choose, Bex?"

CHAPTER THIRTY-NINE

When she got to Daniel's room, she banged on the door before her body could tell her not to.

Part of her was terrified, part of her was excited. She was stuck in a weird sort of limbo that only Daniel could cause.

She banged her fist against the door harder, panic beginning to rise in the pit of her stomach.

Please be in. Please be in.

The best-case scenario would be that he was still asleep. That he was just groggily pulling himself up out of bed and had not realised she'd gone.

The worst-case scenario was that she'd already done enough damage and she would never be allowed in again.

"Daniel!"

"Madam, are you okay?" She turned to see one of the maids standing behind her.

The lie came slightly too easily. "I'm so sorry, I went to ask reception about extending our stay and I locked myself out. I think my boyfriend might still be asleep."

"Men," the woman replied, rolling her eyes, before walking around Bex and scanning her own key card against the door.

That was easy.

"Thank you so much, you're an angel." Bex stepped into the room and closed the door behind her.

The sight hit her so hard she took a step back and hit the door.

Empty.

The room was bare.

The bed they'd slept in was made, the carpet was spotless and the bathroom was cleared of stuff.

He'd gone.

"Shit! Shit!" she said, feeling her voice grow heavy with emotion. She walked further into the room and something caught her eye.

Her letter. She bent and picked it up. It was on the floor, just beside the bin.

Had he deemed it so unimportant that it was the one thing he would leave behind? Or had he been trying to throw it away?

More pain splintered through her as her face flushed with embarrassment. That letter had been *her*. It had been her completely. If he was okay with losing that, or with throwing it away then he was probably fine with -

She jumped as the door to the room opened and she looked up, her heart in her throat as she expected to see him. Instead her eyes met dark brown ones.

"Bex," Maria said, the door swinging shut behind her. "What are you doing in here?"

"I...err..." She hated the fact her voice sounded gravelly. She hated how it gave her emotions away. Her hands curled around the letter and she placed in the back pocket of her jeans. "I kind of hoped Daniel would still be here."

Maria's eyes ran up and down her, assessing but gentle. "You're soaked to the bone."

Bex looked down and realised she was right. Her jeans were practically stuck to her and her hair was clinging to her face. It had really begun to rain and from the cab to the hotel lobby she had got drenched.

"It's nothing." She looked down at the floor. "Did he check out?"

"He wanted to. I couldn't understand why." Maria paused for a second. "Now I think I have a clearer picture." She walked further into the room. Her expression had the kindness of Lottie but the sharpness of Patricia about it. "He's downstairs. Amy wanted to go to the pool and he couldn't refuse. I came to get her goggles."

"But none of his stuff is here," Bex said, her shoulders refusing to relax whilst she couldn't see any evidence of him having been in the room.

"Like I said, he wanted to leave. He had packed everything away. But Amy wanted to use the pool." Her eyes moved to the wardrobe.

"I've been told to get them from in there."

Bex's body sagged momentarily.

He was still here.

He was still in the hotel.

She straightened up quickly, feeling Maria's eyes on her.

"I have to go and find him."

"Bex...if you need to go and talk to him, you have to be certain. I need you to be certain about what you're going to say."

Bex met Maria's eyes. The seriousness in the older woman's face made her want to run, made her want to box herself up again and pretend none of this had happened. But the line between the older woman's eyebrows made her think of Daniel. Made her think of the man she loved with all her heart.

"I am certain."

"Do you love him?" she asked firmly.

Bex stuttered, her mouth opening and closing at the direct question.

"After everything I learned the other day I have to protect him. He may be thirty-eight but he's still my son."

Bex straightened up and met Maria's gaze with determination. "If you don't mind, Maria, the first time I tell your son how I feel about him, I want it to be to his face, not to anyone else's."

Maria smiled. "Good answer. Do you still have a key card on you?"

"No, I checked out." Colour flushed her cheeks. "And then I came back."

"The important part is that you came back." Maria handed Bex her key card. "The pool is on minus four. I'll look after your luggage outside."

The pool was designed to look like an underground cavern. The walls were curved, made from dark grey slabs of stone, and it made every sound echo loudly. The only thing lit was the pool itself, glowing turquoise as it twisted in and out of columns and under fake bridges. It meant blue light dappled across the rest of the room, occasionally lighting up those lying on stone loungers near the walls.

Bex felt like she had walked into a fairy's playground.

A dark fairy.

A medieval kind of one.

In any other scenario Bex would have stopped to admire the architecture but right now, she needed to keep walking because she thought she might be sick. There were a few people scattered around but she couldn't see their faces in the darkness, they were hidden, talking to one another on the loungers.

If not for the happy screams and shouts coming from the pool, it could almost be seen as a romantic location.

Bex scanned her eyes across the dark spaces trying to see if she could see Amy or Daniel, or any of the other members of the wedding party, but she saw no one she recognised. She walked past a couple more loungers, nearly slipping on the floor as she hit a particularly wet spot, before heading over a small stone bridge to the other side of the cavern. She could see more loungers and more of the swimming pool's twists and turns but she couldn't see him.

"Daniel?" she hissed.

Someone nearby turned to look at her but then turned away. It wasn't him anyway. Even in the darkness she knew his profile.

"Daniel!"

God, she hated this. What if he was deliberately not answering? What if he didn't want to ever see her again? Her mind cast back to the letter and the way it had laid right next to the bin.

What if it was too late?

Suddenly, a splash to her right caught her attention and she saw Amy throw herself out of the water, flinging her hair back as she gasped for air and one of Patricia's sons hopped up next to her. He howled with laughter as she spluttered and coughed.

"No fair! Go again! I wasn't ready!" Amy said, slapping her hands against the water.

"I've won the last few times!" he said smugly.

"I'll be able to beat you, I promise!"

She stepped forward just as the pair submerged themselves in the water, holding their breaths and blowing bubbles from their lips.

If they were here, Daniel must be somewhere nearby.

Movement caught her eye and she looked up to see a boy sitting on a lounger on the opposite side of the pool. She could just make out his features in the darkness. Like her, he was also wearing normal clothes and he was also watching where Amy and her cousin had just submerged themselves. His green eyes met hers and for a second she almost lost her footing.

Him.

The boy at the crash.

The thirteen-year-old with the curly blonde hair and the dark green eyes. He was right here. In this hotel. He looked ever so slightly older and his face more rounded and soft, but it was definitely him.

The familiar way he smiled at her made her chest tighten.

He couldn't remember. Surely he couldn't have remembered.

But there was something else about that smile. Something she could not put her finger on. It was so familiar and yet so different at the same time. Like she was looking at a distorted photo of someone she knew.

And that's when she remembered her dream, and the way he had smiled then and how…how it had looked just like Charles.

"Leo," she whispered, staring at him. The boy grinned, his green eyes shining even in the darkness.

Got there eventually.

She blinked as a voice sounded in her head.

He tilted his head to the right, gesturing over to another dark corner.

She followed where he had pointed and her heart slammed in her chest. Daniel stood with his back to her. He was wearing a t-shirt with swimming shorts. Around him, grouped together, were Lizzie, Charles, Patricia, Simon and Kenneth. As she watched he glanced over his shoulder, keeping an eye on his daughter before swinging his head back to the group.

Now she could see him, the confidence she had walked in with fled from her body.

What was she going to say?

What was she going to do?

Feeling Leo's gaze on her, she glanced back at the teenager.

As their eyes met, a familiar laugh whistled through the air just beside her ear and then, like smoke, he faded away.

Bex blinked, trying her hardest to keep her heart steady.

Had she just seen a ghost? Was that what else was happening to her on this crazy day?

Ghosts couldn't age could they?

Ghosts aren't bloody real!

Shit.

What the hell was happening?

She looked to the left, and then to the right. There was literally nowhere for him to have hidden.

Leo had gone.

And it had definitely been him. The more she thought about it the more she couldn't believe she hadn't realised how closely his eyes matched Lizzie's. And hadn't he called Amy by her first name before she had even told him it on the night of the crash?

Amy's imaginary friend…

She shook her head, glancing along her side of the pool to where Daniel stood. She must have been imagining things. A new hangover effect. Or maybe it was this underground pool. Or maybe she had got so cold from the rain that she was actually getting the flu and hallucinating. She looked at Daniel again. Or maybe it was a side effect from being so panicked over facing him.

She was literally going insane.

This is what love did to people.

Throwing her shoulders back, she mustered up every bit of courage she could and walked over to them.

Lizzie clocked her first. "There you are sleepy head! What time do you call this?" She was sharing a lounger with Charles, both perched on the edge and her new wedding ring proudly displayed on her hand.

"Had a long night."

At the sound of her voice she saw Daniel's body stiffen. Slowly, very slowly, he turned to look at her. In the darkness she could make out his cheek bones, his eyes and his hair.

"Where's your swim stuff?" Lizzie asked. "Thought you'd have loved to have gone for a swim! Jenni will be down in a minute, you two can race if you want?"

Bex flicked her eyes between Lizzie and Daniel, her words getting stuck in the throat. He very gently shook his head.

He hadn't told them.

He had kept it a secret.

And any other day that would have felt like a huge relief but today it didn't. Instead it was coupled with the sadness.

She wanted to be sat here. Next to Lizzie, giggling about all the things she had done with Daniel the night before and thoroughly making Lizzie turn red with her honesty. She wanted to keep throwing him looks that made him blush and slipping her hand around his back when she stood by him. She wanted to tell him he didn't need to wear his t-shirt and that he didn't need to hide his scars.

"I... ummm..."

"Are you still hungover?" Patricia said stiffly from behind Lizzie. "I have some Berocca in my bag if you'd like. Or Jean gave me some stuff from Spain that she swears by. It's like a balm for your head."

Daniel was still watching her, leaning against one of the columns. His arms were now crossed.

What was she doing here?

Was he really worth it?

She looked at him again. Properly. Taking in every little thing about him. From the arms she knew could hug so tight, to the hands that would brush her hair when she was sad, to the eyes that would lock with hers, to his mouth. The mouth that had said the most loving, caring and trusting things any human had ever said to her.

Was he really worth it?

Yes. Always yes.

Even if she fell down and embarrassed herself right here, right now, in front of her best friend and her best friend's new family in this weird dark cave.

She had to do this.

"I'm in love with you."

Lizzie, Charles, Patricia and Simon froze, their eyes widening as they glanced at Daniel. Kenneth smiled, shaking his head and placing the newspaper he had in his hands to the side.

Daniel didn't even react. He simply continued to watch her.

"I'm in love with you and I'm terrified," she said slowly, licking her lips and keeping her gaze locked on his. "I'm scared you'll hurt me, I'm scared you'll run, I'm scared I won't ever believe that you really love me back, I'm scared you won't believe I love you, I'm scared that me running out on you this morning has destroyed any chance I ever had." She took a shaky breath. "I love you Daniel. I love the way you smile, I love that not many people get to see that smile although at the same I wish more things made you laugh. I love the line between your eyebrows - it lets me know when you're thinking or worrying. I love how well dressed you are... for purely selfish reasons." The corner of his mouth twitched and Bex felt her heart kick sharply. "I love that you are a good person - you're kind and wholesome and generous and you never expect anything back in return. I love that you wear your heart on your sleeve and that you don't play games or try and mess me around." She winced. "I am actually more of the fuckboy between us." She clenched and unclenched her hands, noticing Amy and her cousin, who had been joined by another of Patricia's sons, swim up to the side near Daniel's feet. "I love what a good dad you are. I love how much you care about Amy. I love that you put her first. I love that when you're nervous you rub the back of your neck. I love the way you never interrupt me, you always let me finish speaking before you make your point. I don't understand how you can't see how utterly gorgeous you are. I don't get how you can have gone through life and not realised how handsome and sexy you look. You should be a big-headed idiot, but you're not. Not even in the slightest." She saw Daniel shift and she knew he'd have winced at hearing those compliments. It made her chest rise with even more affection for him. "I love that you trusted me with your secrets and I hope you know how much it means to me that I finally trusted you with mine. I love that I can trust you Daniel."

He stared at her, his chest rising and sinking ever so slightly and despite how hard she was trying, her insecurities were truly beginning to rattle inside of her, urging her to run or laugh or to pretend the whole thing was a joke.

Everyone else sat in silence and watched him too. Lizzie kept throwing her concerned glances and even Patricia looked sympathetic. Charles was smiling, and Simon and Kenneth were partially hidden behind Daniel so she couldn't see what they were doing. She tried her hardest not to let Charles's smile give her too much hope.

"So, I love you, Daniel. This is me," she gestured at herself, "looking like a drowned rat, telling you that I am in love with you and wondering if you could, maybe, trust me enough to love me back. Again."

There was a short silence. Everyone looked at Daniel. Even Amy and her two cousins were looking up at him. Time stretched out between them and despite how cold she was, Bex felt sweat prick along the back of her neck.

"I think," Daniel said, straightening up and pulling himself off the stone pillar. "That we should talk outside."

The sentence hit her with the power of a sword through the chest and she had to use every bit of her strength not to stagger away. She was grateful for the darkness. Grateful that it could hide her utter humiliation.

"Okay." She was surprised she managed to get the word to leave her mouth. Had it ever hurt to speak before?

Lizzie made some sort of strangled grunt and she saw Charles squeeze her knee.

"Dad," Amy said, in a very matter of fact tone from the edge of the pool. "You don't have to be all secretive because I'm here. You're underestimating my maturity."

Kenneth let out a bark of laughter and Amy grinned.

Daniel turned his head to look at her. "If you're sure, boss?"

"A gazillion per cent."

Bex looked between them, not really having the mental energy to register what was going on.

Daniel turned back towards her, his eyes meeting hers.

Was he giving her a pitying look? Was he watching her with sympathy? Was he about to-?

"You're overthinking, darling," he said softly, striding forward and pulling her into a kiss. At the touch of his lips, her heart soared, happiness and relief making her sag against him. He caught her, easily, one arm around her waist and the other on her neck. Bex gripped his t-shirt, feeling tears run down her face and Daniel wiped the few he could away with his thumb. It was an innocent kiss, it was only Daniel's lips against hers, but it held a promise. A gentle, sweet, promise Bex could feel through her entire body. It made her shake and she leaned into him even more.

"Didn't mean to make you panic there," he whispered, pulling away only slightly but keeping her face close. "Still feels weird kissing in front of Amy. In front of everyone, in fact."

Bex laughed, happiness bubbling over inside of her. "You bastard."

"Sorry," he winced.

"I'll make you pay for it later."

"I don't doubt it." Their eyes met and she felt her face blush with the look he was giving her. She could feel her cheeks were turning red and although it was a rare feeling, she welcomed it, smiling up at him. "I told you I'd wait Bex."

"But I left? And I found the letter on the floor?"

"You dropped it on the floor, remember? Last night?"

She giggled. "But it was right by the bin?"

"I'm flattered that you think I am that magical but I can't control where the thing lands."

She laughed against his mouth, looping her arms around his neck.

"And anyway," he brushed his thumb across her cheek again, catching more tears that had fallen like an afterthought. "The letter's your past. I want to be your future. And yes, you left. It hurt. But I also know you." He kissed the tip of her nose. "I kind of hoped you'd be back again."

"I panicked."

"I know." He smiled down at her. "I have told you I've never loved anyone as much as I love you, right?"

"You may have mentioned it. But at the time I don't think I replied that I felt exactly the same way." She swallowed. "That I *feel* exactly the same way." She glanced sideways, watching Amy beaming at the pair of them. "One more?"

She rolled her eyes dramatically. "If you must."

EPILOGUE

Bex walked into the house, her gym kit under one arm and a little pull along suitcase in the other. It wasn't uncommon for her to turn up like this, especially on a Thursday night as she usually had Friday through to Sunday off. She chucked her keys in the bowl by the door and took off her shoes.

"Hey!"

"Hey," Daniel stuck his head out of the kitchen, an apron wrapped around his waist and a smile on his face. His hair was ever so slightly wavy. Over the last few weeks he had relaxed somewhat. Bex's presence in his life, full-time, seemed to have made him less precise and she liked watching him unravel at the edges slightly. He gestured for her to follow him in.

"Something smells good!"

"Thanks, it's not that big of a deal." He pulled her into the kitchen and as the door closed he pressed her up against the back of it, his mouth coming down hungrily onto hers.

She sighed into him, enjoying that his lips tasted of white wine and a bit of whatever he was cooking. She ran her hand up through his hair and tugged on it gently, which caused Daniel to smile.

"I missed you," she whispered as their mouths explored one another.

"It's been two days."

"Too long."

He pulled away, smiling at her. "So, how was work?"

"Good, same old really. Jill's invited me over to hers for dinner next week. She said you're welcome to come."

"What day is it?"

"Thursday?"

He winced. "Sorry, I'm on a shift." He turned away and walked over to the oven. "Shit, sorry."

"Daniel, it's your job. Don't apologise. Want me to bring Amy? Jill has kids around her age."

He looked over at her, the smile on his mouth making her heart lift. "If you're sure?"

"Positive." She looked around the kitchen. "Was someone baking in here too?" There was the shadow of flour on the work surfaces and she could see tupperware had been loaded in the corner.

"Lottie," Daniel said with a smile. "She was stress baking."

"How's she doing?" Bex said softly.

"Not great," Daniel shrugged. "Trying to take every day step-by-step but I think she's making up for lost time. She used to bake all the time until Bry made her feel it was a bad habit." He rolled his eyes, reaching for a glass in the cupboard to hand to Bex. "So, she came over to bake with Amy earlier."

Bex took the glass and headed over to the fridge. She glanced at Daniel as she took out a bottle of wine. "You look good in an apron."

He laughed. "No, I do not but thanks."

"You do!" she insisted, pouring herself a glass of wine. Leaving the bottle on the table, she walked over to him, wrapping her arms around him and kissing his cheek. For a moment they just stood there, leaning into one another and listening to the hum of the kitchen around them.

"Where's Amy?" Bex asked, pulling away first.

"In the other room. Working on a project."

"A project?"

He smiled at her coyly.

"This I've got to see." She walked towards the kitchen door but as she was about to leave, her eyes caught on something on the side. She frowned. "I didn't know you were into *fancy* coffee."

Daniel glanced over his shoulder. "Oh, no. It's not for me. I have no idea about coffee but Lottie mentioned that it was her favourite a couple of weeks ago, and she couldn't find it anywhere as most of the branches had shut down. Had to order it through a friend of a friend at work, thought it might cheer her up. Amy insisted we had to wrap it up before we give it to her though."

"Matt has that coffee."

"He does?"

"Yeah, ask him for some next time."

"Thanks."

Walking into the hallway, she followed the sound of music into the living room. Amy was sat on the floor, huge knitting needles in her hand. She was wearing a rainbow patterned Alice band on top of her head and she was humming along to the music before she spotted Bex.

"Hey Bex! You look pretty."

Bex laughed. "Thanks, kid. So do you." She walked up to her, sitting down opposite her on the floor. "What are you doing? I didn't know you knitted?"

"Dad and I are learning."

She raised her eyebrows in surprise. "Are you?"

She heard a huff of laughter behind her and she looked to see Daniel stood in the doorway.

"Since when did you knit?" She narrowed her eyes playfully. "And are you following me?"

A grin tugged at his mouth as he walked in. He had her glass of wine in his hand. "You forget this."

"Ah, my hero," she said, taking the glass from him as he sat down beside her. "So," she elbowed him, "knitting?"

"Amy and I are making a gift."

"What kind of gift?"

Amy's eyes sparkled and she looked at her dad.

"Can we tell her?"

"Hmmm...I don't know-"

"Please, Dad!"

He smiled good heartedly, turning his gaze back to Bex. The look in his eyes made her stomach dip.

How did he still have the ability to do that to her?

"Kyle's birthday is in a few weeks, and as you know, his number one fan is sat right in front of you."

Bex laughed, looking at Amy. She grinned and wiggled her fingers. Kyle had painted her nails at the weekend and they were still multiple colours. Apparently, the teachers at her school hadn't noticed it yet -

much to Kyle's horror.

"So..." Daniel looked at Amy, nodding for her to continue for him.

"So, we wanted to make him a Christmas jumper. Dad said he didn't have one."

Emotion lumped in Bex's throat and her chest tightened. She stared at Amy's hands and felt something quiver inside of her. "You...you're making Kyle a Christmas jumper?"

Daniel squeezed her hand. "We thought if anyone could make him fall back in love with Christmas, Amy and an ugly Christmas jumper could."

She stared at him, her eyes brimming with tears as she took in his stupidly handsome face. "I bloody love you so much."

Daniel laughed, his eyes lighting up.

"And you," Bex said, turning her head to Amy. "I bloody love you too."

Amy giggled, clapping her hands together. "I love you too."

She stared at Amy's gleeful face. It felt too much. There was too much love and happiness in her body at that exact moment. She had never felt anything like it. She opened her mouth to speak but she couldn't. Daniel brought Bex's hand up to his mouth and kissed her knuckles.

She practically melted under the look he was giving her. "Kyle is going to love it. Thank you. And he's going to love that you're going to spend Christmas with us."

"We're looking forward to it. Surprised Jason wanted to book us in so early."

"Don't be surprised," Bex laughed. "Never be surprised. But honestly," she looked between the two of them, "this is the nicest present in the world."

Amy smiled. "Wait until you hear about the other surprise."

"Amy!"

"What?"

Daniel winced, pinching the bridge of his nose with his free hand.

"What surprise?" Bex said, turning to look at him. "What was the other thing?"

"I wasn't going to ask you in front of Amy."

"But I know, Dad-"

"Amy," he said sternly and she swallowed her words. For a second she saw nervousness scurry behind his expression. "Come on," he stood up, holding out a hand. She took it curiously, standing up and looking at Amy with her eyebrows raised.

"Am I in trouble?"

Amy giggled and Daniel gave Bex a look that said *Really?* He led her into the hallway and shut the door to the living room, throwing Amy a disapproving look as he closed the door. His daughter simply grinned at him.

"What's going on Daniel?"

He winced, running a hand behind his neck. "How do you feel about making this more permanent?"

"About making what more permanent?" she replied, reaching up and taking his hand in hers. He smiled at the small gesture but pulled away to quickly take his apron off and toss it over the bannister just behind him.

"Did the apron need to come off for this conversation?"

"I thought you might be slightly more amicable if you could see I was wearing a suit."

Bex laughed, putting a hand to her mouth as he looked away, a blush forming on his neck. "Sometimes you do know me too well." She stepped forward and tugged his shirt playfully. "I do love you in a suit but if you'd added a blazer it would have been sexier."

"Noted. The more layers the better."

"Oh that is definitely not the guidelines I want you to follow."

He laughed but the frown line was still present between his eyebrows.

"Come on," she said with a smile, "what did you want to ask? What do you want to be more permanent?"

He took a breath as if was readying himself for something. "You, you being here. You living here."

She waited, keeping her face completely neutral whilst her heart raced hard inside her chest. The blush moved up to his cheeks and he blinked a couple of times.

"Forget it," he said quickly. "Forget I-"

She closed the distance between them, slipping her arms around his neck. "I'd love that." She laughed at the look of confusion on his face. "*That* was revenge for the pool. For making me wait so long for an answer. Told you I'd get my own back."

"From what I remember, I am pretty sure you got your own back that evening."

"Oh, you're getting a lifetime full of revenge."

She pulled him into a kiss, loving the feel of his mouth on hers and loving the fact it still gave her a slight kick every time she did it.

"So, that's a yes?"

"That's a hell yes!" She brushed her hand over the side of his face as if she were tucking strays of hair behind his ear. "I was going to ask you if I could on the night of the accident." They had stopped calling it the night he died, hoping it would make it a little more bearable to think about. Not that Bex wanted to think about it often.

He smiled. "So, what you're saying is that I'm late in asking."

"Very late."

"And I'm due a lifetime of revenge, huh?"

"You can bet on it."

"I won't bet," Daniel whispered, his eyes showing just how much he loved her. "I'll wish for it."

Elsewhere

Lottie sat on the floor, her back against the door and her feet stretched out in front of her. In her hands she held a tupperware full of salted caramel brownies. Nerves jumped around in her stomach but she was optimistic. Optimistic and hopeful with a dash of crippling fear and a sprinkle of *oh my God, what am I doing?* As the hours ticked by her insecurities began to get louder. She hadn't baked brownies in ages. What if they were rubbish? Should she have waited till she had at least tested them first before bringing them over? What if they tasted bad?

She clicked her tongue back and forth in her mouth before biting down on her bottom lip, her teeth pulling at the skin painfully.

The minutes continued to tick by. She had stopped looking at her phone a while ago because it seemed to make time go slower and if it got much later, she'd need it to have some power left in it so she could ring a taxi.

Her back was beginning to ache and she kept having to switch her legs over as they kept getting pins and needles. The hallway was quiet, the sounds of people from the street occasionally filtering through the walls but other than that, there was nothing. She put the tupperware down between her knees, before picking it up and putting it on the floor, before picking it up again and holding it to her chest. She'd brought a book with her but the words kept swimming in and out of focus and her head wouldn't let her get involved in the story, not with her nerves on a knife's edge inside her stomach.

The sound of keys caught her attention and she quickly stood, staring as the door opened and the man she had been waiting for walked in. He was wearing jeans and a dark grey hoody. As he caught sight of her his pace faltered.

Lottie's stomach pinched together. "Hi," she said unsurely.

"Hi," he said, his gaze running over her and his face giving nothing away.

"I…I brought you brownies." She held out the tupperware, forcing a smile on her face.

"I don't eat sugar." He glanced at the box and then back towards her face, his expression impassive.

Her shoulders slumped ever so slightly. "On certain occasions you do."

"Not anymore," Matt said coldly. "What are you doing here, Lottie?"

"I came to apologise," she said, her voice dropping to a whisper. "I came to say I'm sorry. I know I depended on you a lot on Charles's wedding day and I ruined your night and I'm sorry."

He stared at her, his lips pressing into a thin line and his green eyes striking her with a sense of disgust. Everything inside of her shrunk away at the sight.

"That's what you want to apologise for, is it? Ruining a wedding for me?"

She nodded. "Yes."

She knew she had upset him. Regrettably, she hadn't even thought about it. It was his little sister's wedding to his best friend, and he'd had to spend the night with her, making sure she was okay. He'd found her in the toilets when a few other women reported her in there and he'd stayed with her, forcing her to eat and making her sip water. At one point she had dosed off on his shoulder and the next thing she remembered she was being carried up to bed. He'd stayed with her until she'd fallen asleep again, the pair of them reminiscing about when they'd used to live together. He hadn't seemed angry at the time. He'd been kind and gentle, teasing her like he always had. It had been stupid of her not to realise she'd been ruining his day.

It was her reckless decisions that had caused him to miss most of the fun. That's what Bry had said.

He shrugged. "Well, you've said you're sorry. Can I get into my flat now, please?"

Her skin bristled with discomfort. "Do you forgive me?"

He stared at her, his eyes causing her skin to flush in an unpleasant way. "No. But you said you're sorry so I hope you feel better about yourself. Can I get into my flat now?"

"Matt, please-" She stepped forward but he took a step back. "We used to be best friends."

"Used to be." He eyes flicked over her again. "Past tense."

She felt tears begin to fill her eyes and she gripped the tupperware harder. God, she was crier. She cried after everything and she hated how her eyes were the first things to give her away. It always made her look like a child. "What's gotten into you? Why are you being so mean?"

A huff of mocking laughter left his lips. "Call it genetics, hey, Lottie?"

Genetics? What was he talking about?

"I don't understand," she whispered.

He shrugged. "That's not my problem. Now, I've asked you twice to move out of the way. I'll ring the police if it's a third."

"Matt, come on-"

"I'm being serious, Lottie." He narrowed his eyes at her. "I don't even want to look at you right now." Self-consciousness reared its head inside her. He was probably repulsed by the sight of her, probably mocking her in his head. If she was some pretty, slim, flirtatious thing sitting on his doorstep he'd have probably invited her in. He'd have at least smiled at her. But no. She pressed her elbows into her side, the way she always did when she felt insecure, trying to make herself that bit smaller.

"Okay," she said, her voice wavering. "But don't say I didn't try, Matt."

"I assure you I won't need to mention you were ever here."

A tear slipped from her right eye and she wiped it away. Before she left, she turned and left the box of salted caramel brownies by his door. He took a step back as she passed, as if he couldn't bear to be within a few metres of her.

"Lottie?"

"Yes," she said, inwardly wincing at her own eagerness.

God, she was pathetic. Just like he had said.

She turned to look at him, hoping beyond hope he would be smiling at her. He wasn't. He held out a hand.

"Your key?"

"What?"

"Your key. That's how you got in the front door I presume. I'm grateful you didn't just let yourself into my flat too. Both keys, please."

Her hands shook as she reached into her pocket and handed them to him. When she didn't move he looked at the door pointedly.

"Go on then."

The door shut behind her, exactly six hours and thirteen minutes since she had opened it. Her hands trembled and she felt her tears scorch down her cheeks, clinging to her chin before they dropped down.

Stupid, foolish, idiot girl.

What had she been thinking? Embarrassment threatened to bend her spine as she walked away, the wind slapping at her face. Crossing one arm across her body she held her head with the other and began to cry.

Matt stared at the closed door, his heart racing in his chest. Words he wanted to say stayed locked in his mouth and his stomach tightened as his brain registered just how tearful her voice had been.

You dick.

He shook the voice away and flicked his eyes to the brownies by the front door to his flat. His mind went back to the morning years ago. The morning he'd stared at his front door as she had walked out of his flat declaring that he was just some mistake. Bitterness overpowered the guilt that had started to build in his chest. The words Bry had – correction - the words Lottie had said to Bry, rang in his head. Loud and clear. The pain of them bit into his torso and with it, his feet unstuck from the floor and he walked towards his flat. Leaning down, he grabbed the box of brownies, weighing it up in his hands.

Inside his flat, he walked up to the bin and tipped the contents of it into the black bag.

Lottie Williams had been a mistake.
A mistake he never planned to repeat.

ACKNOWLEDGEMENTS

Okay, first thing I have to say in my acknowledgements is an apology. A big one. Helen Atwood, I am so sorry to have used your lovely name on a nasty character. I met Helen, two years after I had started to write *Forget Me Not* and already had Helen Williams story mapped in my head. Apologies as my Helen is one of the sweetest people you'll meet. And sorry to any Helens out there, I only picked that name as I didn't know any at the time!

First thank you, HUGE THANK YOU, goes to Demi Dabasia-Dunwoody. This girl helped me so much with everything lawyer land and child protection wise. She was a HUGE help. I can't tell you how many times I voicenoted her a 'quick' question and it was fifteen minutes long. She helped me at midnight, at six in the morning, at random times in the day, she was always on hand to give me her opinion and she read a beta copy of my book in a day to help give me feedback (especially on the courtroom stuff). I can't thank her enough. She is a star and I love her to bits.

Thank you to my girls, my number one team (in alphabetical order so I don't offend anyone), Becky Dale, Chloe Lewis, Gemma Bicknell and Maxine Wright. You have been my support team from the get go, always believing in me and I will never, ever, be able to repay you. You have no idea how much your presence in my life has changed my life. And thank you for also being on my beta reading team and giving me such good feedback (and laugh out loud phone calls!). I am so lucky to have you. I will never take it for granted. Can't thank you enough.

Thank you to Karen Sweeney for being one of the sweetest people I ever have met. She was also part of my beta reading team and helped me so much with the progression of this novel. She has become a firm friend who has picked me up on many occasions and never let me doubt myself. I am so happy bookstagram brought us together.

On the note of bookstagram, thank you to all the book friends I have met on there who have supported *Forget Me Not* and been excited for this novel. I really hope I didn't let you down. I can never tell you how much you've all changed my life but you made my dreams come true. Thanks for being so lovely. Every post, ever message, every story means the world.

Thank you to my mum. Her support behind this novel has meant the world to me. Thank you for everything Mum and thank you for informing me that if you take the hub caps off tyres, they won't deflate...which is what Matt was originally going to do (hehe). I love you to bits. Thanks for letting me be an anti-social hermit in my room. Thank you to my sister for being so sweet and supportive of my writing as always. She has been working so hard as a junior doctor and I am so proud of her and love her so much. And thank you to my dad for letting me get on with it and letting me move my trampoline into his bike area so I could get out my frustrations during lockdown (hehe, love you!).

Thank you to my family. Thank you to my Grandma, who I dedicated this book to. She is my biggest cheerleader, sending my books to all her friends. She is honestly the cutest and best dressed Grandma in the world, I love her to pieces. To my Leicester family who continually read my work and tell me how proud they are of me, I love you to pieces. To my twin cousins, Pippa and Tamsin, who are the best cheerleaders a girl could ask for, I love you both and could hug you forever. To my Wigan family who have been in my corner from the get go who I never see enough, I love you so so much. Wish you lived closer. And to my Garstang family who make me laugh no matter how I am feeling.

Thank you to my editor, Catherine Collier. Always there to pick up after me and she has been doing so since school. Thank you so much gorgeous girl, I love you. This book would be a mess without you.

Thank you to (alphabetical again) Emily Smith, Jessica Gottardo, Lauren Conlon, Maeve Scarry, Rachel Marber and Sarah Polley, who never stopped asking me about my writing and who helped me talk through stories. I love you to pieces.

Thank you to Ruth Early. My inspiration and writing buddy.

Thank you to my friends. From St Margaret's Sports Centre, to ((BOUNCE)) instructors and attendees, to my WGGS Diamonds, to other countries, to WB, to Project 2020, to work friends. I am not going to name you all as I will forget someone and feel insanely guilty but you know who you are. I'll have told you. I love you all to bits. So many of you have been so supportive of *Forget Me Not*. You didn't just smile and nod, you read it, you got involved and I honestly keep expecting to wake up from some sort of dream. Your love and support truly made me cry. I can't thank you enough. I really hope you know how much I love you.

Thank you to Justin and Josh, working with you two makes work literally somewhere I look forward to going. I am so bloody lucky to work with the pair of you. Josh also gets a credit as he came up with Matt's line 'you only have to get it right once' when talking to me when I was moaning about internet dating. I had to write it down immediately! So, thank you Josh!

Thank you again to the teachers who inspired me – Cyndy, Mrs Joyce, Mrs Smith and Mr Fletcher. You have taught me so many things and I will never forget how much I've learnt from you.

And thank you to YOU! For reading this. For reading my book. If you have come this far on the *Forget Me Not* journey I really hope you've enjoyed it. I really hope it made you smile and helped you escape even for a little while.

And to whoever is reading this, I hope you're okay.

Never doubt yourself, I believe in you.

ABOUT THE AUTHOR

Melissa Morgan is a scuba diver who spends most of her time underwater, looking after her favourite eels at the Ocean Conservation Trust. When she isn't underwater, she's either writing or on a trampoline as a ((BOUNCE)) Instructor.

At the age of six, she knew she wanted to be a writer and began writing stories about horses to read to her class mates. Spending most of her time with her head buried in a book, she loves falling for fictional characters and finding worlds she can escape too.

She is extremely lucky to have the best friends in the world and a beautiful, supportive family. Oh, and the cutest two poodles you will ever meet – Saxon and Bonnie.

She'd love to hear from you.

Instagram @melissawritesthings

Printed in Great Britain
by Amazon

64097484R00231